As I kiss this barrel my heart follows

The Lady *in the* Barrel

GEORGE E B CROZIER

First published in Great Britain in 2025

Design, typesetting and publishing by UK Book Publishing.

www.ukbookpublishing.com

ISBN: 978-1-918077-14-8

Acknowledgements

I would like to thank my wife, Pat, who has assisted me through thick and thin and devoutly listened to my ramblings and throughout the writing of this book. My family and friends that kept telling me to do it and finally I have succumbed.

George Crozier 2025

Foreword

A swashbuckling and exciting tale set in 18th century England and France during the Napoleonic wars. Packed full of adventure, intrigue, treachery and mystery.

An infant girl who was set for a royal upbringing in the Montpellier dynasty filled with glamour and luxury, but fate and incredible misfortune intervened.

Lost then brought up among common fisherfolk of Tyneside.

Following a tragic shipwreck, she was seemingly discarded in an old wine barrel by her own father and mother to save her life at the cost of their own.

The story written within this book requires careful attention. There are layers to peel back, connections to be made, and truths that are not always what they seem. The characters you will meet are shaped by their circumstances, driven by their desires, and haunted by the choices they make. Their journey is one of discovery, not just of the external world, but of themselves.

Back in France, the Count Artois instructs a wily Scottish adventurer, Archie McPherson, to seek out the truth and answers to what happened to his family.

There will be moments of doubt, fear, and uncertainty. The story before you are a testament to the power of perseverance, the resilience of the human spirit, and the enduring quest for meaning in a world filled with chaos and ambiguity.

As the story unfolds it is full of humour, tragedy and unbelievable courage over twenty years, making sure you will want to keep on reading.

Prepare yourself for a tale that will challenge your perceptions, engage your intellect, and stir your soul. The path ahead is winding, filled with twists and turns that will keep you on the edge of your seat.

How could it possibly happen in the first place you may ask, and why wasn't she found sooner.

Treachery, twists and turns all the way through make this book a compelling read. The interaction between the common folk and the ruling classes are a joy to behold. Questions you will be desperate to find the answers to, will she ever be found, you may ask, and will she ever become the rightful heir and Countess of the Royal House of Montpellier?

Welcome to a story that is as much about the journey as it is about the destination. Welcome to a world where the past is never truly gone, where every secret has its price, and where the search for truth can lead to places you never imagined. Welcome to the Lady in the Barrel.

GEORGE CROZIER

Preview

It didn't seem like a celebration, not in the true sense of the word anyway, but it was, most definitely a moment to remember, there was no disputing that. The occasion, although very special, was a few weeks earlier than expected, Nevertheless, Captain Jon Marcel and his wife Eleonore were overjoyed to welcome their very first child into the world. Even if the timing, and the place were not ideal. They were still on board The Montpelier, quite some miles away from their next scheduled stop in Edinburgh.

"She's beautiful Jon," exclaimed Eleonore, "magnificent, she really is. She is a credit to us both, and in fairness, to all our families." Eleonore's expression said it all. No one could have been prouder or more overjoyed, her face and her entire demeanour simply radiated happiness and satisfaction. Jon, her husband was just as pleased and totally overcome with joy as only a first-time parent can be.

He excitedly said to Eleonore, almost blurting out the words, "We will have to send news to France to my Father and Mother, they will be so happy." He could hardly contain his excitement.

Eleonore though, interrupted at this point. "Of course they will, Jon," she said, "but to be honest we have been at sea for so long they are not even aware I was pregnant. They think, quite rightly that we are on our honeymoon." She paused for a minute, before carrying on. "Let's wait until we reach Edinburgh and safety before we tell them anything. Then, we can let the whole world know." She lay back for a moment and rested against the beautiful linen of the old oak bed. She turned and smiled at the newborn baby. "And that will also, "she said, "give us time to think of a name for her. A perfect name."

Having said this, she glanced outside and noted the weather was good, as indeed was the forecast.

The Montpelier was in full sail and making fine progress towards its destination. The following few weeks on board were very happy. Indeed, the birth of the child had somehow managed to bring every soul on board even closer. It was no exaggeration to say this was a happy ship.

The Lady *in the* Barrel

CHAPTER 1

It was now 23rd September 1797, a night when fate conspired with nature to test the resilience of both man and machine. The time: 8.14 p.m. The French schooner Montpelier fought the savage waters of the North Sea; it's hull groaning under the relentless onslaught of towering waves. Bound for Scotland with a cargo of French wine and other luxurious goods, the ship was far more than a simple merchant vessel – it carried the hopes, dreams and lives of all aboard. The sea, however, unyielding and vicious, cared little for such matters.

Soon the Montpelier began to approach the treacherous coastline of north-east England, near the ancient ruins of Tynemouth Abbey, the storm quickly took on a cruel intensity. Sheets of rain lashed the deck, while gales howled and tore at the sails with a vengeance that seemed almost personal. Captain Jon Marcel, a man hardened by years of battle with the elements, gripped the helm tightly. His knuckles were white, his eyes fixed on the jagged outline of the English shore – a sight as foreboding as the storm itself, safety lay ahead, but only just, it was laced with the perils of the infamous Black Middens and Trow Rocks, places where ships, it seemed, had been swallowed whole, taking their crews with them to a watery grave, never to be seen again.

"Captain Marcel, sir!" the First Mate's unmistakeable voice cut through the storm like a blade, panic lacing his words. "We simply must be making for shore soon! If we don't we're done for!" His eyes darted nervously toward the land, now barely visible through the storm's fury. "We can't delay any longer, Captain!"

Marcel nodded, though his mind was elsewhere. He knew his man was right, but his thoughts were not dwelling on the ship's immediate peril. They were on the precious cargo below deck. Not the wine, not the cargo, but his wife Eleanore, and their newborn daughter, both now more important than life itself and who had been born just three weeks ago on this very ship amidst the endless expanse of the sea. His heart pounded, not with fear of death but with the almost certainty of what he might lose.

"Aye, I see it," Marcel growled; his voice steady and resolute even as the ship threatened to break apart. He glanced at the waves and felt their power crashing against the hull he then turned back towards his First Mate. "Unfortunately, the sea isn't our only enemy tonight, Louis. If we do make it to shore, we won't be welcomed by the English," he turned to face his companion, "that's for sure … but hopefully we can survive." The words hung in the air, bitter and final, encompassed by an air of resignation.

The Montpelier was a two-masted schooner crafted from the finest American oak, it had weathered many storms in the past, but tonight's assault was like none experienced before. Under normal conditions, they would have easily reached shore within an hour but tonight was no ordinary night. Captain Marcel summoned his crew of twelve, each man loyal, battle-hardened, and drenched to the bone. Their eyes locked onto his, searching for hope in his weathered and experienced face.

"My friends," he began, his voice hoarse yet unwavering and clear as he sincerely said "we've sailed through calmer seas and darker times together. Tonight, we face a test – not just of our seamanship, but of our courage and faith. We've done all we can. The rest … is in God's hands." He said quietly, pausing, his eyes misting over. "We must prepare for the worst lads and hope for the best." He tried to look at everyone directly, but the ferocity of the storm prevented further dialogue.

The crew nodded, solemn yet determined. Marcel offered a silent prayer before turning back toward the cabin where his wife and child awaited him. The storm, though, had other ideas.

As he fought his way back to his quarters the door blew open violently, letting in a torrent of wind and rain. Unbelievably, the storm had grown even fiercer, the ship groaned under the weight of its torment, its main sails had been ripped apart and the good ship Montpelier, strong as she was, was in great danger of capsizing, its very soul being torn apart.

Eleanore, the captain's wife was terrified, her face was pale but resolute, clutching their daughter close. Her voice, barely audible over the storm, she trembled with anxiety. "Jon," she whispered as she stared at the child, "You must save our baby; she must not die Jon, she cannot." Desperation was now creeping in, all logic and common sense disappearing with each second.

Eleanore's aristocratic poise had now been replaced by primal terror. She clung to her child as the ship lurched violently, throwing them across the cabin. As water surged in, the ship was inching closer to the rocks that would spell their doom – there was no escape.

Marcel caught hold of his wife and child, pulling them close. "There is a way," he said while staring out across the sea as though he had something on his mind, but his voice filled with dread, endorsing his words. He turned to face Eleonore, "you won't like what I am thinking," he said, stumbling over the words, "you'll need to be brave, more than ever before." He now gripped her more tightly.

Eleanore turned a tear-stained face to him searching for any hope or answers, but before she could speak, another wave slammed into the ship, sending them sprawling, Desperation choked her voice. She was now so distressed she could hardly speak; she was also soaked to the skin and freezing cold, bleeding and desperately clinging on to her baby. They skidded across the cabin floor. Crashing into furniture and grabbing hold of anything they could. Her voice let out a desperate whisper "Are we going to die Jon? Is this the end? Is this, what we have lived all our lives for?" Tears were rolling down her cheeks as she tried to come to terms with this predicament.

Captain Marcel hesitated for a moment unable to lie. "I don't know," he admitted, his voice a low rumble, heavy with grief. "Probably... But if we are to die, our daughter must live, we must make sure of that." He turned to face Eleanore who gripped the baby tighter as Marcel gently wrestled the child from her "She needs a name," Eleanore screamed, her voice trembling, "she must have a name before we do anything else." After a moment's thought Eleonore whispered, "Auriel Celeste, our golden girl, a gift from God."

Marcel repeated the name, a flicker of a smile touching his lips even as the weight of despair threatened to consume him. "God will watch over her," he cried, his words both a prayer and a plea. His eyes, weary from a lifetime of struggle, looked upon his wife and child. He thought of the life he had been destined for, the life he would now never see.

Captain Jon Marcel, son of the Count of Artois, heir to the Montpellier estate, had never imagined this would be his final voyage.

As the ship creaked and groaned dragging ever closer to the rocks, Marcel knew the end was near. But his daughter, Auriel Celeste – would survive. She had to. The sea, the storm, the very forces of nature – none of it would take her. Not tonight.

Jon stood at the bow of the Montpelier, the cold sea breeze whipping across his face as his thoughts drifted back to the moment everything changed. He remembered that day with haunting clarity. The sun had cast long shadows over the courtyard as he prepared to set sail for England – his final voyage before assuming the title of Count of Montpellier, a role second only to the royal kingdom of France. The tension in the air had been palpable. The weight of the moment pressing down on everyone present.

Captain Marcel had been unmoved by the concerns of the count, his weathered face betraying no sign of the gravity of their discussions. But Jon's parents, the Count and Countess, had been visibly shaken. Their son's voyage was more than just a matter of duty – it was fraught with danger, especially with Eleonore, Jon's new bride, accompanying him.

The journey to Edinburgh would take almost twelve months, considering the number of ports they must visit, each passing day a reminder of the dangers that lurked at sea.

However, when the Count pressed the family's gold seal into Jon's hand, his expression darkened, his demeanour changed. "No man, woman, or child can claim the title of Count without this medallion," his father had said, his voice low, barely above a whisper. The shadows seemed to grow longer as he leaned in closer. "Jon, as you know, my health falters. If I do not pass this to you now ..." He paused before taking a deep breath, filling the silence. "Other forces may intervene – forces we cannot afford to contend with or ignore."

Jon knew what his father was alluding to. "Uncle Francois?" he questioned, his voice laced with suspicion. The name hung heavy in the air like a curse. Francois had been exiled to Tunisia after his treasonous attempts to overthrow the French monarchy, he still to this day plotted from the shadows. Dangerous and unpredictable.

The Count's weary nod had confirmed Jon's worst fears. "You understand then why I hesitate to let you sail... The threats are too great."

But Jon had made up his mind. His loyalty to France was paramount and in no doubt, but the voyage was a test of that devotion. With a final embrace and a tearful farewell from his mother, Jon boarded the Montpelier, full of confidence and self-belief.

Now, as the storm raged around him, the memory of that day felt like a lifetime ago. The ship groaned and creaked beneath the onslaught of the waves. Captain Marcel's face, normally so calm, was etched with worry and anxiety as he barked orders to his crew.

"Louis!" Jon shouted, his voice cutting through the howling wind. His First Mate appeared, face pale but determined, "I need help, we need to save our daughter. Find Pierre and bring him also.

Louis didn't hesitate "Of course sir, what can I do." He looked genuinely afraid, but his devotion to duty was unmistakeable.

"Fetch me that barrel of Portuguese port wine, it's over there," Just then, before anyone could move there was another huge crash as the main mast smashed its way through the cabin roof, narrowly missing the five occupants, there was glass and debris everywhere.

"Quick," Jon said, dusting himself down "take the top off the barrel and empty it and please hurry." Louis and the cabin boy raced over to the barrel. In a flurry of motion, they pried open the lid with their knives dumping its contents indiscriminately on the deck. The sweet scent of wine mixed with the salty air filled the cabin as Jon worked quickly, his hands shaking and inconsistent. Auriel the baby, was swaddled in thick blankets, and placed gently inside the barrel, her tiny face serene despite the chaos surrounding them.

"Is this the only way?" Eleanore asked once more, her voice breaking, desperately hoping for another way.

Marcel nodded: his eyes filled with unspoken sorrow. "It's the only way she will survive. She will get off this ship. There is no other choice."

They could hear the crew outside now, shouting and cursing and jumping around in understandable confusion and panic. Land was approaching fast.

Marcel was busy writing out a note, which he was about to put in the barrel with their daughter, the note would explain the child's lineage and asked that the finder would locate her rightful guardians, either his parents or Eleonore's. He promised whoever would do this would be looked after and handsomely rewarded. He tucked the family's solid gold medallion within the child's clothing, a symbol that might one day save her life and reunite her with her true family. They had little time to do anything else, other than see that the barrel was watertight but for a couple of air holes in the lid.

Together, with the help of the young cabin boy, Pierre, they lowered the barrel into the raging sea. Eleonore kissed the top of the barrel and said a prayer, her lips trembling, before letting go. They watched as the waves swallowed their child, carrying her away from the doomed ship, their tortured minds full of fear and apprehension.

Suddenly an explosion ripped through the night; the ship's magazine ignited. Fire consumed the deck in one blinding flash. Jon was thrown to the deck, his leg shattered by the blast.

When he eventually struggled to his feet, Eleanore and Louis were gone and young Pierre knocked cold. Blood streamed down his face, blurring his vision, but even through the haze he saw the barrel – still afloat, and still moving farther away. Amidst the pain, Jon almost laughed out loud.

Auriel would live. She had to.

His thoughts, however, were soon interrupted by the sound of Pierre's voice, who had regained consciousness. "Sir, Captain Marcel sir," the boy cried, his young face streaked with fear but his hands steady as he held out a bottle of brandy. "For you, sir. One last drink?" he said with a grin. He had awoken and found the bottle rolling around the deck.

Jon smiled weakly through the pain. "You're a good lad, Pierre. You've got spirit." Pierre was aged only eleven and an orphan and it was because of this the captain took him on board in the first place as a young apprentice … It didn't seem like a good idea now though, he thought, which prompted Marcel to apologise to the young lad "You deserve better than this Pierre I am so, so sorry."

"With respect captain you have given me hope and friendship, I will always be grateful for that, however short that time may be, I will never forget you, may God rest our souls." It was an amazing piece of dialogue for an eleven-year-old.

Captain Marcel lay back and smiled, young Pierre just nodded and uncorked the bottle of brandy and handed it over to the captain who gulped down rather a substantial amount, its warmth spreading through his chest, before handing it back. "There you go son" he said, "make the most of it, it's probably your first drink --- and I suppose likely your last" As he winked at the young lad, Pierre hesitated for a moment before taking a deep gulp, coughing as the alcohol burned his throat. He spluttered and hiccupped for a few minutes before smiling and turned to face his captain. He was about to speak but the captain, his mentor, had already slipped away. He was at peace now.

Almost simultaneously the ship, the Montpelier, suddenly reached high out of the water and came crashing down onto the rocks with unearthly power, breaking apart around them, it's strong beams and timbers splintering like match sticks. Within seconds everything and everyone was below water, the crewmen who were still alive were fighting and thrashing about in a valiant but hopeless effort for survival. Pierre watched the wreckage in silence, safe for the moment as he held on to a netful of cork floats, his heart heavy but his resolve strong. He would survive. He had to – for Auriel Celeste and to fulfil his promise to his captain.

On the shore, the storm raged on as would-be rescuers gathered. "No-one will survive that," said one of the onlookers on the beach. "It's just too severe, the devil himself would perish, we best come back tomorrow when it's calm." There were bits of boat and debris bobbing about everywhere. With no human voices that could be heard or bodies to see it appeared there were no apparent signs of life anywhere. As the winds howled, Pierre made a silent vow to himself – he would find Auriel, and he would ensure her legacy lived on. For Jon, for Eleonore, for France.

The storm had battered the coastline, turning the sea into a merciless beast. The following morning as the dawn's pale light crept over North Shields, revealing the wreckage in brutal detail. The Montpelier lay scattered across the shoreline, debris bobbing in the water like a graveyard of splintered wood and broken dreams. Locals from North Shields began to gather around the rocks and nearby beaches where the Montpelier had sunk, they were more interested in what they might find for themselves, like the odd bottle of wine or items of clothing. The unwritten law of the land dictated that small finds were theirs to keep, but anything of true value, gold or silver, was the crown's property, and failing to report such discoveries could mean a night in the stocks, or worse, deportation. Soldiers and customs men patrolled the shoreline, their eyes scanning for illicit finds among the wreckage.

The wreck was, after all, a French ship. Few in North Shields cared if any of its crew survived. To them each drowned sailor was one less enemy on the battlefield.

The customs men, much to their disappointment couldn't find anything of any value, not real value any way. The sea was calm now and there was very little noise, apart from the odd seagull trying to get in on the act. The comparative silence however was punctuated by a child shouting, "Hey Ma, I think I've found a live one here," he said, "he's twitching. He's alive but only a kid".

In an instant the soldiers were there, rushing across the beach, kicking up sand, quickly followed by the customs men. They surrounded the hapless child; it was Pierre the cabin boy. The soldiers quickly dragged the barely conscious boy, his small frame battered by the sea, he was their prisoner now. They dragged him across the beach and up towards the Priory at Tynemouth, followed all the way by an unruly crowd who were shouting insults towards young Pierre. To them he was not a survivor, he was a prisoner of war.

Kids were hurling insults, throwing stones, spitting at him and kicking out as he passed them by, a frightened boy among a sea of cruelty. Pierre, so young, was understandably terrified, bearing in mind he could barely understand the language, stumbled forward, his vision blurring, his body shivering with fear and exhaustion.

The soldiers hauled him into the shadowy remains of Tynemouth Priory, where they threw him into an old monk's cell, disused for over two hundred years. The iron door was badly corroded but they managed to get it open. Truthfully, they didn't know what else to do with him, some straw was scattered on the floor like an afterthought. Pierre collapsed with exhaustion, his bruised and battered body aching, the darkness closing in around him.

What seemed like hours later, the local Governor and Chief Officer arrived. They ordered the guards to bring out the prisoner. Pierre had been stripped of all his clothing now and was standing naked and trembling in the cold, some of his hair had been ripped out during his arrest, leaving his face pale and drawn, he was clasping his hands in front of him with his head slightly bowed.

When he saw the men staring at him, he silently attempted a feeble gesture – sticking out his tongue and touching it with his fingers, a plea for water. His captors didn't see it that way however and assumed he was making a rude gesture and swiftly began punching him in the face, breaking his nose in the process. Pierre immediately fell on his knees, bleeding and crying and totally distraught. The soldiers grabbed him by the hair and ears once more and pulled him back onto his feet again before returning him to the cell.

That night, Pierre barely slept. Feverish and delirious, he dreamed of Captain Marcel. In his vision the captain's voice echoed in the darkness, urging him to stay strong. "You have a great future ahead of you, Pierre," the captain whispered, "but you still have work to do – for me, for Eleonore, and for the country.

The following day a local French speaking monk arrived at the priory from Lindisfarne, he was cheerful and full of energy. He had hopes of communicating with the boy. He was a genial chap called Bartholemew.

He was immediately taken to Pierre's cell, where he met the guards. "Don't expect too much" said one of the jailers "he just mumbles and what he does say doesn't make sense anyhow."

Bartholemew entered Pierre's cell and immediately saw the boy's dire state, naked, bruised and shivering in the cold, and missing clumps of hair, Pierre was a shadow of the boy he had once been.

He stared at him for a few moments and then spoke to Pierre in French "Pouvezvous parlez Francais" the monk asked.

Pierre's eyes flickered open. "Oui" the boy croaked, his voice barely a whisper. "Voulez vous un peu d'eau (would you like some water)," Bartholemew offered, holding out a flask of water. Pierre seized it with trembling hands, gulping it down in one go. For the first time since his capture, there was a flicker of hope, after an act of kindness.

Over the next few days, Pierre told Bartholemew and the officers everything he knew – the details of the Montpelier, the crew, the goods they were transporting. He spoke of the wine and the journey, but one secret kept locked within his heart he would never tell.

He said nothing of Auriel – the golden girl – hidden away in the barrel and sent out to sea. It was his secret to know and to hold on to for now.

It didn't take long after that for Bartholemew and Pierre to strike up a relationship. As the authorities concluded their inquisition, Pierre was officially recorded as the sole survivor of the wreck. The report was signed off, and the officers seemed satisfied with the information. But Pierre, with the weight of a solemn vow pressing down on him, never revealed the truth of the child who floated somewhere in the vast, unforgiving sea.

To the world, Auriel Celeste – the golden girl – had never existed. But in the shadows, her destiny was still unwritten but very much alive.

CHAPTER 2

Two days had passed since the Montpelier met its grim fate, crashing against the Black Middens, a stretch of treacherous rocks notorious for their hunger, and sinking to its watery grave. The storm had subsided leaving the town to its uneasy peace with only one survivor: Pierre, a young cabin boy, who bore the weight of the wreck's mysteries alone. The wreckage had been thoroughly scavenged; the bodies cleared to be laid to rest in common graves. Disappointment grew like a shadow over them; in the end, the wreckage yielded little of note.

On the jetty of South Shields, two formidable fishwives, Florrie and Mary, sat like sentinels, expertly gutting the morning's catch. They worked in practiced silence, the sea breeze carrying the smell of brine and fish as they smoked their clay pipes, their legs dangling over the edge swinging in time with the gentle rhythm of the waves. As they stared across the Tyne, the rocks where the Montpelier had met its grim end loomed like a memory half-forgotten but not forgiven.

"You went over there, didn't you Mary?" asked Florrie, narrowing her gaze as she worked, looking towards the North side.

"Aye, I did," her friend replied "by the time I got there, the place was bare. Not a scrap worth the bother," she said with a huge sigh, the memory of the wasted effort still fresh. She paused, glancing out over the river.

"Nowt?" said Florrie as she took a long drag on her pipe. She narrowed her eyes, a mixture of disbelief and curiosity flickering across her weathered face "You saw a couple of deed bodies though Mary, you must have, I'm sure there must have been more than bones and seaweed."

Mary shook her head, frustration creeping into her tone. "Nae kidding Florrie, it was boring as hell. All I saw was them dragging some kid up to the Priory, nae clothes on him." They stared across the river in deep thought both drew on their pipes and nodded in acceptance of lives lived on the edge of the world. "I expect the soldiers and that lot from the North side grabbed anything of worth." She turned and looked at Florrie who was barely listening.

Both women sat back in comfortable silence, smoking as they contemplated the barren shore across the river. They might have been around thirty, but the harsh life had aged them prematurely, their faces etched with lines carved by years of toil and saltwater.

As they sat, a young boy passed by, whistling a tune that broke the silence, until he spotted the two women. In a burst of impish courage he shouted, "Hairy Mary! Hairy Mary!" before dashing away, his laughter scattering on the breeze like a taunt. Florrie, shaking her fist, cursing after him, promising a swift clip around the ear if he dared return. Mary winced at the nickname, the words stinging despite her tough exterior. The nickname was an old thorn, never quite dulled by time, a taunt rooted in the slight moustache that had earned her years of teasing. She and Florrie were as strong as any man, hands roughened by the nets and knives, able to hold their own in drink and brawl alike, and yet here was the world, quick to remind them of every imagined flaw.

These hard women were up at six each morning, collecting the fish. Gutting them and cleaning them, all for a penny a box if they were lucky. On top of this they had husbands and children to see to.

Mary grumbled about the hour, sighing about her husband, Harry, who was likely drunk as a skunk by now. Florrie chuckled, her laugh rough and dry. "Better a drunk husband than none," she teased. "Besides, he does work, doesn't he?"

Mary replied "Aye, so does your Anders, and he has the bairns involved too." Florrie laughed at Mary's funny remark she always tried to look on the positive side no matter what the circumstances were.

Florrie's husband, Anders Guttenberg, a Danish mariner who had settled in England years before, eventually finding his way to the shores of South Shields and into Florrie's life. He had learned the lobster fishing trade in North Shields but decided to move to South Shields where he met and married Florrie Grey when she was sixteen, she was the daughter of the local tripe shop owner Dolly.

Their home, a modest, rough-hewn cottage of scavenged timbers and stones perched by Trow Rocks, with a view rivalling any manor's. It was a place cobbled together from whatever the sea hadn't claimed and yet it had become a sanctuary, a shelter against the storms outside and within.

As she made her way home, Florrie spotted Anders and their eldest son Amos pulling in the boat with today's lobster catch. Her younger son, Erasmus was gathering firewood along the shore, his arms laden with driftwood.

"Hi, Ma!" Erasmus called out, waving both hands. "I've found loads of firewood I don't know where it's all come from!"

Florrie smiled with a mixture of pride and curiosity swelling in her chest as she approached the pile. "Well done, lad," she praised. As she examined the driftwood Florrie started to wonder if the collection of broken timber had once been part of the Montpelier, the shipwreck of the day before. It didn't matter of course, the idea just hung in the air, unanswered and irrelevant, as Anders and Amos returned from the sea.

Anders shouted to her "Give us a hand Florrie before she drifts back out. "He was referring to the coble-style boat he'd crafted himself, a Viking-inspired vessel, complete with a dragon head carved into the bow. The boat was his pride and joy, and he had made a great job of it. He was happier with this than the typical yawl style common for the day. For all intents it was like a longship, his designs did not alter the performance of the boat, but it pleased him, and he joked that it would one day be his funeral pyre, set alight and pushed out to sea in a blaze of glory.

Florrie rolled her eyes at the thought and shook her head but helped secure the boat, nonetheless, with the help of Erasmus. Once it was safely ashore, they all retreated into the cottage, the boys carrying their firewood inside.

"We caught four lobsters today, Anders said, settling in front of the low fire. "We should get a decent trade for them."

"Good," Florrie replied, glancing at the nearly empty meat hook above the hearth. "We'll take them to Geordie Barclay's: we're running low on meat." Geordie Barclay being the local butcher and was only too happy to trade.

The flames leaped in shadows from the fire, casting a dim glow across the small stone room. Amos crouched by the fire, tossing a handful of wood pieces into the blaze. The response was almost immediate; smoke billowed thickly, curling through the room in sinuous plumes, stinging eyes and filling lungs,

Florrie's temper sparked just as swiftly, her gaze fierce as she glared at her sons and husband.

"How many times must I say it?" she shouted. Her voice was like steel. "Wet wood doesn't burn. It smokes!" Her gaze fell on her husband, Anders, with a look that seemed to sear him as deeply as the fire. "And you, you're just as bad as they are!" she snapped, pointing at him, punctuating her words with a sharp toss of her sack of vegetables onto the cold floor.

She stormed outside, pulling a clay pipe from her apron pocket, striking a match with the fury of a woman forced to repeat herself one too many times. The boys, cowed but eager to redeem themselves, turned to Anders.

"Look lads, go and find some dry driftwood. If you go into the cave near Frenchman's Bay, you may find some there and hurry." he added.

Outside, Florrie puffed her pipe as her youngest, Erasmus, offered an apology. "Sorry Ma, we are going for some dry wood now, we won't be long," Florrie nodded, she couldn't hold her anger for very long.

Enthusiastically the two lads shot off, keen to please their mother. In no time they were both in the dark cave with an armful of dry driftwood, but as they were about to leave Erasmus froze, his eyes narrowing. The young lad stood there for a moment. "Amos," he whispered, a shiver threading through his voice, "what's that over there?"

Amos squinted into the shadows, setting down his collection of wood to approach the dim outline of a large, weed-covered barrel wedged against the cave wall. He nudged it cautiously, feeling its weight. "It's a barrel, it's caught up on some pebbles," he murmured, his tone hushed and wary.

"Quick, fetch Ma and Da. This isn't something we should handle alone.

Erasmus dashed back to the cottage; his voice shrill with excitement as he called out for his parents.

Amos pressed his ear against the wood, his hands trembling slightly as he slid a slender stick into one of the openings. No liquid. But something else – a palpable presence – hung within. His curiosity got the better of him. Biting his lip, he pried the lid open. A gasp echoed in the cave. There, swathed in fine, impossibly soft cloth, lay the pale form of a child. Amos stumbled back, his breath catching, his hand flying to his mouth. "It's a baby," he whispered to himself, his voice hoarse. He peered inside, fearing it was already dead. Feeling braver he looked further and detected a piece of paper, then something else caught his eye – a large gold coin, engraved with unfamiliar writing. His mind raced, he could hear his family approaching, and in an instant, he pocketed the coin, it was a secret he didn't intend to share.

Anders squeezed into the small space, and peered at the barrel, on observing the three holes he asked if there was any wine in there and was disappointed when the answer was negative. They looked in the barrel and found its grim contents. As Florrie gently lifted the child from the barrel, happily noting it was still alive, the scrap of paper fluttered out. A note, nearly washed beyond recognition by dampness and time. Her motherly instincts kicking in as she examined the baby girl, she saw the clothes were exquisite, the skin flawless. "Anders, this is no ordinary child" she whispered. A mixture of awe and fear in her voice. "No ordinary child at all."

"Who could have left a baby here? Surely, they will be coming back for her. We need to inform the authorities," he said firmly! "This is beyond us."

Florrie gazed at the baby and agreed it was the only thing to do. She hurried back to the cottage to get a blaze going for warmth for the child.

Once the baby was safely inside the cottage Anders rushed off to find the local magistrate and doctor, the Reverend Trevelyan. After hammering on the door, the reverend's housekeeper, Mrs. Watson, opened it.

"What on earth is going on here, have you seen a ghost man?" Her eyes widened as she saw the panic on his face. He apologised for his manner of intrusion and gave a description of what had happened and how he needed the reverend or his wife. After hearing his frantic account, she promised to track down the reverend and get him to the cottage as soon as possible. She grabbed her hat and coat and made her way to the Council Municipal Building.

Anders, appreciated the housekeeper's help, and then decided he had better find Mary, knowing her sister Becky would be needed. As he approached, he saw she was outside sitting on an old barrel, relaxing and drinking a tankard of ale. "Quick Mary is your sister in, the one with the bairn?" Anders managed to splutter out.

"Our Becky?" she whispered, "she's not in any bother, is she?"

"No, no, she's not, but she's needed up at the cottage, as soon as she can."

Becky was just eighteen and recently a mother herself, and would be soon, unknown to her, the wet nurse for this mysterious child. He quickly explained the situation and the three of them hurried back to the cottage. As they approached the small house, they could hear a child crying. Anders was alarmed at this, but Mary calmed him down by saying it was just her way of letting them know she was hungry.

Becky quickly took charge, soothing the baby and feeding her while the others looked on in silence, the enormity of the situation sinking in. The note found in the barrel was almost illegible, the ink smudged and faded, but Anders clung to it, knowing it might hold the key to the child's identity. He said to Florrie "I can't read it, most of it has washed away so the barrel must have been in the water at some time. I suppose we could try drying it out, but we can't risk tampering with it."

Florrie exclaimed "No, don't do anything, we're not getting the blame for this, you know what the authorities are like."

Amos sat silently, listening to the talk, the weight of the gold coin heavy in his pocket, his mind racing. The coin's strange engravings tugged at his memory, summoning stories of ships lost to the sea and treasures hidden in remote caves. But as he looked at his family and listened to their concerns, he kept his discovery to himself, it's mystery too intoxicating, too powerful, to share for now.

Speculation crackled through the small room each question unanswered. The baby's past hidden behind veils of damp ink and strange symbols. Yet, as Florrie held the child close, a small reluctant smile crept across her lips.

No-one could fathom how the barrel had ended up in the cave, nor why such a child would be abandoned. The only consensus was that someone had deliberately placed it there, high above the tide line, ensuring it would be found.

"You boys did a fine thing today," she said softly. If it wasn't for you both this child might never have been found."

Florrie invited Becky to stay the night, an offer readily accepted as the child fell into a peaceful sleep. The fire crackled warmly as shadows played on the walls, as the family gathered close, knowing instinctively that this was only the beginning. The true story was waiting, an enigma hidden deep within the tides of Frenchman's Bay, and as the fire smouldered low, each of them felt it; a mystery as thick and shadowed as the smoke that still lingered in the air.

The next day, Florrie was up before dawn, her mind already racing with the day's tasks. The news of the barrel and the child had spread like wildfire through the town, and everyone had an opinion on the matter. But Florrie's focus was on the baby, who was now feeding contentedly in Becky's arms.

As Florrie returned home from work, Amos approached her with a proud smile, holding out a smooth ebony-black pebble. "Found it where the barrel was, Ma" he said, "Thought you might want to keep it as a reminder, there's just a little crack at the bottom but I've filled it in with lime and sand."

Florrie took the stone, her eyes softening as she admired its polished surface. "I love it," she said, placing it on the mantle beside the fire. "It looks well there, now go and finish your chores."

As she watched her son leaving, Florrie thought, this is my first present from him, but she couldn't shake the feeling that this stone – like the child – was just the beginning of something far greater. Something that would have the power to change their lives forever.

CHAPTER 3

The dawn broke over the village with an eerie stillness, as if the world itself were holding its breath. By midday, the entire town buzzed with the scandalous discovery – a baby, found abandoned in a barrel, no less. Whispers passed like wildfire through the cobblestone streets, igniting every corner with speculation and gossip.

Inside Florrie's modest cottage, the atmosphere was a world away from the frenzy outside. The small kitchen was a sanctuary, where the weight of the world seemed to pause, Florrie, a sturdy woman with a heart as fierce as her love for the child, sat cradling the baby, her eyes scanning the tiny features with meticulous care. Each delicate finger and toe were examined as if she were piecing together a puzzle, the answer to which eluded even her.

Florrie and Becky were still in full attendance and devoting every minute to their new little visitor. Florrie spoke first as she rocked back in her chair, "Mind, I don't care what anybody says" she ruminated, "she's a real beauty, this one," her voice almost reverent, "she is so perfectly formed."

Becky standing by the window, turned slightly, her face half-lit by the pale morning light filtering through the grimy glass, "Aye she is that" she replied adding thoughtfully, "I suppose that will help when the authorities arrive and have to decide what to do with her or even who might have to take her on." A shadow crossed her features.

The words hung in the air like an unspoken threat.

"Eeh aye you're right" Florrie said, "I never even thought about that mind, someone's going to be very lucky."

"Aye very lucky," agreed Becky finally, with a tight-lipped smile, the words carrying an undercurrent of something more.

The morning passed in a blur, very quickly with lots of visitors coming and going with curiosity, each eager to catch a glimpse of the mysterious foundling.

Florrie knew most of them of course, but there were quite a few actually just being plain nosey, admittedly though everyone was full of good will and they endured the intrusion with a tight-lipped smile, her patience fraying with each passing moment. To be honest though both Florrie and Becky probably wished these moments would go on forever, but they knew in their hearts, of course, this could never be.

Becky on top of everything else, had her own child to think of as well, who was now staying with Becky's sister Mary and, of course, Florrie also was an extremely overworked housewife and mother.

Becky had reached for the kettle to make a cup of tea when she glanced outside of the tiny kitchen window, the glass panes used in the windows in those days weren't particularly clear as they were of poor quality, but she instantly recognised the Reverend Doctor Trevelyan, and his wife Fiona approaching. Accompanying them was the local police sergeant Billy Burns flanked by a young officer who was unfamiliar. Becky's heart skipped a beat, her instincts screaming that the calm was about to shatter.

Whilst still peering through the glass Becky had her hands up to her eyebrows in order that she could see with greater clarity. "Hey Florrie," she said, "the vicar's here and his posh wife as well."

Florrie's response was immediate, her body tensed as she rose from her chair. What's she after she wondered. She opened the old cottage door, giving it a gentle persuasive kick on the bottom as it creaked under her firm grip, it often got stuck. She managed a thin smile as she greeted the group, she left the door open and said, "Come on in, make yourself at home while I go and fetch Anders he's just on the beach."

Whilst doing so, she nodded in the direction of Becky and said, "you go and make everybody a cup of tea hinny," she paused once more before saying quietly "and when you do make sure you put a sip of brandy in mine, I think I might need it," as she looked in the direction of the vicar's wife.

Inside, the tension mounted as the guests settled into the cramped room, the air thick with unspoken questions.

Florrie didn't mind the vicar, but she didn't care much for his wife, she was a bit too posh for her liking, she spoke with an upper crust accent and, apart from that, she always washed her hands before she would accept refreshments from anybody and she washed them immediately afterwards, as though us common folk had the plague or something, Florrie would say.

Florrie arrived back with Anders a couple of minutes later and once the familiarities were over, they all proceeded to discuss the matter in hand. It was obvious to everyone in attendance that the final decision would obviously have to be made by the local law courts and the Alderman of the day but there were still lots and lots to discuss and indeed, not least, who was to have temporary care and control over the child until these matters were resolved.

Billy Burns, the sergeant in attendance, ever the professional, kept his tone neutral, but his eyes were sharp, calculating as he guided the conversation towards the inevitable.

Although a good friend of Florrie and Anders he was here for answers, but the truth was far from simple.

He had to be impartial and had to be seen to carry out all his investigations within the context of the law and no favouritism shown. Everyone was aware of how serious the affair was and the implications of such. He made sure his young officer P.C. Wilson, wrote down every relevant piece of information, even to the exact times surrounding the various issues.

Sergeant Burns went over every detail repeatedly, until he was satisfied there was nothing left for anyone to add. "Well," he said closing his notebook and putting away his pencil in his top pocket, "I think legally and officially that's all we can say about things now. Of course," he said with a twinkle in his eye, "that doesn't stop us from speculating, does it?"

Taking off his helmet and placing it on the table, therefore making the meeting officially over, he looked around the room and noted, apart from himself, there were another six adults present along with Florrie's two children Amos and Erasmus and naturally the baby girl herself.

He looked straight at P.C. Wilson. "Right Wilson, who do you think left the barrel in the cave?"

Young Wilson who was only about twenty was decidedly uncomfortable with being questioned. Wiping his brow with a handkerchief he tried to stutter out a response when Florrie intervened.

"Take no notice son," she said, "he's only having you on." She turned her attention fully now to Sgt Burns, "howay Billy," she said sarcastically "leave the lad alone. Get real for goodness' sake" she added.

Sergeant Burns laughed as a young, relieved Wilson took an extra drink of his now cold tea. "Even so," Sgt Burns went on," somebody out there knows the answer, and by now will almost certainly know the child has been found alive and well and they must know an enquiry will now be underway."

The conversation shifted and theories were flying like arrows.

Fiona Trevelyan, who had remained aloof until now suddenly spoke, her voice laced with certainty of privilege. "Well," she said in her superior manner "I think it's the mother who has dumped her there, who was more than likely a servant girl and just wanted to get rid of the child to hide her shame," she added with a flick of her hair and a touch of arrogance, "These things happen all the time."

"Fair enough Fiona" said her husband "but then who would be the father?"

"I don't know," Fiona answered rather agitatedly, "how would I know that? But it's more than likely a farm hand or a randy stable boy," pausing for a few seconds, while silence filled the room, "someone like that I would imagine," she added quietly.

Florrie looked up shaking her head and said, "Aye that's possible" she agreed, "but I'd wager it's more than likely the Lord of the manor or a man of position and power who's at fault ... when you look at the quality of the clothes she was wrapped in." She pointed and looked at Fiona with piercing eyes and a sense of loathing. "It's your sort that does this kind of thing, not us." She felt rather pleased with herself now.

The room fell silent, the air charged with tension. "Now, now," said Sgt Burns "let's not get too carried away or personal, it's all about opinions after all," but he went on to say "but Mrs Trevelyan is right though, she does have a point. I also think the person who dumped the child wanted her to be found alive. One thing I am surprised at though, there was no money, or provisions left with the child, nothing to plan for the child's future, like it was all done in a hurry." He was deep in thought as he pondered over his last remark.

Amos, standing in the corner, felt his heart slam against his ribs. The secret he carried burned like a brand. He had found something with the baby – a gold medallion, hidden away in his pocket. But now, it was too late to confess he had found some gold and had removed it he knew it was important, but now,the stakes had risen too high.

"Provisions" said Anders "like what, food and milk and that".

"No, no not food," said Sgt Burns "money though, I suppose, even a couple of coins, something like that or even a proper note not just a scrap of paper. It just seems strange, given the quality of the clothes she was wrapped in, that there was nothing else … it's just odd really."

All the time this was happening Fiona had been scrutinising the faded piece of paper that had been left. There was writing on it, but you couldn't make it out. With deliberate care she pressed it against the slate table, her fingers tracing the faint outline of words until it became clearer. Fiona turned the note upside down onto the greasy slate and began rubbing the areas where the writing was more apparent.

Once turned back over they noticed some of the letters became very clear. The writing was indeed in English, and the words Auriel Celeste was quite clear, however, nobody knew what that meant. They could now make-out other letters as well, but not full words. It was evident she was someone's daughter alright, and it seemed like the father had been named, it was someone called Casper or Casper Mercer. The revelation sent ripples of excitement through the room, though none knew what it meant, but at least there was something to work on.

Florrie despite her earlier disdain, found herself impressed with Fiona's diligence, so much so she offered her a small brandy, which for Florrie was very rare, but was a sort of olive branch.

However, much to everyone's surprise Fiona accepted, without I may add, foregoing the necessity to wash her hands first. A couple of drinks later and Florrie and Fiona got on famously, the tension of the evening dissolving in the warmth of shared spirits, with Florrie teaching Fiona a few well know Geordie phrases. Now whenever Florrie asked Fiona if she needed another drink Fiona answered, much to the delight of everyone present, "Wayaye man, why not." She learned the word hinny and used it in all the wrong places followed by further laughter from all present.

As the night progressed, with lots of different thoughts and ideas tossed around, nothing of any real value came to light from any of them and time was now getting on.

It was unanimously agreed by all present that for the time being at least, Florrie and Anders look after the child with the help of Becky until a date was set for the authorities to make a lawful decision. Also, Sgt Burns said he would continue his investigation in the hope the mystery that surrounded the town would be solved.

The last word of the evening came from the Reverend Trevelyan when he was speaking to Anders, "You know what Anders," he said, "after all that's gone on tonight and yesterday, the most surprising thing of all is the camaraderie between your Florrie and Fiona".

Anders followed his gaze towards where the two ladies were sitting, one a posh aristocratic lady and the other a local fishwife and they were still drinking and laughing totally unaware of the social differences between them. Anders smiled and shook his head in amazement, a smile of disbelief playing on his lips. "Aye" he murmured, admitting he hadn't seen that one coming.

It had now been four days since the ship had sunk. Young Pierre the cabin boy, being the only known survivor, his fate hanging in the balance, was being held in the old priory prison just across the river.

He had already given the authorities his account of what had happened and was, therefore, of no further use to them. Now, he awaited whatever decision the English authorities would impose.

Being French, of course, they couldn't just let him go but they couldn't put him in an ordinary prison either as the other prisoners and inmates would, undoubtably, carry out their own form of justice, you must understand and accept the English and French, at this time, hated each other and no quarter would be asked for or given.

The authorities didn't know what to do with the boy. Father Bartholomew, the monk, had just arrived burdened by compassion and carrying a small meal and some fresh clothing, they were only monks' habits, but they were clean and warm and after a little alteration they fitted rather well. "There you are" Bartholomew said, feeling quite pleased with himself "you look just like one of our own monks back at Lindisfarne".

Young Pierre wasn't too bothered about that he was just too pleased to have warm clothes to put on, he didn't care what he looked like and to be honest he was far more interested in the smell of the food Father Bartholomew had brought with him which consisted of roast pork, potatoes and Lindisfarne mead, a type of wine. He devoured all in front of him most enthusiastically, washing down each mouthful with the delicious tasting mead. After his meal he fell blissfully asleep unaware his future was being discussed and indeed his very existence.

The Sherriff of Northumberland, the supreme commander of all prisons in the local area had come down in person to see the lad to decide what his future would be. He had absolute power to make this final decision and that could include solitary confinement for life or even execution if he thought fit.

The Sheriff and Father Bartholomew were looking over Pierre as he slept when the Sheriff, a good man by nature shook his head and made an unusual request. "Do you think it might be possible," he said, "that the order of the Lindisfarne Monks may take the boy into their charge, at least until he is eighteen years of age and then we can decide what to do with him," he added quickly before Bartholemew could speak, "I think under the circumstances, that would be most acceptable." His eyebrows rose accordingly.

Father Bartholemew caught off guard by the suggestion was surprised at the request but agreed saying, "If it suits Your Grace, and of course, if you can obtain permission and approval from the courts, then that would be fine."

"You leave that to me" nodded the Sherriff "but keep the lad in isolation for the foreseeable future and teach him English and give him an English name, and don't, under any circumstances let anyone know his true identity, not even your fellow monks, no one" he went on.

Father Bartholomew nodded his agreement. "So, when shall I take him?"

"This evening when darkness falls" the Sherriff replied, "and Father Bartholomew" he said very solemnly "I thank you for your co-operation, but we will not speak of this matter again".

They shook hands and went their separate ways. The cell door was left open that night and for the first time there were no guards on duty. Obviously, the Sheriff's influence had already become apparent.

Father Bartholomew and Pierre wasted no time in making their escape. They moved swiftly out of the ruins and made their way to Lindisfarne and relative safety. Their journey was quick and without incident.

The following morning, the news was breaking that the young French lad had escaped but not without speculation. He had apparently fell to his death on the rocks below, his body then being washed away by the merciless sea.

Following a major search of the surrounding areas and no clues as to where he might be or even alive, the authorities agreed amongst themselves that he was missing and presumed dead.

For the next couple of days there were all kinds of rumours going around, that he overcame and killed the guards and disposed of their bodies and that he was last seen swimming out to sea.

Eventually, all rumours and enquiries came to nothing and, for the time being at least, Pierre the cabin boy was safe.

The boy who had survived the wreck of the Montpelier was gone, replaced by a nameless monk-in-training, his past buried deep in the cloisters of Lindisfarne.

CHAPTER 4

Montpellier, a jewel in the crown of southern France, stood proud in the late 1700s, it boasted a population of around 150,000 souls its, proximity to the Mediterranean Sea gave it unparalleled access to global shipping lanes. The city's international trade, particularly in wine, had transformed it into a hub of wealth and influence, making it the administrative capital of the Languedoc region. Paris may have been France's heart, but Montpellier was its pulse. At the centre of this thriving empire stood the Marcel family – wealthy, powerful and deeply connected to the royal lineage of Louis X1V himself.

They were one of the richest and most powerful families in France, ranked alongside the Guilhem family, their vast fortune built on vineyards and overseas trade.

Although the family, led by the patriarch, Count Artois Marcel, commanded respect in every corner of France he owned several residential properties. Their chosen residence was the magnificent Palace del Rois, set against this backdrop of a historic 16th century cathedral dating back to 1536 and it epitomised the wealth of the owners where opulence just became another word.

"Come, my dear let's join our guests for some refreshments before the dancing commences" murmured Artois to his wife "I fear the night is young and we should waste none of it."

Hand in hand he ushered Celeste, his wife of thirty years, into the most ornate, grand dining room you are likely to see. They were applauded in on sight by the carefully curated selection of nobility. As they approached their seats he gestured with his hand and all those present sat down immediately and patiently awaited his further instructions.

A single nod of his head in the direction of the chief of household started a frenzied response of action from the servant ensemble. Their precise steps delivering the most excellent wines together with all manner of exotic dishes, together with dozens of mouthwatering canapes. A feast people would say fit for a king, and if the food and drink wasn't sufficient to awe, provided by Artois with his wife's approval, the finest musicians in Southern France enchanted their guests, lifting the room's energy to a near celestial level,

"May I compliment you my dear" Artois whispered, leaning forward to kiss his wife's hand "you look so beautiful tonight" he paused "but then again, you always do" he added with a twinkle in his eye.

"Why thank you Artois" Celeste replied, "as ever, your compliments are treasured."

The evening was proving to be a total success, which was soon to be followed by enjoyable dancing and entertainment. The night was by no means a rare singular affair; indeed, it was a regular occurrence, happily enjoyed by one and all.

The evening unfolded like a well-rehearsed play – lavish, perfect, timeless. Regrettably, however, the wonderful atmosphere was about to end in the most devastating of ways.

As the guests revelled Artois and Celeste had slipped away for a few moments into one of the many opulent salons surrounding the great hall, as they relaxed and settled in with a glass of their prized wines, content to watch others enjoy themselves from afar. The couple were sharply interrupted however, by their most senior Major Domo.

"Your Grace" he said, "I have the most serious news for you of which I can hardly bear to speak of it."

"What is it man that can be so serious, you can hardly dare speak of it" demanded Artois, sensing the gravity he automatically seized hold of Celeste's arm.

Before any other word could be spoken the Major Domo swallowed hard before announcing, "It's your ship Sir, the Montpelier, it's been lost, sank with all hands missing," he went on "just off the coast of England, near Scotland."

Upon hearing this news Celeste fainted almost immediately, she was aware her son Jon and wife Eleonore were on board. The shock was too much for her to bear. "What do you mean, no-one survived" Artois quizzed "that's impossible, there must have been. Our son Captain Marcel and his wife were on board, surely, they are safe" he asked in desperation, he was looking for miracles, which weren't there, "They must have made it ashore."

The major Domo could only shake his head. They were, understandably, overcome with grief and shock and Celeste's world tilted, nothing being said was sinking in. "There must be some mistake" Artois went on "who for God's sake told you all this, they must be lying."

After a few moments' silence the Major Domo said quietly "It was your personal manservant Sir, Mehdi Aziz, and the news is spreading all over the town." Loyal and incapable of deceit, Medhi's word was gospel to Artois.

Artois sat motionless and quiet for what seemed like an eternity before asking for Medhi to be brought into the room.

Moments later he was brought into the room. His usual smile, the one that brightened even the darkest of days was absent. Medhi was of Tunisian descent, and he had lived with the Marcel family for over twenty years, since he was a two-year-old, in fact. If anyone could speak the truth it would be Medhi. He was a small young man, but he was very fit and athletic, his demeanour usually cheered up everyone who met him. Today though, Medhi walked into the room without speaking. Artois and Celeste immediately knew the information they had just received must be correct.

Celeste burst into tears, leaning forward and hanging onto the silk sleeves of Artois's coat. He placed his right hand onto the back of her wrist and squeezed it tight, too tight probably, as he uttered the words "It's true then, the Montpelier is lost?"

Medhi just nodded, again no words were spoken, the sadness in the room was too profound.

"And no survivors, is that correct?" Artois asked with tears in his eyes. Medhi shook his head and very quietly replied "That's correct sir, no survivors."

After two or three minutes of absolute silence Medhi went on "There were rumours that the cabin boy may have made it to safety. But no one knows for sure, Your Grace, it's just rumours."

"The cabin boy" Artois interrupted "that must be Pierre, we've met him Celeste" as he stared into her eyes "Jon took pity on him because he was an orphan and gave him a job on the Montpelier, it was his first trip away, do you remember."

Celeste just nodded saying nothing.

By now Artois was deep in thought, his mind was racing, could there be an explanation of what had happened, could there be some news, he thought that may bring them a crumb of comfort.

Ever puzzled, he looked over towards young Medhi, he noticed his left hand was bandaged heavily and was still showing signs of fresh blood, indeed there were some drops on the marble floor.

"Have you had an accident Medhi" Artois pointed to his hand "what has happened? Cut yourself in the kitchen?" he queried.

Medhi bowed and shook his head before answering "I am so sorry sir, but I have urgent business I must attend to immediately, please forgive me" he then rushed out of the room as fast as he could.

Artois turned his attention to Jon Paul the butler "What's all that about? Has he been careless," he paused "that's not like him."

Jon Paul shook his head and took his time in replying, "No sir" he replied, "I'm afraid it was no accident, Medhi cut off his own finger."

"Cut off his own finger" replied Artois rather loudly, "for what purpose, I mean, what on earth for?" he went on "Why would he do something like that."

Celeste had now recovered and gained her composure. Both she and Artois were as confused now as they ever had been.

Jon Paul spoke next with great deliberation and compassion, "Medhi Aziz" he explained "comes from an ancient, very proud Tunisian lineage who are fiercely loyal to everyone in the family and their loyalty would stop at nothing, sometimes beyond even death, such is their custom," Jon Paul went on "and it is part of their belief sir "he said "that if a respected member of the family who unfortunately suffers great pain then someone has to share the pain with them, for example by drawing blood, usually by a simple cut" he paused for a time "but in some cases if the pain is too great to bear, such as the loss of your son," he said very quietly, "removing a finger or an eye is as great a sacrifice he can give, it shows absolute compassion and loyalty, beyond expectations and this is what Medhi has done sir."

The weight of Medhi's devotion left Artois stunned. "My God" he exclaimed, "on a day when Celeste and I have lost our most treasured son and daughter in law we have been most humbled and deeply moved by a young servant boy whose love and devotion has shown no bounds, he has laid bare the deepest bonds of sacrifice ... we must at least take comfort from that."

The following day, as the sun rose over a grief-stricken household the Marcel family were still in deep shock, they knew they could not rest until the full truth of what had happened to the Montpelier. The normal, happy go lucky atmosphere was now non-existent, but as always, life goes on and everyone tried to carry on and make life as normal as possible. The count and countess did their best to lead by example. They ordered the resident musicians to continue playing happy continuous music throughout the day.

"You have to stay strong now for their sakes" insisted Artois,

"I agree" said Celeste "but my heart is heavy, and I can hardly breathe" she went on "I cannot bear to face the future, not without hope or proper answers" she added"

Artois was deep in thought before replying "I think, I think we should send someone over there to find out what they can and exactly what might have happened, we need to know everything."

He again looked over to Celeste and with raised eyebrows said, "Even if it's just to protect our sanity."

"To England?" Celeste exclaimed "Who would you send to England?"

"No, not quite, my dear" said Artois "whoever we send would have to go to Edinburgh first, and travel down to a place called Newcastle, in the North-East of England – an industrial centre where they build ships."

Celeste replied quickly "I can't see any Frenchman getting within a couple of miles of Newcastle before they would kill him."

"No, your probably right, in fact, I know you are" he replied, "but I was thinking more of an English-speaking Tunisian and a Scotsman."

"You mean Medhi?" Celeste asked with a puzzled expression.

"Yes, I do mean Medhi" Artois replied, "he has shown today his utter loyalty has he not?"

Celeste nodded immediately, "So who's the Scotsman then?" she asked lifting one eyebrow in the process.

"That would be a certain Archie McPherson," he replied, "among other things he is a whisky purveyor in Leith, and he has no love for the English."

Celeste smiled, she had heard of Archie, but he had a reputation of being a backstabbing, money-grabbing scoundrel, but in the past, he had been helpful to the Marcel's and with Medhi in close-proximity perhaps McPherson could be trusted. Nevertheless, it was a risk they were prepared to take hoping it would get them some kind of closure. Over the next few days there were all kinds of details to cover, letters of introduction to write, a list of all the questions to be asked, bribery money, as nothing would come cheap and, of course, the commissioning of a small seaworthy craft which would have to depart from either Belgium or Holland and not from France for obvious reasons. Medhi would have to make his way overland by coach to meet the ship when ready. The condition of the craft would have to be of paramount importance as the family felt they could not afford another disaster.

Before Medhi was due to leave, Artois and Celeste requested an audience with him. They wished him good luck and prayed for a safe return. In addition to all the information he had, he was given a few gold sovereigns and a gentleman's set of clothes, in the English style, of course.

With a final farewell, Celeste and Artois watched as their last hope – the young, loyal Medhi set off towards an uncertain fate, the weight of their grief pressing down on every step. As Medhi left there were tears in the eyes of the countess and even though her heart was filled with dread and apprehension she, and of course Artois, still clung to the tiniest speck of good news.

The fate of the Montpelier may have been sealed, but for the Marcels, the story was far from over. Their entire hopes now rested with Medhi and the wits of Archie McPherson.

Leith, Scotland and England awaited.

CHAPTER 5

The cold wind whipped through the narrow alleyways as the sun dipped beneath the horizon, casting long shadows across the village. It had been nearly two weeks since the baby had been discovered in that cursed barrel. Two weeks of unanswered questions whispered conversations, and mounting tension. The town was abuzz with rumours, yet all agreed, at least for the time being, that Florrie Guttenberg would care for the child. The courts slow as they were, had scheduled a hearing for the last day of September 1797, where the fate of the baby would be decided. Until then, Florrie and her family took on the task with a quiet, determined enthusiasm, though an undercurrent of unease stirred beneath the surface.

Inside the small cottage, a fire crackled weakly in the hearth as Florrie looked up from her work, turning to her friend Mary. "Well, it's been a couple of days since you saw her last, what do you think of her now?"

Mary gazed upon the beautiful child, all safely wrapped up in her cot. She leant over and tugged on the baby's ears and toes and pinched her skin ever so gently before replying "She is magnificent Florrie. She really is. Have you decided on a name for her yet?" Her voice carried a mixture of warmth and curiosity.

Florrie sighed; a distant look crossed her face. "Funny you should ask that it's an interesting thought," Florrie replied "me and Fiona were recently looking at the note, the one found in the barrel with her. We've found a word that looked like a name, Auriel Celeste, neither of us knew what it meant so we altered things a bit and thought Celia might be a good name, even if only temporary."

"Oh aye," said Mary "so Fiona, the vicar's wife is suddenly your best friend now?" she retorted sarcastically.

Florrie chuckled, shaking her head, at Mary, "Eh I knae who would have thought me, and Fiona would become friends?" She paused "A few weeks ago I couldn't stand her, it just shows you though, doesn't it?"

Mary joined in the laughing saying, "Aye, she's changed I suppose, still a snob like, but I do like the name, what does our Becky think?"

"What does Becky think" Florrie hooted "she loves it actually, except of course, she wanted to call the bairn Rebecca, understandable I suppose, it was her milk that saved the bairn in the first place … she still thinks she's the mother."

The sound of their shared laughter filled the room, a rare moment of levity in otherwise uncertain times. But just as quickly, the mood shifted. The conversation was interrupted by a knock on the door.

"Come in," shouted Florrie "it's not locked." A chill ran down her spine.

The door creaked open to reveal Sergeant Billy Burns the local constable. His presence, though familiar, brought an air of authority that stilled the room. He was a burly man, very authoritative, tall and slightly overweight with a ruddy complexion, that had earned him the nickname "Ginger Billy" long before he put on the uniform. He wasted no time with pleasantries. "I've been to see Jack the Blaster from the Grotto Ale House," he said, "I showed him the top of the barrel."

"And" Florrie enquired "did he recognise it?"

"No, Billy replied "Not as such, he agreed it was a Portuguese wine barrel all right but not from around here," he carried on, "more than likely it was from the Whitby area where there are a lot of wine merchants."

"Whitby," Florrie queried "how did it make its way all the way down here?"

Billy shrugged, the weight of the unknown heavy on his broad shoulders. "God knows. We've asked around, young Wilson, you know the young policeman that was here last week?" Florrie and Mary both nodded "Well, he's been making enquiries all over Shields, Boldon, Sunderland and Jarrow and honestly no one has a clue. It's as if it appeared out of nowhere."

"What happens now then?" Mary interrupted "Can we just … keep her?" she enquired with a voice tinged with both hope and apprehension.

"No, no," said Billy, shaking his head. "It's up to the County court next week, it's for them to decide. Until then, we wait, we haven't any option."

Mary shook her head and shrugged her shoulders, aye that'll be right, she thought, they won't let us make a decision.

The conversation was abruptly interrupted by Becky, bursting through the door, her energy a stark contrast to the sombre mood.

"Well, where's me bairn then" she said with outstretched arms "look what ya Ma's got for you."

"It's not your bairn mind Becky," Sergeant Burns, ever the realist retorted, "don't get too attached," he said in his deep policeman's voice.

Becky's smile faltered for a moment, but she quickly recovered and replied, "Doesn't stop me loving her now though, does it?" she said.

"No, it doesn't," Billy went on, "I'm just saying." He turned his attention back to Florrie and Mary. "So, it looks like we've gone as far as we can with our investigations and this morning I submitted my report to the Chief Constable, the whole thing is now in their hands and apparently they will be in touch very soon." He finished his tea and made his goodbyes, leaving the house quieter but no less troubled.

As Billy disappeared Becky asked, "What does that mean like?" she queried, "can they just come and take the bairn away whenever they feel like it?"

"Not at the moment," Florrie answered.

Becky then enquired if Sergeant Burns had mentioned PC Wilson and if he was seeing someone.

"Not really, only to say he had finished with his enquiries. Why like, do you fancy him?" she laughed.

This brought a sharp retort from Becky. "I most certainly do not," she said in the most corrosive of manners. She paused, "Well, maybe a little bit," she giggled as she thought about the question.

The sudden shift in conversation caught Florrie off guard, and she laughed despite herself. "Oh, so that's what this is about."

The banter continued as both Florrie and Mary burst out laughing, they knew Becky fancied the young policeman and they were taking great pleasure and delight in Becky's embarrassment. Becky already had a child, a little boy, Tommy, who was a year old now and a real handful, as of course most children are at that age, his father was a soldier in the Dragoons, and he had left with his regiment before he even knew Becky was pregnant and as they weren't married or had any intentions of being so the child was never an issue, certainly not to him anyway. Becky herself was only eighteen years old and still rather attractive; the ravages of time and the abusive workloads hadn't yet got hold of her and above all else Becky needed a future. Living with her sister Mary and her drunken husband Harry was not an ideal situation. The truth now, however, was let out of the bag, she fancied PC Wilson and she knew Florrie and Mary well enough, once armed with the information they would try their best to get involved and make things happen, it was just something they did.

Later that evening as Anders and his boys returned from their days on the water, they came into the house soaked, weary and absolutely starving. "I hope we've a hot meal on tonight," said Anders, "me and the boys could certainly do with it."

"Aye, it's almost ready," replied Florrie, pointing towards the pan boiling on the fire "it's boiled fish and potatoes."

Anders and the boys weren't impressed. "Fish," said Amos, "I'm sick of fish Ma, that's all I've seen all day."

"Well, it's good for you" insisted Florrie "it'll make you big and strong and its good for your eyesight as well."

Amos, quick as a flash replied under his breath, "To be honest I'd rather go blind." "What's that" Florrie enquired.

"Nowt, Ma," he said quickly, "have we got anything for afters?" "Yes, we've got rhubarb and custard."

At this point Erasmus's eyes lit up. "Can I just have the rhubarb then Ma," he asked, full of expectation.

"No, you can't" she replied, "you'll eat what your given and be grateful" she paused for a minute "I'm sick of this every mealtime."

Before she could go off on one of her rants, a common occurrence, she was interrupted by a loud knock on the door. The type of knock that made your blood run cold.

Anders rose slowly and stepped in front of her, his hand instinctively moving toward the sword mounted above the fireplace, "I'll go," he told her, "That's not a friendly knock, not friendly at all."

Everybody stopped what they were doing, Florrie still had the large wooden spoon in her hand, she had been stirring the rhubarb and the two boys just stared at their father as he went to open the door.

As the door creaked open, Anders was shocked to find two red coated soldiers, muskets in hand, devoid of emotion at the door. Taken aback he enquired why they were there, what business they had here.

Before any conversations could proceed any further a court official accompanied by the Chief Constable of Durham Assizes stepped forward, in a cold, detached voice he read out a short statement to the now silent family standing in front of him. The official informed them "By order of the court, the infant known as the baby in the barrel is to be removed to a place of safety until custody can be legally determined." He then folded up his parchment.

Florrie's breath caught in her throat but managed to say, "The court hearing, but that's a week away," she protested, "so where's the bairn going until then?" her voice was trembling.

She was distraught and in full panic, frantic even. "Stop them Anders, stop them" she screamed. She made a dash for

Anders sword above the fireplace, only to be held back by her husband himself. A very serious Anders grabbed hold of Florrie so tight she could hardly breathe.

All she could hear was Anders saying "Sh, sh, it's going to be alright."

The official didn't flinch. He merely nodded and stepped aside as a large brutish woman pushed into the room, she was in her mid-thirties or thereabouts, not the least bit pleasant looking, she was expressionless and said nothing, other than, "Is this the infant?" She strode to the crib, scooping up the infant with the same care one gave a sack of potatoes, before stuffing her into a coarse wicker bag. The room seemed to freeze in shock. Without another word being said the police commissioner and bailiff left the now hysterical Florrie and her family alone with the empty cot.

The armed soldiers stood directly in front of the door and remained there until the officers had gone. The family repeatedly asked where the child was being taken but received not a word in reply. Apart from reading the official statement no conversation had been entered. To say Florrie was devastated would be a gross understatement. Anders could barely contain his rage.

As the soldiers filed out, leaving the house in oppressive silence, the family stood frozen in shock, the empty cot a stark reminder of their helplessness.

The following day blurred into a haze of despair. Florrie, once the heart of the household, descended into her grief, her duties neglected, her spirit shattered, her self-esteem gone. Even when Billy Burns came with news that the child had been taken to the workhouse in Sunderland, the information did nothing to lift her from the depths of despair. Anders was talking to Billy Burns, and confided, "Honestly Billy, I have never seen a woman cry as hard as she did last night and for so long, she was totally wiped out."

Billy, at this time just nodded. Anders went on, "Not helped either mind," he went on, "when Mary and Becky came over, it was like being in a hoose full of scalded cats." Billy wanted to laugh but he knew not to, he just nodded.

"On a more cheerful note, what's P.C. Wilson's first name" enquired Anders. "Charley," replied Billy, "why are you asking that?"

"Oh, it's just Becky fancies him and wanted to know, I'll tell her when I get back."

As they parted company it was notable once again that the news of the "abduction," in their minds was swiftly travelling around the town, with nearly all the support leaning towards Florrie and the family. Doctor Trevelyan and Florrie's newfound friend Fiona were away on church duty and weren't expected back until after the court hearing had been held, so they were totally oblivious of the circumstances. Most unexpectedly even Harry, Mary's drunken husband turned up with some sausages donated by Geordie Barclay, much to the delight of Amos and Erasmus.

As the days went by Florrie's mood worsened. She was unkempt, she hadn't been washed or changed her clothes and on top of that she was foul tempered, she went into a state of depression. She didn't want to see or talk to anyone, not even Anders.

Support of the local community, however, was building up fast and there were hundreds of protestors outside the local

Shields courthouse, although she was totally unaware that she was not alone.

A day before the hearing, Sergeant Billy Burns came over to see the family. The hearing had now been changed to Hebburn as the police and courts in South Shields were afraid of trouble if the hearing went ahead in their own town. He looked at Florrie directly and spoke kindly, "Everyone is on your side you know Florrie; they really are."

There was silence for ages before Florrie answered without looking up, "I'm not interested, I couldn't care less."

Anders turned to face Billy, "She's been like this all week, we just can't seem to get through to her." He glanced back at Florrie who was now crumpled on the woolie mat beside the fire, like a wounded animal would, totally oblivious of the conversation. The night went over with Anders carrying out the duties that Florrie would have been expected to do.

It was now seven a.m. on the day of the hearing. Florrie was still lying in the same place: she wasn't in the best frame of mind following a few too many drinks the day before. Anders came into the room and gently shook Florrie by the shoulder.

"Florrie," he said, "we've got a visitor."

Florrie half opened her eyes and said, "I don't care, how many times have I got to tell you, and whoever it is can get lost." She was dishevelled and beaten down by the past week's events.

Suddenly a loud female voice interrupted Florrie. "And you, young lady, can get yourself out of that self-pitying mode," she shouted, "and you bloody well will care as well." She then proceeded to shake Florrie to liven her up.

It was Dolly, Florrie's mother. On seeing her Florrie burst into tears. "Ma, they've taken me bairn and we won't see her again."

"Right, you can stop that now Missy. Who's told you that?" she asked, "you've got an army of friends out there ready to swing for you lass." She pointed to the window. "Now, get yourself ready and get out there and join them, and I mean now."

Florrie, caught off guard by her mother's fierce demeanour, wiped her tears and nodded weakly. Deep down she knew Dolly was right. It was still very early in the morning but there were dozens of people standing there. The numbness she had felt for days began to lift, replaced by a flicker of hope and anger. She thought of the baby – Celia, or whatever her true name was – and how they had taken her so cruelly without a word. That helplessness turned into a slow-burning rage.

"Are all these people waiting for me?" Florrie asked her mother.

Dolly replied, "Aye they are and there are hundreds making their way to Hebburn courts as we speak." Dolly looked at Florrie with an affectionate glare.

"Really," Florrie whispered, "what for?"

Dolly lowered her voice for once, taking hold of both her daughter's shoulders, stared at her for a few precious seconds and said, "Because they are your friends Florrie, that's why, and they believe in you. Now get up and get a move on," she raised her voice now, "and tidy yourself up you little trollop, you aren't going to shame me."

Florrie now jumped into action straight away which gave Dolly time to address Anders. "And you, useless, you go and make a cup of tea," winking as she did so. Anders was only too pleased to do so, he had been quietly observing. He stepped forward and placing a reassuring hand on Florrie's back he said "She's right, Florrie. You're stronger than this, let's show them what you're made of."

Dolly's presence was like a lifeline, yanking her out of the quicksand of despair she had sunk into. Slowly, she began to dress, her movements sluggish, but her resolve strengthening with each step. By the time she was ready, Dolly had already started organizing. She turned to Anders, "Get the boys fed and dressed, we're all going to Hebburn. We'll make sure that court knows what they are up against. We'll let them know they are in for a fight."

Eventually, they were all outside suitably dressed for the occasion. Sergeant Billy and Charley Wilson were there with a horse and cart they had borrowed from Geordie Barclay. It was all cleaned and washed ready for the occasion.

"Your carriage awaits, my dear," Billy said, grinning from ear to ear "you shall not miss the ball," he laughed.

Outside, the community was gathering. Word had spread quickly, and people from all over South Shields were prepared to stand in solidarity with Florrie. They moved off to a great cheer from the gathered crowd, they were a good-natured lot, all shouting out messages of goodwill and support. "You'll do it Florrie," they were saying "You'll do it."

The protestors were no longer just concerned citizens – they had become a force, rallying around her and the baby, demanding justice. Their party arrived at the Hebburn courts well before time. Just as well really as they could not have foreseen the hundreds of well-wishers that awaited them. "So much for it being quieter here" Billy remarked "I bet they didn't expect this."

Florrie and Anders were over-whelmed; her mind was spinning. Would the court really take the baby away for good? Could they possibly fight the system? She squeezed Ander's hand, feeling his silent support. Dolly sat next to her, a formidable figure, watching the road ahead with a steely gaze. When they eventually arrived at the courthouse it was just as bad, people were waving signs, chanted slogans and offered words of encouragement as the family made their way through the throng. It seemed the whole town had turned up. There wasn't a seat to be had or any spare standing room, except for the seats which had been reserved specifically for them, which included Becky and Mary who were already there.

"See, Florrie," Dolly said, gesturing toward the crowd, "They're here for you." Florrie nodded, the weight of the support finally sinking in. She wasn't alone after all. She had an entire town behind her. Inside the courthouse, the atmosphere was cold and foreboding.

Although it was a very serious affair, Becky couldn't believe her luck when Charley Wilson was going to be sitting right beside her, she was flushed with excitement and giggled at every opportunity. She kept glancing over to Charley and he did likewise, like you would do at Sunday school. To those watching it was at least a little light relief before the seriousness that was about to unfold.

The hearing was scheduled for eleven and was expected to last no more than half an hour which was the norm for this type of case. There were murmurings and idle chatter from around the courthouse, such was the massive interest this case was generating.

Sergeant Burns looked at his pocket watch, it was 10.55, five minutes to go he thought.

The judge, an older man with a stern expression, presided over the hearing. Florrie sat in the front with her family, her heart pounding in her chest. The sight of the officials who had taken the baby made her hands clench into fists. She had to hold herself back from screaming at them. As Billy turned round to have a quick chat with the family before commencement of the hearing, there were suddenly gasps from the public gallery with cries of astonishment. For the first time ever known in a hearing of this type, the child Celia was brought into the court.

She was placed in a makeshift cot on a couple of lightweight stands, as though she was up for sale. Gone were the clothes Florrie had kept her in, they had been replaced by standard workhouse grey, a type of hard-wearing cloth. She had the customary tight bonnet pulled over her head with the tiniest of aprons tied around her waist. She was accompanied by the same unsmiling assistant that had taken her away from them in the first place.

Florrie managed to restrain herself but couldn't bear to look at little Celia, not dressed like that anyhow. She bowed her head and remained silent.

The chief Magistrate spoke first, "Is this the child in question?" he asked with little or no compassion, as he made gestures towards the infant.

"It is Your Worship," answered the court official. "And whose charge is he or she in at the moment?"

The usher quickly replied, "She is in the temporary care of the Sunderland Workhouse at the moment," he went on. "The child is she your worship, and about two months old. She is the so-called child found in a barrel."

The senior Magistrate nodded "Has anyone expressed an interest in taking the child on?" he asked with once again no compassion or warmth.

"Yes, your Worships, the Convent of Our Lady in Durham are quite happy to take the child, into their care if nobody else will or can."

They spoke as if the baby were nothing more than a piece of property, not a living, breathing human being. The Magistrate looked up at the public gallery where Florrie and her family were sitting. He asked for Florrie and Becky to be pointed out. Once they had been successfully identified, the Magistrate for the first time showed a little bit of humanity and compassion.

He lowered his tone of voice and said "This child over here owes her life to you and your family and your friend. Had it not been for your decisive actions that child would not and could not have survived, you must take immense pride in what you have done and the way you have looked after her since she was rescued and taken care of as you would your own child. This court recognises and wholeheartedly congratulates you on what you have done."

There was a ripple of applause from the public gallery. "Quiet please" interrupted the usher.

The senior Magistrate continued, "Unfortunately," as he was addressing Florrie and Becky "your financial and personal circumstances mean you are not allowed by the law of this land to adopt such a child, especially in these unusual circumstances, therefore, regrettable as it may be, we have no other alternative but to award the child into the care of those people who can."

Florrie just closed her eyes, she was sick to the stomach, and she couldn't bear the thought of it, but she knew he was correct, of course, but had to try. "Your honour," she began "this child – Celia, as we've been calling her – was found in the most terrible circumstances. But in these past few weeks, she's become part of our family. We've cared for her, loved her, and we just want the chance to keep doing that."

She paused, swallowing back the lump in her throat. "We don't know who left her in that barrel or why. But we do know she deserves love and care, and that's exactly what we've given her and what we want for her."

The courtroom was silent. The judge listened carefully his expression unreadable. Florrie looked at him, trying to gauge whether her words had reached him, but it was impossible to tell.

The judge continued, "I will expedite this process. A decision about this child's future will be made as soon as possible.

The public gallery was now silent as the three Magistrates discussed the entire proceedings. In the meantime, a couple of nuns had arrived from the convent and stood next to the lady from the workhouse. They had also brought some clothes with them. There was a tiny replica of a nun's habit, in case the decision went their way. Their eyes were downcast, not looking at anyone. The leading Magistrate turned his attention to the matron from the workhouse. "If the child is put into your care," he asked, "will you have honest and healthy work for her?"

"Yes," replied the matron, "it should only take a couple of years or so before she can be put to work in the washhouse, it's as clean and healthy as you can get," she went on, "and strong for the soul and mind" she added as she looked toward the nuns.

Florrie closed her eyes again and, once more, lowered her head. Becky also had her eyes closed and her fingers in her ears, she wanted to see or hear nothing. The Magistrates were now ready for their decision. Just as they were about to make the announcement, there was a sudden activity, a ripple of commotion swept through the gallery. Heads turned, whispers spreading like wildfire.

" Silence, please," the usher shouted, "settle down or you will be asked to leave the court."

Naturally, as you might expect everybody looked up to see what all the commotion was about. At the back of the room, a figure emerged from the shadows Fiona Trevelyan, the vicar's wife. She had somehow made it back from York sooner than was expected, no doubt it was to lend her support to Florrie and Becky.

Fiona moved with purpose, her gaze never leaving the Magistrates. Florrie acknowledged her presence and managed a warm smile, amazingly though Fiona offered no response whatsoever, it was as though a knife was slowly being pushed into Florrie's heart.

The Magistrates paused, clearly unsettled by the sudden arrival. One of the ushers leaned in, whispering urgently to the senior Magistrate. The proceedings ground to a halt, the court held in a suspended breath.

Once again there was silence in the court. Tension though, was building, as was the confusion. This resulted in their Worships withdrawing from the court for at least fifteen minutes.

"Silence, please," shouted the usher on their return. "The court will now give out their verdict." You could hear a pin drop, even the crowd outside, who until now had been unruly were extremely quiet.

After what seemed like an age the Magistrate spoke and said, "There has been a last-minute request," he said slowly, his voice betraying a trace of surprise. "Reverend Dr Trevelyan and his wife have requested custody of the child, pending certain conditions. We have agreed an approval in principle to this request once these conditions are approved." Minor pandemonium broke out and there were gasps of astonishment. Surely this was good news.

"Silence, silence or you will all have to be removed, silence I say." shouted the usher. "Mrs Trevelyan," the Chairman said, "will you stand up in order that I may address you. You have conditions? Are they important…"

Fiona answered most articulately and firmly, "Absolutely essential," she answered, "and I regret without these conditions being met I cannot proceed." She said all of this without emotion or taking her eyes off the Magistrates.

"Then, Mrs Trevelyan, pray tell us what these conditions are and what you have to say."

At last Fiona relaxed her serious demeanour. For the first time in the court, she turned around to face Florrie and Becky, she had tears in her eyes.

She spoke very softly and quietly for the first time since she had arrived, she faltered slightly but carried on, her voice filled with emotion. "I became friendly with these two wonderful, hard-working ladies only a few weeks ago," she pointed out the two women "they showed me and my husband in a few hours what love, and kindness can achieve. Therefore,I can think of no better human beings alive that could bring up a child as good as my friends. My conditions, therefore, are, I will accept the child Celia into my home as my own and bring her up within the Christian values of my household, providing these two ladies are allowed to remain a part of her life. I cannot raise Celia without their help. They are as much a part of her family as I am."

A murmur of disbelief spread through the crowd. The Magistrates turned to Florrie and Becky, his eyes narrowing. "How do you respond, ladies? What is your answer to that?"

Yes, yes, yes, they both shouted together as they jumped up from their seats. Becky even went a step further, shouting "I do, I do, I do." The intensity of the moment overwhelming her.

Sergeant Burns who sat beside her smiled and said, "Calm yourself down Becky, it's not your wedding you know. Not just yet." He laughed.

After the court's last statement, the whole room exploded into applause and deafening cheers, it was so loud you could probably hear them in South Shields. The day had started out as possibly the worse one they had ever had but it was ending one of the best.

Fiona rushed over to the women, the fear and inhibitions were all gone now, she was smiling and obviously overwhelmed by the whole proceedings.

She was thinking, only a few minutes ago she was classed as the pompous vicar's wife with no real friends to speak of. Now here she was the hero of the moment, mother of a beautiful little girl named Celia and best friends with Florrie and Becky and not forgetting Mary.

At long last she was being accepted by the whole community, and deservedly so.

Florrie couldn't help herself though, she paused and looked at Fiona with a distrusting stare. "You had us worried there for a few minutes mind when you wouldn't look in our direction, me and Becky thought you wanted to take Celia for yourself."

"I had to play my part that way," she retorted seriously, "if I hadn't acted like that, we were certain the other parties involved, particularly the nuns from the convent, were going to object, we couldn't take that risk."

Now Becky intervened and made a sensible but rather astute remark. "You said we thought, who's we?" she asked.

Fiona smile broadened as she looked at Becky full in the face, "My husband of course, Mr. Trevelyan, he has been working in secret behind the scenes ever since we found out.

Indeed, if it were not for him, none of this could have happened."

There was silence for a moment, and Becky answered rather enthusiastically, "Well, if that's true, I think I'll start going to church again" everyone laughed and hugged each other.

Even PC Charley Wilson had to join in the laughter. There certainly had been evidence of more than one miracle that day, and the contented smiles and pure satisfaction on everyone's faces said it all. It was a new beginning, and the future did indeed look bright.

CHAPTER 6

After weeks of speculation, the Marcel family back in France had now been made fully aware of all the circumstances surrounding the disaster, but because the relationship between England and France was at an all-time low the information they received was not as accurate or as conclusive as they would have liked. After long hours of discussion, the Marcel's decided to conduct their own investigations, this was to be done by sending over their most trusted of servants, a Tunisian, Medhi Aziz, for two reasons, one he could speak perfect English and the second he didn't look French.

It was agreed they would send him over to Scotland, the port of Leith to be exact, and there he was to enlist the help of Archie McPherson. Archie was well known to the Marcel family, as he had helped them many times in the past. Archie classed himself as a purveyor of fine whisky, but he was also recognised as an unregistered investigator who acted within the law some might say, and acted outside of the law most would say, his methods were unusual to say the least – but very effective.

Young Medhi Aziz had never been to sea before, and he was so much looking forward to the experience. Once on board and underway, however, he swiftly changed his mind.

Regrettably, he was sick more often than he was not. The journey itself took less than a few days to reach Leith, (the port of Edinburgh).

"Right Ho, sailor boy," said the captain "you can drag yourself out of bed now we have arrived in bonny Scotland."

The grinning captain took great delight in Medhi's agony, watching him suffer was an experience enjoyed by all.

"I must get off this ship" pleaded Medhi "I couldn't manage another minute" as he raced to be sick one more time. The captain and the crew once again laughed with great enthusiasm as they threw off his belongings and cases indiscriminately from the ship onto the jetty.

He stumbled ashore still wobbling over his recent experiences. "You see that yon building over there, young sir" the captain said pointing to what looked like a load of old planks and bricks precariously balanced on the edge of the jetty, it certainly didn't look like a building. Medhi looked up and saw the unruly pile of materials when the captain interrupted his thoughts and said "That's where you'll find Archie McPherson … If you're lucky" he laughed.

Medhi stood alone on the dockside; to say he looked out of place would have been an understatement as he was dressed in the impeccably designed clothing given to him by his master, Artois. He stared at what he thought looked like the devils own back yard, the locals who were passing by were speaking in what seemed like English but was very different somehow. Some of them even dressed differently, the likes of which he had never seen before. The men wore bright woollen skirts, he later learned these were Scottish kilts, these kilts exposed their knees, and they seemed to have some kind of furry animal sewn to their belts, again he later found out this was a sporran. It was indeed a strange land.

He couldn't be sure if the people were friendly, or if in fact, they wished him harm, for whenever he spoke to them, they mainly just shook their heads and uttered what he considered to be gibberish.

He gradually made his way up toward the timbers and bricks. This was no house he thought to himself, there can't be people living here. More to the point, surely Archie McPherson, a friend of Count Artois couldn't possibly live here.

To get to what looked like a front door, and the supposed main entrance, you were expected to walk across single planks, very loosely cemented into the brickwork, each plank was placed roughly two feet apart, one slip or one foot wrong would send you twenty feet below into the fast-flowing river. The very first plank Medhi put his foot on moved quite significantly, which in turn, was met with roars of laughter and great expectation by the crew of the ship he had just left. There were many sighs of disappointment as Medhi made it safely to the front door.

He was still precariously balanced, however, on the last plank with nothing to hold on to. The space between the door and plank he was standing on was only about twelve inches and he was worried that if the door were to open out over, he would be swept off and into the river. Fortunately, he noticed a very large nail had been hammered into the wall near the door and he held on to that for safety.

As he prepared to knock on the door the whole situation wasn't going anywhere near his impressions of what he had expected. Holding on to the nail though made him feel a bit more secure and he knocked on the door with his other hand. Moments later the tiniest of windows opened above him and out came what Medhi perceived was the very head of the devil himself. This horrifying vision looked at him with his red eyes, a rather dark beard and teeth that could surely chew through iron chains he thought, and on top of his head was a small dark blue beret with a little silver tassel.

"Aye, and who might you be wee man" a voice said "and what business would you want with Archie McPherson" he drawled in a typical Glaswegian voice.

Medhi, thankfully, understood most of it and answered, "I have a letter for you Mr. McPherson sir," said Medhi "it's from the Count Artois Marcel from France."

There was silence for a few minutes before Archie spoke again "Aye, I ken him!" he said quietly and rather slowly "has he given you any money lad?" he asked, raising his upper lip, allowing his already large eyes to bulge out even more. Medhi, although afraid and feeling alone still hung on to the nail.

"Yes, he has, sir" he replied, "gold sovereigns and a note signed by himself."

"Well hand them up here laddie" Archie demanded, "and I will open the door for thee."

Although you could say Medhi was still wet behind the ears and had a lot to learn he wasn't that stupid. "I'm sorry Mr McPherson" he said, "but I can't do that, my orders are that I can only pay as we proceed.

"Then you'll need to stop there aal neet laddie" said Archie "your no getting in here." With that he shut the window leaving Medhi standing on the flimsy unsteady planking outside the door.

The cold night seemed to wrap itself around Medhi as if conspiring to test his resolve. It seemed hours before he encountered Archie again, and somehow, despite the chill, he had fallen asleep and it was now dark, and the rain drizzled down relentlessly as he found himself shivering. He looked up at the small, dim window, the only beacon of light in the dreary Scottish night.

A creak echoed through the silence as the tiny window above slid open and Archie's grizzled face peered out. "So, you're still here then," a voice said sounding almost surprised "are you going to hand up that money now?"

"I am not" Medhi replied, his breath misting in the cold air, "I have the Count's orders and know what I must do."

Archie grunted and cursed a little, still staring at the young Tunisian. "Aye, well you're a stubborn wee soul right enough, I'll give you that lad … I suppose you best come in out of the cold."

Medhi stood up waiting for the door to be opened only to see a rope snaking down in the rain from the window above.

"What's this sir?" Medhi asked, confused, his face twisted and contorted due to the smell of the old rope.

"It's your way into the hoose lad" Archie grinned, drips of ale dropping from his mouth. Medhi was very confused by this, "Why can't you just open the door" he protested.

"Aah cannae dae that laddie, I dinnae open the door to strangers" he said matter-of-factly.

With that last remark Archie left to go inside with the smelly rope still swaying in the wind. It was pitch black now save for the light coming from the window itself.

Medhi thought he had no alternative but to climb up, his hands stung from the wet and cold, but he couldn't go back because he couldn't see a pathway, so he began climbing. Fortunately, he was very fit and agile and after a few moments he was at the window opening itself. He managed to throw his belongings through the window onto the floor but not before checking the pouch containing the sovereigns remained tucked safely in his coat.

As he pulled himself through the window the warmth of the fire hit him like a wave. Archie was cooking some meat over what looked like a spit, the smell from the meat was intoxicating. The desire to get over there was overwhelming.

Archie looked over to the window from where he was sitting, his grin catching the firelight and said "Well come doon bonny lad, come doon, I expect ye'll be wantin a bite of supper and a drop of ale?

Medhi's stomach growled in response, and despite the odd circumstances, he couldn't deny the overwhelming desire for warmth and food. He lowered himself to the floor, shaking off the rain, and gratefully accepted the tankard of ale being handed to him.

"Get that doon ye" Archie said, his smile becoming nearly friendly "It'll soon warm ye up."

He liked Medhi already he thought, he had courage, and he had a mind of his own and seemed very loyal, he reminded him of himself when he was a boy.

Medhi was glad of the ale but if truth was known he was more interested in the food and the warmth of the fire before anything else. Archie took his eyes off the meat for a second, as he turned the spit, he looked at Medhi and said, "You can call me Archie laddie," he paused for a minute and added, "I only allow friends, good friends, to call me that."

Medhi smiled, "Thank you Archie," he smiled back, the tension between them easing, he realised Archie wasn't as frightening as he had first thought. He was rough but had a strange kind of charm. His home was like something you would expect. Nothing of real value and generally untidy.

They ate in companionable silence, the crackle of the fire and the occasional pop from the roasting meat the only sounds in the room. The flat bread was fresh, and the meat – though unidentifiable to Medhi – was delicious.

He glanced at Medhi smiling, the devilish appearance was beginning to diminish now. Medhi also smiled, perhaps this Archie McPherson wasn't the devil incarnate after all. After about half an hour Medhi and Archie were still enjoying their meal.

Archie said, with food remnants still in his mouth "I expect this is a bit of a come doon from the meals you've had at the Palace" he said whilst sucking and licking the last of the meat from the bones, wiping his mouth with the back of his hand.

"Not at all" Medhi answered "in fact this meat is probably the most enjoyable I have ever had."

"Aye that's because you're starving" Archie replied, "but there's plenty more where that came from, I have as you might say a daily supply."

They talked and drank more ale through the rest of the evening, Medhi felt himself relaxing as they discussed themselves, who they were, and about the mission Count Artois wanted them to carry out. Medhi realised Archie had lived a full life, that much was clear, but he also possessed a deep, cunning intelligence, he could see why the count had chosen him as a guide.

The next day Medhi arose first, as was usual for him, and he started clearing away the plates from the night before. He looked at the bones on the plates but couldn't recognise them, perhaps it was some strange Scottish animal he had never heard of, like the haggis monster the ship's crew had been telling him about, so he just shrugged it off.

Archie emerged soon after and immediately began making breakfast, naturally it was the old Scottish favourite, porridge.

Medhi however, like most people, especially the young, felt the need to attend to an urgent matter, an urge to visit the toilet. He politely asked Archie whereabouts this most private of conveniences might be. He didn't want to look at him directly as Archie still hadn't put on his kilt yet.

"Sir," he began hesitantly. "Where, if I may ask is the … necessary?"

Archie grumbled. "There yae go laddie, you see that hole in the floor. Right there, well that'll be it laddie," he said.

Medhi looked shocked. "But that's just a hole in the floor sir" he protested.

"Aye so it is laddie, but it is next to the fire so it's warm." He then added with a smile "whatever goes in there goes straight through directly into the river so it disnae smell" he seemed rather proud of the fact.

Medhi blinked, horrified, but what could he do? However, he couldn't get used to the idea that the room where you had just finished your meal, where you had slept the night before and carry out your bodily functions were all in the same tiny space with no privacy.

"Not quite like that in the Palace," said Archie.

"Not quite sir," Medhi replied. "Could you please look the other way at least sir" asked a rather uncomfortable Medhi.

"Of course, laddie of course." Archie turned around to face the other way until Medhi had settled himself down and succumbed to natures demands, chuckling all the time.

"Oops" Archie said laughing, "I heard that big boy hitting the river.

Medhi was so mortified his eyes rolled over, his face was burning up, his embarrassment was now complete. The sooner he left this place the better he thought.

As Medhi tried to regain some semblance of dignity, he couldn't help but think of the luxury of the palace, how far he had fallen. Nevertheless, he found himself having a grudging respect for Archie.

However, hunger still got the better of him and Medhi couldn't resist the hot porridge Archie had made, for the second time in twenty-four hours he had again tasted something he had never had before. As he enjoyed the experience it naturally got him thinking. "That meat we had last night Archie," he asked, "was that a haggis?"

"A haggis," Archie answered loudly with a smile, "no bonny lad, haggis is not an animal it's a mixture of oats and mutton and boiled in a pan with vegetables and tatties but it's no an animal."

Medhi instantly knew the crew from the ship had been telling tall tales "So it's not a huge hairy monster with razor sharp teeth then?" Medhi went on to say.

Both Archie and Medhi had a good laugh, he had been fooled once again but even he could see the funny side. Medhi finished off his porridge, licking clean the very last bits from the wooden bowl.

Licking his lips he then said to Archie, "So, it wasn't chicken, was it?"

Archie carefully looked at his new friend, his expression grew serious, though there was a mischievous glint in his eye. "That my wee Tunisian laddie was the well-known rattusnorveicus," he said in all seriousness, pausing for seemed like ages, "otherwise known as the common water rat, such as the one that's hanging over yonder there on the meat hook, and a fine specimen indeed, even if I do say so myself."

Medhi froze, his stomach churning, he hardly dared turn round to look but he had to, he felt compelled. Eventually his eyes fell upon the large pink, skinned, unmistakable shape of a water rat. Its discarded fur simply left in a pile on the floor where it had been scraped off the unfortunate animal ready for disposal. Once again, our young friend found the open hole in the floor most helpful, how many more times could a man be sick he thought to himself. He barely made it back in time.

The rest of that day was spent in a blur of preparations and discussing the many tasks ahead as were proposed by Artois Marcel. It was agreed they should buy a strong healthy horse and a covered-in cart. Not quite the luxury coach Medhi was used to but adequate, nonetheless. The journey to Newcastle they were about to embark on would take, in their opinion, a couple of days or so, their fact-finding mission had now begun. There was something invigorating about it – an adventure that had just begun.

Meanwhile back in South Shields the Rev Tobius Trevelyan and his wife Fiona had come home after taking charge of their now beloved new daughter, Celia. It was almost two weeks since the court had given them custody. Every day, without fail, Florrie and Becky called to the house for at least an hour, it was after all, what they had agreed to in court and no man or men or any number of wild horses would ever stop them from doing that.

St Hilda's vicarage where the Reverend and Fiona lived was a superb building and was only yards from the church. It had been built over six hundred years ago, and the house must have been built about two hundred years later, they were surrounded by fine gardens and a huge ornamental fishpond. There were lots of mature trees and a grazing field for the horses, in short it was an idyllic place to live and be part of. Inside, the building was no different, it was run by the housekeeper Mrs Watson, she kept it looking immaculate, but it was also a very happy environment.

It was Saturday afternoon, and Mrs Watson was busy cooking and preparing meals for the following day, the Rev Trevelyan, whilst being the most agreeable man and loved having fun with his parishioners, always made sure that Sundays were always kept in the best tradition of the church. In his mind, and Fiona's, Sundays were a time for prayer and bible instruction and, of course, a fine selection of hymns, the more joyous the better. Naturally no one worked on Sunday's, so this was the day they hoped to attract as many people as possible to their church.

The Reverends wife, Fiona, was preparing her Sunday school lessons, which was becoming more popular each week that passed, and she had a fondness for the group of children, whose curiosity and energy never ceased to amaze her. She watched as they filed in and was delighted to see Becky among them. Fiona was overjoyed as she had been hesitant at first but was now a vital part of the group and often helped the younger children with the readings and took part in the discussions with surprising insight. Becky kept to her promise, she had said in court she would join Fiona's Sunday school and she as good as her word, made sure she did attend. As the lessons began, Fiona spoke of love, kindness and the importance of looking after one another, that felt especially poignant given all that had happened with Celia. Becky listened intently, her thoughts drifting to the baby she had grown so fond of in these short weeks. She couldn't help but smile as she thought of the little girl's giggles and the way her tiny hands reached out for comfort. Her newfound position at the vicarage had given her life structure and a sense of belonging. It's worth mentioning this was the very first time, apart from her christening Becky had ever been back in a church, and she was now eighteen years of age. She was shocked but impressed by how friendly everyone was to her and how humble they all seemed to be.

Meanwhile, Florrie, standing by the fish stalls with Mary, wiped her brow and looked out toward the water. There was something deeply satisfying about returning to her familiar routine, even as life around her seemed to be changing. She knew things could never go back to exactly how they were before, but that wasn't necessarily a bad thing, The unexpected events had opened doors, created new opportunities, and more importantly, healed wounds that Florrie had thought might never mend.

She enthusiastically asked the housekeeper, "Can I help you in any way to prepare the meals Mrs Watson?"

"You most certainly can," was the reply as she was only too pleased to receive any type of help. "Here," she said as she threw a bagful of potatoes towards Becky, "get on with peeling these then if you would be so kind … It's a horrible job though," she went on.

Becky just laughed "Not if you compare it to filleting fish on a winter's day it isn't."

"No, no I don't suppose it is when you think about it," Mrs Watson chuckled to herself. Initially she'd had misgivings about Florrie and Becky coming round to the house daily, but these early signs were encouraging. The days passed by with baby Celia being treated like a celebrity by everyone who saw her, they all wanted to visit her and talk about her, there was even an article in the local press about how she was found in the barrel by Amos and Erasmus Guttenberg which, understandably, made the boys feel like heroes. They couldn't walk down the street without someone pointing them out and saying look there's the kids that found the bairn in the barrel. There seemed to be an air of excitement and expectation everywhere.

It appeared the whole area had gained a new purpose and there was a confidence about that was a joy to behold, at long last there was something to smile about. Life indeed, was feeling a lot more agreeable, as the conversations were drifting toward the more serious business transactions.

"Funny isn't it" Becky mused aloud, more to herself than anyone else. "What's that dear?" Mrs Watson replied, looking up from her pot of stew.

"How things can change so fast, one day it's just another hard slog, and the next, you've got a new family, a new job … a whole new life."

Mrs Watson smiled knowingly. "Aye, life has a way of surprising us all. Sometimes for the worse, but often for the better, if you keep your heart open."

Becky nodded, her thoughts drifting once more to Celia. She wasn't sure where the road ahead would take her, but for the first time in a long while, she felt ready to face whatever came her way. South Shields with its quiet streets, ancient church and close-knit community had become more than just a place to live – it was home. In that moment Becky realised that maybe, just maybe, she had found her place in the world too.

Mrs. Watson initially a little stern, had grown fond of Becky's enthusiasm and sharp wit. She had proven to be a quick learner, and she handled her tasks with care and precision, never once complaining about the work.

Over time Mrs. Watson had started sharing stories about her own life, and the two women found common ground in their love for hard work and no-nonsense attitudes. One afternoon as Becky peeled yet another bag of potatoes, she looked out of the window toward the fishpond. The light filtered through the trees, casting a golden hue over the water. She thought about how different life had felt just a few months ago and marvelled at the strange and wonderful turns it had now taken.

CHAPTER 7

As Medhi stood on the windswept hill overlooking the ancient town of Berwick, a shiver ran down his back. He turned to his companion, the brooding Scotsman at his side.

"So, this is Berwick is it, Archie?" asked Medhi "Is this where Scotland ends, and England begins?"

Archie, his jaw clenched, stared ahead, his gaze hard and unforgiving. "Aye it is laddie, once we cross over yonder bridge, we'll be in England" replied a rather agitated and sombre Archie "into a land of greedy, treacherous people, in my humble opinion, of course, so it is."

Medhi just nodded and spoke no words, he knew little of England or its people other than they always seemed to be at war with France and most Scottish people had a disdain for them. His heart thudded in his chest as they approached the narrow stone-built bridge across the River Tweed.

As they trudged southwards towards Newcastle, Medhi more through boredom than anything asked Archie about the English and why he hated them so much. At first, he just turned away, his face a mask of tight-lipped resistance. As they passed a milestone, halfburied in the earth, something in Archie snapped. He stopped abruptly, his eyes narrowing as they fell on the inscription: Inverness, Culloden.

The stone itself had now partly collapsed and was only half visible above the earth but to Archie McPherson its very presence was like a knife blow to the heart.

"That" he said with incredible venom, pointing at the stone "is why I hate the English, they and their kind murdered my entire family. All of them. I have vowed by God to take vengeance whenever and wherever I can."

His voice, usually rough, was now laced with venom, he now went silent and never spoke another word, leaving Medhi to contemplate the reasons and to wonder what circumstances must have happened to initiate such a response.

The next day at about 8.30 in the morning as they arrived at Tynemouth the air turned bitter. Typically, it was raining and very cold, they looked across at the jagged rocks of the Black Middens and both assumed this was where the Montpelier had run aground and sunk.

"Aye," Archie muttered darkly, the wind tossing his hair wildly, giving him the look of an ancient spirit, "this looks like a perfect place to sink a fine ship. You widna have much chance of surviving in that lot, especially when a storm had blown up."

Medhi shivering in his fine summer clothing that the Count Artois had given him agreed. He couldn't believe how cold it was, yet he noticed the locals were wandering around in half their clothes, as though it was midsummer.

"What manner of men are these?" he asked Archie "Are they superhuman, the cold doesn't seem to affect them at all. Are they immune to the cold?" He seemed genuinely surprised.

"No, they are not superhuman laddie" replied Archie "these people are known as Geordies, they are more like a cross between the Scots and the English." Archie thought for a moment "They are a decent lot though, hardworking and very loyal." He looked at Medhi and winked saying "Ah widna kill one of these just for the sake of it." He laughed as he turned back to face the town of North Shields. "Come awa laddie and let's see if we can get lodgings for two nights."

Strangely enough Scottish folk were always made welcome in this part of England, as were indeed people of Arabian heritage, so it was of little surprise they found a decent place to stay, in fact the establishment they found, The Wooden Dolly, was only a stone's throw away from the Black Middens, an ideal place to rest and a great base to carry out their investigations. It was warm and welcoming, its hearth ablaze, casting light into the room.

"When we relax and have a drink tonight Archie will you tell me the real story of why you hate the English so much, they seem a fair sort to me" questioned Medhi.

Inside, the atmosphere was merry – a stark contrast to the tempest raging outside. Lanterns swayed from the ceiling, their soft glow flickering across the faces of seafarers and townsfolk alike. In the corner, an old man played a squeezebox while a boy no older than eight danced on a table, his bare feet drumming with the tune.

Archie stormed into the tavern, a towering figure in his kilt and plaid, his face set in a stern expression which silenced the crowd. "Now then," he boomed, "who among ye will share a drink with Archie McPherson and my young friend Medhi?"

Without waiting for a reply, he pulled two bottles of whisky from his bag and held them high." Archie looked at the landlord saying, "With your permission sir, if it pleases you, these are on the hoose."

The landlord, a small rotund chap with little or no hair beamed "It surely does please me Mr. McPherson, you and your friend are most welcome."

The night stretched on in a haze of whisky and laughter, but beneath the revelry, Medhi's mind lingered on the mystery of Archie's hatred. Later as they stumbled up to their room, they found it to be small with only space for two beds and a small table. As they settled down Archie pulled out yet another bottle of whisky saying, "Me reserve son, ye should always keep a wee something in reserve."

He fell back onto a bed and said, "I'll take this one laddie if you have no complaints, you take that one."

Medhi just nodded only too pleased to have a place to rest after being in the back of the cart. They lit the oil lamps and Archie started his clay pipe, seemingly deep in thought.

Medhi could no longer contain his curiosity. "While we are relaxing Archie, will you tell me the real story? Why you hate the English?"

Archie, to his credit, took his time to answer. "I haven't telt many men or women for that matter, my story Medhi, because when I do tell people I nearly always end up killing somebody."

As he was saying this, he pulled out a pistol from inside his coat. The barrel gleamed in the lamplight, he levelled it at Medhi's temple, his voice a low dangerous, growl.

With all the hatred and pent-up feelings, he had built up over the years. "Aye I'll tell ye I'll tell ye alright but divvn't be surprised if aah kill ye in the process" he replied, shaking with emotion.

Poor Medhi was shocked and rooted to the spot "Only if it's convenient Mr Mc Pherson" he croaked. This remark and the way it was said from the young lad made Archie laugh out loud.

The tension broke and Archie roared with laughter, clapping Medhi on the back with enough force to send him sprawling.

"Well, I'll gie ye this canny lad, aal gie you this, your no a softie that's for sure, I'm taking a wee liking to ye so I am. You've certainly got nerve." With that he tucked the pistol away and allowed the warmth of the tavern to seep into their bones.

Medhi just nodded, "I think I may call you my friend now, so it is with interest and compassion I would hear your tale." Archie took a deep breath, sniffed and cleared his nose for a while and stared at the lamp and for a few seconds he watched the reflections dance across the room. "Right then, my wee Tunisian warrior" said Archie "let's see if I can tell the whole story without killing you" he winked reassuringly.

Archie poured both himself and Medhi another whisky. He lay back on the bed, resting on his elbow, he took a few seconds to sort himself out and then said, "You have to go back to just before the Battle of Culloden, that was in 1746 "Archie went on, staring into the dancing flame, "my grandparents and my faither lived on a small farm, near Dumbarton, the whole family were cousins of the McDonalds, you may have heard of them, but they were not fighting folk, nevertheless they were loyal to Prince Charlie and sympathetic to the cause. After the battle the English redcoats came. They razed our lands. Killed our men, raped our women and hung our children."

"What was the cause?" interrupted Medhi.

"Freedom lad, freedom and independence, we wanted to rule ourselves and still do as a matter of fact, but in them times the only way the McPherson's could help was by supplying meat and other foods for the clans, which we did right up to the final battle of Culloden. My faither was only ten years old at the time but he had an older brother and two younger sisters, one wee bairn was only a few months old" Archie went on after a moment's thought "a few weeks after the battle, which we Scots lost, the English redcoats started returning South back to England. Every farm or smallholding they came across was raped and pillaged."

Medhi interrupted again "Your family – did they?"

Archie nodded, his voice barely above a whisper now. "Aye my faither was – he was just a boy, but he saw it all. They left him hanging from a tree with his sisters, but he survived. God knows how. A band of gypsies found him, took him in. That's how he lived. That's how I'm here now. But he never forgot, never forgave."

Did no-one ever warn the farmers or people so they could protect themselves or even escape."

Archie shook his head "No laddie, they didna have time, but in any case, the farmers and their wives were no match for the redcoats. My grandparents knew what they would do once they overran the farm, it was common knowledge the men would be killed once they had witnessed their women being raped and their children hung from any available tree, they were just left there, sometimes for weeks."

Archie went on, "Aye you see laddie this is where I usually kill somebody or bash their heeds in, it's as though I am telling lies you understand and ma temper gets the better of me" he stared straight into Medhi's eyes "but in your case I'll make an exception" he went on "yes indeed, the redcoats did all of these things, and they even burnt down our farmhouses and scorched the land for good measure." On their travels my father, who was about twenty at the time, met a young Scottish lassie in Edinburgh, they got married, in the gypsy style and then had me."

"They loved Edinburgh, and they settled doon there and acquired a wee bit o land where they kept a couple of sheep. Nothing fancy you understand, just enough to keep them gannin."

By this time Medhi was completely enthralled "Surely that's a good thing though isn't it Archie, things were looking better now."

Archie shook his head; he was beginning to sweat profusely now and was finding difficulty in choosing his words. He poured himself another glass of whisky and gulped it down in one go. The room fell silent, the weight of Archie's story hanging in the air like a storm about to break. Medhi could say nothing, could offer no comfort. He simply watched as the Scotsman, so full of rage and fire, finally broke. With another deep sigh he turned to face Medhi who sensed he was struggling within himself for what he was about to reveal. It turned out gypsies, apparently, weren't allowed to own sheep or any land for that matter so the redcoats were ordered to confiscate my parent's belongings and chase them off the land. My faither and mother protested, they wouldn't leave and in the fight that followed they were both killed, and I was left alone in the field to fend for mesell, I was just over two years old." Archie looked up at Medhi again "Aye that's right Medhi" then he said very slowly "two years old, that's how old I was."

Medhi carefully interrupted, "How on earth did you survive Archie, it would seem impossible?"

"Aye, it was" Archie grumbled "but in a way, I suppose, I only half survived, part of me is human but the rest of me Medhi, I think you know by now, is more beast than man."

There was absolute silence in the room after that, absolute silence. What made matters worse, during the course of the night, although it was pitch black, Medhi was sure he heard that tough giant of a man, Archie McPherson, crying to himself There was no more to be said, nothing to suppose, nothing to defend.

In the flickering glow of the fire, Medhi understood there was no peace for a man like Archie. Only the endless shadow of vengeance.

CHAPTER 8

Medhi awoke with a start. The room was empty, bathed in faint morning light filtering through the curtains. He instinctively checked the time 7.30 am give or take – but the emptiness gnawed at him. He was immediately worried about Archie especially following the discussions they had the night before, concern burrowed deep into his mind. He wondered had he said too much, had he put too much pressure on Archie. These thoughts were racing through his mind, did he push Archie harder than he should have? The questions swirled like a storm as he dressed hurriedly, his heart hammering.

Descending the creaky wooden stairs, Medhi entered the pub's modest kitchen. The landlord, Walter, was already there, bustling about preparing breakfast for his guests. "Good morning, Walter" Medhi said forcing a smile "You wouldn't have seen Archie this morning, would you?"

"Aye, I have actually" Walter replied lifting his head "he's away to the fish quay for some kippers, at least I think that's what he said," mumbling under his breath,

"Kippers?" Medhi's brow furrowed in genuine confusion, "what on earth are kippers?" he asked with as puzzled an expression as you are ever likely to see.

Walter stopped for a moment, his weathered face breaking into a slow, amused grin. "Ah" said Walter, slowly and deliberately "so you've never had kippers before then, eh? They're a delicacy round here lad. Herring smoked until they're cured. Quite the treat if you ask me." Walter just laughed as he carried on peeling his onions.

"I never have had kippers, and what is cured?" Medhi was unfamiliar with the term.

Walter answered "Well Medhi, kippers are a wellknown delicacy among Scottish folk and us Geordies alike. Cured means that they've been prepared in a special way, smoked with brine, then once they are done, they are cooked and usually served with scrambled eggs. You'll see."

Medhi just nodded and looked totally bemused, he knew Walter had said everything that was needed, and he had been very sincere, but it left him still in the dark.

The sound of heavy boots snapped Medhi from his musings. Archie filled the doorway, his arms outstretched, holding out two bundles of oily brown fish tied with string. His grin stretched wide; his voice boomed through the kitchen. "Kippers! A feast fit for a king, Medhi! You won't find these in Montpellier."

Medhi however, wasn't so easily convinced, especially after tasting Archies rattus coravecious (water rat stew) but following Walter's testimonial he did agree to give them a try. To his surprise, the kippers were delicious, a savoury revelation, indeed he was now beginning to embrace all these traditions and tastes that were gradually coming his way, The custom, though of serving beer with breakfast was a concept he was still struggling to accept.

Nevertheless, breakfast was now over, and it was time, at last, for him and Archie to start the real task of the day. They must ask questions and gather information on behalf of Count Artois, the mysterious owner of the sunken ship Montpelier. Archie, ever pragmatic, knew he would probably reveal more from the locals than he would from the official report, but decided he would start with the local constabulary to see where that would lead.

They Georgian façade of the local constabulary greeted them just after nine am. "A grand morning to ye sir" Archie said in his typical larger-than-life style to the desk Sergeant, with his arm forward and outstretched in a gesture of goodwill "I am hoping you might have some information of the shipwreck on the Middens here just recently" he went on with his hand still out in front of him, but there was no response from the Sergeant. "Might you be able to help?" He was met with a blank stare.

"All information on that night is in the report covered by the local newspaper" said the rather dour police sergeant "and there's nothing more I want to or can add so I'll bid good day to you" as he began to turn away from them.

Archie's smile didn't waver, but a flicker of steel flashed in his eyes. "Aye, I understand" replied Archie, the smile now gone from his face "but ye see, I have a wee token here that, I hope, may change your mind" he said throwing a gold sovereign onto the tall solid counter, the heavy dull sound of the gold on wood cut through the air. The sergeant's hard demeanour cracked ever so slightly as his gaze lingered on the coin. Archie's grin returned as he thrust out his hand once more. "Archie McPherson," he said with renewed warmth, "and this here is Medhi Aziz, my assistant."

This time, the sergeant took the offered hand and said, "Good morning, Sir, my name is Albert Parker, the resident sergeant of Arms in this establishment, how can I be of assistance, Mr McPherson?"

Medhi was slack jawed, he'd heard of Archie's ways of obtaining information, but this was the first time he had experienced such a transformation, witnessing it in person was something else.

Archie now fully in control of the situation went on "Before we start Albert" he said, "may I call you Albert?"

"Of course," replied the sergeant, his eyes still fixed on the gold coin.

"Good, good, first things first, you might want to tuck that sovereign away somewhere safe, you never know there are thieves and vagabonds everywhere, ye canna trust anybody these days" he said winking at Mehdi; however, the irony of the statement was lost on Sgt Parker who quickly slipped the sovereign into his top tunic pocket.

The police station itself was only a few yards from the Priory where young Pierre was taken after his capture and where he reportedly escaped from. "Would it be possible for us to go and see the place, where the young laddie was imprisoned?"

Albert was only too pleased to comply he didn't want any other person, especially police officers to be privy to this conversation. "Yes" he replied, "I still have the key for the cell door, it's here somewhere."

He rummaged around for a while, knocking things over here and there and then he produced the largest key any one of them had ever seen, it was made of brass and must have been twelve inches long. It was beautifully engraved if not a little uncared for. The three of them left the police station en route for the Priory, although upon arrival there was no need of a key as the door had been left open. Archie stood there thinking for a moment before saying "You see what aa canna understand is why bring the laddie here to this god forsaken place when you could have just kept him in the polis station."

There was a slight pause. "That's simple enough to answer" replied Albert "with him being French no one wanted to take responsibility, and everybody knew if he had been put with other prisoners, he would more than likely have been murdered, or worse if you follow my drift" Albert paused again "he was only a young lad after all."

Archie nodded "Aye, good point that, in fact I have had experience of such matters over the years, so I have, none of which I feel like repeating." He erased such thoughts from his head.

"So, this is the actual cell he was kept in and escaped from is it" Archie asked, "and has not been touched since."

Sgt Parker nodded saying "Aye sir, it is and it's not been touched since. "

Following a moment or two of reflection Archie went on to say, "this window halfway up the wall is the one Pierre crawled through and escaped from?" He paced slowly, letting his fingers brush the rough walls.

"Aye that's the one" Albert went on "look there's still a bit of blood where he must have wriggled through" he answered proudly.

Archie turned round to face the Sergeant and said, "I can see why you've made Sergeant, there's not a lot gets past you Albert is there?" His tone was sharp, like a blade slid quietly from its sheath.

Albert looked genuinely pleased with himself and went on "Aye he must have lowered his self onto the rocks below and swam away. Brave lad, he was," he said feeling like the oracle himself at this stage.

"So, after he escaped into the water, where exactly did he swim to? France? Holland? Scotland?" This asked sarcastically.

Albert's face flushed as he struggled to find an answer, eyes rolling to the ceiling in search of answers that weren't there." I'm not sure, to be honest. No one's ever figured it out. The lad just disappeared."

"Disappeared?" Archies eyes gleamed. "But no body washed ashore. No trace of him at all?" As he said this Archie raised his eyebrows and fixed his eyes firmly on Albert', "And why did he crawl out of the window when he could have just walked out of the door?"

Albert stammered and stuttered for a few seconds "Well, we think it was because he was French and rather thick and just did the first thing that came into his mind" he answered rather smugly.

"Aye that's most likely it" Archie nodded "when you put it like that."

A heavy silence filled the cell. Albert uncomfortably, wiping a band of sweat from his brow, "I think that answers all your questions now, Mr. McPherson."

Archie's grin was wolfish now, dangerous in charm. "Oh, you've been a tremendous help Sergeant, it's not often you get to talk to someone who is so knowledgeable and has such a superior intellect. One last thing though. Was Pierre alone that day or did he have any visitors?"

Albert thought for a minute, "Just the monk, Fr Bartholomew from Lindisfarne, he used to bring food and drink every day for the lad," said Albert.

"Really, that's interesting," said Archie now very alert "has anyone spoken to Fr Bartholomew about the boy's disappearance?" he asked in a surprised response.

Albert's discomfort deepened, "Well, not really" answered Sergeant Parker "he hadn't been anywhere near for a day or so before the prisoner escaped so we didn't bother as what could he know?"

Archie had a little smile to himself "Aye your right once again I succumb to your superior intellect Sergeant, you see people like me never think of things like that, who, indeed, would have thought of interviewing Father Bartholemew. It's been a pleasure talking to you, an absolute pleasure Sir, truly." His sarcasm hung in the air, heavy and biting. He clapped Albert on the shoulder, hard enough to make the sergeant flinch. He glanced over to Mehdi who just stood there shaking his head, what next, he must have been thinking.

Archie and Medhi spent the next hour sitting on an old bench within the Priory overlooking the River Tyne and the Black Middens. Medhi spoke first "I was just thinking, are we going to speak to the monk Bartholomew."

"Aye we are indeed laddie, we certainly are, but not today or tonight" he put his huge arm around Medhi's slim shoulders' "there is valuable drinking time awaiting us first." He turned to look at Medhi, and grinning he said, "Unless you have any objections of course."

It was with those few words of wisdom they headed back to the Wooden Dolly more than willing to accept the evening's challenges and entertainment and join in they most certainly did.

The Lindisfarne Priory is situated on Holy Island just off the coast of Northumberland, it was built around 535AD although most of its grand architectural buildings and imposing columns are now destroyed, a band of local monks still loyal to St Aiden and St Cuthbert live among the ruins and have created habitable buildings within them. The monks still carry out their duties as were agreed and set down from ancient times by their original masters. For instance, they still rose at 6 am every morning and waited until the sun appeared on the horizon, they would then commence their daily routines which included various prayers and meditations which could last for several hours, this was all before breakfast. The rest of the remaining hours of the day were spent reading the scriptures and writing books on the subject.

Other duties included cultivation of the land and wine making or to be more precise the development of Lindisfarne mead, which is a kind of honey wine blended with local grains and barley, very popular and very delicious. Although the monks were busy for most of the working day, they were allowed a couple of hours in which they could virtually please themselves and therefore speak freely on any subject.

It was on one of these moments that Fr Bartholomew spoke to young Pierre the only survivor of the Montpelier shipwreck. "How are you feeling today Pierre" he asked in English, utilising some sign language as he did so.

Pierre answered "I think I am how you would say okay" he smiled as he said this as he had only been learning English for a few weeks, and he was already grasping the meaning of the words and not just saying them.

"Good" said Fr Bartholomew "over time I shall endeavour to explain why you have to be here, but I must stress you are not a prisoner but unfortunately it is not safe for you to be among the local population just yet so you must be patient." He repeated these last few words in French just so there would be no misunderstanding.

Pierre nodded, he understood alright but nevertheless he asked Fr Bartholomew would he ever be able to leave and if so when. The kindly monk thought for a few moments before answering "Look" he said "always remember I am your friend and I desperately want you to be happy and content and eventually free, of course, and not live in fear. However, your safety is my main concern but as soon as I am sure you are capable of mixing with the people outside of this monastery you will leave with my blessing and best wishes."

Once again Pierre answered in rather broken English "Then I start learning from now" he said in English with a beautiful French accent.

Bartholomew laughed he couldn't do anything else and clapped his young pupil "I am most certain you will my dear boy" he said "but as from today you will be known as Peter Bartholomew and apart from you learning English and other trades which I will endeavour to teach you, you will also have to speak in the local dialect.

Young Pierre looked at Fr Bartholomew and resigned himself to the fact that he would have to change his whole identity, simply to survive, even for a young boy of his age he recognised this and readily accepted the challenges.

At least, he thought, I am still alive and have food and shelter, thanks mainly to Fr Bartholomew and not forgetting of course the High Sheriff of Northumberland who helped make good the escape by making sure the cell door was left open. Before he had arrived in England he had heard a lot of bad things about the

English people, but here were a couple of men who had shown huge compassion, and he would never forget them.

The following morning, they arrived at the windswept ruins of Lindisfarne Priory. The ancient stones stood like sentinels, weathered by centuries of salt and wind, a testament to the island's turbulent past.

To get to Holy Island and the Priory you must wait until the tide goes out, when that happens you have a few hours where you can cross the causeway and make your way to the island. One of Pierres (now known as Peter) duties was to sit in the high tower and make note of all new arrivals to the Priory. This was a tradition going back hundreds of years, it was mainly following the invasion of the Vikings, but the practice was kept on.

Peter already knew most of the visitors as they were the same regular group of local trades people. It was quite boring but today was slightly different. He noticed a covered in cart being pulled along by a fine looking horse, although he couldn't make out the strange looking occupants, one was a young dark skinned man, he looked slim and had very expensive clothes on, not the normal type you might expect and his companion was a much larger man in what looked like a woollen skirt, this was definitely not normal so he quickly left his post and reported his finding to Fr Bartholomew.

After hearing Peter's account, he said "You've done right lad, you go quickly and hide inside the prayer room and don't come out until I tell you, don't come out for anyone. It's probably nothing but better be safe than sorry."

Peter agreed and hid in the private prayer room and waited for further instructions. Fr Bartholomew continued with his business which today included the bottling of the mead (honey wine). He could hear voices outside and thought one of them was of Scottish denomination which under the circumstances meant nothing to him. Seconds after hearing the voices there was a slight gentle knock on the door which was then opened. Father David, one of the younger monks at the Priory popped his head in "Sorry to interrupt you Father" he said, "we have a gentleman here, a Mr McPherson who would like a few words with you."

"What about" he asked cautiously with more than a little scepticism.

Father David went on "He says he's a whisky merchant and would like to talk business with you if he may."

As this conversation was going on, Mehdi was quietly asking Archie why he didn't tell the monk that he was after information about young Pierre.

"Never show your cards at the first time of asking" said Archie "make your opponent feel relaxed and comfortable, he'll talk when the time comes" he added.

"Right" said Fr Bartholomew "show the gentleman in if you'll be so kind".

Archie and Medhi breezed into the room full of confidence and enthusiasm. "Pleased to meet you good sir" said Archie, his right arm outstretched in a gesture of friendship "have you got a name I could address you with" beaming as he did so.

"Fr Bartholomew is my full name here, but most people call me Father."

"Aye, aye grand, that'll do for me" said Archie "My name is Archie McPherson, and this is my young assistant Medhi Aziz, who for all his sins is an expert on Portuguese wine."

Medhi upon hearing this, almost fainted as he didn't know the first thing about Portuguese wine, as a matter of fact he knew more about kippers than he did about wine, he just stared at Fr Bartholomew with a blank expression hoping he wouldn't spot his utter disbelief in what he had just heard.

Momentarily Fr Bartholomew was relieved, and he began to relax a little. "So how can I be of service to you" he asked.

Before Archie answered he beckoned to Medhi to open his case and followed this up by presenting the monk with two fine bottles of blended whisky. As he was doing so, he said "This is my business father, I blend and sell fine whiskies all over Scotland and in the North of England, none more so than in Wylam and Hexham. It was there, in fact, that I heard them talk about your famous Lindisfarne mead and believe there's an opportunity to expand your reach. Perhaps into Scotland?"

"Oh" said the monk "I'm pleased to hear that, any news is welcome, but good news even more so."

"Aye well that's what I thought" replied Archie."

Medhi, now schooled in the way Archie operated and was thinking, automatically poured out two large whiskies for Archie and Father Bartholomew, but deliberately none for himself.

"Thank you, kind laddie," said Archie "bottoms up as they say" then they both downed their drinks in one swift action, no sooner had they finished when Medhi filled up their glasses again. This was repeated on no fewer than four occasions.

Mehdi, of course, having had no drink was still very sober, which by now was more than could be said for Archie and the father. As the time passed and more drinks were consumed, the business side of the conversations were slowly disappearing and Archie being Archie was slowly adding little pieces of interest he had heard in the local pub, making sure he wasn't forewarning Fr Bartholomew about anything untoward, he was rather hoping he would, by this stage, begin to discuss something about the shipwreck himself.

Fortunately, he didn't have long to wait. After the first bottle of whisky had been consumed it was Fr Bartholomew's turn to offer Archie some of the Lindisfarne mead.

It was while he was uncorking the bottle the monk became a little unsteady on his feet and started to giggle to himself, he was now enjoying the company.

He then, uncharacteristically and quite unexpectedly asked "Has anyone in the pub mentioned the shipwreck on the Black Middens to you Archie?" he wanted to know if they were aware of Pierre. Bartholomew was now completely full of the ambience and rather chatty.

"Aye, one or two of the locals in the Wooden Dolly have talked about it in passing but I wasn't that interested really" as he leaned back in his chair, for all the world to assume he was about to fall asleep,

"Did they mention the young cabin boy who escaped? He was the only survivor you know," Father Bartholomew went on. Medhi interrupted although he was sure Archie was only pretending to be half asleep, he guessed correctly this might be a good time for him to continue the conversation.

"Well, the manager of the Wooden Dolly, Walter, thought he escaped, and swam back to France or something like that" he said.

Bartholomew snorted; his laughter bitter. "Swam back to France you say?" he said in a raised slightly sarcastic voice "He couldn't swim across a pond, never mind the North Sea" he added with contempt.

"Really" Medhi said "how do you know that then?"

Archie, feigning sleep, stirred slightly but said nothing, letting Mehdi take the lead.

Bartholomew glanced at Archie, who was now apparently asleep and totally oblivious to any conversation, good he thought I can carry on, he really wanted to confide in somebody. He then took a deep breath and said "Because I happen to be the monk who cared for young Pierre and ensured he was alright, I also made sure he had plenty to eat and drink" he went on.

"So, you cared for him?"

"I did," Bartholomew muttered, his eyes clouding.

"Do you think he escaped then" Mehdi asked rather cautiously. It seemed ages before he got a reply

"Let's just say I don't think he's dead. No – but I don't think we've seen the last of him either." once again glancing over towards Archie, making sure he couldn't hear what was going on, the signs were, he couldn't as he was now snoring very openly.

"So, in your opinion, where do you think he might be" asked Medhi, again trying not to be too inquisitive.

"No idea" said Fr Bartholomew shaking his head, although his voice spoke of not knowing anything his eyes suggested other alternatives.

Just then Archie appeared to come out of his drunken sleep and yawned massively with both arms stretching up into the air. "So, my wee friends" he asked, "have I missed anything?"

Immediately, Bartholomew said "No, not at all Medhi and I were just discussing the finer points of making Portuguese wine, isn't that right Medhi?"

Medhi realised at once that Bartholomew didn't want to continue any further conversations and was inwardly considering he had said too much already, the amount of drink he had just consumed had indeed loosened his tongue, probably a bit too much for his own liking. The next half hour or so was spent discussing the supply of the Lindisfarne mead, which they hoped would be of benefit to them both and they agreed to have further discussions in the future and left on very friendly terms.

As they rode back over the causeway, the tide rising ominously around the horse's legs, Medhi turned to Archie, unable to contain his curiosity any longer. "So, you heard everything?"

Archie eyes never left the swirling waters beneath them. "I did lad, everything, but it was well worth it. Every word laddie, every, last word. We've barely made it in time though." His voice held a hint of exhilaration as though the danger itself was a reward. He proceeded to pat Medhi's shoulder and quite sincerely added "You've done well, You're a quick learner.

Bartholomew knows exactly where that boy is hiding. But the full story will come … when the time is right," a grin tugged at the corner of his mouth, an unsettling one.

Medhi was feeling pleased with himself relishing Archie's praise. But the feeling was fleeting. Something deeper, darker, lurked beneath their triumph, and he could sense it. The waters beneath them seemed to reflect more than just the sky – they hinted at dangers yet to be revealed.

"The answers will come in their own good time Medhi, we have other pieces of this puzzle to fit together. There are others who might have seen something other people's opinions, in particular the people who combed the wreckage the day after the ship ran aground and the fishwives who sit on the jetty every day, they're a sharp-eyed bunch. Someone knows more than they are letting on."

Medhi nodded in agreement his mind racing ahead, but stayed silent, but he could see the wisdom of Count Artois employing Archie McPherson, even he could see how Archie's methods, unconventional but undeniably effective achieved results. He sensed that they were just scratching the surface of something far deeper and far more dangerous than they had anticipated.

As they journeyed back to North Shields, hours spent discussing all manner of subjects, some serious, some light-hearted banter. Despite their differences – Archie, a grizzled Scotsman with years etched into his face, and Medhi, the young, eager apprentice – there was an unspoken camaraderie between them. They had only known each other for a couple of weeks but their age and cultural differences seemed not to matter at all.

Medhi, being the younger of the two travellers was naturally becoming more curious with each passing hour. He was gaining confidence now and he certainly felt comfortable enough to ask one or two, pertinent questions. Particularly regarding his mysterious relationship with his master, the Count Artois. Questions like, how they met in the first place and what could have forged such a bond between the two men who, on the surface, seemed so different? What had he actually done to obtain the Count's full trust and confidence. Whilst Medhi was thinking of such matters, he studied Archie, looking him up and down, taking in his dress, his physique and finally focussing on his face. A weathered face that seemed devoid of any feeling or compassion. A ruggedly built man, he was intimidating but there was something – more.

The silence between them thickened until Medhi finally spoke, his voice tentative. "So, how did you and the Count actually meet Archie?" enquired Medhi "Was it in France or Scotland?"

Archie turned around slowly, his gaze locking on the Tunisian with a measured intensity. His raised eyebrows suggesting Medhi was asking a little too much.

Medhi, undaunted, pressed on "Only if it pleases you, of course." He said rather quietly, bowing his head slightly in deference.

For a moment Archie, said nothing. The rhythmic clop of the horse's hooves filled the air as he adjusted his worn collar, seemingly lost in thought.

"No, laddie, its alright. You probably have every right to know, so you do." His voice was gruff but there was a strange weight to his words. Archie carried on with his explanation. He had first met the Count of Montpelier in Scotland. Leith to be exact, he mused. "As you are aware, Medhi" he said "I am in the whisky trade, and fine liquors. I was going about my usual business, passing the warehouses where huge stocks of whisky and all kinds for that matter, are stored. As I was passing one of these warehouses, I heard a commotion, sounded like a bit of a scuffle going on inside a scruffy disused building. There was some agitated shouting, and I could quite clearly hear raised English voices and mingled among them was a lone French accent. Curiosity got the better of me, made me open the warehouse door." Medhi could sense the conflict in him, "I always remember opening that door as it was rusting away and quite heavy. Truthfully, I wasn't really bothered what anyone was getting up to. I really wasn't."

"It was their business" interrupted Medhi "is that why?"

"Exactly, laddie. It was their business and nowt to do with me." Archie once again paused for a few seconds. "But then after watching the skirmish for a few minutes I noticed six Englishmen, armed to the teeth, surrounding a single Frenchman and he was fighting back and holding his own. Momentarily, he stared back at me and saying nothing continued his fight back against these unruly hooligans. For a moment I thought to walk away, it wasn't my fight. But then the Frenchman looked at me, straight in my eyes. Credit though Artois, who I now know as Count of Montpellier did not ask for any help although he was bleeding profusely from his wounds, he didn't need to, that look said it all."

"Then did you offer some help?" asked a surprised Medhi, knowing the nature of his newfound friend. "You couldn't have just left him on his own" he whispered, the suspense almost unbearable.

"Well, the thought had crossed my mind Medhi. Englishmen and a lone Frenchman fighting, really meant nothing to me."

"So, what happened then. Did you just walk away?" Asked a surprised Medhi "It doesn't sound like you." Once again there was an uncomfortable silence before Archie continued.

He began thinking deeply for a few moments. Suddenly and deliberately, choosing his words carefully he said "Aye, I stepped in. Took down two of the Englishmen before they even knew what had hit them, broke another one's leg, the rest scattered like the cowards they were. You see Medhi, I was to find out a little later Artois has no love for the English, none. A bit like me actually" he added laughing. "So, I was on the very point of leaving the warehouse when I heard Artois shout out, this time in perfect English you can have my money, and you can take my life, but you will never take the Frenchman that lives inside me."There was silence for another few seconds. "That man was no ordinary Frenchman. He was a patriot. A man of pride, willing to die for his country. Exactly like myself, I couldn't stand by and watch him fall."

Medhi intervened, once again, full of curious interest he could not help himself "So, what happened then Archie" he wanted to know in almost desperation. Archie initially just smiled, he knew Artois servant Medhi was dangling from a piece of string under the full control of Archie, who was loving every minute of it. After what seemed like ages Archie replied.

When it was all over, the Frenchman was unconscious, bleeding out on the cold cobblestones. I lifted his head, and he whispered where his ship was docked. I got him there, no questions asked. He turned to face his companion, once again "I had no choice, you see. Mind you, they were all big lads and armed, but as you may have gathered six English were no match for Archie McPherson, no match at all. Once on board, however, we found out from the captain, the authorities were looking for a wild beast of a man with the strength of a lion who had killed a few Englishmen. Artois, who had now regained consciousness persuaded me to stay on board the ship while in dock for a few weeks. It was then he and I got to know each other very well and formed a common relationship. We spent weeks together after that. He nursed his wounds while I stayed hidden from the authorities. It was agreed from then on, I would give the Count some useful classified information, for a fee, of course." Mused Archie.

"What, like a spy" Medhi interrupted, his eyes wide with admiration.

Archie's grin returned, but this time it was colder, calculated. "Aye, if you like Medhi, just like a spy." He smiled to himself, the silence stretched between them, Medhi now realizing how little he knew of this man and the secrets he held.

CHAPTER 9

The sun hung high in the crisp autumn sky as Medhi stepped on to the soft sands of North Shields, excitement thrumming through his veins. This was the day he had been waiting for. After all the stories he had heard from the pub landlord – the wild humorous tales of the Geordies and their indomitable spirit – he would finally meet them face to face. At long last they would be meeting and talking to the ordinary local, working class, folk who were scraping their livelihoods from the seashore. What was it, he wondered, that made these people so distinct, so legendary? Soon, he thought, he would be able to judge for himself, just what it is that makes these people so special.

Archie and Medhi approached the exposed rocks of the Black Middens, the low tide revealing a large mass slick with seaweed and mystery. The rocks, treacherous underfoot glistened in the afternoon light, but the locals moved over them with ease, driven by necessity. Families – mostly children – worked together, scavenging for mussels, crabs and winkles. It was a hard life, relentless in its demands, but the hope of finding a stray lobster or a shipwreck's bounty kept them going. To be honest it was a hard and unrelenting task with little or no reward, but something was better than nothing, so they just got on with it.

Medhi's eyes swept over the scene. These people, he mused, were more resilient than he'd imagined. The two men made their way over to where some lads and their mothers were busy searching for crabs.

Archie broke the silence, "Have you had any luck then," he spoke to a couple of kids who looked no older than seven or eight years old, his voice carrying over the beach as he approached, "what are you looking for exactly" he asked, genuinely interested.

"Crabs or mussels mister" said the older of the two children, eyes gleaming with determination.

"Good, good luck then," Archie said, glancing all around him, and then went on to say, "by the way, were any of you here when the ship went down a couple of weeks back?"

Before the boys could respond, their mother approached. Although she was wearing a long skirt she was drenched right up to the waist, and in her bare feet, caked in sand and saltwater, but her hands carried a basket full of the sea's treasures, winkles and mussels and at least one large male crab the size of one of Archie's huge hands.

"Would you be interested in buying any shellfish sir?" she asked politely "I've got some winkles and mussels and a crab if you want it."

Medhi recoiled slightly, his stomach churning at the sight of the writhing crab. He shook his head even before she finished asking the question.

Archie though, had other ideas "Of course lassie" he said "I'll take all you've got" as he handed over a few shillings, which was far more than the haul was worth.

It was at this moment that Medhi could foresee the outcome his stomach would betray him before the day was out.

Archie, undeterred, pressed on. "I was just asking your boys here" Archie said, "were you here a couple of weeks ago when the ship went down. Find anything interesting?"

The woman shifted her weight thinking, "Aye we were here but there wasn't much, I found a couple of goblets, a spoon and a plate. Not much else."

Her young son Charley piped up "But aa fund the deed kid Ma didn't aa," his voice full of pride.

"You did Charley" the mother replied with a chuckle, "but he wasn't really deed was he?" she went on.

"Nah but he could have been" he paused slightly, "he looked it" Charley replied, "he only came alive when the soldiers pulled half his hair out."

The mother laughed, he was a character Charley was, no doubt about that. The boy's words hung in the air as Archie's mind raced. There as a mystery here, one that hinted at something more than a mere shipwreck.

"I heard the lad escaped, is that right?" Archie asked, his tone cautious.

The woman's expression darkened with thought. "Well," said the mother, "that's the story we've aal been told, in fact he was supposed to have been killed when he jumped out of the window in the Priory. But most folk think he was moved – somewhere secret. Not dead at all."

By now there were a few other beach combers who had gathered around looking for handouts I expect from the strange looking but apparently affluent Scotsman, their eyes filled with curiosity and expectation. Archie nodded thoughtfully, the eyewitnesses felt the same way, he agreed, but said nothing. He handed out a few more coins, thanking them for their time.

As they moved on, Medhi glanced across the river to South Shields, where fishwives clustered on the jetty, surrounded by a mass of seagulls.

"Where to now then Archie" asked Medhi "are we heading across the river" he asked, watching the scene.

Archie's gaze followed Medhi's. He could hardly make them out individually because of the number of seagulls that were swirling around them, hoping no doubt for their share of the discarded fish guts the women were throwing over the side "Aye we are that Medhi" said a man deep in thought. Stroking his chin he went on "I feel we may learn more over there than anywhere else, just a thought" he muttered, his mind already racing with possibilities. He ended by saying we go there tomorrow.

The following morning after bidding a farewell to Walter, they thanked him very much for his friendship and hospitality. They promised him that before their return to Edinburgh they would call in and see him and have a few drinks.

As Archie was shaking Walter's hand, he glanced round towards Medhi, the young Tunisian, his companion over the last few weeks, had tears in his eyes. Over the few days they had stayed with Walter they had built up a strong relationship. Archie laughed inwardly and silently, he shook his head slightly, but it was nice to see the lad showing genuine feelings.

They boarded a local ferry big enough and safe enough to take their horse and cart across the river to the South side. Surprisingly, Medhi held his composure, his usual seasickness absent. A good omen perhaps. The journey itself took less than ten minutes and thankfully with no undue problems or mishaps.

It was still a couple of hours before midday, so they had plenty of time to compare the two towns, which they did, but for amusement only.

Their conclusion, by all accounts, was one of huge similarity between the two although South Shields did seem more industrious, with more warehouses and workshops lining the riverside. Intermingled between these commercial buildings were all manner of small shops and houses. They were all tightly packed in as though it was deemed to be essential to occupy any spare piece of land, in a way it reminded Archie of his place in Leith. As they passed through, the locals greeted them warmly, and Medhi, for once, felt a strange sense of belonging. Dressed in more fitting attire, he looked every bit the part of the local community.

"I feel much better like this, "Medhi said, smoothing down his new jacket.

Looking at him Archie replied "Aye I think you're right there Medhi, I suppose gold and silver hand stitched silk isn't exactly common around these parts" he laughed just as they were passing a large bundle of what seemed like discarded rags, these rags suddenly and quickly got up and moved out of the way of the cart. Medhi realised there was somebody within these rags.

He thought for a while and said to Archie "How long are we going to stay over here?" "Oh, just a couple of days or so" answered Archie "but first we need to find some lodgings."

Their search for lodgings was unappealing until they came across a quaint tripe shop owned by Dolly Grey, a stout woman, with a sharp tongue and a warm heart. The shop was a delightful little building with traditional bull's eye glass in the windows and looked cheerful, looking right over the river and was advertising rooms for hire above the shop. As Archie sealed the deal for their stay, Medhi found his attention wandering to the strange produce Dolly sold – tripe.

"What's tripe, Archie?" Medhi asked, eyeing the wool-like pieces with suspicion.

Archie grinned. "Ach, it's a local delicacy lad" he replied, "they say once you've tasted tripe you will never forget it as long as you live" he added most enthusiastically.

They both went into the shop and introduced themselves and explained to Dolly Grey their requirements, Archie of course, did most of the talking which in turn allowed Medhi to survey all around him and in particular look at the merchandise on display. All he could see was layers of what looked like woollen pieces of damp cloth, he wondered if perhaps the local delicacy, the tripe, was placed on these cloths. He also noticed someone had spilt what looked like sawdust on the floor and hadn't had time to clean it up yet. It gave him time to slide on the sawdust, much to his own amusement.

In the meantime, Archie and Dolly had come to an arrangement for one of the rooms. The one Archie chose had a small window, it opened, and it looked directly onto the River Tyne and had the benefit of having two beds in it. The price included a tripe supper every day you stayed there. Although it was noted there was no heat in the room Dolly accepted the patrons could dance and sing as an alternative way of keeping warm, she now turned her attention to Medhi.

"Mind you're a bonny wee lad" she said to him "do you have a wee lassie hanging on your arm by any chance?"

Archie interrupted. "She means have you got a girlfriend lad."

Medhi was shocked and taken aback rather mortified, he didn't know what to say, nobody had ever asked him that question before, so he said the first thing that came into his mind.

Glassy eyed he replied, "What's tripe Mrs Grey, is it a fish?"

Dolly laughed out loud. "Dear gawd" she said, "I dare not think what state you might be in if the local lasses get hold of you." Archie loved this answer and readily joined in the laughter.

"Saying that mind Dolly, it may well do him some good, I don't think he's that well versed in the ways of romance."

Medhi was still reflecting on what the old granny, Dolly had said. What could she mean when she said the young lasses had finished with him, finished doing what with him he thought? Plying him with drink perhaps, teasing him about his accent, his style off clothing he mused. Yes, he thought that must be it. After all, the ladies he had been acquainted with at the palace were mostly delightful, shy creatures with very good manners who read poetry and danced beautifully and all in all they were extremely polite. These thoughts made Medhi think he was rather looking forward to meeting these delicate young ladies in a way. He was, however, none the wiser what tripe was.

Later as they ventured down to the South Jetty, where all the fishwives laboured over gutting and preparing the fish, the older ones were sitting along the jetty and the younger girls were working around huge pots of boiling water, cooking crabs and the like. Archie reckoned there must have been thirty females there, in between twelve and thirty years of age.

Archie was looking for two women – Florrie Guttenberg and her friend Hairy Mary. As they approached, Medhi noticed the attention shifting toward him, particularly from the younger women. One of them, bold and laughing called to him direct.

"Get yer clothes off then, lets have a look at ye!

Medhi froze, blushing furiously as the women erupted in laughter. Archie shot him a wink before making his way towards the women, leaving Medhi stranded, surrounded by a crowd of playful, exuberant girls. His cheeks burned as their laughter echoed around him, but even through the embarrassment, something deeper stirred within him. Here, among these rough, but kind-hearted people, he was beginning to understand the true spirit of this place – the resilience, the humour, and the unbreakable bond between the people and the sea.

And Medhi despite himself, was about to be caught in the thick of it.

"Good morning, ladies" breezed in Archie, with a smile seemingly stretching from ear to ear "I wonder if any you beautiful lasses could point me in the direction of Florrie Guttenberg and her friend Mary?"

There was silence for a few seconds, nobody spoke or stopped, they carried on working. Suddenly, one of the crab boiler's asked, "Who wants to know and what's in it for us if we tell you?"

Archie replied, "Well, I have a bottle of whisky to share among you."

The oldest of the women shouted "Right, that'll do for us, let's see your whisky first though."

As Medhi handed the bottle of whisky over the speaker pointed over towards the end of the jetty saying, "That's Florrie and Mary sitting over there."

Archie was about to make his way over towards them when he asked Medhi to remain with the other ladies and try and glean whatever information they might have. "See what you can find out laddie" he said "try and use your charm and your good looks, you'll soon get the hang of it, I'm sure of that" he winked at Medhi before leaving him stranded on his own with, you might say, a bunch of over exuberant young females.

"Good morning, ladies, may I introduce myself, I am Archie McPherson. I am currently staying with Dolly Grey, who is, I understand, the mother of one of you delightful ladies, am I correct" he asked.

"Aye you are" said Florrie "Dolly's my mother and this here is my friend Mary" she answered rather suspiciously "what is it you want from us; it's not fish I take it?"

Before Archie could answer he was interrupted momentarily by shrieks of laughter from where Medhi had been abandoned.

He glanced over just in time to see a gentleman's waistcoat being triumphantly held aloft, Florrie and Mary both laughed as they watched the proceedings with Florrie adding "Mind, you won't be able to leave the young lad with that lot over there for too long Mr McPherson or there will be nowt left of him."

Archie, glancing back towards Medhi agreed and said "Aye you're probably right, of course, but let's see how he gets on with it for the moment. He then started asking questions, he wanted to know did they know anything or see anything of the shipwreck.

He explained he was from the Edinburgh's wine co who's cargo had been on the Montpelier and the insurance company wanted to know as much information as they could, however trivial. He didn't mention, of course, he was employed by the Count Artois.

"Well, aah never seen owt, more's the pity" said Florrie "but Mary did, didn't you hinny, the day after the boat was sunk."

Mary shifted uneasily, her hands twisting in her lap. "Yea know what it is Florrie, yea keep saying that" said Mary "but I telt yae I didn't see that much either, just the kid being dragged up to the Priory, and he was half deed" she concluded.

"But he was alive" queried Archie "you saw that much at least."

"Oh aye, he was alive alright, they pulled half his hair out mind, but he was definitely alive" she stated. "He was the ship's cabin boy we think, at least that's what they told us afterwards."

"Aye, aye that's what most people are saying" said Archie "so Mary doll, what happened do you think? What's your opinion?"

Before she could answer there was another loud high-pitched shriek from the circle of excited young females around Medhi, they had managed to remove the young man's white shirt exposing his young, fit, dark-skinned torso.

"Sorry ladies" said Archie "I'll be back in a wee moment." Only this time he said this with a bit of concern in his voice "I think my wee friend may need rescuing."

Fifteen minutes later, after much negotiation and many sighs of disappointment from the girls Archie managed to separate Medhi from their grasp and retrieve the items of clothing he had lost. There were distinct sighs of disappointment from the girls as they allowed Medhi to be taken away which prompted Archie to say "Are you alright lad, was all that just a wee bit too traumatic for you, are you sure you're okay"

"Medhi, breathless but visibly elated, shook his head "Traumatic?" he laughed. "Not at all! That was … an experience I won't soon forget. Believe me." His grin broadened, and Archie couldn't help but chuckle. These young Geordie lasses were totally different in the ways of the girls he had known and met at the palace, to say otherwise would be a huge understatement.

Back with Florrie and Mary, Archie resumed his enquiry. "Right Mary doll, what was you saying just then."

Mary answered immediately. "Nivver mind the Mary doll bit" she snapped, her tone catching Archie off guard, "just make sure you keep that young lad away from my Becky, she's already got one bairn, and she doesn't want another."

Medhi leaned toward Archie "What's a bairn?" he whispered.

"Ach it's some sort of gift" he replied with a wink, "young lads, such as yourself tend to give them to lasses for free. But they end up paying for them for the rest of their lives."

The joke was lost on Medhi, of course, but the rest of them just laughed heartily and they loved Medhi's innocence. In the short time Archie had spoken to Florrie and Mary, he had charmed them and liked them, so he asked Florrie if they could perhaps meet again the following day where he could meet both their families and perhaps talk a bit more. He also promised to bring along a couple of bottles of fine whisky, a gesture that tipped the scales in his favour. More pieces of the puzzle had fallen into place today, but the larger picture remained elusive.

As evening fell, the men returned to their humble lodging house. It was round about five o clock now and the air carried the scent of the nearby harbour, salty and damp, mingling with the ever-present stench of fish and decay. As they approached the shop, they checked over their horse and made sure there was nothing of any real value in the cart itself. Although it has been described as a cart it was more than that, it was more like a gypsy caravan but without the frills or hand painted decorations, but just as comfortable and sturdy, nevertheless.

The little brass bell jingled as soon as they entered the building, "Evening lads," said Dolly as soon as they set foot in the shop "just in time for tea."

"We certainly are," Archie replied, his stomach growling in anticipation "what's on the menu tonight?"

Her face lit up with pride. "My speciality – fried tripe with onions and lemon sauce."

Medhi paled visibly, his eyes widening with horror. "And … where exactly do you keep the tripe," he asked nervously.

Dolly pointed toward the pile on the counter. Medhi's stomach churned at the sight of what appeared to be discarded animal skins. His horror only deepened as Dolly threw the mass into a pot of boiling water.

"It won't take long.," she chirped.

Medhi leaned toward Archie, his voiced hushed. "What exactly is tripe?"

Archie, stifling a laugh, replied, "It's the lining of a cow's or sheep's stomach. Might not sound appealing, but I'll tell you lad its delicious."

Medhi eyed the bubbling pot with dread, wondering how he had gone from the grandeur of feasts to this bizarre corner of the world, eating tripe off a wooden crate by candlelight. Did Geordie people look for all the most revolting bits of animal flesh they can find and think I might just eat this. It certainly seemed that way.

Archie was totally oblivious to what Medhi's thoughts were at this moment. As Medhi silently shook his head.

By now though he was getting used to these strange foods and customs, so like it or not he was determined to try this 'tripe' even though he felt sure he may very well be sick soon after.

An hour or so passed before Dolly came into the back room and there was no light in there other than a tiny candle. There was a large unsteady wooden crate situated between two chairs, the crate was to become their dining table.

His mind wandered back to the palace, where they would sit around grand tables, some of them forty feet long, with fine silver cutlery, silver and glass candlesticks and all accompanied by the finest French wines and top-quality cuts of meat and fresh fruit. There was usually game birds and sweet meats and every delicacy you can imagine.

Reality set in when Archie began to tuck in, saying, "This is good laddie, very good."

"There's a spoon each, if you want one, it's up to you" Dolly said, "as for me I just use my fingers,"

Medhi was still looking at the bowl of tripe or whatever it was, and he began sniffing at it like a nervous cat would. Eventually, after much probing and pushing the food around he decided to make an effort and very carefully began to eat the tripe.

"Hmm" he said, "that's not that bad actually, not bad at all." He was surprised himself, and within a few minutes they had both cleared their bowls. After that they were quite happy sampling some of Dolly's homemade beer, truthfully it could only be loosely described as beer, nevertheless it tasted better than water and by all accounts did have a kick to it.

The time passed over very quickly and before anyone realised, it was after 11 pm. "Well, Medhi" Archie said leaning back on his chair and yawning extensively "we've got an early start in the morning so we have, I say we should turn in for the night."

Dolly on hearing this locked the front door and made sure the back doors were bolted up, her own room which was downstairs next to the shop was also well secured with bolts and locks everywhere, probably better than all the other rooms combined. "Well goodnight lads, see you in the morning" as she took her last sip of beer "six thirty sharp mind and its eggs for breakfast" she went on.

"That's good" said Medhi "what are we having with them, kippers perhaps?"

"No, just eggs, hard boiled ones" answered Dolly leaving no room for further discussion.

He was disappointed and slightly shocked but accepted the situation. Archie just smiled to himself, he knew this was the only way life could be around here, mostly no frills.

Hours passed. Archie had long since drifted off to sleep, his heavy snoring filling the room. Medhi, though, was restless and sat upright in bed. The faint flicker of candlelight played across the room's rough-hewn walls, casting strange shifting shadows. Just as he began to drift off, a soft tapping pulled him back to full consciousness. Stones, hitting the bedroom window.

Naturally, full of curiosity, he went over to investigate. The window itself, which was fully glazed, would only have been around two foot square but at least it did have a handle on, and it did open. He managed to squeeze his head and shoulders outside, peering round the frame where he was confronted by three of the young fisher lasses, giggling and hiding behind the horse and cart, barely illuminated by the pale moonlight. Their giggles reached him through the still night air.

"Come on down, Medhi!" one of them called, her voice teasing. "We've got something to show ya."

His pulse quickened. Being a young red-blooded male he was more than happy to go along with the shenanigans and therefore quite eager to participate in any activities the girls may have been planning. Without a second thought, he slipped out of bed, climbed through the window, and landed on the cobblestones below. The girls laughed softly, beckoning him toward the cart, Bessie, her eyes gleaming, stepped forward, unbuttoning her blouse, showing her voluptuous breasts. This was his first sight of breasts, and he was captivated. The moonlight caught her skin, and Medhi's breath hitched.

It was then he suddenly realised he had no shirt on. "Wait" he said, "I've left my shirt upstairs" glancing up at the open window "I'll have to go back for it."

One of the young lasses was busy opening the canvas cover at the back of the cart, while the other girl, was stroking his chest and torso, she was kissing his shoulder one minute then kissing his neck. "Don't worry about your shirt," Bessie said "you definitely won't be needing that tonight or anything else for that matter" she said almost to herself, in the most seductive manner.

He barely had time to react before the girls were upon him, their hands guiding him into the cart. To his credit he wanted to say something in response, but he couldn't, he just allowed himself to be led into the rear of the cart, his mind was racing, whatever they had planned, he was ready to surrender himself to it. He did guess correctly; however, they weren't there just to speculate on the weather.

The next morning Archie descended the stairs at 6.30 just in time to see Dolly attending to breakfast. "Morning Archie" she said cheerfully "slept well I hope, and where's your young friend, not up yet?" She turned to face Archie full on.

He smirked, glancing out the window toward the cart. "I suspect," he said slowly, "I think that boy will come back a man.

Dolly thought for a moment or two "well I'd better give him two eggs then" she said "and hard-boiled ones at that" she laughed.

About two hours later Medhi emerged from the cart outside, he was a picture of contentment, his chest was now fully expanded and to say the least he looked rather pleased with himself. His demeanour had changed, and his beaming smile left no-one in any doubt as to his conquests and pleasure the night before and with an air of apparent nonchalant ease he leapt from the cart with his bare chest gleaming, and like a proud peacock strutted across to Dolly's front door. "

Good morning, Miss Dolly" he said rather cheerfully," and you as well Archie, I hope you slept well" as he glanced across the room.

"Aye we did lad" he answered, "which I assume is more than you did methinks." Archie was grinning from ear to ear as he looked at young Medhi and old Dolly Grey just smiled and shook her head, she knew this was a night the lad would remember for the rest of his life.

How ironic she thought that a well-educated young man brought up in the confines of a royal palace would lose his virginity with three young fisher girls in the heart of a dockside town.

Medhi was beginning to like England now, particularly South Shields. He now gratefully accepted Dolly's breakfast of two hard boiled eggs and home -made bread. He was now ready to face the world.

CHAPTER 10

The sun hovered over the horizon, casting a golden hue across the calm sea. Archie McPherson and Medhi Ali stepped out into the morning air, the tag of saltwater lingering in the breeze. It was just after breakfast, and the two men were making their way toward Florrie Guttenberg's stone cottage nestled by the beach. It was a Sunday – a day of rest for most – but for Archie and Medhi it was, it was the beginning of something more. The clock hadn't yet struck 9:30 a.m., but already the day had the crisp clarity of early summer, with the tide gently lapping at the shore.

As they walked, Archie felt a familiar energy in the air, something beyond the idyllic scene in front of them. The sound of a fiddle floated on the wind, its melody precise and haunting, like the whispers of an ancient tale not yet fully revealed, A thin line of smoke spiralled from the cottage chimney, curling lazily into the sky. The scent of woodfire mixed with the sea air, inviting them closer.

Approaching the cottage, Archie's eyes were drawn to two young boys crouched near the door, mending lobster pots with practiced hands. Without missing a beat, Archie called out," Anyone in the hoose lads?" His voice, though friendly, had a curious edge. He always did like to ask questions – especially when the answers might change everything.

One of the boys, Amos – sharp eyed and already wise beyond his years despite being barely ten – looked up from his work. "Aye there is," he replied with a wry grin and they're expecting you. "I hope you've brought the whisky you promised them" he said with a hint of sarcasm "or you won't be stopping long." His tone was light, but Archie knew well that in these parts, a promise was as good as gold.

Archie chuckled. He respected Amos's audacity; it was the kind of sharp mind that thrived here on the rugged coast. With a nod, he and Medhi knocked on the wooden door of the cottage, the sound disappearing into the sea breeze. The fiddle music stopped for a moment; Harry had paused. Inside, voices hushed.

"Howay in lads" Florrie Gutenberg herself had opened the door and with a hurried glance up and down the beach, pulled them inside with surprising strength. "Daen't let everybody knae wor business." There was something in her voice, a caution bred from a life lived with secrets.

Archie, ever the gentleman, took off his blue tam o'shanter beret as they entered the lowceilinged room.

"A fine wee place you have here Florrie" he remarked, taking in the cottage's modest charm. glancing around the cottage "a fine place indeed" he went on. His eyes lingered on a figure standing by the fire – tall, broad-shouldered, and watching with folded arms. "And you, sir," Archie continued, "must be Florrie's husband, Anders."

"Aye" he replied, his eyes locking with Archie's in a silent, mutual assessment. "And you must be McPherson."

The two men shook hands, an unspoken challenge exchanged between them. But for now, the tension dissolved, and the room eased into light conversation. A bottle of whisky was produced, its amber glow catching the light as Harry, Florrie's brother, resumed playing the fiddle. Laughter echoed through the cottage, but Archie's mind never rested.

Soon, the reason for the visit emerged – questions about a recent shipwreck, the Montpelier. Archie probed for details, but each answer seemed to lead back to what he already knew and there was nothing to be added.

As the visitors were about ready to leave, and return to Edinburgh someone arrived at Florrie's front door. It was Becky, Mary's sister and she had baby Celia with her.

"Oh, you're just in time" said Florrie "I'd like you to meet Archie, the mad Scotsman I was telling you about and Medhi, his assistant."

Becky's face lit up in amusement, but Archie's attention soon shifted as he said, "Not quite mad Florrie, different perhaps but not mad" he laughed. Archie took off his beret once again which he clasped with both hands, clutching it to his chest, "Pleased to make your acquaintance" he said staring into Becky's eyes "yet another bonny face I'll remember always".

Becky just stood there giggling. Although she knew he was just teasing she loved the attention all the same. "Mind you though" Archie said in all seriousness "as pretty as you are, your child is undoubtably magnificent".

Becky turned around and looked at Celia in her cot "Aye well" she said, "I must agree with you there, unfortunately though she isn't my child more's the pity". Her appearance lit up the room, her laughter infectious. She bent over the cot "Our Celia here is the Golden Child we found in a barrel, aren't you, my darling?" she gurgled to the baby.

Amazingly, baby Celia seemed to smile back as though she knew exactly what Becky was saying. Archie was both enthralled and curious at the same time.

"Found in a barrel?" Archie repeated, his curiosity piqued "where was this"? He looked back to Florrie and Anders who recounted the story with great enthusiasm of the child's discovery. Archie's mind raced, connecting fragments of information, forming new theories.

Archie was listening intently. "So, this was a day or so after the Montpelier had sunk"?

"Aye it was" interrupted Anders, his tone grew cautious "but the discovery was proved it had nothing to do with any shipwreck, the Montpelier or otherwise. There is no connection."

But Archie's thoughts were already drifting toward the impossible.

"Why, do you think it might be?" Anders asked, looking rather suspicious.

"No,no,no, not at all Anders" Archie answered quickly "coincidental mind but nothing more than that" was all he would say.

His eyes were gazing into space as he gathered up his thoughts, but no doubt, further investigations would undoubtably be beneficial. It was too late to carry on with any further investigations today.

As the day wore on and the whisky flowed, he quietly made plans for further enquiries. Florrie had things to do, and Anders had to get back to work, Sunday or not he still had pots to pull in, time was against them, as was the alcohol.

He asked for permission from Florrie and Anders to talk to Amos the following day as he and Erasmus had found the barrel and the baby. It was purely a matter of personal interest and nothing more, Archie insisted. They were both more than eager to comply, it could not do any harm and besides, they liked Archie anyway, so why not they thought. That night as he and Medhi lay in the dark, Archie posed a simple, unsettling question. "Just for the sake of argument and discussion for instance "What if the child did come from the Montpelier?

What if this baby – wasn't supposed to survive? Medhi couldn't understand the logic of the questions, but Archie was different to most people. "What circumstances could have occurred prior to Celia being found?"

As the hours passed, even Medhi began to wonder. Could it be? Could a desperate act have led to a child being placed in a barrel, in a last-ditch effort to save her life?

Archie carried on "Let's say for the sake of argument" his brows raised as he gently nodded his head "let's say the barrel and the baby did come from the Montpelier. If so, we must ask the question why, and again how could it be possible for the barrel to have even been found?" asked Archie.

Medhi thought for a moment as he extinguished the candle with his forefinger and thumb, possibly more than a moment actually, before he went on to say "Right then, problem number one, the Coroner's and the official report in accordance with the cabin boy's testimony, there was no mention of a child on board the Montpelier and according to the records in France, the crew and the passenger list did not include any infants aboard when the ship set sail. In fact, the only passenger was captain Marcel's wife Eleonore and the crew, of course. To be honest not even the captain's nor his wife's bodies have been found to this date."

Although it was dark in the room now Archie nodded instinctively, still deep in thought, but of course, listening and considering every word as his obsession with the mystery deepened.

"So, when did the Montpelier set sail for Scotland?" asked Archie "because I must also ask, why was Eleonore even there?"

"Well, the ship left France on 1st February 1797 and on its way to Scotland it was due to call into various ports, including Portugal and other places hoping to arrive in Scotland by late September".

"Mmm about nine months then" said Archie "and I'm just thinking why his wife was there at all?" He looked in Medhi's direction although he could not see him. "Unusual that, wasn't it" he went on "women as a rule don't accompany trading ships."

"Ah well, that's simple enough" answered Medhi quickly "it was their honeymoon" he said, feeling pleased with himself.

Archie never answered, he just stared in front of himself focussing on a mouldy piece of plasterwork the light from the window had picked out.

Medhi carried on "come on Archie, you don't think for one minute that the baby found in the barrel could be the child of the Marcel's surely"?

Archie lit the candle once again and looked directly into Medhi's eyes "Is it that impossible then"? he queried.

"Of course, it is" Medhi answered frustratedly as he watched the shadows of the candlelight dance across the walls, but then after a couple of moments thought he retracted his last statement and mumbled "I suppose it is actually possible although highly unlikely".

With raised eyebrows Archie said. "But that's what I said when we first began to discuss this matter" and with a soul-searching expression he went on "but then again, for the sake of argument, let's assume the baby was the child of the Marcel's why would they put her in a barrel and let her sink with the ship"?

"Well, they wouldn't" interrupted Medh "why would any father or mother do anything like that and then abandon their child"?

"Aye, you're probably right, so you are" said Archie "it's probably my imagination running wild again as usual".

With that last remark they both decided to get some sleep, but even that was proving difficult. However, after a while they both managed to do just that. Round about two or three o'clock in the morning Medhi suddenly sat up and spoke "Actually, if they were trying to save the child's life and the child was about to drown and die" he said in a tormented voice "they probably would put her in a barrel and hopefully try to save her, wouldn't they Archie?" his mind was racing over the possibilities of the night of the shipwreck when certain death was the only outcome.

"That's right lad" came the reply, although he was half asleep "as I keep telling you, think outside the box, sometimes that's where the truth is and not the more obvious choice." He smiled to himself, Young Medhi was learning and learning fast.

Still, something about this case haunted him, tugging at his every thought. The truth, it seemed, was just beyond reach – buried beneath layers of time, sea and secrets.

The cave where the child had been found seemed to offer no immediate clues, but Archie saw something that others had missed – the way the sea could carry an object far beyond where it seemed possible. The barrel, the child – it could all be connected. But the deeper Archie dug, the more elusive the answers became. He wasn't ready to make any grand declarations just yet. Not to Florrie. Not to Anders. And certainly not to the Count and Countess Artois who had been searching for answers about the lost ship.

After a few minutes' walk along the beach, they approached Frenchman's Bay where they caught up with the two boys and this time the lads were busy sorting out the day's catch, the father had just dropped off for them.

"Good morning to yea lads" called Archie as cheerful as ever "looks a good catch that mind" he said pointing in the direction of the lobsters and crabs "better than most days I would think" he went on, but Amos wasn't impressed.

Without looking up from his work he said, "So what exactly are you after Mr. McPherson" never once glancing in the direction of the huge imposing Scotsman "we are, as you can see, quite busy".

Archie and Medhi looked at each other, their eye movements giving away their thoughts "Aye, I can see that young sir" Archie replied, "me and Medhi here were wondering where exactly you found the barrel and the bairn".

"Ah that was a few weeks ago now Mr. McPherson" young Amos replied "my memory is not as good as it could be, if you know what I mean" he said staring straight into Archies eyes.

Archie initially said nothing, but he thought to himself 'bloody amazing, still a child but a grown up in mind and not the slightest intimidated' he then spoke "ten years old and your memory's fading already"?

"Aye sad isn't it" Amos replied with a straight face.

Archie reached down into his pocket and after rumbling about said "here" tossing over a loose penny in the direction of Amos "this might help you remember".

The lad picked up the penny and gave it to his young brother "actually Mr McPherson" he went on "another couple of pennies may well help my memory return altogether".

Archie turned to Medhi, they both had to laugh as they knew they were in the process of being fleeced by two scallywags. As soon as Amos pocketed the extra two pennies, he took them over to the caves at Frenchman's Bay. As they got closer Amos pointed out the area in which the barrel had been found.

"That's the actual cave over there" he said, "it's difficult to get in though, but Medhi should manage taking into account his slim frame" Amos went on "we were busy collecting driftwood for the fire at home when Erasmus noticed something strange in the corner, it was the barrel sitting among some pebbles further into the cave".

"Quite a distance up from the sea then" said Archie "even with a high tide, does the sea normally reach this high"? he queried.

"No, not really, we've never known it" replied Amos.

Archie nodded his head and thought for a few moments. He had managed to squeeze inside the cave, and he could see the location of where the barrel had been found. He took note there was at least twenty feet from where the incoming tide would rest and where the barrel was found.

"Wasn't the barrel wet when you found it Amos"?

"Aye it was but I don't know how" there was a pause "perhaps it was raining when it was brought here, I don't know".

"Aye, of course laddie" said Archie "that will be it right enough. When is the next high tide, do you know"? Amos responded again,

"About another couple of hours I would imagine, why, what for like?" Archie paused for a few seconds and then laughed.

"Actually, I'm going to show Medhi here how to skim pebbles across the sea, he hasn't seen that done before."

Amos shook his head "Aye fair enough, it takes all kinds I suppose."

Medhi looked at Archie, if looks could kill, as they say. A few hours later the two men returned to the cave, only this time they brought with them a small wooden barrel to which they attached a length of string, around twenty metres long.

Fortunately, and good news it was windy that day which meant the waves were ferocious and quite high. For the first ten minutes or so they just sat and watched the action of the sea and how the waves changed direction every so often. They watched them coming in and crash onto the pebbles inside the cave and noted where the sea came to rest. One thing was obvious, the sea never reached the point where the barrel was found.

Archie then asked Medhi to venture out into the sea at waist level and throw some bits of driftwood onto the waves as they were coming in.

Although Medhi did as he was told, as you can imagine, he was not the slightest bit happy with it, much to the amusement of the two lads watching the proceedings. Archie had noticed, when the waves came into the cave the wooden debris floating on top of the waves was thrown a little further up the pebbled beach, still about fifteen feet away though from where the barrel was found.

"Right Medhi" Archie said "now you take this barrel back into the sea and wait until the biggest wave arrives, and when it does try and throw the barrel right on top of the incoming wave. I will keep hold of the string, so we do not lose it."

Medhi, now soaking wet and freezing was grumbling under his breath. Why does it have to be me all the time he thought, as he fought against the waves.

When the next huge wave came in Medhi managed to throw the barrel on the top crest. When the wave came trundling into the cave it suddenly stopped as is normal in this case, but then threw forward the still moving barrel onto the pebbles, this time however, unlike the debris the barrel did not stop moving and it rolled up to even beyond the point where the original barrel was found. This was all conjecture, of course, but it did indeed seem possible that the original barrel could have acted in the same way and therefore, as far as Archie was concerned, the barrel could have come from the Montpelier.

They lit a small fire within the cave and began drying out Medhi's clothes. Naturally, they were discussing the day's findings and Medhi asked Archie if he was now convinced the barrel was from the ship, the Montpelier.

"No" Archie replied, "I just can't say for sure, there are too many unanswered questions, but what I would say is, it is possible".

Medhi interrupted Archie "Are you going to say something to Florrie and Anders then?" he asked.

"No laddie, I am not, nor am I going to say anything to the Count and Countess Artois, in my mind it will just bring back false hope without any evidence."

"Then what will we do now then?" he asked disappointedly "Do we just give up?"

Once again, deep in thought, Archie replied "For the time being lad we do just that, we have no alternative but to wait for any developments that may or may not come along, and that unfortunately can take some time". He patted Medhi on the shoulder "so it's now back to Edinburgh for me and back to France for you laddie" he said with a thoughtful and friendly smile on his face.

There was just one more thing to do, however, and that was to honour a promise they had made to Walter, the publican from the Wooden Dolly in North Shields. On their way home to Edinburgh, they were to call in and have a last few drinks with him before they departed.

Having said their goodbyes to Florrie and Anders and of course, to Mary, Harry, and Becky they made their way over the river back to North Shields.

It was a miserable evening with rain just beginning to fall but at least a night of great entertainment lay before them. They arrived at the pub at 7p.m, Archie as usual breezed his way into the pub full of his usual enthusiasm and exuberance. "Good evening, Walter" he boomed in his most cheerful voice "let there be drinks all round on Archie McPherson" with a wide grin he ushered in Medhi" and do not spare the horses" he laughed.

It is understood, a wonderful night was had by all and, if I am honest, a few happy tears.

The next morning, although a little the worse for wear our intrepid duo made their way back to Scotland.

CHAPTER 11

During their return to Scotland, the cobble streets jolted the cart violently, shaking Archie and Medhi as they made their way north. The uneven roads seemed endless, but finally the dense woodland of northern England began to stretch out before them. The rain, relentless and cold, hammered down harder than either man would have liked. Archie pulled his weathered coat tighter around himself, while Medhi grumbled under his breath, shifting uncomfortably as the cartwheels sank into yet another deep rut. They hoped they would be arriving soon at the Lindisfarne Monastery, here they would meet up again with Father Bartholemew and I would imagine, om arrival, they would be thinking of some warmth and welcome refreshment. The rain was now becoming more persistent than ever, and their general humour was gradually being replaced by downright annoyance and foul temper.

Nevertheless, after what seemed an eternity the silhouette of Lindisfarne Priory was now in sight as it emerged from the mist. The jagged stone towers loomed ahead, barely visible through the sheets of rain.

"This blasted rain," Medhi muttered, twisting his wrists and punching the air to relieve the stiffness that had crept into his joints. His breath clouded the air in front of him, mixing with the downpour that had chased them since dawn.

"Thank God" mumbled Medhi "I can't wait to get off this damned cart" he exhaled sharply; relief tinged with exhaustion.

Archie glanced toward his young companion "Aye Medhi, welcome to England. The weather's not quite like this in France, eh?" he laughed.

Medhi's response was just a cold, silent stare as he looked along the path. Words weren't necessary. They eventually crossed the fairway, which was connecting the mainland and the Priory grounds, although dangerous they managed this task without further mishap. Eventually arriving at the Priory at 8 o clock. It was getting quite dark now and the two men were looking very tired as they had been travelling for more than ten hours non-stop.

"Horses first, Medhi. They need to be fed and dried, they need to be fresh for the morning." He was saying this between sniffs and sniffles "And make sure they are under cover for the night."

The nearer they came, the more imposing the Priory seemed – ancient and weather-beaten, a fortress that had withstood countless attacks. Archie then made moves toward the Priory and as usual left Medhi to just get on with it.

He arrived at the Priory entrance and whilst in the process of hammering on the great brass knocker he couldn't help but notice the many battle scars the old entrance door had endured over the years. There was different sized axe marks and various holes made by spears and arrows and large dents made by various battering rams, though still intact --- he was filled with admiration, certainly this door would have a lot of tales to tell. By now Medhi had arrived alongside him, looking slightly more miserable than he had before. He mumbled it was still raining and once again Archie knocked firmly, the brass knocker which echoed through the eerie quiet of the night. Suddenly, at last, the great door, with all its iron bolts, locks and hinges finally opened, creaking and groaning its displeasure all the way. A single flickering candle appeared first, casting a dim glow over a small round gentleman with a most unwelcoming expression as he looked up at them with suspicion. His robe was loose and tattered, his face a mixture of annoyance and weariness.

"Good evening, Father, "Archie said, smiling as he did so, "I apologise for calling at this late hour, but we have urgent need to speak to father Bartholemew. He does still reside here, I take it. "Archie was clutching his well-worn Tam-O-Shanter and trying his best, in his way, to look normal "I trust he hasn't turned in for the night" he went on.

The monk who had answered the door was busily adjusting his home-made clogs as he went on to explain, that Father Bartholemew hadn't gone to bed yet, but he wasn't sure if he would see them or not, especially at this late hour, The monks' feet were not allowing the door to fully open and his clogs jammed the foot plate "Could the pair of you not come back tomorrow? Can't this wait until morning?" he questioned, the candle flickering in the wind.

As Medhi peered into the grand hall he could see a large log burning fire looking particularly inviting, he cleared his throat impatiently. "It can't" he said firmly "Please. Tell him it's Archie McPherson and Medhi. He'll understand." Archie nodded towards the priory interior.

The monk hesitated, his hand gripping the door as if he might slam it in their faces. But before he could reply, a voice echoed from deep within the priory.

Before any other words could be exchanged a voice shouted through "Let them come in Father Michael, they are indeed who they say they are and are actual friends of mine. They are expected"

Father Michael, on hearing this, removed his jammed clog and rather begrudgingly let them pass through. The door slammed shut behind them with the ominous click of heavy locks sliding back into place. The Priory, though lit by many candles scattered around, was still dark but the roaring open fire provided a much-needed contrast to the darkness, its warmth drawing both men in like moths to a flame.

Father Bartholemew was standing by the hearth smiling with his arm outstretched in a friendly and welcoming gesture, although his face was lined with years of experience, his eyes were sharp and calculating. "Good evening, gentlemen. Archie -- Medhi it's a pleasure to see you both once again. I trust your business was concluded uneventfully, and I hope" he added quickly "to your satisfaction" he continued smiling as he looked at them both, a rather inquisitive smile, but smiling all the same.

"Well, almost, "Archie replied "but we're here and I was hoping we may be able to discuss a proposition with yourself regarding your mead, thereby introducing your delicious product into Scotland."

"Ah, so it's business, is it? Come, sit and we can talk. Is it a drink your needing? I thought as much" he said laughing I'm quite happy with that."

All three of them laughed with Bartholemew's eyes sparkling with interest. Without waiting for a reply, the monk retrieved two large bottles of mead from beneath a pew, no glasses but it was so cold no-one cared about formalities.

They sat up close to the fire, with Medhi absent mindedly poking at the flames with an iron rod, sending embers swirling into the air. Father Bartholemew noticed, his eyes narrowing slightly.

"Enjoying that, Medhi? He asked, a curious tone to his voice. "Why, yes I am --- but I can stop if it bothers you."

"No, no, not at all, it just reminds me of a boy we have staying here. He does the same thing, staring into the fire as if searching for something in the flames" he explained before continuing with the conversation.

"Who's that then?" enquired Archie, his interest piqued, trying not to be too interested.

"Why, just a young boy we took into our care a couple of weeks ago" replied Bartholemew "he's doing alright."

"Two weeks ago," Archie asked with a lot of interest "two weeks ago" he said again, gazing directly into Bartholemew's eyes.

"Sorry, sorry I should have said two months ago he's been here much longer" he quickly amended with a nervous laugh.

Archie quickly replied, "I was going to say, that would have been about the same time, or there abouts of when the cabin boy from the shipwreck went missing" there was a pause before he went on and simply added "wasn't it?"

Medhi intervened, taking his eyes from the fire for a moment "Can't be him can it, he's dead isn't he?"

Of course it couldn't be," laughed Archie. Still laughing, when he was swiftly joined by Bartholemew who quickly asked, "Another drink? before we all turn in for the night." His hand was trembling ever so slightly. Archie thought he seemed nervous.

Life indeed, was feeling a lot more agreeable, as the conversation was drifting towards the more serious business transactions, when Archie turned to Medhi "Are you having one laddie?"

Medhi took his eyes from the fire for a moment he was now well versed in the way Archie did things and guessed he wanted to be alone with the monk.

"No, I don't think I will have any more now, I must admit to being rather tired so excuse me for seeming to be a little disinterested."

Both Father Bartholemew and Archie nodded their heads and accepted his seemingly indifferent approach. For the next two or three hours the two men carried on drinking and chatting away, both asking and answering questions with an irrelevant disorder. While discussing various interesting situations Bartholemew did indicate or suggest that the cabin boy could be still alive and might possibly be in England somewhere and in hiding. Although Archie was shaking his head, he seemed to agree that the wily monk knew more than he was letting on. Archie realised he could not force any more from him. At this stage, however, Archie did mention that a baby had been found in a barrel close to the proximity of the shipwreck. And, of course, the obvious question of coincidence meant nothing to Father Bartholemew, suggesting of course, that he knew nothing, but Archie, as wily as ever, was sure he was holding something back.

Although the monk was in daily conversations with Pierre (now Peter) there had been no mention of a baby or a barrel, Pierre had made sure of that.

The next morning as they prepared to leave, Archie thanked Bartholemew for his hospitality. Yet the unspoken questions hung in the air, unresolved.

Archie turned to him and remarked how the simple breakfast had set them up for their return journey home to Leith and Edinburgh, "Well Father, I thank ye for all the help and hospitality you have shown us, but it is with regret I have no comforting news for the Count Artois when we return."

"One day, Archie," Bartholemew said quietly as they stood sat the gate. "One day the answers will come, I am sure of that."

Medhi, standing alongside Archie, just nodded in agreement adding with sadness that the master would be upset there was nothing to report or indeed gain comfort from.

Archie met the monk's gaze, the weight of hidden truths pressing down on him. Without a word, he turned away, leading Medhi toward the waiting cart, he knew this wouldn't be their last visit to Lindisfarne.

Our intrepid pair returned to Edinburgh without incident and spent the next few days writing their reports and findings. Although there would be no satisfactory conclusion they felt no more could have done at this stage. It was, therefore agreed, at least for the time being, their report was complete and delivered back to the Count Artois in Montpellier.

CHAPTER 12

After an arduous and difficult journey Medhi arrived back at Montpellier alone, having left Archie back in Edinburgh. Her was tired and a little dishevelled but was glad to see the sunshine and the better weather than he had experienced in England. He felt the weight of the palace's secrets pressing down on him as he crossed the dimly lit corridors of the Chateau de Montpellier, the scent of old stone, polished wood, and dust lingered in the air, mixing with the subtle perfume of rich tapestries that lined the walls. His thoughts raced, intertwining the conversations he'd had with Count Artois and Countess Celeste, their unspoken fears, and the grim realities of his own mission. Unfortunately, he had no constructive news or even any hopeful information to give the Count, he had arrived empty-handed, no closer to the truth they so desperately craved and whilst he wasn't looking forward to meeting his master he still felt as though he had arrived back home.

As he approached the palace gates, bathed in sunlight but shrouded in an invisible darkness it all felt far removed from his time with Archie in Edinburgh. As he watched the many royal staff going about their business, it felt wrong, the very air felt charged, as if it held its breath. It felt as though he had been away for much longer than a few weeks, things seemed different somehow and it felt as though there was a definite sadness around the whole palace. The good news was the sun was still shining brightly, and the locals appeared to be going about their business as normal. Still, something wasn't quite right, he thought. He shrugged his shoulders with an air of resignation as he made his way past the attentive guards and into the palace. As he made his way into the inner confines a familiar voice cried out, "The Count is waiting for you" it said, "we all are, and we welcome you home." Medhi recognised him as Francois the head of household. Medhi and Francois embraced each other with the latter suggesting he take some refreshments before he made his reacquaintance with the Count. Medhi nodded his agreement, and without saying too much he followed his old friend into the reception and kitchen area. There he reminisced with other members of the counts personal staff. Although taken up with essential duties they all took time to welcome him back, which he gratefully accepted. A small glass of unsweetened black coffee was handed to him, and he drank with enthusiasm, not quite like the hot tea he had been getting used to. Whilst taking a few sips quite a few of the kitchen staff were gathering around, naturally curious as to what information he had found, however, Medhi politely refused their requests, pointing out that the information he had gathered was for the count and countess only and for no-one else at this stage. Of course, everyone present agreed and were more than happy to welcome him back.

The count had now been informed Medhi had arrived and wasted no time in having him brought up to his private chamber. Even as Medhi walked, his mind kept returning to the missing golden seal, the "Grand Seal of Commission" the one thing that could save the Count's line. Without it the Artois family's centuries-old reign would come to an end.

Artois instantly called out to Celeste to join him. "Come quickly" he said "Medhi has returned." They had no further time to discuss anything further when Medhi approached. The Count walked over to him as soon as he entered the room and gathered both of his hands and squeezed them gently, his eyes never leaving the young man, as though transfixed. He went on "I hope you have the information we so desperately crave" he enquired with a hopeful and desperate smile. His wife took hold of the count's arm and added "We live in eternal hope that we may get comfort from your findings" but even more quietly said "however, I feel, as a mother, the news will not be good."

The young Tunisian servant stood before Artois and Celeste and the Count asked Medhi was he feeling well "A little tired, perhaps but well nevertheless."

"Come, come and sit here between Celeste and me," Medhi took a seat on the most comfortable and beautifully decorated cushions he had seen in a while, slightly different to Archie McPherson's ramshackle apartment above the River Leith. Before any further discussions were entered into Medhi explained that most of the information had been meticulously written down and placed into his leather-bound satchel, but thought he would briefly mention some details before they had chance to read the full report.

He glanced over toward them both, who were listening intently, but they seemed oblivious to the words spoken, especially as Medhi said he had no good news. "It's probably going to take a couple of days for you both to read and digest the contents of the report."

Such was the anxiety of the general situation that Medhi found himself in the role of asking rather than answering questions. For instance, at one stage, asking the disappointed couple, could captain Jon's wife, their daughter-in-law, who was obviously missing, be in fact pregnant.

This stunned the royal couple "I don't think so" he replied looking to his wife "not when she left, anyhow, or we would not have let her go on the trip. Why do you ask that?" he queried "that's a strange question?"

Celeste went on "It's a heart destroying question, do you know something you are not telling us?" Medhi then remembered something Archie McPherson had said regarding not giving them any false hope.

Medhi apologised immediately and stumbled over his words "No, no" he went on, feeling very nervous, "it's just that a child was found near the shipwreck and was about six weeks old and Archie and I wondered if there could possibly be any connection, but obviously not."

There were lots of other discussions during the next hour or two, which seemed somehow to appease the Count and Countess, at least for the moment.

A couple of days went by, while the report and written information could be absorbed in detail, In the meanwhile, Medhi had time to contemplate his luxurious surroundings, he couldn't help but marvel at the opulence of the Palace del Rois with the rather dilapidated dwellings and buildings of the fisher folk of the North-East of England. There were times when he laughed inwardly to himself when he recollected the various buildings, particularly Archie's riverside abode. Nevertheless, strangely enough, he still found them most welcoming and the local people of the North-East were among the friendliest he had ever known. He smiled to himself once again as his head shook from side to side with his eyes tightly shut, he remembered most distinctively, his first encounter with Dolly Grey's tripe shop and even more so the eating of the tripe with boiled eggs and beer.

His thoughts were interrupted by the palace housekeeper; he was to attend a meeting with the count immediately. Medhi stood up and made note of the time, it was about 1 p.m. The actual time itself, as it happens, was of no importance, however, he did feel that some refreshments were now apparent. He put his thinkings to one side, however, as he made towards the huge double doors of the private meeting rooms. As he arrived the doors were opened by two guardsmen and Medhi was ushered forward.

"Good afternoon, Sir, Madam" Medhi remarked as he approached the couple "You summoned me?"

"Yes, we did, and thank you for being so prompt" Medhi just nodded silently "we have just finished reading Archies report and findings and I have to say that whilst a little disappointed at the content I am convinced you and Archie did your very best" he paused like what seemed ages before carrying on "however, there are one or two questions I would like to clarify if you can, and to be honest get some of your personal opinions of some matters" pausing again he asked" is that okay with you?"

"Of course it is" replied Medhi, coughing slightly as he answered. He was still rather subservient and a lot nervous but ready, nonetheless.

The count beckoned his servant's and made provisions for Medhi to sit down comfortably; drinks being served by the service staff before they commenced.

To Medhi's surprise a type of tea was offered. "The countess thought you might like that" the Artois surprised him by remarking "as good as Madame Guttenberg I hope." They both laughed. It certainly put Medhi at ease.

The count went on "Am I to understand that the cabin boy Pierre, who as you know was brought up in the confines of the palace, was found alive, and in fact, the only person found alive. Is that true Medhi?"

"That's correct sir he was the only one." There was silence for a few seconds.

"Well, that's what the report goes on to say" added Artois "but he escaped apparently, did he not?"

"As far as we know, your excellency, he did escape, but no sign of him has been seen since, either dead or alive."

"Hmm" Artois murmured, running his fingers through his meticulously coiffured black hair, staring intently into Medhi's eyes. He twizzled his beard around and vehemently asked "but what do you think Medhi?"

Once again there was silence for a few seconds as Medhi replied "Before I answer I must stress that both Archie and I have no proof either way of what happened to Pierre or indeed, where he or his body might be."

Medhi was now beginning to stumble with his words as he was now becoming very nervous and was wondering if he was saying the right things or not.

Slightly leaning forward, the count said in a sympathetic manner "It's okay I understand it's just your opinion I'm interested in."

Medhi felt immediately relieved and a little more relaxed before going on "To be honest, both Archie and I think he may have escaped, and someone could be helping him."

The count simply stared at Medhi, adding "Seems more like it, doesn't it or you would think a body would have been found by now" he paused a little longer than before as he said, "do you think it's possible then that my son and his wife could have survived."

"Unfortunately, and regrettably, I do not and neither does Archie. It appears your son and his wife were killed during the shipwreck and simply disappeared into the river and were washed out to sea."

The count seemed to accept Medhi's opinion with a heavy heart, together with his wife Celeste. They were having to get used to this news of the tragedy. Medhi had never seen the Count like this before and he knew that although he was a brave and gifted soldier, he was also the current and legal count of Montpellier, who on many occasions, had defended the exalted position and had sworn his allegiance to the people and to France, It was sad for Medhi to see the count and countess in such low esteem.

"Even in this time of personal loss, I have to say we are now entering the final few years of our reign here" Artois continued, "which is, of course, the position of Count and Countess of Montpellier."

Medhi, although a little puzzled listened with intense concentration. Naturally he wasn't aware of the legal matters of inheritance, why would he be, he thought, but it still concerned him, nevertheless.

The Count revealed, in a low, deliberate tone the looming deadline set by the royal courts: July 29th, 1815. A fixed point in time that would seal the fate of Montpellier. The current laws of the royal family in France meant that without a natural heir then the position must be handed over to the nearest living relative of the Count Artois, which meant, if no other actual heir could be found, such as his son captain Jon or his wife, the Count would have no choice but to abdicate and hand over the position to the nearest relative, even though his direct relatives had held this exalted position for over three hundred years. Medhi listened in complete silence, he had not been aware of such rules, and he certainly wasn't aware that a final date was now already in place and indeed why he was being told this. In addition, the new legal heir would have to be in possession, if possible, of the "Grand Seal of Commission, the symbolic object of their rule or golden coin as it was often referred.

Without it, the Artois family's centuries-old reign would come to a swift and bitter end.

The silence in the room was broken only by Medhi who interrupted most briefly "Was that the cold coin captain Marcel was given before he set sail and told to protect with his life." Artois nodded "Yes, indeed it was" was the answer "and without it, no-one in our family can rightfully make a claim. Without an heir, or that seal, out title is finished" the Count said, his voice devoid of its former strength, "everything we have fought for will be handed to whoever can claim it."

Nothing was heard in the room save the chink of glasses as they drank without merriment and pondered his words.

Naturally, conversations began, if a Marcel could not be found who could make a claim? Speculation was rife with some ridiculous names being offered, like Napolean Bonaparte, though with a smirk of irony, a promising young soldier who was swiftly climbing the social ladder and had illusions of grandeur.

The room went quiet when it was stated the most likely of all though, was someone like Mad Abdul the Black Heart, an exiled tyrant with royal blood and a thirst for power who could become the new Count. Medhi had shivered at the mention of Abdul. Even in Tunisia, the stories of his cruelty were whispered with fear and hatred. His dark reputation sucking the air from the room like a black hole. Medhi felt a similar chill. Abdul had always been a very real threat. If Abdul claimed the title, Montpellier would be lost to an era of unimaginable horror. Medhi had seen it before. He knew what Abdul was capable of. "

Well, surely then, that must apply to others who wish to be the new count" Medhi spoke with a fearful voice.

At this statement Artois pursed his lips and blew out a small puff of air and with a hint of resignation remarked "Afraid it is Medhi, that's the rules of the royal association. We've lived by them for hundreds of years and we can do nothing but accept them."

Medhi interrupted once again, this time with more disappointment "But that's nearly twenty years away from now, isn't it? Surely anything could happen in twenty years." He almost pleaded. His face a picture of despair.

"Not without the seal, or a legitimate heir it can't," said Artois. He patted his servant on the shoulder, something he had never done "You and Archie have done your best, more than I could have expected" he said glancing at Celeste who was also listening intently. He took hold of Medhi's hand and made mention of his missing little finger "You cut this off yourself Medhi" he went on "as a sign of absolute loyalty. But alas it appears it may have all been for nothing."

Medhi barely touched his wine as these thoughts swirled in his head, his mind racing to connect the dots, to find something – anything – that could help, could the boy Pierre, the cabin boy found alive after the shipwreck, be the key? He was the only survivor, but even he had vanished, leaving only speculation and unanswered questions in his wake.

The corridors of the palace felt narrower now as Medhi moved through them, each step echoing off the stone walls. He longed for the simple, rough life of the North-East of England where things were clear, where loyalty and friendship meant something tangible. He thought of Archie McPherson, still in Edinburgh, and the fishermen's huts, life there for all its hardships had felt real, not weighed down by royalty. He remembered Archie's rough laughter, the warmth of simple conversations. But those memories felt distant now, fading under the palace's heavy canopy of intrigue and political tension.

As he walked his heart was heavy. Realising that the seal was lost, there was nothing left. They were running out of time, and without a miracle, the fate of Montpellier would soon be out of their hands.

For the time being, at least, nothing more could be done or said, all there was now was to write back to Archie and thank him for his efforts and in addition to keep hold of the information and keep his eyes and ears open for any developments that may arise. The FrenchAnglo war was now beginning to advance and travel between the two countries was almost impossible.

CHAPTER 13

Archie and Medhi's works were now complete, and the accepted opinion between the two of them and Count Artois, it would be best if they let matters rest. The three men had agreed to let matters rest, for the time being they could wait. The next few years moved on without incident, broken only, perhaps, by the odd letter between Artois and Archie. The war between France and England had accelerated, it was gaining momentum now as each nation tried to gain the upper hand. As the year passed England knew, at this precise moment they could not match Napolean or France on the open battlefield. But on the water, they were a formidable match. In the shadow of this great conflict, life at Lindisfarne Priory continued with an almost eerie stillness, as if the horror of war were something distant, something beyond the secret island's shores.

Within the ancient stone walls of the priory the candlelight flickered, casting shadows as they danced in the quiet night, change was stirring. Father Bartholemew now nearing his 70th birthday stood on the threshold of a decision that would alter the course of one young man's life. Pierre, the cabin boy rescued from the wreck of the sailing ship Montpelier, five years earlier. Pierre, of course, who was now being called Peter in order that on his release may soon slip back into society and to the outside world that awaited him, he would be a different person entirely.

"Well Peter" Bartholemew's voice was steady, "you have been with us nearly five years now and it is time for you to leave the confines of the monastery. You have been here long enough, my son" he said while glancing around him. As he spoke a flicker of emotion crossed his weatherbeaten face, the truth being he really did not want Peter to leave but he knew in his heart it was the right thing to do. "Your new life outside these walls awaits."

The boy, now a man, stood tall before him. His once soft features had sharpened, his frame had filled out, but his eyes – those piercing eyes – appeared to hold the weight of his past. "I am quite happy to stay here" Peter replied, "I am not in any rush to leave, really I'm not." The boy now known as Peter Bartholemew, retained his French knowledge but spoke perfect English with a Northumbrian dialect. But beneath the veneer of his new identity, Pierre still lingered, haunted by memories of the shipwreck, of the cries of his fellow sailors, Captain Jon Marcel, and of the promise he had made – the secret he had guarded all these years. He knew the monk was right. His destiny lay elsewhere.

Father Bartholemew, a man who had seen too many winters, studied Peter and smiled a grateful but proud smile. "I know lad, but it is time."

He looked toward Peter who had become something of a prodigy at the priory. His intellect had blossomed under the monk's guidance and his once clumsy hands had become deft and sure. He had mastered the art of winemaking, crafting mead with other secret ingredients so exquisite that some whispered it rivalled the finest blended whisky. The lad was now a tall and quite handsome young man, a little under six feet tall, his interests were varied and many, but Bartholemew knew he would have to let his young champion leave and make his way in the outside world. He smiled sadly; Peter was destined for more than a life of quiet seclusion. In a sense he also wanted to watch with interest Peter's progress.

The date was 17th May 1802, and the monks had gathered in the courtyard to celebrate Bartholemew's 70th birthday, the mood was festive yet with the knowledge this would mark not only the monk's birthday, but Peter's time with them was ending.

The smell of roast pork was in the air. Most of the monks were now gathered outside the monastery when Peter spoke first. "You know we are having this pork as a memory of the time I first met Father Bartholemew at the priory" said the young lad with eyes rolling up and looking skywards. He thought for a few seconds more, turning towards Bartholemew, grinning he went on to say, "I want a huge portion of crispy roast pork, like the one we had when we first met."

"Can you still remember that! Father Bartholemew laughed "that's a long while back."

Peter nodded and a little quieter, but with a lot more sincerity. "Yes, father I remember it --

--- I remember all of it, and I will never forget any of the many conversations we had, nor indeed will I ever forget all the monks standing here before me who have helped me." He flashed a grin at the monk, his gaze filled with warmth and respect.

"Pork it is then Peter, well done. I like your choice. And I suppose we are going to wash it down with lots of mead. Would that be correct?" Peter nodded.

They all laughed, and preparations were instantly commenced. If nothing else, it was going to be an unforgettable experience. By now everyone in the Priory was excitedly awaiting the cooking of the pork, the delicious aroma seemed to be within everyone's nostrils. With each drink of mead anticipation was growing by the minute. Talk of Peter's future was now gaining momentum. It was agreed that he would leave the Monastery within the next few days. Talks had been held with Bartholomew and a Mr. Edward Dunwoody over the last year and it had been agreed in principal that Peter be taken on as an apprentice brewer. Mr. Dunwoody was a well-known wine merchant and an amateur distiller, a part which he loved dabbling in, although not strictly legal. He had been known on many an occasion to make his own brand of whisky which apparently the local community all loved. Visits were often made by the constabulary, but nothing ever came of them, presumably because Mr Dunwoody or Steady Eddie as he was known often gave the authorities a certain amount of free drink. Peter was to be given an introductory letter from all the monks in the priory, describing his exemplary manners and their assurances of a great future for the young lad. Suddenly all thought and conversations stopped momentarily 'aha' here it comes Peter" enthused Bartholemew "your hot roast pork, and very crispy by the look of it" he added, turning round on his stool he fixed his eyes on Peter "I'll bet you won't forget this pork either" he enthused, in fact they all did. To say the meat was devoured extremely quickly would be a grand understatement. Everything edible seemed to disappear along with the local delicacy of crusty bread, in addition, they had made their own kind of sauce which seemed to compliment the pork in a most delightful way. Everything was, as expected, washed down with tankards of mead. It was a brilliant end to a birthday celebration and a poignant and emotional end to Peter's sojourn with them.

The next morning, before dawn, Peter was given his letter of recommendation from the monks, which he carefully placed in his home-made leather carrying case. In the actual holdall he had placed a few meagre provisions, a bottle of mead and a small pouch of coins to assist him on his journey. All the brothers and fathers of the monastery turned out to wish him well. It was around 6a.m. the early morning mist curling around him like a spectral shroud, but nothing was going to stand in his way, and he was ready.

"Well Peter, this is it lad" said Father Bartholemew, with tears welling up in his eyes "Tis the end of an old life and the beginning of a new one." He had always known this day would come, he smiled warmly as he embraced Peter one last time, holding longer than he intended, the weight of it all pressing down like a leaden sky. Naturally he was worried as anyone would be, but he knew in his heart that this parting of the ways was the right thing to do, and he thought, while looking, at Peter, this lad will make it through anything.

Peter, however, couldn't help but show his emotions, after what seemed like ages he eventually let go of his great friend. He knew as long as he lived, he would never forget him or indeed the time he had spent at the priory. He walked slowly away, walking down the mistcovered pathway, looking back every so often. When he finally waved goodbye, he thought to himself 'no looking back now' I'm a free man and while a bit afraid he knew his future and destiny lay elsewhere.

Peter unfolded the map he had been given, its edges crisp, the parchment smooth beneath his fingers. The inkwork was precise and had been done by the monks skilled in cartography, giving directions guiding him on his journey ahead, with detailed instructions as to how to get to Mr. Dunwoody's home and business premises. They were beautifully drawn and informative; the monks had done a great job, and they were comprehensive. He calculated his route and reasoned to himself, if he walked briskly enough and with purpose he would arrive at his destination within a couple of days.

Each part of the map was intricate, with notations for landmarks and subtle hints of what lay ahead. If was as if the path itself was testing him, urging him forward.

As Peter walked, his mind wandered. Despite the urgency of his mission, he couldn't help but think of that fateful night, of the actual shipwreck, he had experienced all those years ago. He remembered the cries of distress and anguish of his crew mates in their final moments on board the ship and in the water. He hadn't realised at the time that tough, hardened seamen could panic and cry. He also remembered very well indeed the final moments of his master, Captain Jon Marcel, he remembered him more than anyone, along with putting the small infant child into a wine barrel and letting loose the most cherished cargo into the raging North Sea in the hope that someday it would be recovered, a desperate gamble that haunted Peter every waking moment. In some ways he felt guilty he had never mentioned this fact to Father Bartholemew or anyone for that matter, but he knew he couldn't as it was far too important a matter and he had made his promise to the captain and Celeste, but he now thought this information along with his new life would be of paramount importance to him over the next few years.

The mist that had shrouded his path was lifting now, revealing the silhouette of Tynemouth Priory. Its towering spires loomed like sentinels, watching his approach. His stomach churned with a feeling he couldn't quite place – not fear, nor elation but something n between. The iron gates stood as they had years ago, rusted and unlocked, a testament to the time he had spent imprisoned within its stone walls. He passed the threshold, there was no bitterness, only a strange sense of relief, as though the place released him from its grip. He had no time keeping device so he was very pleased the clouds had disappeared slightly in order that he could see the sun and, therefore, travel in the right direction. He also guessed by the amount of walking he had done it would be around midday, another sure sign, he thought, as he also felt quite hungry. As he passed the iron doors Peter glanced in more than once into the room, noticing the contents, the straw and other things that were there at the time of his confinement had been removed. He decided, however, it would be of no advantage or consequence to wander inside.

Peter pushed forward, his eyes narrowing as they scanned the horizon. The river now lay before him, its surface low and sluggish.

The infamous Black Middens, jagged and treacherous, emerged from the waters like the spine of some ancient sea beast. These rocks had claimed countless ships over the years, and now, exposed by the low tide, they seemed almost sentient. A chill ran down Peter's spine a strange compulsion pulled him toward them. The wind, cold and restless, carried a faint whisper, ghostly and unintelligible, but unmistakeable in its urgency. It beckoned him to stop.

He hesitated at the river's edge, feeling the weight of unseen eyes upon him. His hands fumbled as he unpacked his meagre provisions. Bread, mead, dried fish. He ate quickly, his hunger momentarily sated, exhaustion overtook him, and he drifted into a fitful sleep.

When he awoke, the landscape had transformed. The tide was creeping back in, swallowing the Middens once again. The air had grown colder, heavier, as though the sea itself was speaking in hushed tones, its whispers grew louder in his mind, fragments of voices long silenced by time. He felt strange again, feeling that the past was reaching for him, tugging at his consciousness, demanding something he desperately tried to forget.

He sighed, he couldn't forget the past, it was impossible, he kept thrusting his walking stick into the soggy ground around him and indiscriminately flicked up tufts of grass and soil into the air as he vented his frustration, the weight of the past pressing down on his conscience like an anchor. Even in his torment, he felt the pull to keep moving.

With a sudden burst of determination, Peter shoved the remnants of his provisions into his holdall and made his way past North Shields, its streets bustling with life and noise, a stark contrast to the silent priory he had left behind. The city seemed chaotic, alive with the clamour of industry and trade, the scent of coal and human toil. It was not the quietude he had grown accustomed to. Peter glanced at his map every so often and followed the winding path towards Newcastle.

He marvelled at the new buildings as they rose around the city's stone walls, their architecture and the powerful message they sent out, a far cry indeed from the confines of the priory and the cloistered life he had led.

All along his route Peter had been looking for places he may stay the night before moving on finally to Wylam.

A darkness began to settle, and he noted he was nearing Blaydon just shy of his destination. His gaze fell upon an old coal barge unattended, still tied up to the jetty – called the

Staithes apparently – at least that's what his map said. He circled it once, twice, before deciding it would do for the night. With a grunt, he threw his belongings on board and clambered after them, although it was dark he could still see enough of the barge to form lasting impressions. It reeked and filthy with remnants of its coal days hanging in the air, thick with decay. Yet, it was dry enough, and after Peter had inspected every corner decided he would say a prayer and resign himself to staying the night.

Sleep eluded him as regrettably, he spent most of the time awake listening to the unfamiliar creaks and groans. Unfortunately, it was the most uncomfortable time he had ever encountered. In a way it was like the time he was confined between the cold, stone walls of the old priory, many years ago.

At dawn, he awoke to find the sunlight piercing the clouds, pulling him from his uneasy rest. After surveying the area around him he found there weren't many people about, so he assumed it was still early morning. He quickly gathered his belongings together and ate the last of the provisions he had brought with him. Gathering his thoughts together, he studied the last few instructions on his home-made map. If they were correct, he would be at his destination about noon. He trudged westward, the road grew narrow and cobbled. At he walked further along he noticed a stone marker which was half submerged in the cobbled roadway, Wylam 2 miles, was all it said, relief washed over him. "Thank God, he muttered, the words hanging in the cold air. Peter, although tired was almost there. His pace quickened, driven by the knowledge that his journey was nearly at an end.

Once he arrived in Wylam it was a quiet village, its modest buildings a stark contrast to the fine buildings of Newcastle or indeed North Shields, but at least with a place this size he reasoned, he should find it easier to find Mr. Dunwoodie's residence.

It took him only a short while to locate his destination. An imposing old building, he thought, full of architectural character, exuding history. Before he knocked on the door, he took a few extra minutes to run his eyes over the building itself and the surrounding area. The building's weathered façade spoke of a different era, its stone walls worn by weather, but still strong, still resolute. After a while, he felt ready to knock on the wonderful, handcrafted oak door. In doing so he noticed a huge brass ring attached to a steel rod. Underneath the word PULL etched in the stone. With a deep breath he grasped the ring and pulled. This he anticipated was another way of letting the residents know of potential visitors (this must be for people like me, he guessed). He simultaneously heard a melodic ringing sound, like a cluster of small bells, each playing their own tune. He couldn't help himself smiling, for the first time in what felt like an eternity. First impressions of the household were indeed very, very favourable. Before the door was even opened Pierre, the young cabin boy, felt he had arrived. He was ready for his new adventure to proceed.

CHAPTER 14

The wind swept mercilessly across the docks of Tyneside, carrying with it the scent of saltwater. Darkness had already begun to descend on Dolly Grey's tripe shop, an inconspicuous building tucked away from the main street, where the usual chatter of fishwives and boatmen had turned into something far more sinister.

Inside Dolly sat behind the counter, her fingers idly drumming along the edge as she hummed to herself. The shop was dimly lit, casting long shadows over shelves that now held more than tripe. In a desperate bid for survival, she had begun selling fish an act that had stirred the waters of discontent with her longtime neighbours. She had broken an unwritten law, and the consequences were closing in fast.

Outside, a small crowd had gathered – angry, restless and growing louder by the minute. Fishwives weathered by years of labour on the docks, flung abusive insults and objects toward her window. Rotten fruit hit the small glass pane, the thuds echoing like distant thunder. Dolly however, remained unmoved, her gaze somewhere beyond the horizon. She had faced worse. Her survival instincts were becoming sharper than ever as the situation was spiralling out of control.

Suddenly, the commotion outside stopped, and the noise was interrupted by the sound of a little brass bell that cut through the growing tension. Dolly didn't bother looking up, she assumed it was another brave soul, perhaps willing to purchase something amidst the chaos. The voice that followed froze her in place.

'Mother, what have you done?"

Florrie ever so gently closed the door behind her, she stood in the doorway, the figure of someone caught between two worlds – her mother's unyielding defiance and the fury of the mob outside. Florrie didn't need to raise her voice; the disappointment in her tone was sharp enough to slice through the thick air of the shop.

"Do you realise what's happening out there? They're furious, every last one of them," Florrie said in a low yet carrying voice, an urgency forcing attention, "The fishermen, their wives – they're all mad at you."

Dolly, never one to back down, slowly lowered her spectacles and fixed her gaze on Florrie. "They can all run up a shutter for all I care," she said with a calm indifference, shifting in her chair with a creaking coming from the old wood.

Florrie leaned in, her tone suddenly serious. "Hold on, Ma. Let me bring in Andy – Andy Tate. He's just outside, and he can explain it better than me."

Dolly gave a dismissive nod, more out of curiosity than interest. "Go on then. Get him in here." Her cackle rang through the room, her tobacco-stained teeth catching the dim light in a menacing way.

Florrie opened the door and called out to Andy, who was hovering near the growing crowd." Andy, can you come in for a minute and explain the situation to my Ma?"

Andy, a gruff man built like a tank, shook his head at first, his voice booming over the low murmur of the crowd. "Don't need to come in," he barked. "We just want her to stop selling fish. Simple as that." He glanced over his shoulder at the restless mob, then added with a pointed edge "How would she feel if we started selling tripe down by the river?"

Dolly shot up from her chair, her eyes narrowing as his words sunk in. For a moment, she said nothing, only muttering something inaudible under her breath. Then, in a low, dangerous voice, she growled, "He's got a point there … Tell him to get in here, unless he's afraid of me." Her laugh was hollow, filled with something darker than amusement.

Andy, clearly not one to back down, stepped into the shop. The atmosphere inside seemed to shift the moment he crossed the threshold. The tension was tangible, like the charged air before a storm. Florrie, ever the mediator, gestured for Andy to come closer. As he did, she noticed more people gathering outside, the situation teetering on the edge of chaos.

"It's bigger than I thought, Dolly." Andy remarked, his eyes scanning the interior of the shop. "You could store a lot of tripe in here, and a few eggs."

Dolly responded, nodding as she did so "Too big, by a long way, I suppose, but that's life. Anyway, get to the point, what do you want?"

Andy gathered his composure and stood back for a moment, he was the sort of person it would be difficult to guess his age, especially considering his receding hairline. Rather unkempt, as well, with one glass broken in his well-worn spectacles. Florrie, however, reasoned he would be about 50 years old and not married, she knew that much, and he was proud of the fact he ran his own shellfish cabin right on the river itself, so close to the river, in fact, at high tide half of it was submerged. He reasoned that's where he got a substantial number of mussels and winkles at low tide. It was also a perfect venue to observe the various comings and goings on the river.

In a rather disgruntled voice, he went on "I see the lads from over the water delivering fish here Dolly."

She looked straight up at Andy without answering. "Aye that's right" he said, "we've seen them."

"Aye, so what" she shouted back "it's still a free country, at least it was the last time I looked" she said still mumbling under her breath adding "and besides they are cheaper." As she said this, she was pointing her scruffy finger directly at Andy. "Put that in your pipe and smoke it" laughing out loud as though she had made some kind of point.

"That's the point though" interrupted Andy "the fish aren't any cheaper from across the water."

"Ah they are" interrupted Dolly "I've been to your place loads of times, including our Florrie's little spot."

Florrie couldn't help but intervene "Well me Ma has got a point Andy" she pointed out "if they are cheaper over the water, you have to say that's fair enough. Is it not?"

Andy sat back in his chair and nodded in agreement. "That may be, I suppose," he went "that's probably because they're cutting us out, you're getting trade prices from them and ordinary prices from us."

Dolly's eyes narrowed, but she remained silent. The sharpness in her expression softened just a fraction, though her posture remained rigid.

Florrie, sensing an opening, once again interrupted "Ma. Andy's got a point," she said carefully "You can't blame him for being upset. If they're undercutting the locals, it's bad for everyone."

Andy's jaw clenched, but he nodded, his voice calm now. "That's right. We're all struggling to keep afloat, and every pound you save is another nail in our coffin."

For the first time, Dolly seemed to consider his words. "So, what are suggesting?" she asked, her voice losing its edge, just slightly.

Florrie jumped in before the tension could rise again. "There's got to be a way around this, Andy, why don't you ask the folk outside to go home for now? Let's sit down and talk about this properly."

Andy eyed Dolly for a long moment, then nodded. He stepped back outside, speaking to the gathered crowd. Slowly, they began to disperse, though their frustration still hung in the air like a storm waiting to break.

When Andy returned, the tension had eased, if only slightly. He closed the door behind him, his shoulders visibly relaxing. "All right," he said, "let's see if we can figure this out."

Florrie smile faintly. "Ma, put the kettle on. I think we could all do with a cup of tea."

Dolly grumbled, but for once, she didn't argue. She moved toward the back, leaving Florrie and Andy in the charged silence of the shop.

For the first time that day, there was hope. But the storm wasn't over yet.

Florrie looked at them both, nervous about the suggestion she was about to make. "I might have an idea."

The other two looked on nervously. Florrie continued, "Andy, you thought this place was big, maybe too big."

"Well, it is for selling tripe and nowt else" he continued looking about the place "Why, like, what are you thinking of?"

Florrie went on "You also said it was a good spot or position, near the town centre. "I did" Andy replied slowly "but what's your point, what are you going on about?"

Dolly interrupted!" Hold on, hold on, it's my shop and I don't even know what she's talking about."

Both Dolly and Andy turned towards Florrie, their gazes heavy with confusion. As if they expected some divine intervention. Florrie paused, her eyes locked on Andy, but her words were aimed at her mother. "Sorry ma, I'll get back to you in a minute" she said knowing her mother was easily huffed. Shifting her focus back to Andy, she continued, her tone calm but purposeful. "Am I right in thinking your stall is the one right under the wooden jetty where the pilot boats are tied up?"

Andy hesitated, his words dragging as though weighed down by suspicion. "Aye it is." he replied very slowly, with more than a little apprehension and curiosity "It's a bit run down like, not saying it isn't" he added the embarrassment clear in his voice.

Florrie pressed on "I expect it's not easy to get down there, scrambling over the rocks and it can't be much better for your customers, especially the older ones, can it?" she was saying all these words with hint of a solution in her mind, none of which, it must be said were registering with Andy. A thick silence settled over the room.

Florrie knew she had to spell it out before the tension snapped. Taking a deep breath, she addressed them both, "Will you hear me out? Just listen, no interruptions until I've said everything." Dolly and Andy exchanged a glance and reluctantly agreed. Dolly, more intrigued than Andy, leaned back and muttered, "I think we should have that cup of tea now ... We're going to need it."

Florrie, feeling the weight of the moment, took a deep breath and adjusted her clothing to make herself a bit more comfortable and sat down, her eyes scanning the shop as though seeing it for the first time. After a tense pause, which felt like an eternity but was only a few seconds, she began. "Let's be honest with ourselves – none of us are exactly well off, are we?

Both Dolly and Andy nodded in agreement, with Andy cleaning the only eye piece in his spectacles.

"We are all in the same boat, not just us, but everyone outside too. If we don't find a way to survive together, we're done for," their agreement was more empathetic this time, both Dolly and Andy nodded again.

Dolly finally broke the silence, "So, what are you getting at then, Florrie" her eyes darted to Andy for support but found none. The silence stretched again until Florrie spoke, her voice suddenly strong "Amalgamate" she said, with a tone that left no room for doubt, "Amalgamate."

"Nivver heard of it" Dolly shot back, her face scrunched in confusion "what's that like, some kind of soup?"

Florrie couldn't help but smile at the absurdity. It means we band together, That's you, me and anyone else down on the river. We pool our resources" but she added very quickly "but we keep control of our own stalls. It's about working together while staying independent.

And when I say we, I do mean everyone on the south side of the river who wants in." Andy blinked, the concept still eluding him. "But what does that actually mean?"

"Be quiet" interrupted Dolly "she's getting there, let her finish."

For the first time in a long time, she was impressed with her daughter. Florrie accepted her mother's intervention, and went on "We all, know my mother's got a big building here, especially for tripe and fresh eggs, but my thoughts are, after some changes we could make this place twice the size it already is." Both Dolly and Andy exchanged doubtful looks and almost simultaneously protested "Well, what good is that going to be, twice the size to sell nowt." Dolly scoffed.

Florrie, unfazed, smiled knowingly, and said "Aye that's right Ma, we could turn this into a proper market. Big enough to take at least twelve retail units, each selling their own produce, fresh fish, shellfish, your winkles Andy, and your tripe Ma."

Dolly raised an eyebrow, her voice heavy with scepticism. "Well, that's great, that is" replied Dolly "how am I going to manage twelve shops when I can barely manage my own?"

"That's the beauty of it," Florrie explained, her enthusiasm mounting. "Each stall would pay you a rent. They'd manage their own upkeep. You wouldn't have to sell a thing, Ma, you'd be the landlord."

Dolly's reaction was immediate, but before she could speak Andy interrupted "It's a brilliant idea Dolly, and I know most of the folk would jump at the chance, and as a bonus we would all be under cover, no more dealing with the rain." He turned to Florrie, admiration in his voice. "If you think you could make this work Florrie, I think we should get everyone together and get things started."

Before he could finish, Dolly chimed in, quickly and purposefully, "I think our Florrie's the one to do that Andy, don't you agree?"

Andy nodded eagerly, turning to face Florrie, who was now sitting very quietly. Andy was smiling as he said most enthusiastically "Well, I can't think of anyone more determined or better suited than your Florrie, she's perfect for it." He put his spectacles back on and peered through them at them both and agreed whole heartedly.

Not long after, a meeting was called. The local fisher folk gathered, and whilst everyone had their say, most were enthusiastic, a few were hesitant. But in the end, the decision was unanimous. Consequently, all stalls were claimed. Minor reconstruction began, and the building was ready for the new venture. It later became known as 'Dolly Greys Indoor market' the very first collection of shops under one roof in the northeast of England.

A new chapter had begun.

CHAPTER 15

The year now was 1805, the world teetered on the edge of chaos. The air buzzed with the tension of a continuance of England's bitter rivalry with France and had reached fever pitch, and at sea, the meteoric rise of Horatio Nelson and Cuthbert Collingwood had tilted the balance in Britain's favour. Yet, in South Shields, far removed from the thundering cannons and war cries of Trafalgar, the soft church bells marked a different kind of battle – one of faith, tradition, and identity.

Oblivious to all that was going on, Celia Trevelyan, was in the middle of her first Holy Communion, her heart fluttering with excitement. She was, after all, the focus of every eye in the room, or so it felt. Of course, she wasn't the only child taking communion that day as there were also 20 of her friends lining the pews alongside her, but to Celia, this was her day alone a shining star in a sky full of lesser lights.

Celia, dressed in pure white, was the adopted child of the Rev Tobias Trevelyan and his wife Fiona, following the discovery of the infant child in the barrel, six years ago and now she stood tall, taller than the other girls, in fact, and strikingly beautiful with her olive-toned skin and flowing fair hair. The mystery of her origins clung to her like a shadow, whispered about among the congregation, a tantalising enigma that no-one had been able to fully unravel.

Among the congregation and well-wishers sat Florrie Guttenberg and her friend Mary, Celia's godparents, who had never forgotten the miraculous discovery of their little ward.

"She looks brilliant, mind" Florrie enthused, carefully looking Celia up and down, checking her appearance.

"Aye, she does that, all right" answered Mary "and she looks quite comfortable with it" taking time to grab hold of Florrie's hand and squeezing it very gently, both ladies smiled contently as their beautiful godchild took part in the proceedings.

Florrie's lips curled into a knowing smile. "Well, we don't know who her real parents are, could be royal blood, for all we know?" Her tone was light, but the implication was heavy, hanging between them like a secret too dangerous to speak aloud. Both women laughed, the sound catching Celia's attention as she passed them, frowning slightly, her mind already shifting to the feast that awaited.

Mary's daughter, Becky, was also there with her now boyfriend, Constable Charley Wilson. Becky herself was now a much more assured lady, very competent and forward thinking. Her young son, Thomas or Tommy as he preferred, was also a guest. Becky had always been attractive but her newfound confidence and extra stability in her life brought a new side to her no-one had ever seen. She was a church member and held an important position within the church itself and was on lots of committees in and around the town, probably too many, she thought, as she did not have enough time in the day to carry out each individual duty.

St. Hilda's Church, though modest in size, was grand in spirit with lots of ornate architectural structures within the building. It's ornate golden eagle lectern, which stood in pride of place near the altar was a beacon of beauty in the room. It seemed even more lovely today though as the sun shone through the stained-glass windows, which in themselves told beautiful stories of this fine old church, and was casting vivid patterns of colour across the ancient stone floor. All the little girls and boys were beginning to make their way out of the church, glancing every so often into the side aisles where their proud parents and friends were watching.

Eventually all the congregation were leaving followed by Fiona and the Rev Trevelyan. It must be said everyone present was as proud as they could be and were looking forward to the rest of the day. The children, of course, being by far the most excited, including Tommy, Becky's son who was pushing past everyone to be first at the food on the tables.

In the churchyard, preparations were well under way. Mrs. Watson, the Vicar's housekeeper, commanded the scene with the precision of a seasoned general, directing volunteers and children with authority, helped, of course, by her most trustworthy assistant Becky. "You sort the sandwiches, if you will, Becky love," she said "and I will bring out the cakes, and the little gifts for the children" patting Tommy gently on the head. Becky immediately dived into her tasks and was busying herself with the ease of someone well accustomed to organizing chaos.

"Charley" she shouted amid the excitement to her boyfriend, Constable Charley Wilson, "can you lend a hand over here, there's some ham to be cut."

Charley grinned, more than pleased to help. They would be married soon, and the thought brought warmth to his chest, so any experience in these matters would prove to be invaluable. Charley had been a constable now for over seven years and was used to handling rowdy crowds, but dealing with enthusiastic kids and their mothers was proving rather more difficult, but to his credit and good humour he performed his duty in a very exemplary manner.

Watching from a distance Charley's superior Billy Burns was now a detective Sergeant and quite the disciplinarian, but today he was proudly watching his young protégée. He couldn't help but smile remembering him as a nervous lanky youth with virtually no confidence at all." Now look at him he thought strong, accomplished and quite the rising star and it was also great to see, full of enthusiasm. Sergeant Burns could foresee a great future for Charley.

As Burns drifted into his thoughts, a familiar voice broke thorough, "Hello Billy, you look unrecognizable without your uniform on, almost normal in fact" he added "not as tall either, without your helmet." Both men had a good laugh. Anders, Florrie's husband, approached, his laughter filling the air.

Billy chuckled, "Hello Anders," Billy replied "aye, almost normal. I see your Florrie's into the thick of it as usual." He glanced over to a group of volunteers and guests laughing.

"Aye, so I see" replied Anders "right in the middle of everything, as usual, just like her mother, that one" he said, shaking his head ever so slightly "she's talked about nothing else but this day for weeks."

The two men shred a knowing glance, their thoughts momentarily aligned on the day Celia had been found. It had been a day like no other – a day of discovery, of questions, of mysteries yet unsolved. "You remember when Amos and Erasmus found her, don't you?" Billy asked, his voice quieter now, as if the memory, demanded reverence.

Anders nodded slowly, "Aye. I'll never forget it."

One of the volunteers walked by with two glasses of home-made wine and handed them to the two men.

"Me neither" said Anders "not for one single moment," Both men were silent, but it was charged with the weight of that long-ago event, a moment that had bound them all together in ways they could never fully explain. As the children laughed and played, the adults drank their wine, and the church basked in the glow of another sunny day, the mystery of Celia Trevelyan lingered – waiting, as all secrets do, for the day it would fully come to light.

Both men were reflecting on circumstances when a chap walked by. "And neither will this lad, will you son" he said, holding on to Erasmus's arm, holding him back as he tried to walk by. He was on his way to the refreshment table and frowned impatiently.

"Forget what?" asked an impatient Erasmus, eyes darting between the food and his father. He was seventeen now, and like most lads his age, he didn't have time for his elders' musings, especially not when his friends were waiting.

Billy grinned, his eyes twinkling, "When you and Amos found Celia in that barrel at Trow Rocks."

Erasmus' expression softened for a moment, his mind flashing back to that day. "No," he muttered, "I certainly won't forget that. Can I go now Da?" He shifted his weight from one foot to the other, eager to be away from the intensity of the moment.

Anders nodded, gesturing toward the crowd of young men at the far side of the yard. "Go on then join your pals," said Anders as he indicated the direction he supposed Erasmus was headed.

As Erasmus disappeared into the throng, Billy's gaze followed him. "Fine young man that Anders," he said with genuine affection, then slowly and quietly turned to face Anders, unlike your Amos eh Anders? Have you seen him lately?"

At the mention of his other son, Anders' face tightened. He glanced away, trying to mask the bitterness in his voice. "No, neither do I want to see him" he answered. He paused for a moment "Well, that's me anyway. I know for a fact Florrie would welcome him back in a heartbeat. That's mothers for you."

Billy shook his head slowly, his voice low and heavy with regret. "Aye Amos, he's a wrong one, that one" reiterated Billy shaking his head "no good will ever come from the path he has chosen."

Billy's words trailed off into silence. They both knew what had happened – how Amos had once been a boy full of promise but had chosen a dangerous life instead. Billy remembered the christening, the laughter, the shared dreams. But now, when Amos' name came up in conversation it was in connection with police records and criminal investigations. Smuggling, petty theft, and worse. His so-called friends had become hardened criminals, and his world now revolved around excitement, danger and the lure of easy money,

"Gunpowder Bob," muttered Billy under his breath, his eyes clouding with memory. Bobby Bolingbroke – Amos' partner in crime – was dangerous in ways Amos never could be. Where Amos was charming and clever, Bobby was all sharp edges and rage. They were a bad match, feeding off each other's worst instincts. Bobby's parents had died when he was only ten years old, and his family were eventually split up by the local authorities. He had a younger sister, Jessie, who he loved very much, and they were virtually inseparable, but the authorities, of course, never gave that matter much thought and she was moved South somewhere, never to be seen again. Bobby, even at a young tender age, blamed the authorities for everything that had taken place, he vowed then, on his mother's death if he could ever do them any harm, or anyone connected with them, he would. It was a solemn promise he made. Bobby Ran away to sea when he was only eleven years old, fuelled by anger and hatred from losing his family, he was quite a small lad and slim with it, which is more than likely why he was given the job of a powder monkey on one of the naval ships. The job, as you may know, entailed carrying bags of gunpowder from the ship's dry store, located in the bowels of the ship. He had to pick up the gunpowder there and run with the packages to midships and upper decks towards the guns. It was an extremely dangerous occupation and physically demanding, but without them, it must be said, Lord Nelson's ships would not have been as effective as they were. Strangely, though, Bobby enjoyed the excitement and the camaraderie of his shipmates immensely and it was here he earned his nickname Gunpowder Bob, likely because of his reckless speed and bravery. After a few years at sea his ship docked in his native port of Newcastle and more out of curiosity than anything else he jumped ship. It was here he met up with Amos, it was from this meeting their crossed paths had been sealed in a grim pact, one that only led their futures deeper into crime.

Meanwhile, Anders and Billy were still discussing the disappointing paths that the boys had chosen. Suddenly a bright cheerful voice interrupted their thoughts.

"Hello Grandad" she said "I hope the party is going to start soon" her voice was full of excitement and expectation.

Celia stood before them; her eyes wide with excitement. The communion party was in full swing now, the laughter of children filling the air. She gazed expectantly at Anders, her innocence a stark contrast to the dark memories swirling between the two men.

Anders knelt to her level, forcing a smile. "I think it's already started," he beamed, looking at all the young lads, racing forward to the table, laden with all sorts of fancy foods.

Celia's gaze, however, was piercing. "Or why don't we go and find Grandma Florrie and Aunt Becky?" she said, her voice firm but soft.

Anders blinked, his smile faltering. There was something searching in the way she looked at him. A tension passed between them, a tension that Billy, sensing the shift, was quick to step away from.

"See you later, Anders," he muttered, disappearing into the crowd.

Anders turned back to Celia, his brow furrowed, "What are you getting at, lass?"

Without hesitation, Celia's small hands found his. Her voice steady, almost too mature for her age. It gave Anders time to reflect for a few moments. "Oh my God ...." he thought, "It's time."

Just at that very moment he caught the eye of Florrie, who was quite happy making sure everyone was enjoying themselves. "Florrie, Florrie" he quietly shouted, making circular movements with his arms "come over here a minute," he deliberately paused a few moments before adding "I think our Celia here has a few questions she needs answering," he said in a bemused kind of way.

"Oh aye, and what's that like" she asked enthusiastically "something on your mind lass?" stroking her head "Come on then, let's hear it."

"Well" said Celia without a hint of hesitancy, or nervousness "you're not really my grandparents, are you? And none of you are really my family, not even Mama Fiona or Aunt Becky or Aunt Mary" then she added in almost a whisper "Of course, I love you all … very much, but I hope you understand, I need to know who I really am, and who my real parents are." She then paused what seemed an age before continuing "Why would they just leave me, in a cave? In a wine barrel."

For a moment time seemed to stand still. Around about then they were joined by Fiona and Mary, who had noticed there was something slightly amiss about their conversation.

"God, why all the long faces, something serious going on here" laughed Fiona nervously. It was an attempt to diffuse a difficult situation, but her voice was strained as she attempted to mask the rising panic.

Florrie looked stricken, she exchanged a look with Anders, who gave a small, resigned nod. "She knows," he whispered.

Celia stood with her arms folded, now the centre of attention. "I know about the barrel, where it was left, I have even been to the cave and seen the exact spot where the barrel stood. Or are you telling me this is not true?"

Fiona knelt beside Celia, her face pale but composed. "Celia, your part of our family." She said softly, "and you've never been abandoned. We found you in that barrel, yes, but it wasn't because anyone wanted to leave you behind. We love you – so much."

Celia nodded, but her eyes, far too wise for her age, didn't waver. "I believe that" she said quietly. "But I still need to know the truth. I need to know who I am."

Fiona was hoping to conceal her shock and the inner sickness she felt in her stomach.

There was an unbelievable silence from everyone for a few moments. Eventually Fiona found her composure, she beckoned Celia towards her and took her in her arms. With tears streaming down her face, she admitted "It's true, you were found there, and yes, you were found in a barrel. But I have to say, and it's most important to say this, you were not abandoned Celia Trevelyan, you were most certainly not. Yes, you were left there, but it was for us to find you and to bring you up as part of our family, all our family, including Florrie and Becky and it goes without saying, we have loved you from that very moment I hope you believe that."

Celia nodded and answered, beyond her years "I know that" she replied as she looked directly into everyone's eyes and simply said "But I still want to know who I really am."

Anders placed a hand on her shoulder, his voice gentle but firm. "We'll tell you everything, Celia. But not here, not today. Soon. The whole family will be there, and we'll explain."

This proposal appeared to please Celia for the moment as she gave a satisfied nod, and the weight of the conversation seemed to lift. Following this explanation, the noise and joy of the communion party resumed, and a wonderful day was spent in a very enjoyable manner. But in the back of everyone's mind, there lingered the same burning question – who was Celia Trevelyan, really?

The weeks that followed were filled with hushed meetings and difficult conversations. Florrie was particularly heartbroken, learning it was Amos had been the one to reveal the truth to Celia, perhaps with malicious delight. But Erasmus, unlike his brother, had shown kindness, guiding Celia to the spot where she had been found, offering what comfort he could.

The mystery of Celia's origins remained unsolved. But the girl in the barrel, now determined more than ever, was set on discovering the truth. However long it might take, she would find out who she really was – and why she had been left to be found.

CHAPTER 16

The years marched on, relentless, as the great powers of Europe clashed once again. France and England, ancient adversaries, were locked in the throes of a bitter war, and now the Spanish, allied with France had thrown their own weight into the chaos. Battles erupted across the continent, bloody and decisive, England's navy held dominion. Under the ruthless command of Lord Nelson, England was unassailable on the water. But on land, a new power loomed: Napoleon Bonaparte, whose iron grip on Europe's soil left no room for English pride to breathe.

It was whilst discussing these matters in the old Ferry Tavern that lives in the local community were about to change forever. The building was old by anyone's standards, dilapidated may have been a better way of describing it.

Amidst the hushed but frenzied whispers of this war the tavern continued its own existence, nestled like a secret along the river's edge. It nestled between two equally run-down buildings right on the river's edge, almost half submerged, especially round about high tide.

Roughly it was about 100 yards or so from St Hilda's church, locals were amazed that it never fell into the sea of its own accord, which seemed miraculous. Rumoured by the locals, if the church tower was in sight from the smoky main bar no harm would ever come to the pub. They held this half belief with reverence and defiance. The tavern was barely a building more a part miracle of flotsam, wrecked ship timbers, and stones from the old churches, some of which still had the writing on. The Ferry Tavern sat as though on the edge of oblivion, it was a miracle, they said, the tavern hadn't been claimed by the currents. But the old timers in town were fond of such miracles, and even more so of the roaring fire and a cup of ale on nights when the sea and sky seemed to wage their own private war. It was scarcely large enough to fit twenty souls, yet somehow, it had a way of welcoming the whole town within its cramped walls when the fires roared.

The tavern was only a stone's throw away from Dolly Grey's tripe shop and was run by Walter Smith. All the locals used the Ferry and gathered there on most evenings, strangely enough, no-one knew who the actual owner was, but Walter was the ex-landlord of the Wooden Dolly from North Shields, everyone knew the pub and most people had been there. Walter was a well-respected publican, right across Tyneside really and he was famous for his booming voice and keen knack for stirring a conversation, be it profound or purely absurd. It was on one of these nights of dubious discussions that certain events unfolded. It was around November 9th, 1813, when Walter's wife Maisie, a woman who embodied both patience and a fiery spirit, was in charge of placing buckets under the now badly leaking roof, due to the weather becoming very rainy and there was a steady drip from the ceiling in various places, which prompted Walter to build the fire up again by scratching about for loose coal and bits of firewood scattered around the hearth, to offer warmth to his customers.

"Never ending job Anders," he said, slightly groaning under the weight of his oversized coal scuttle, "job for a younger man, this, he went on through his wheezes "certainly not me," he added, laughing along with anyone who would listen, "and the blasted roofs at it again."

Anders, a patron as local as they came, offered a sardonic smile, "You should get your lass to do that," he said, glancing over to Walter's wife, "she does nowt else."

Well, there's a saying everyone's familiar with … if only looks could kill … and never was it more apparent than on this occasion.

Maisie paused, dripping bucket in hand, couldn't help herself, "If he" she said, looking at Walter "does an honest day's work, or any work for that matter, Anders, I'll have it read out in church on Sunday," she snapped, her words as sharp as the cold wind seeping in through the tavern's cracked windowpanes.

Anders realising he might have just dropped a clanger, leaned over the bar, "Here," he said to Walter "get Maisie a drink, would you?" while throwing a shilling on the bar counter "and change back, mind."

Walter smiled and pocketed the coin with a wink, but didn't offer to help his wife with the buckets. "We're going to have to fix that roof," he sighed, though he'd said it a hundred times before.

Anders looked across to where Maisie was busy mopping up and physically shoving the disgruntled customers out of the way "Move then" she was saying "don't let me disturb your drinking time for Gawd's sake." She was in full throttle now and no stopping her. "Your ale will still be there when I'm not."

Ander smiled to himself and chuckled, she reminded him a lot of his Florrie, a good hearted, kind natured woman but as tough as nails when needed to be. He took another pull from his mug, saying to Walter, leaning both elbows on the counter. "So, what's wrong with the roof, Walter?" he said with curiosity getting the better of him, "are the tiles missing then?" he went on, insinuating he had some expertise in the matter.

"As far as I know, there's one or two slates loose and dislodged, but not actually missing, why like?"

Anders took another sip from his ale "Just wondering Walter, just wondering." Anders, nevertheless, appeared to be in deep thought, as though he had something in mind.

Walter, also now curious as to what Anders was thinking surprisingly said "You can mend it if you want. You know I haven't got the time" as he busily carried on pulling pints.

Just then, the church bells struck eight, their ominous toll echoing over the river and slipping like a ghost through the cracks of the tavern's old walls. The bells marked the hour, but they also signalled something far darker – an omen of the events about to unfold.

Anders took a long, thoughtful sip of his ale, his gaze fixed on some distant invisible point. "Just thinking, Walter. Just thinking." His voice trailed off, yet his expression betrayed a deeper contemplation, as though he were piecing together some hidden puzzle. "I'll tell you what, me and Stevey here will do it tomorrow." Stevey who had been quietly nursing his drink, went slack jawed. This was as much a surprise to Stevey as to anyone else. His stunned silence said it all.

Walter raised his eyebrows in surprise, then gave an approving nod. "You're on" replied Walter, who was most impressed with Anders reply. "But do you know anything about roofs?" he queried.

"Nowt, but it can't be that hard, can it?" Anders replied with a quick grin, almost immediately. "Anyway, Stevey here can do all the hard work isn't that right lad?"

No sooner had Anders got the words out than Stevey's face paled, shaking his head just as quickly. "Not me Anders. Heights aren't my thing" he muttered, taking a nervous gulp. Then after thinking for a few moments, "but I can hold the ladder steady for you."

Just then Maisie bustled by them with her bucket, sloshing water over the floorboards as she went. She shot a grateful smile at Anders, clearly more impressed by his offer than by the drink he'd bought her.

The next morning dawned with a crisp chill in the air. The rain had stopped, but the roof was slick with morning dew. Anders and Stevey arrived at the tavern, bleary eyed but resolute.

"Right, Walter, did you say you had ladders?" enquired Anders, scanning the assortment of dusty debris piled in a corner.

"Aye, I have indeed, they're in that corner over there," pointing to what looked like a pile of unwanted ropes and sticks.

"Where" interrupted Anders, who, along with Steve couldn't see anything of use. "All I see are bits of old ropes and bamboos, where's the ladders?" he queried again, his face a picture of bewilderment.

Walter's face twisted in exasperation. "That is the ladder. It's a rope ladder, same as they use in the navy," said a surprised Walter. He seemed serious enough and surprised at the men's reluctance that they were really ladders.

"Well, I'm definitely not going up them," said a terrified Stevey, "not in a million years."

Anders gritted his teeth and turned to Walter, who was standing there with his arms folded totally bemused before muttering under his breath "That's all I've got like. Good enough for the Royal Navy mind .... Just saying"

"Aye, Okay Walter, they'll have to do," he muttered, rolling up his sleeves and settling to work untangling the ropes. It took half an hour of fumbling, but they managed to assemble something that loosely resembled a ladder. A crowd had gathered, watching the endeavour with the keen interest of spectators waiting for a spectacle.

Walter, ever the opportunist, had opened the bar, ensuring a steady stream of ale for his customers, prompting Anders to remind Walter to keep enough ale back for him and Stevey when they were done. Walter was more than happy to do just that, but insisted Anders had a beer before he went on the roof, for Dutch courage. Anders, didn't need to be asked twice and virtually drained the ale in one go, spilling and dribbling down his now greying beard. He burped loudly afterwards. "Best pint I've ever had" he said, handing back the tankard to Walter, who smirked.

"Aye, well the next one will be even better," Walter laughed. "Be careful, though" he went on "those slates look slippery from here."

Anders heaved himself onto the ladder, which swayed ominously with each step, each rung twisting beneath him like a serpent. The onlookers cheered as he wobbled, laughing at his expense. Finally, Anders reached the top, pulling himself onto the ridge and carefully edging towards the loose tiles.

Upon hearing their cheers Walter came back out from the pub and caught a glimpse of Anders, now nearing the top still struggling.

"Howay, Anders, get a grip. It's more like a circus than a roofing job." People good naturedly started cheering.

After examining the tiles for a few minutes, he shouted down "Nail rot, the roof's got nail rot."

"What's that?" enquired Walter, holding his hand to his ear "What's it got?" He turned and looked directly at Stevey.

"Don't ask me" he replied, "I haven't got a clue, I'm just thankful I even know what a roof is, never mind anything else."

Across the street, Dolly Grey had been peering through the shadows, watching proceedings with growing concern. She shaded her eyes against the glare, unease flickering across her face.

"Now watch what you're doing you clumsy oaf," she shouted over "Wor Florrie needs you in one piece." Her laugh rang out, yet a thread of worry wove through it.

Anders balanced precariously on the roof's edge, laughed back over his shoulder, feigning ease. "Will do, now, get back in your shop and sell some tripe." He leaned down, reaching to test a loose tile. His grip faltered as the tile shattered beneath him and the rope ladder slipped through his fingers, and with a cry that was lost to the sudden, cold silence of the square. The crowd gasped, frozen in horrified awe, as he plummeted, flicking backward as his body sailed through the air, crashing onto the cobblestones below with a sickening thud. His head struck the ground, and an awful silence fell over the onlookers.

Dolly standing outside her shop, paralyzed as she watched Anders fall, her hand pressing tightly over her mouth.

Witnessing the fall, she went rigid, clutching her chest as if she could somehow hold her heart in place, but her body betrayed her. With a weak, shuddering breath she staggered, then collapsed on the steps of her shop, her body crumpling in a final devastating stillness, her face pale, her eyes rolling back in a final, vacant gaze, the shock had apparently caused a massive heart attack, she was silent, lifeless. A scream tore through the silence as onlookers rushed to her side, but it was too late, Dolly Grey's spirit had left, snuffed out by the tragic event which had unfolded in mere moments.

Stevey, standing near, was dumbfounded, he felt his knees weaken, his face ashen, his hands clasped to his head in helpless disbelief. He couldn't believe what was happening. It was impossible to process what was happening before him. Eventually, he sank down onto his knees, his heart pounding. Walter the publican said something to him, but nothing seemed to register. All he could do was stare, first at Anders then at Dolly's lifeless body. He was trembling and sobbing uncontrollably.

Maisie approached him, her face a portrait of stunned composure, though her eyes betrayed a searing grief.

"Here, Stevey," she murmured, "put this on," as she handed him a thick warm coat. Maisie looked into his eyes, her gaze searching, but all she saw was raw, unfiltered despair. She patted him gently on the head before making her way over to the lifeless body of Dolly Grey. Each step felt like a lifetime.

A passer-by with a trace of medical knowledge rushed over to see if he could help. He knelt beside Anders, his fingers tentative on his neck, hoping against hope for a pulse. His eyes were open but lifeless and seemed to follow the path of his own blood, trickling over the moss-covered cobbles. He looked up to the growing crowd and shook his head, confirming what everyone thought. The reality was inescapable, written across his sombre expression: Anders was gone.

Maisie reached Dolly, who lay crumpled on the cold, unforgiving stone steps. She knelt, straightening her disarrayed clothing. She bent down beside her and whispered quietly. "Here lass, let's get you covered up, we don't want this lot talking aboot you, do we?" Maisie leaned close, pressing a kiss on her forehead and clutched her hand while she waited for the inevitable authorities to arrive.

Within minutes, the quiet marketplace was alive with a flurry of activity. The police and medical staff who attended Dolly gently moved Maisie aside offering her a most welcome cup of tea. Their faces filled with quiet sympathy as they also gave confirmation, Dolly was indeed dead.

Meanwhile, Billy Burns had been summoned to the scene and immediately went over to where Anders lay. He also confirmed his friend's untimely death. It was said by the many onlookers no-one had ever seen Sergeant Billy Burns so sad and distraught, nevertheless, he still carried out his duties and took notes of all matters of legal interest.

News of the incident was now gaining momentum and travelling fast. Billy felt a pressing urgency of the grim duty that was his alone. He knew he had to be the person to inform Florrie before anyone else did. He, more than anyone, knew Florrie Guttenberg's world was now shattered. She had lost her beloved husband and mother in one cruel twist of fate. He took a breath, steadying himself, it was now up to Sergeant Burns to deliver the news.

CHAPTER 17

Following the aftermath of the accident and the subsequent deaths of Anders Guttenberg along with Florrie's mother Dolly Grey, Florrie was in a major state of shock and unbelievable grief at the news that upended her world. Sergeant Billy Burns had the unenviable task of informing Florrie and her son Amos of the full circumstances. Her beloved husband and her mother had died. They sat in a darkened room in Florrie's little cottage, right on the sands only a few metres away from the ferocious North Sea. A single candle was the only source of light, throwing its weak light across her face, hollow and etched with grief, she hadn't even bothered with the fire, which was normally on night and day. Nothing seemed worth it now, and what was there left to live for, she wondered.

"I can't stand this, Billy" said Florrie, interrupting a gloomy silence. She added tearfully, "what have I got to live for now, Billy, what have I got."

In a deep and calming voice, as he was accustomed to this type of hardships in his line of work, did his best to answer. "You've got Erasmus Florrie and that other bugger Amos, if he ever turns up like, they will still need you, now more than ever." He cleared his throat, the tension in the room tightening as he spoke.

Florrie just sighed her response, without uttering any words. Erasmus, now a young man, felt the same grief as his mother. His eyes were red with tears and his heart as heavy as all the stones on the beach. "Thanks, Billy," he said, his voice barely above a whisper. "My mother understands what you are saying, she just doesn't want to talk about it, that's all." Sadness was emanating from his empty soul.

Billy nodded in response. "Have you heard anything from Amos? Has he been in touch?" This brought a wry smile from Erasmus and prompted Florrie to look up towards Billy.

"Well, I'm hardly likely to tell you Billy, am I? Even if he had been in touch."

Billy gave a resigned sigh. "No, you're probably right," replied Billy, but added "but remember lad, and you as well Florrie, I'm your friend first before I am a policeman." He paused for another moment, "you should know that."

Florrie managed a faint smile as she spoke to Billy. "Aye, we know and he's very upset as you can imagine. He's a good lad really and not as bad as some folks make out." She was constantly glancing at the black shiny pebble on the mantlepiece, Amos had given her this many years ago.

"She polishes it every day, Billy," smiled Erasmus, "every day, mind, never misses, and she touches it for good luck if she thinks she needs it."

The sorrow hung heavy in the air until the door creaked open. Mary, Florrie's oldest friend swept into the room with her daughter, Becky. Without a word Mary rushed over to Florrie and hugged her with so much force she nearly squeezed the life out of her, and then of course, it was time for the inevitable tears and sorrow, which fell upon all present.

Billy coughed, breaking the reunion momentarily. "Sorry, ladies, please accept my apologies. You too Erasmus, but I must go now and deal with some urgent business, but I will call again tomorrow to see how you are coping and if possible, discuss the funeral arrangements. If that's agreeable, of course."

Florrie looked up, her hand on Erasmus's shoulder. "Aye, we'll see you then, you know what me and Erasmus wants," she said, "and naturally what Anders wanted, which is the most important."

Billy hesitated, "Aye, I know only too well, Florrie, but the kind of funeral Anders wanted is not legal, you know that. They'll be watching."

Her response was quiet but firm, "Like that's ganna bother me," she said, "don't think so, do you."

Billy just shook his head, there was no point in discussing it." See you tomorrow, pet and try to get some rest."

As soon as the door closed, talk of Anders funeral became the main topic of conversation. A bottle of dark rum was produced by Becky from beneath her long grey skirt. She placed it on the table. "Now, just as a matter of interest," she said, "just in case you're wondering I haven't told Charley anything about this little get together tonight or your plans for the funeral.

"Good," said Florrie, rather sharply and to the point, "you know Charley has ambitions in the police, so the less he knows the better." She began rocking backwards and forwards in her chair, deep in thought. "Right, she said" with a purpose, "Erasmus, put that fire on lad. I am sure Anders, wouldn't want us to be like this." She wiped away the few tears that had been running down her face. Erasmus was only too pleased to light the fire. He leapt into action straight away, leaving the girls to talk among themselves, and possibly discuss any arrangements that may take place.

Becky spoke first "Has your Amos been in touch then?" she queried.

"Oh aye, he has," Florrie answered, "he was here last night, with his friend, Gunpowder Bob."

"Taking a chance, wasn't he?" interrupted Becky, "He's a wanted man, him and Gunpowder Bob and well … the town knows." Her eyes were raised in concern.

"All reet, all reet, we knae your betrothed to a polis, but what do you expect, he's still my son."

Aye, and he's still my brother as well," said Erasmus, poking the fire, which was now well alight.

Becky had to agree and promised she wouldn't say anything to her fiancé, Charley, not a thing.

"So did he mention anything?" Mary questioned.

"About what like?" asked Florrie, feeling like she was under interrogation herself. She was still looking at Mary as she had asked the question, then went on. "Well, he did say, he didn't kill that smuggler from Whitburn. He's adamant about that. He agrees he was killed by somebody, but it wasn't him,"

"I agree, but he's still getting the blame, along with his little pal Bob, isn't he?" Becky retorted.

"Well, he would, wouldn't he," interrupted Mary, "he hasn't been a shrinking violet all his life, has he."

For once, everyone agreed, including Florrie and Erasmus.

"So, are you still going to carry out his wishes? That's assuming you can, of course," asked Mary.

Florrie leaned forward, her voice low and steady, "If I can, I will, but it won't be easy, the police and the authorities are well aware of Anders wishes and will certainly have a presence on the beach that day."

"Well, I can guarantee that," said Becky "Charley's already confirmed that."

Florrie pondered for a moment then glances around the dim room, gathering her thoughts over the comments and surprisingly mentioned, "Archie McPherson's coming down for the day. Walter from the pub must have told him."

"Is that relevant, like," asked Becky.

"No, no it just came in my mind, I don't know why."

There were a few seconds while everyone considered their thoughts. The faint crackle of the fire filled the stillness. Erasmus finished his glass of rum off in one go, "Drop of good stuff that, Becky," he smiled, "my da would've loved that," as he lifted his glass up, as if in a toast to an unseen memory. It seemed to ease the tension, and the little gathering seemed more at ease, if only slightly.

"So," Mary said, "about this funeral pyre, how exactly is it going to work."

Florrie gaze sharpened, and she stood, positioning herself near the fireplace where the warmth seemed to fortify her, "Well, first of all, no-one can know about it, other than who is in this room, and I mean no-one," she looked straight at Becky.

"Point taken," Becky answered returning her stare, "point taken, well and truly."

Florrie carried on, she was standing up at this point near the fireplace, warming her knees. She ran her hand over the black pebble for luck before continuing. She thought long and hard about what she was going to say. "Legally", she continued, there's nothing in the law stopping us from laying Anders to rest on his boat, if that's his wish. Think of it as a floating coffin." She paused, gauging the effect, they all nodded in agreement, "The authorities may see it differently, but if anyone asks, he's simply lying in state," she went on "and as you all know, Anders wanted a true Viking's end with honours, with his boat set ablaze, sailing into the distance, and eventually vanishing beneath the waves of the North Sea. In a blaze of glory, if you like."

At this point, everyone was quiet, contemplating and imagining the old warrior's ship blazing across the cold northern waters.

Becky then spoke "But you do know the police will be watching, Florrie," her voice edged with caution.

"Aye, they certainly will," interrupted Erasmus, "so, we will have to be one step ahead of them all the time, exactly as our da would want it."

As the night deepened Becky went home feeling sick with worry, she knew Charley would ask questions, probing and insistent about the funeral arrangements. She didn't want to lie to him, her future husband, but as much as she loved Charley, her loyalties still lay with Florrie and Erasmus and her mother Mary. She resolved to misdirect him, a futile effort perhaps, but necessary all the same. Charley was a clever young man, he wasn't easily deceived, he would weigh up every word.

Meanwhile, back at the cottage, while discussions were still taking place, the proceedings were now interrupted by a very strange warbling sound, almost birdlike, but not as raucous. "What the frigs that" exclaimed Mary, who had remained behind. It was after ten now, and quite dark. To her amazement she turned round and looked at Erasmus, upon hearing this sound, he cupped his mouth and issued a call in return, matching the call. A response was quickly followed by another strange birdlike call. A few seconds passed in silence, then footsteps crunched outside, coming towards the cottage door. Erasmus snuffed out the lone candle, casting the room in shadow.

"I don't like this," Mary muttered, "who's there?"

They didn't have long to wait for an answer, the door creaked opened, bringing with it an icy blast of cold autumn weather and in walked Amos, Florrie's son and older brother of Erasmus." Hi, Ma, he said quietly with an edge of both sorrow and resolve. He turned to Erasmus, and the two brothers embraced briefly. He went on again, just as sincerely, "How are you coping, all of you?" he asked.

"Getting there," was all Florrie could say. Amos turned his attention to Mary," Has Becky been? he asked," does she know about the Viking funeral we're planning." "She does, but she's sworn to secrecy, and we all believe her," Mary replied.

"Good, good," Amos replied, "the fewer who know the better. But what about Billy?" A wary look crossed his face. "Has he got any idea what we are going to do?" his voice was more serious now with a hint of menace and a little nervousness. "You know what he's like ma, he's a crafty old soul that one, he's got a nose for secrets."

Erasmus was standing by the fire with his brother, their expressions sombre as the firelight flickered over them. "Good to see you Amos," as they hugged for a fleeting moment. "Where's little Bob?"

Amos looked towards the door "He's outside keeping watch; he'll signal if anyone's coming. He's okay, we can trust him." This seemed to pacify Erasmus, and the group relaxed as they resumed their whispered planning, each step honed with careful precision. Together they crafted a scheme that, if successful, would leave the town of South Shields breathless. Hopefully this would be the grandest, unlike anything they had ever seen, a fierce and final tribute.

Anders Guttenberg and Dolly Grey deserved this final tribute, at the very least.

CHAPTER 18

Sergeant Burns arrived back at the cottage the next day, his boots crunching against the gravel path leading to the modest dwelling, The early morning mist clung to the ground, wrapping the landscape in a veil of mystery. and as he approached, he could see a wisp of smoke rising from the chimney. He pushed open the door, feeling a surge of relief as he spotted Florrie inside, seated by the hearth. To his surprise and joy, he found her in a more settled and calmer mood, something not seen for days.

"Must have slept well last night, did you Florrie?" Billy asked, he couldn't hide the relief.

"I did," mused a rather sleepy Florrie, and added "still feel dreadful, of course, as you might expect." She reached over for the brass kettle sitting on the hearth. "Cup of tea okay for you, Billy?" she offered. "The rum's all gone though," she glanced at the empty bottle on the kitchen table.

"Tea's fine for me Florrie, too early anyway," answered Billy, rather apprehensively, "plus, I am on duty now, as it happens."

"Are you?" Asked a surprised Florrie, "On a Sunday, how's that like?" she further questioned him.

Billy shifted his weight uncomfortably, before eventually replying, "Well, to tell you the truth, we are on the lookout for your Amos and Little Bob," Billy said with reluctance. .... We've found some more information about the death of that smuggler from Whitburn," he stopped for a moment as his gaze met hers, he shook his head, and his expression darkened, "can't see us finding anything," he went on, "but we are obliged to look, it's more a formality."

Florrie upon listening to this gulped down a mouthful of cold tea before adding, "I can't be doing with this, Billy. You and I both know he wouldn't murder anyone." She paused for a few seconds. "A thief, mind, I can't argue with that, but not a murderer, not our Amos."

Billy gave a slow nod, his agreement evident which pleased Florrie somewhat, and the tension between them eased.

He broke the silence, and in a quieter voice asked," What about Dolly? Have you made any arrangements for her?"

"No, not exactly," she replied, giving some thought to the question. "The bairns they wanted something special for her, something fitting, what mind you, I don't know." She paused, her mind drifting to her mother, took her time to answer but after a little pause said, "Dolly, after all, was their grandmother."

The conversation was suddenly broken by a burst of ladies' voices, high pitched and hurried, fast approaching the cottage. It was Fiona and Celia, making their first visit after hearing the catastrophic news of the untimely deaths of Anders and Dolly. They moved with purpose, as if bracing themselves to bring solace amidst sorrow. Florrie was in no mood to be vindictive, though, she was only too happy to see them.

Fiona's eyes glistened with sympathy, but it was Celia, who was now almost twelve years old, and much to Florrie's obvious delight, was blossoming into a fine young lady, tall, with long fair hair, magnificent complexion and classical features, her eyes wide with a maturity beyond her years. Seeing her like this caught Florrie's attention, she's such a beauty, Florrie thought, nowt like us lot.

Fiona broke the silence, hesitant yet comforting, "How are you managing, love? Are you coping okay?"

Florrie just nodded, her eyes brightening with a hint of gratitude, "I'm alright," she said quietly, then raising her voice added, "but all the better for seeing you two, especially our Celia here." She reached out and took Celia's hands. "He loved you, you know," she said.

Celia tilted her head, puzzled," Who?"

"Your granda, of course, "replied Florrie with a voice that was thick with emotion. "Oh right," said Celia, her lips parting in a small smile, "and I loved him as well."

A fragile silence filled the room, memories surfacing. and the room was filled with tears of sadness and memories, and the air grew heavy when either Anders or Dolly were mentioned.

Finally, Celia spoke, her voice barely a whisper. "Grandma," she asked, "could I leave a personal message, for granda Anders, and nana Dolly."

Florrie was confused, "Of course, darling. Of course you can, what is it you want to say?"

Celia's gaze held steady; her expression solemn. "Ah well," she said, "that part is private, between me and granda." Her voice was barely above a whisper.

Florrie watched her as she contemplated her response, she rubbed her finger over her chin, deep in thought. Then replied, "whatever you have in mind, that's alright with me," she murmured.

She looked over to Fiona, Celia's adoptive mother, and just shook her head, confirming she didn't know what Celia meant, but Fiona gave a reassuring nod of approval.

The small interlude in the conversations allowed Fiona to discuss the funeral arrangements. It was agreed her husband,

Tobias, who was the local vicar, would say a few words. Even though Anders hadn't ever been to church, but Dolly had been once or twice, so it was agreeable Tobias Trevelyan would officiate.

Billy Burns took this moment to step aside, leaving the ladies to get on with the matters in hand. The day's light was slipping away, and Celia was becoming more restless and anxious to leave, when yet another knock on the cottage door interrupted proceedings. Florrie, visibly annoyed at the interruption, gestured to Celia. "Go and see who that is, pet, and don't let anyone in, you have my permission," she flashed a wry smile as she said it.

Celia nodded, relieved for the break, and eagerly opened the door. What she saw left her shocked to say the least. There standing before her was a towering man, a rough, brawler type, he was threatening and very imposing and wore strange clothing. A thick woollen kilt and a Tam O Shanter hat, it was Archie McPherson. His appearance radiated danger, but almost immediately, his smiling expression and heartfelt condolences suggested otherwise. He was most welcomed by Dolly and everyone present, even Celia who was initially afraid, felt the warmth in his expression disarming, even perching on his knee, enraptured by his stories.

For hours Archie captivated them, his tales weaving through shared memories, laughter replacing any hint of sadness in the room.

Celia, although anxious to leave earlier, was more than happy to stay now and listen to his wonderful tales, drinking in every word. He painted vivid pictures of his past adventures with Florrie and Anders, years ago, recounting how Florrie's mother Dolly had put up Archie and Medhi when he first came up to the northeast. They all roared with laughter when they remembered Medhi eating tripe for the first time. Celia was spellbound with each little story.

"Eeh, I wish there was some rum Archie, I could really do with some," they all laughed and there was a small pause before they began again. It was during this time, Fiona was making a cup of tea which amazed everybody present, Fiona making the tea, that was a surprise.

Out of the blue Celia voice broke through. "Were you looking for me, Mr. McPherson, when you came from Scotland? I was the girl they found in the barrel at Trow Rocks. Her tone held a desperate plea, with a hint of urgency.

Archie froze, his entire body stiffened, as he gazed back at her. He now saw a beautiful young lady standing in front of him, who from her very appearance seemed to have a familiarity. He could only draw comparisons with others he had met in the past. Unfortunately, however, he could not make sense of his own thoughts.

"You were the baby in the barrel, then?" he turned to Florrie, "She knows about that?"

"She knows, all right, in fact she's almost obsessed with it now, she's been searching for answers, wanting to know who her real parents are and why they just abandoned her." Archie just nodded and turned his attention to Celia.

"Och, I am sorry, my wee darling, I was here on other business at the time, never knowing your story. I'd have come for you, I swear if I'd known, perhaps I should have done."

Celia's face fell, though her tone remained hopeful as she added, "Will you help me find my real parents now Mr McPherson?" It was almost a plea, a delicate request.

"I fear, I cannot at this moment Celia, I can't yet," he said. Strangely enough though he could not shake this uneasy feeling he had in his stomach. An unsettling feeling that gnawed at his gut. There was something here he couldn't shake, an image, a memory. What was he missing, and why did young Celia look familiar.

Excusing herself Fiona broke the tension, promising to return the next day. She bade farewell to Archie, who by this time, was in a world of his own and obviously preoccupied. "Aye, aye, see you later," he said with a glazed, tormented stare. Once again, this crafty, whisky purveying, Scottish investigator seemingly had other things on his mind.

It was only two days away now before the actual funeral was about to take place. Most of the townsfolk were aware of what kind of send-off Anders had asked for. It was common knowledge, among his friends, that he wanted a full Viking send-off, a fiery spectacle the authorities were fully aware of and, predictably, planning to prevent. The townsfolk, however, were buzzing with excitement, and were placing bets in pubs and alleyways, some insisting Anders would get his wish, others certain the authorities would shut it down. It was odd that all this festivity should be happening in the face of such a sombre topic.

Meanwhile Amos and his brother Erasmus, were making plans of their own, assisted by the ever-scheming Gunpowder Bob. It was uppermost in their minds; they had to make sure the funeral pyre was about to happen. They agreed they had to come up with a complex alternative plan to fool and divert the authorities away from Anders Viking longboat, carefully orchestrated to keep officials looking the other way. The service was to be held on the beach next to Trow Rocks, only yards away from the cottage and the sea. Hundreds of people were expected to attend, alongside a formidable police presence. A palpable tension hung over everyone involved.

In the quiet of the police station, right opposite St Hilda's church, Sergeant Burns and Charley prepared for the looming funeral. A kettle was still simmering on an old stove, as it had that morning and every other morning. They had been going over the events for the following day, "Apparently there are going to be over four hundred people there," said Billy, deep in thought, "and that's without us," he went on.

"Aye and there's going to be twenty of our own there, "added Charley.

"Mmmm," contemplated Billy, "I just hope it goes off okay, for Florrie's sake," he muttered to himself.

"Well, it will, if they keep to the arrangements," said Charley, "that's all they have to do."

"That's true," pondered Billy, "I still can't help worrying though."

Billy topped up the little paraffin lamp that was burning nicely. He looked over towards Charley, puffing on his new Bakelite pipe. He said it gave him a sense of peace and made him feel relaxed, and more time to think. He leaned further back onto his old, slatted bench.

Charley took his pipe out for a moment and answered in a measured way, saying in a calm, calculated voice, "I don't think," he said, pointing his pipe toward the window, "they will try anything, Billy. We've got everything imaginable covered, especially since Florrie has asked for permission to lie Dolly's body beside Anders on the boat. For viewing purposes, of course."

Billy nodded thoughtfully, though a nagging doubt lingered. Charley went on, "Becky says Dolly isn't going to be buried until next week, so they aren't going to push her out to sea are they," he went on," doesn't make any sense that."

Sergeant Burns just bent his head and nodded. "The locals are still betting like, they think they will see a Viking funeral but I can't shake this feeling, Charley. Something's going too ….. too smoothly."

Changing the subject altogether, Billy asked if he had seen or heard anything about Amos or Gunpowder Bob. "No, not a thing, people are saying he has done off somewhere and they have been spotted over Carlisle way."

"Well, that's good then, at least we won't have them to contend with."

Billy shrugged, his gaze shifting to the worn, cracked floorboards. As they sat in the dimly lit office, the weight of the coming days settled heavily on their shoulders.

CHAPTER 19

Sergeant Billy Burns squinted against the biting morning wind as he scanned the growing crowd that had assembled along the shoreline. The day had arrived. The dual funerals of Anders Guttenberg and Dolly Grey were set to commence, and the anticipation in the air was thick. Both Anders and Dolly were well respected members of the community, figures of such stature that few could resist paying their last respects. But the allure wasn't just out of respect – it was Anders final request that had stirred the excitement. He had requested a typical Viking funeral, his boat set alight and sent out to sea. However, this type of funeral was illegal in England. Word had got around and now the police were out in force to make sure it didn't happen. Sergeant Billy Burns was there along with PC Wilson and a strong contingent of officers. They were bolstered by a few sharp-eyed council officials, all intent on seeing this event remaining a dignified service, free from any unlawful spectacle. All formalities were exchanged with lots of mutual respect from each party, which initially on the surface at least, pleased PC Burns.

"Glad to see there doesn't appear to be any trouble Charley," he muttered to his number one officer, Charley Wilson, unable to shake the unease tightening his stomach, "I am still a bit nervous though," he added, glancing around the huge crowd that was now beginning to gather. Billy Burns was struggling to see why there were so many people there, especially as it was only nine o-clock in the morning, yet people had flocked to the beach hours ahead of the planned service which was due at four thirty this afternoon.

Charley nodded his head in agreement, his eyes never ceasing to roam the crowd "Aye, that's why I have arranged for a coble to sit between the shore and Anders' boat. Just as a precaution."

"Have you?" queried Billy, "Whose idea was that?"

Charley puffed on his new pipe and shrugged. "It was just something Becky mentioned last night. It was odd really; she was going on about Amos not being around. She couldn't understand that ….. as he loved both his father and his grandmother. It made me think," said Charley pausing, his gaze sharpening as he spoke. "You notice there are plenty of people still putting substantial money on there being a traditional Viking send off."

PC Burns interrupted, "Did you not ask her why she was talking like that. What was she going on about, anything specific?" he went on.

"I did ask," returned Charley, "but she just waffled on about family values and expectations, then just as quickly changed the subject …… made me think, though," he went on.

Because of the conversations, both men were on high alert, looking in every direction for something that may not be quite in order. They were scrutinising every passerby and every movement. The weather, although cold was fine now and dry. Anders little ship 'The Ragnar' seemed a mile away from the actual water, although it was on the beach in full view for everyone to see.

"To be honest, it's not likely that Amos will turn up is it, Charley?" Billy ventured quietly.

"Not really." said Charley."They'll arrest him on sight."

"Right, if he does try anything, it'll be from a distance," Billy replied, glancing meaningfully at the coble out at sea, which drifted lazily, manned by officers keeping a close watch on the Ragnar. "That'll stop any Guttenberg schemes from going further, and he'll know that," added Billy, "which is a bit of a worry, to put us off the scent, you might say."

Charley just nodded, as though answering him. Then he spoke. "Well, they won't get past that coble, Billy, even if they wanted to.

Billy looked across at the boat drifting in the sea. "No, that's true," he answered, "plenty of men on there as well. Let's just hope it stops any illegal action that the Guttenberg family may attempt.

A procession had begun. Slowly people moved toward the boat, awed by the Viking detailing and the solemn tribute. The main sail was set up with blue and white stripes, its gold and white dragon head on the bow standing proud, with leather and timber shields along both sides and four oars standing upright in the centre. The bow was facing the North Sea. At the centre lay two coffins, side by side, wickerwork masterfully crafted from woven lobster pots and fishing lines. The details had been meticulously planned by Anders' widow, Florrie and her family, with the heartfelt knowledge Anders would have adored such a tribute. The whole deck area was covered by dried flowers with little personal mementos nestled among them. Naturally, pride of place was given to Anders sword and one or two items Dolly treasured and held dear. This was the way of the Viking culture.

Rumours were filtering through to Billy and Charley, betting was still going on and the consensus was, there was going to be a Viking funeral. Florrie and Mary, helped by

Becky, had done them proud, and with the help of Erasmus, Florrie's youngest son, was standing tall as an unelected guardian of the boat. He was helped by Thomas, Becky's fourteen-year-old son. The two boys, solemn and dignified, were dressed up in Viking attire, including ceremonial swords, shields and horned helmets they were aware they were not merely guardians of the ship, but of a tradition itself. They had made the special shields of leather and wood studded with brass rivets.

Both men stood either side of the Ragnar, solemn and silent.

People were now beginning to pay their respects, but once having done so only a few were leaving the area. Whispers threaded through the crowd, predictions still rife that despite police presence, a true Viking farewell was about to unfold. This, temporarily, worried Billy and Charley, they thought better of asking questions at this point. Billy's brow creased, but Charley merely shrugged, sharing the tension.

A tall figure approached, familiar to them both: Archie McPherson, who had been especially invited by Florrie and endorsed by Celia, who had taken a special liking to Archie. He moved with a quiet reverence through the gathering. After watching the procedures for a while, Billy once again reminded his officer, Charley, to keep an eye out for anything unusual, especially for the unlikely appearance of Amos and that rascal Gunpowder Bob.

Although the event could be described as highly charged, it nevertheless attracted a calm serenity held sway, calming Florrie and her family and close friends as they waited with bated breath. The time was nearing almost three thirty, and from the stone cottage just yards away, platters of refreshments were carried to the beach by steady hands, awaiting the arrival of Tobias Trevelyan and his wife, Fiona.

Suddenly someone shouted. They're here!" A ripple of excitement spread through the crowd and murmurings were spreading all around the beach like clouds of buzzing bees.

At the front Celia, though a mere child, stood tall with a solemnity beyond her years. Anticipation was now running high; the ceremony loomed near, the clock ticking toward three forty five. Officials accompanying the Reverend, came right over to the Ragnar, watched most intently by the two lads. The officials appeared to poke the timbers of the boat and peered inside. Physically disturbing both coffins with small sticks, probing around here and there.

"What on earth are they doing?" whispered Florrie.

"I haven't the first idea," answered Fiona, "Nothing good, I'll bet."

Suddenly one of the officials asked, "Might it be alright if we took a look inside one of the coffins?" he spoke quietly removing his beret to show respect.

A flash of anger passed over Erasmus's face, his grip tightening on the hilt of his sword. "It most certainly would not be alright," his voice a growl. He was severely agitated by the request. "Disturb my father and grandmother, and it'll be the last thing you do," he went on to say, in a very strong unmistakable manner, his eyes bore into them, a warning as ancient as the sea itself.

Mumbling a few Anglo-Saxon expletives, the two officials moved away, feeling rather chastised. The gathering crowd had stopped moving now, hundreds of them, and were standing patiently waiting for the service to begin, every eye on the Reverend.

Trevelyan stepped on to a small crate of around two-foot square which had been given to him to stand on, it was felt it gave him an elevated position from which to address the congregation. His words were a balm to them, a tribute to the lives of Anders and Dolly, stirring emotions. The tide had come in fully now and while only a couple of hours ago the sea seemed miles away, it was now only yards away from the ceremonial boat 'The Ragnar'. This thought PC Wilson was a little too close for his liking, once again he removed his pipe, spitting out some residue before saying, "get some officers down there between the boat and the sea," he barked. "And get that coble alongside, ready for any problems.

The young constable was taking charge like a true professional. It pleased his sergeant who was standing a little further back on a raised sand dune, he could now see everything around him.

Fiona took over momentarily from her husband and suggested that everyone should sing the hymn which was '*For those in Peril on the Sea*'. It was a wonderful end to the Rev Trevelyan's service. The tide was now at its highest. So high, in fact, it could almost touch the Ragnar itself, even to the point where Erasmus and the officers on duty felt the sea milling around their ankles.

Charley shouted from afar "Hands on the boats, lads. Keep it tight." The coble he had ordered, although drifting about was still in position, ready for any last-minute attempts to shove the Ragnar out. There was a mixture of dignified applause and silence following the service. Someone lit a beacon as a final homage. The flames took hold and were leaping up to the sky, seemingly for onlookers. This appeared to be a last gesture of the funeral. People took their hats off and women stood with their heads bowed in silent recognition.

As the beacon flared, a thunderous explosion suddenly erupted in the distance, shaking the ground beneath their feet. Gasps scattered through the crowd as the sky split open with fire, two silhouettes emerging from the flames, firing pistols into the air. It was at Trow Rocks, close to the cave where Celia had been found in the barrel. So great was the explosion, it lit up the now darkening sky, like a sun descending. It was awe inspiring.

"Look," said one of the officers, pointing his finger, "it's Amos Guttenberg and his accomplice Little Bob."

The pair continued to taunt the officers from their perch, dancing and fooling around until someone barked, "After them! There's a bounty on their heads!" Within moments a scramble ensued, officers and locals alike charging in pursuit. Both men were wanted for all manner of activities, including the said murder of the fisherman from Whitburn. Then one PC shouted out "They've got a small boat, look. Get to them before they can reach it. Don't let them escape."

This prompted the last remark for the coble to join in the chase. It shouldn't take the ten men long to reach their position. Pandemonium broke out and there were scenes of disarray all round.

Back on the beach, only Sergeant Burns and PC Wilson remained, unnoticed by the frantic throng, Charley's voice rose in a whisper of urgency. "Look, Billy look, they are pushing The Ragnar out to sea."

"Who?" answered Billy quickly.

"The crowd, and our Becky's helping them."

Billy looked across and answered quietly "Aye, so they are lad, so they are." Wilson anxiously replied, "We should stop them though, shouldn't we, Billy?"

"Aye, we should, Charley, we should, "said Sergeant Burns, pausing. He then turned to Charley, "but we won't," he said most emphatically.

The tide surged outward, carrying the vessel and its precious cargo further from shore. The wind caught The Ragnar's sails, filling them, propelling the boat as if guided by unseen hands. Watched all the way by Celia, standing motionless.

They were almost a hundred feet offshore when Erasmus was handed a bow and arrow, which up until then had been concealed in Archie McPherson's kilt. The arrow's heads were covered in pitch. Erasmus took the arrows and lit one of them from the nearby burning beacon, watching as its tip glowed a fierce red. As he was doing so a lone official raced across and tried to intervene, only to be held back by Archie.

"Dinna try that laddie," he said almost apologetically. "It won't do your health much good; I can guarantee that." At this, he grabbed the fellow by his neck.

With grim resolve Erasmus took aim. The arrow arced through the twilight, a line of fire across the darkening sky, embedding itself among the dry flowers which caught light immediately. Flames licked at the timbers, and within moments the boat was ablaze, a fiery vessel floating ever further from the shore. As the arrow fell on its target he winked at his mother, Florrie.

Erasmus's voice was low, almost a murmur. "That's all the dried twigs we put under the flowers," he spoke as if to himself.

The statement wasn't lost on Florrie, probably the first time in his life he had managed to get some dry firewood, it was a rare thing, dry firewood on these mist-soaked shores, but tonight, as The Ragnar roared to life in crackling flames, Erasmus felt fate itself bending to their will.

The Ragnar was now blazing fully, much to the enjoyment of the waiting crowd. However, the cheering and flames had alerted the crew of the coble to see what was going on and had turned their vessel sharply back toward The Ragnar, intent on dousing the flames and dragging the boat back to shore. A disruption of the ceremony was imminent, and the funeral the Guttenberg's had so much desired could be thwarted in mere moments.

He had only two arrows left. Erasmus, though, on seeing this, lit one more arrow and fired it toward the boat. Unfortunately, though, because the distance between the Ragnar and himself was greater than before the flaming arrow sailed short of its mark. He had one arrow left. He could hear mutterings rippling through the onlookers around him as he carefully lit it and took a deep breath. He muttered a little prayer and caught a glimpse of Celia's steady eyes from the beach. She offered him a quiet thumbs up and something in her calm demeanour gave him strength. That was all he needed. He drew back the arrow and, using all his strength, fired towards the boat.

This time his aim was perfect, thudding in finality. Even though it had penetrated one of the coffins. There was a collective gasp of surprise from the watching crowd.

"He's missed, hasn't he," mumbled Charley, this time appearing to be disappointed.

Billy, however, shook his head slowly, eyes fixed on the Ragnar. “No, Charley,” he said, his voice taut with knowing. “He didn’t miss at all.” He turned round to face Charley full on. “In fact, it was a perfect shot,” he added.

Charley looked back at the boat then back to Billy. “How do you mean, perfect? The coble’s closing in.!”

Billy smiled to himself and suggested to Charley to signal the coble to stop their pursuit of the Ragnar.”

“Why on earth for, they are almost there.” He was totally bemused by it all.

“Remember when Erasmus wouldn’t let the officers look inside the coffins,” went on Billy, “he was most adamant was he not?”

“So, what was the point?” asked Charley, his face clouded with confusion, when he was cut short by another, deafening explosion, This time the beach and sky blazed in a dazzling crescendo as the coffin erupted, shattering into a spray of fire and shattered wood. A fiery glow consumed The Ragnar, obliterating the sails in a single thunderous blast. Flames engulfed the boat, and within seconds, it sank with dignity beneath the waves, leaving only the haunting scent of smoke in its wake.

Silence prevailed for a few noticeable minutes, the beach was still, the stunned crowd staring at the rippling water, only a few flowers floating where the boat had been. And then, there was a round of gentle applause, gathering into a crescendo by all present.

Becky had now arrived at Charley Wilson’s side. Florrie and Mary had followed her over. Celia had decided to stay on the beach beside Erasmus. Anders had finally got his Viking funeral. During the respectful applause a strange smell drifted over from the boat. Both Charley and Billy were still in shock but instinctively turned to face each other, and together said "Gunpowder Bob."

A grin broke across Charley's face, and Billy couldn't help but laugh, the sound reverberating through the cool night air. Although they were policemen, they were friends and family first.

CHAPTER 20

Anders' and Dolly's funerals were now over. Becky and PC Charley Williams were now married, Erasmus had taken over his grandma's business, and his mother Florrie was helping him run it. They moved away from their stone cottage on the beach and moved into the much larger rooms above the tripe shop premises. Although the lure the of the cottage Anders had built with his own hands was too much for Florrie to let go, she returned daily to light the fire and sometimes to relax and do nothing. She would often sit there silently and just stare at the shiny pebble Amos had found for her in the cave.

'What made him think of that,' she mused. Beautiful it certainly was, but at the end of the day was just a pebble, she smiled to herself. Never a moment ever went by when she didn't think about Celia, her little adopted granddaughter, who initially they found abandoned in that wine barrel, "Who are you, my little treasure?" she often asked herself, "and who are your birth family?" She questioned herself daily, often to the point of exhaustion, when she would eventually drop off to sleep.

Meanwhile, thousands of miles away in Montpellier, as the sun dipped below the horizon, casting its amber glow over the windswept cliffs, a tempest brewed in the grand halls of nobility. The Count Artois and Countess Celeste sat beneath them vaulted ceilings of their study, its walls lined with scrolls chronicling the long and illustrious lineage of the Marcel family. The air was heavy with the scent of parchment and beeswax candles, an aura befitting the gravity of their predicament. Artois clenched his fists, his face lined with worry. The royal courts of Fance had spoken. Without a legitimate heir, his title would expire. Originally, his own son Jon was the first and only heir who could and should have taken over from his father, but regrettably had perished in a disastrous shipwreck some fifteen years before, questions remained unanswered, his body never recovered, no news of any survivors, which unfortunately, left open the position of Count, to the nearest living relative. Extensive research had been made all over France for any direct relatives, ideally by birth, however, none could be found. Artois had summoned all his legal advisors and all the most experienced lawyers in the land to conclude matters in an acceptable manner. Unfortunately, without a legal heir, such as a son or daughter or grandchild would mean that Artois, according to ancient rules, would have to abdicate and give up his position without any say in the matter. There was only a certain amount of time he could remain in office. The royal courts of France had given the date, it was to be 29th July 1815, at precisely 12 noon, less than three years away. By ancient decree, the noble line would be open to challenge, even from commoners, such were the rules of France at that time. Many sleepless nights were spent by the Count and his wife, struggling to come to terms with the situation. They were extremely sad for what was to happen and reluctantly accepted the situation, of course, and its inevitability.

Celeste, her brow furrowed, scanned the faded genealogies spread before her. "Francois," she murmured, the name slipping from her lips like venom. "How can such a man claim our family's legacy?"

Artois flinched. Francois Marcel – known to all as *Francois the Blackheart.* His cousin, exiled to Tunisia for unspeakable crimes, embodied a darkness that stained their family for decades. Whispers of his atrocities had reached the French court and made them ashamed to have the same name.

"That monster ..." Artois growled. "To think he might lay claim to Montpellier is unthinkable."

But unthinkable did not mean impossible.

No-one else knew the whereabouts of the golden medallion, which was apparently lost at sea, which in turn of course, was the crest of the Marcel ancient family. Any person found in the possession of such a medallion would automatically become the legal heir. At this moment in time, no such object has been found, this being the case, a new coin or crest would have to be minted, within the confines of the royal mint. Only one seal could ever exist, and this must be agreed by every member of the royal administration in Paris.

France and Tunisia were not in daily contact with each other for several reasons, but if Artois's cousin became aware of the situation, as it was most certainly possible, he then could be assumed to be automatically first in line after the abdication. It was a thought too dreadful to contemplate by the Marcel family. Francois, (the Black Heart) was indeed a very dangerous individual. He was eaten up by hate and jealousy and adamant that one day he would become the Count of Montpellier, this position, second only to the throne of France, and a direct equivalent to Napolean Bonaparte would be a position he could not allow to pass by, he would stop at nothing to achieve his ambitions and in his own words, no-one would ever stand in his way. Even though he was Artois's cousin and distant relative they were nothing alike. They most certainly did not have the same outlook on life and while Artois was a devout Christian he was also kind and compassionate, he very much loved his people and often had days of fun and relaxation where everyone joined in the celebrations. Francois the Blackheart was exactly the opposite, he could not have been more different. He hadn't been exiled for any small reason or misdemeanour, far from it in fact, he had been a cruel tyrant who had committed many murders, all of which he had managed to wriggle out of, but was exiled, nonetheless. He was, by far, the most dangerous individual in France, he was incredibly cruel to almost everyone he met, dangerous to anyone who dared to disagree with him or stood in the way of his ultimate dream. He had been in exile now, for almost ten years, into a sparse part of Tunisia, he was allowed to keep a loyal guard of around a hundred special army personnel, all of them experts in their own field of combat warfare.

Only his one hundred strong guards were seemingly immune to his total disregard to humanity. Francois and his contingent were residing near the ancient Roman amphitheatre, an isolated place, in a desert area, he would visit there most days, just sitting in the middle of the arena, silently contemplating his future. At nearly sixty. His appearance had only grown more menacing with age. His tall frame, honed by years of military training and unrelenting discipline, betrayed no sign of weakness. His sharp features and jet-black hair seemed almost sculpted from obsidian, and his eyes – void of warmth or humanity – were said to strip a man with a single glance.

There didn't seem to be any life in his piercing eyes and there was certainly no warmth coming from him, he had no redeeming features as such, and one could easily see why he had no friends. His loyal guards were the only people he could rely on who he had affiliation with, his cruelty to his fellow man knew no boundaries. The more pain and torture he could inflict on anyone pleased him immensely. These actions helped him cope with his exile. Regrettably he wasn't called Blackheart for nothing. You didn't have to be his enemy to suffer the consequences of his cruel actions, all you had to do was, have the misfortune to be in the vicinity of him. He very rarely tortured anyone and let them live through it, the vast majority, if not all his hapless victims died during their ordeal or were executed soon after.

There were never any witnesses, he never showed mercy or compassion, and he enjoyed their misery and anguish. Nearly all the people he tortured were of Tunisian descent, some female as well as male suffered the same fate, it didn't seem to matter to him. It was almost as if he was living his life like some of the twisted Emperors of old, Caligula being his favourite, he revelled in all things evil. He didn't have a wife to speak of, although he did have quite a few mistresses, all of them young Tunisian girls, but alas, not even they were safe from his debauchery. His favourite method for keeping these concubines under control, even for the slightest of misdemeanours, was to subject them to unspeakable torture and pain, his favourite, however, was to insert the young ladies into a purpose made compartment in the ground in his bedroom, the hole itself would be about six feet deep and approximately eighteen inches wide. These holes were called correction centres, his special name for them, but unfortunately the victims would be trussed up and tied in such a way only their head could move, usually in stressful positions, whenever slight movement would cause terrific pain. He would hang them upside down in these holes, whereby only their bare feet would be showing out of the ground, a special disc covered the rest of the excavation. The other unfortunate concubines, who were invited into the bedroom, usually three or four of them, would be made to tickle the exposed soles of the feet of the victim. Sometimes for up to an hour or so. They were expected to laugh loudly at every anguished scream. As bad as things were, even his kitchen staff were not immune from his evil mind. If certain meals did not, please him, or he fancied some entertainment, he had the cook or cooks sewn up inside animal skins with only their bare legs showing so that they were still able to walk around or run slowly, he would then have the skins covered in antelope blood and place the hapless victims in the centre of the arena. He made sure each victim was blind folded before he let loose a dozen or so starving hyenas which would chase and eventually kill them all.

The Count Artois was aware of his cousin's misdemeanours and his lifestyle and couldn't bear to think one day his subjects would be ruled by such a vile creature as Francois the infamous Blackheart. Time was now passing by, only a few short years were left before the inevitable. The Count and Countess, once again, spent many a night and day mulling over the unthinkable circumstances, if only Jon, their son and the rightful heir had not died in that unthinkable shipwreck, if only a legitimate heir could be found, how things could be so very different.

CHAPTER 21

The North-East of England slumbered beneath a veil of ignorance about the enigmatic Count of Montpellier. His cousin, the sinister Francois the Blackheart, was a figure even more obscure. In truth, no one would have dared connect Celia, their unassuming ward, to the shadowy tendrils of the Count's lineage. But secrets have a way of lingering, silent and potent, waiting for their moment. They couldn't of course, associate Celia, their adopted child, with any part of the Count's family.

Celia's life though was just as complicated, just fifteen years old, and quite the young lady tall, dark skinned, and striking with long straight fair hair, she stood out among the weathered fishwives of her village like an exotic bird amidst a flock of gulls. Adopted by her parents fifteen years previously, the Rev Tobius Trevelyan and his wife Fiona had brought Celia up in the austere Christian traditions and beliefs, within the confines of St. Hilda's parish. Hexham Abbey was a place the Trevelyan's made a monthly pilgrimage to, and it was here under the vaulted stone ceilings Celia had learned to speak French fluently, it had been hoped, among the family, she would enter the clergy in some capacity, hopefully following in her father's footsteps.

This, however, it must be said was not in Celia's thoughts at all. She wanted something different, something exciting, she craved adventure, not being cloaked in clerical robes.

As the firelight flickered across the worn stone walls, she vented her frustration. "You know what, Grandma they want me to go to Hexham with them," she shook her head slightly, "Hexham, of all places, can you imagine anything duller?"

Florrie, her grandma chuckled softly. 'Certainly, got a mind of her own' she thought. "I'm sure, you will be alright lass" she added with a knowing sigh, "it'll do you good in the end. You'll see."

It won't though," retorted Celia, very agitated and raising her voice replied, "And I'm not going either." She turned to look at Florrie, and after what seemed like ages she said, "I could work in your shop, though, couldn't I?" She was almost pleading.

"Don't be daft lass" replied Florrie, "your kind doesn't belong in a tripe shop, now do they?"

Just then, Mary, Florrie's best friend, entered the cottage. "You'll never believe this Florrie," Mary quickly said, "they've found that murderer they've been looking for, and it's not your Amos." She sound rather pleased with herself as she stood there with her arms folded, grinning all the while.

"Well, we all knew it wasn't Amos," interrupted Florrie, "but who was it? Do we know him?"

Mary shook her head, she had only just found out from Becky, who had only just found out from Charley, her husband, so they didn't have any further details. "Apparently though, he had been apprehended by PC Wilson while on duty at the Mill Dam area."

The Mill Dam was a kind of place you would associate the less desirable of people would congregate, more than likely drinking, of course, in the Old Boat House.

Florrie interrupted Mary, while trying to imagine the circumstances, "Still. I suppose it's some good news, at least they won't be chasing Amos so much."

All this time Celia was listening intently, taking in every word. "The Boat House," she said, "isn't that the pub that's notorious for the press gang raids every so often?"

"Aye, so it is," replied Mary, glancing over to Florrie with raised eyebrows, "so you make sure you keep well away from that place." She said the words vehemently, with a hint of menace, "A bonny lass like you, there's no telling what might happen,"The words or the meaning weren't lost on Celia, who just silently nodded, her gaze fixed on the infamous North Sea as she watched the waves going gently back and forth.

"You all right, lass?" interrupted Florrie, "you look miles away."

"Yes, I'm fine," Celia replied quietly, just thinking, you know, as you do," She then paused for a full moment, "about where I was found, you know, after being abandoned in that old wine barrel."

Florrie and Mary looked at each other with sadness in their eyes, she was never going to forget that day, but unfortunately, they couldn't offer any optimism or fresh hope that would stop her torment. They were simply resigned to the circumstances.

Celia stayed over at her grandma's that night and among other things they spoke enthusiastically about her adopted grandfather, Anders, and while he was very popular and loved by most, he never discussed his early life or indeed what made him come to England in the first place, they knew absolutely nothing of his original family, a bit like herself Celia thought. When questioned about it he would say it was just something he had to do, it was a compulsion. In that very instant Celia knew what she must do, she felt like the metal strap she had inadvertently put round her chest, was now becoming loose.

She felt a real sense of freedom, 'I've got to go out there now' she thought, 'I've got to find out who I really am, I can't go on like this'. Her young mind was tormented but she felt, within herself, that the answers were out there, and she felt the note she had left with her grandfather on his ceremonial boat, was urging her to make the same decision, and the answers were out there, in the North Sea.

She puzzled over all the recent conversations, especially the one with Amos, it was he, after all, who had found her in the barrel, and it was him alone who had informed her of where she was found. She remembered how he had watched Archie McPherson and Medhi trying to work out how the barrel had ended up in the cave. There were all types of suggestions at the time, someone or some person from the area of Whitby, had placed the barrel there, but Amos apparently disagreed with all their findings, he personally thought the barrel had been washed ashore somehow, from a passing ship. This theory, however, was dismissed by everyone at the time because Amos was only ten years old. All these thoughts had now confirmed Celia's intentions, she must now escape the well-meaning clutches of her family, the love they had given her and all their hope. She now had to follow her own beliefs, the decision was made, she would find a way to run away to sea and begin a new life. The sooner the better.

Celia knew, of course, being a female was almost unheard of to become a seaman and have a career at sea. She remembered her grandma Florrie and Mary talking about the press gangs on the Mill Dam. They had lots of laughs about it, but it was also terrifying at the same time. Gangs would turn up frequently in the hope of capturing young males to serve as seamen in the

Royal Navy. Gunpowder Bob, Amos's little friend was one of those unfortunates, a slight and unwilling recruit, whisked away to a life of peril. Celia couldn't stomach the thought of sharing his fate. Celia was so obviously a young lady; she wondered if she could try sneaking on board but once discovered would automatically be returned as soon as the ship reached the next port. She went over and over the various options, there was only one answer, she would have to disguise herself and dress as a boy, preferably a young vagrant, who wouldn't get so much as a glance from any interested parties. Celia started out by finding old cast-off clothing and shoes, she gathered them from all over and when she decided she had enough to start proceedings. She began to wait around the quayside until she spotted a Royal Navy ship enter the Tyne, she would count the guns and the masts and anything else that bore significance. She decided it was this type of vessel that would require a regular supply of seamen. One such ship came in that day, and she noticed it was moored up on the north side of the river where the fishing boats were. Not an ideal place for picking up new crew members so perhaps this ship was not on the lookout for any extra crew, but unbeknown to her, she hadn't realised this was a deliberate ploy to fool people on the south side into a false sense of security. The locals, although noticing the ship, would think any recruitment tonight would not happen, at least not on this side of the river, which thankfully, allowed them unrestricted drinking time. Celia was a little disappointed at first thinking this chance was eventually lost. More to the point though, she had just cut off her long hair, almost to the bone, in fact, and it looked patchy and horrible, how was she going to explain this to the family, she virtually pulled out the hairs of her eyebrows and she was dressed in rags. She found some bandage style material which she tightly bound around her upper body to conceal her sexuality. She caught a glimpse of herself in the Customs House windows, her reflection looking back at her, she saw a wiry, tall, bedraggled figure. Her efforts to make her look like a male had not been in vain, to her way of thinking, she looked terrific. 'But what now' she thought 'I can't go home, might as well go into the ale house and show myself off as a scruffy vagrant'.

As she stood on the cobblestones of the quayside, the icy wind biting at her skin, her thoughts turbulent as the churning waters of the Tyne. This life she imagined – a woman braving the high seas – was a fantasy bordering on madness. The Royal Navy was no place for a lady, and even less for the vicar's daughter. But Celia was not one to be cowed by convention.

Her grandmother's stories had planted the seeds of rebellion, the vivid tales of the press gangs that prowled the Mill Dam, had painted a picture of laughter and fear in equal measure.

Her plan, as audacious as it was desperate, began to take shape.

The alehouse on the north side of the river was thick with smoke and the stink of unwashed bodies. It was a refuge for labourers and misfits, a perfect place for a vagrant boy to blend in, or so Celia hoped. As she began to approach the building all the inhabitants were in various stages of inebriation, blissfully unaware that anything untoward was about to happen. Celia counted as least a half dozen young males, and one or two older ones. Alongside these males were a couple of old fishwives, she recognised both as Florrie's compatriots, and they would recognise her instantly, so here was a chance to carry off her disguise. Her fingers tightened around the battered door handle, and pushed the door with her shoulder, gently kicking the bottom of the door to gain access and stepped inside.

The two old women looked up first, and glanced at Celia, "Close the door then," said the smaller one, "you're letting all the cold air in, its freezing out there."

"Sorry I will," answered Celia, "didn't think there, for a moment," she said rather gruffly, hoping she sounded like a man. Suddenly, a sea of bleary eyes turned towards her, looking her up and down.

Then the landlord spoke up "Manners" he said, "coming from a young man, that's a change these days, isn't it?" he went on, "What's your business here? A drink?" His tone was teasing but laced with an edge that made Celia wary.

"Yes please" she croaked, forcing her voice as low as she could muster, much to the delight of all the customers present. Her throat ached with the effort.

"Have you money for it?" asked the landlord, leaning in closer. "Or do you think we run a charity," he went on with a twinkle in his eye, "I expect you've got a purse full of gold, have you?" he laughed.

Celia reached into her pocket, "Only two pennies. Will that be enough?" she answered in a steadier voice. The landlord chuckled and slid a tankard of frothy ale toward her. "Get that down you lad, it'll put hairs on your chest."

The two old fishwives interrupted and waved her over, "Take no notice son, come and sit here with us, we'll look out for you."

Celia didn't need a second invitation and quickly took a seat beside the women. Her heart quickened; would they see through her disguise? She braced herself, but they seemed oblivious, their attention more on her supposed youth than her origins.

"What's ya name boy?" asked one of the women "You don't look as though you come from round here." She was staring at her with rheumy eyes.

"Ben", Celia answered immediately "Ben Jackson, from Gateshead, looking for some work actually." She lied, then quickly went on, "Maybe on the River Tyne" as she nodded toward the river.

Celia couldn't help but smile, only hours earlier she was Celia Trevelyan, the vicar's daughter, now she was Ben Jackson, a provisional riverboat labourer. As one life seemed to vanish, another was about to be born.

As fate would have it, she didn't have long to find out how her life was about to change dramatically. Closing time was just upon the merry group, when suddenly the camaraderie of the alehouse was shattered as the door burst open, glasses, bottles and tables were scattered in every direction, accompanied by loud bursts of fire from pistols being shot into the air, amidst the shock and surprise, a dozen or so very aggressive, brutal seamen proceeded to grab and attack any male person in the room. They moved with precision, the violence swift and calculated. Celia froze, her heart pounding as she realized their intent. Within the blink of an eye, they seized everyone they could. The men were dragged from their seats, their protests silenced by the butt of a gun, women tried to shield her, but her ragged disguise failed to save her. A sailor grabbed her, his fist like iron. What surprised Celia the most, was the seamen, who it was now blatantly obvious, were a Royal Navy press gang, began beating their intended victim's unconscious before entering any meaningful dialogue. Hit them first seemed to be their motto. One swift blow from a heavy pistol rendered her unconscious. It was apparently later found out that the gang had been watching the ale house for some time from across the river and decided to make their approach when the regulars would least expect it.

When she awoke, her head throbbed, and the room swayed unnaturally. She realized with a start she was no longer on land. The faint tang of salt air and the rhythmic creak of timber confirmed her worst suspicions, she was aboard a Royal Navy vessel.

The following day, rumours spread quickly through the town, the pressgang had taken four local citizens along with one young chap from outside the area, river boatman Ben Jackson. What the townsfolk didn't know, what no-one knew, was that Ben Jackson was not the boy they thought. Celia Trevelyan, the vicar's daughter, was gone, in her place was a boy with no past, bound for a future she could barely imagine.

As the ship's sails unfurled and the coastline faded into the mist, Celia felt the weight of her choice laying heavy on her shoulders.

Celia was now at sea, in every sense of the word.

CHAPTER 22

Fiona's voice trembled; her words heavy with unease. "Have you seen our Celia?" she asked, her gaze darting nervously around the dimly lit room. "She's supposed to be back by now."

"By now," Florrie's retort was quick and sharp, her tone betraying fear she couldn't suppress. "Back by now?" she repeated, her voice rising. "She left yesterday, Fiona not today."

The silence was suffocating, a vacuum that seemed to suck the air from the room. Both women now looked at one another, their faces pale, their breaths shallow. A chill of realization washed over them, internally terrified, paralyzing their limbs.

Without warning, Fiona sank down on her knees, totally oblivious of the fine clothes she was wearing. Her bare knees sinking into the soft wet sand beneath her. She didn't care; all she could feel was the weight of dread pressing down on her chest. Florrie immediately caught hold of her in an embrace of shock and impending doom, which was all they could see in this precise moment.

"What do we do?" Florrie's voice broke, her words barely audible over the sound of their sobs. Both women were wailing uncontrollably when they were interrupted by Mary and Becky, who were coming over to visit Florrie, merely for a small get together. They both came running across in blind panic in response to the unnatural cries of Fiona and Florrie.

"For heaven's sake!" Mary gasped, her chest heaving, "What's wrong?" she blurted out, "what on earth has happened?"

"It's our Celia, she's missing" cried out Fiona, "she's vanished, just gone

"What do you mean, just gone, gone where?" Becky demanded, her tone sharp betraying both confusion and fear.

Fiona and Florrie eventually managed to speak. The answers came haltingly, disjointed and interspersed with fresh waves of sobs. Between the gasps and the stammered words, one truth emerged: Celia was missing. Not a delayed return. Not a misunderstanding. She was truly gone, vanished without a trace.

Becky found her composure first. She straightened her spine, her jaw set with grim determination. "We need to act. Now."

She hurried to report the matter to the local constabulary, while Mary rallied the villagers, spreading word of Celia's disappearance like wildfire. The once sleepy town erupted into action, its inhabitants combing the fields, the coastline, and the shadowy edges of St. Hilda's parish.

Everyone was asked if they knew anything or where a favourite haunt might be so it could be investigated. The answers, when they came, were maddeningly uniform, no-one had seen her in over twenty-four hours. Every place that seemed like an extension of herself offered no clues. After extensive searches, two whole days had passed without success and the grim realisation had set in: Celia had disappeared as if swallowed whole by the earth itself, with little or no clues as to her whereabouts.

Inside Florrie's modest cottage, despair hung in the air. Fiona sat slumped in a chair, her face pale and streaked with tears. Florrie stood by the window, her hands gripping the sill so tightly her knuckles turned white. Although everyone offered their support and hope, even they could see nothing but disaster. The police decided they would search the local caves in the hope they would find something that may help them. None of this action gave comfort to Celia's family. Now regrettably, this was a time of speculation as to what might have happened to the girl and could she even be still alive or even abducted. Their tormented souls left no stone unturned, this wasn't like Celia at all, if she could have, everyone reasoned she would let someone know where she was.

It was Erasmus, Florrie's youngest son, who broke the spell. His voice, hesitant but clear, cut through the fog of grief.

"Well, you know," he said, deep in thought, "she just might've left on purpose." The room turned to him as one, his words drawing sharp, questioning gazes. He paused for a few seconds. "She might even have gone looking for her past, you know what she was like Ma," he added quietly. He had hoped his words would bring comfort in an already terrible situation.

"What are you saying, lad?" Florrie's voice was barely a whisper, "Her past? How? Where like, son?" Florrie whispered very quietly, "Where would she start looking? She had no money?" Her words brought about an agreed answer from all present, you could feel the agitation in the room, but at least it was a positive thought.

The boy hesitated, as if reconsidering his words, but then pressed on. "She talked about it sometimes. About finding answers."

A tiny seed of hope in an otherwise barren field had begun to grow. It wasn't much, just a theory spun from scraps of memory and conjecture, but it was the first glimmer of possibility. The room buzzed, each person grasping at the fragile thread of Erasmus's suggestion.

The fear lingered on. What if Erasmus was wrong? What if Celia hadn't left willingly? Lots of what ifs.

No one dared voice the thought, but as the police continued their search into the caves, even the most optimistic among them began to lose hope.

In the meanwhile, the Royal Navy frigate, HMS Unicorn was already cutting through the placid waters of the North Sea or the German Ocean as it was known in those days, like a blade through silk. Twelve hours had passed since she had departed the River Tyne under the shroud of predawn mist. Her destination: the turbulent Bay of Biscay, where Admiral Nelson's fleet awaited reinforcement.

Above deck, the world was unnervingly tranquil, the gentle roll of the sea offering a deceptive calm. Below, however, in the dimly lit belly of the ship, the air was thick with unease.

"Right, you scurvy lot," barked a stocky marine, his voice reverberating off the low wooden beams. His boots thudded heavily against the planks as he surveyed the group of six ragged figures slumped in the shadows. "Let's be having you," he went on, "we'll be having no soft pansies aboard this vessel," he growled, his eyes glittering with a dangerous light, as her kicked out at one dishevelled person who was still half asleep at this moment. He spoke once again, "You're all in the Royal Navy now," he grinned. "A servant in the King's navy, so you are." He looked directly into their eyes and said, "My names Ivan, you call me Boss, nothing else."

Ivan was not a large man, but his compact frame radiated a brutal kind of strength, the sort that suggested he could endure the full brunt of a storm and come out the other side smirking.

Although the men were bruised and battered, they weren't prisoners anymore and they were accepted as equal crew members and were told they would be treated as such. He looked around his motley collection of new recruits, tutting and laughing every time his eyes fixed onto one of the unfortunates. Eventually his stare fell upon a figure curled in the corner, half covered by old ropes and discarded sails. "And who might you be lad," he growled, his tone dripping with suspicion, "you are over ten, I hope."

The figure stirred; the movement sluggish, almost hesitant. Celia answered in a gruff voice, "I am sir, I'm fifteen and people call me Ben," She stumbled out these last words, hoping her real identity wouldn't be discovered. Ivan continued looking her over.

Ivan squinted, stepping closer. The dim lantern light caught the edge of a face which seemed too smooth, too delicate for the coarse world of seafaring. "You're a bit skinny, mind," he said, "and too tall to be a powder monkey but a bit too slight for much else."

At that moment, another seaman entered the hold, his arms laden with a haphazard collection of navy-blue garments. He unceremoniously tossed them into the fray without ceremony, A chaotic scramble ensued, with the recruits clawing for anything that might fit their emaciated bodies, and although the men were below decks, they could hear everything that was going on above. The rolling about from side to side proved without doubt they were now at sea. Sad and unfortunately all anyone could do now was accept the situation and make the best of the circumstances. Ben hadn't been quick enough to claim his share.

Ivan's eyes locked onto Ben once more "Too slow, eh?" he said, shaking his head. "To be honest, lad, you look more like a lass. God knows if you'll survive out here."

Ben, of course, quaking inside, said nothing, his head was touching the low beams of the ship's ceiling, his future now lay in the hands of strangers, tough sailors and vagabonds.

Ivan proceeded to give orders to the others before a group of officers entered the crowded area, it was obvious they were different to the general seamen. They were smartly dressed, with black polished shoes and brass belt and buckles and pristine uniforms were a stark contrast to the grime and disarray below. Apparently, they were called midshipmen. The lead officer was very well spoken and noticed Ben, i.e. Celia, standing in the corner, alone and shivering and not yet fitted out with any naval attire. "What's his story?" his voice cultured and clipped as he asked Ivan, "have you nothing for him to wear?"

Ivan shrugged, "Hasn't got his kit yet, sir." answered Ivan, "we'll have to look in the dead man's locker to see if there's anything his size."

The officer, whose name tag read Hector, stepped closer, studying Ben. "Has he been assigned any duties yet? He's a pleasant enough looking chap; he looks half sensible and doesn't shave by the look of him."

"No, he hasn't been given any duties yet," answered Ivan, "not sure what might suit him to be honest. If it was up to me, I'd throw him overboard." This last remark struck Ben like a thunderclap, his blood turning to ice, but Hector dismissed it with a wave of his hand.

Hector nodded his response, but added "The captain has recently lost his personal assistant, and is now being attended by the ship's cook, a revolting creature with the hygiene of a bilge rat." He turned back to Ivan. "Have the captain look at this one before we assign him to the general crew. He might find a better use for him."

"Understood, sir," Ivan replied though his tone suggested he was less than thrilled.

Hector once again spoke to Ben directly. "You don't look like the rest of us Ben, I think the captain would like to see you first before we throw you in amongst this lot. He might well know where you might be best suited." He then turned to face Ivan, "Keep him here for the next couple of hours and be sure to give him some food and a drink." As he was giving out his orders he looked over to Ben "and don't bind him or put him in chains, he won't be any bother, he doesn't strike me as a troublemaker."

Hector and his officers then turned and ascended back to the upper decks, their polished shoes clacking against the ship's planks as they disappeared into the maze of the frigate. Ben could now feel his fate lay in the hands of strangers a precarious balance between brutality and salvation.

Moments later Ivan brought in some food and drink to Ben, a little bit of salted beef, potatoes and a type of bread Ben had never seen before, accompanied by a tankard of ale, its surface flecked with bubbles that caught the dim light. He had a deliberate step, his demeanour bore an undercurrent of curiosity as he approached and said "Here, eat." The food was on a wooden square palette.

"What is this?" asked Ben, his voice cracking slightly, sounding more like a girl.

Ivan smirked, a flash of white teeth against his weathered face. "It's what is known as a square meal in the navy. Three of these a day we get, plus a tankard of ale, it'll keep you alive."

Ben hesitated, his stomach twisting more from nerves than hunger. "Why's the captain want to see me?" he blurted, his words tumbling out in a rush. "He hasn't spoken to any of the others. Why me?"

Ivan's expression didn't change. His gaze, sharp and inscrutable, lingered on Ben for a moment longer than was comfortable. Finally, he shook his head and muttered, "Questions won't help you, lad. Eat up. You'll soon find out." He then turned to leave, amazingly he gave Ben a friendly pat on the shoulder as he left, a gesture both reassuring and strangely foreboding.

Left alone, Ben stared at his food. His hands trembled as he picked up the bread, his mind churning with unanswered questions. Why had she stowed away? Was it truly worth abandoning the life she knew for this perilous uncertainty? She thought of home, of safety, of the warm familiarity she had left behind.

The rocking of the ship seemed to mirror the turmoil within her. Every creak of the hull, every distant shout from the deck above, fed the gnawing doubt that had rooted itself in her mind. What if they found out the truth? What if the captain saw through her disguise?

Ben's pulse quickened as his thoughts spiralled, his imagination conjuring scenarios of brutal punishment or worse. From now on she would force herself to believe she was Ben the cabin boy.

He closed his eyes for a moment, willing himself to steady. Whatever the captain wanted, whatever lay ahead, there was no turning back now. His fate was bound to the HMS Unicorn, its secrets and the ruthless men aboard. And the captain? He would hold the key to whether he sank or survived.

CHAPTER 23

The next twenty-four hours unfolded with an agonizing slowness, as if time itself conspired against her. Celia the young, frightened girl who was press ganged had disappeared entirely. In her place stood a figure crafted from necessity, shrouded in disguise and the desperate instinct to become the persona as if her life depended on it, because it did. In her mind she could think of nothing else but survival. Her new shipmates thought she was Ben anyhow and she knew within herself, if she was to survive, that's exactly who she would be. The transformation was unsettling but to her Celia was already a ghost. Ben sat crouched in the corner of his cramped locker, knees drawn to his chest, his mind raced contemplating his future. He looked around him and all seemed dark and dismal without any real hope. Then it came, the sound. A key turning in the heavy metal door with a slow metallic groan, a sound that sliced through the silence. With a loud crack the door suddenly opened, and a blinding sunlight flew into the room, illuminating the chaos around him. There were sea chests, weathered barrels, sails and heaps of coiled ropes all around him. He noticed an old battered three -cornered hat lying just feet from where he sat, the tricorn was only feet away from where he had been sitting, before anything else happened he instinctively made a grab for the hat and put it on his head as if shielding himself from the unknown.

Footsteps echoed down the corridor. Two men appeared in the doorway, the midshipman he knew as Hector, and the burly Ivan with shoulders like boulders, walked towards him. Ivan's booming laugh filled the small space.

"Well now, that hat suits you," Ivan said, "I think we should call you the Admiral," he laughed out loudly, obviously making fun.

Midshipman Hector also laughed, 'We may have a character here' he thought. "Come on Admiral," he said, "it's time to meet the captain.

Ben rose awkwardly, his legs stiff and unsteady, he looked decidedly uncomfortable, "Don't worry, lad," said Ivan, "he's going to decide what position may suit you best" he winked reassuringly. Ben, fell into step beside his shipmates, stretching his legs, for the first time he noticed Hector had a strange floral smell about him, whatever it was it was pleasant and seemed at odds with the smell of the brine and sweat of the ship.

"Aye, you're a big lad alright," Hector said, "Well, tall anyway," he went on, "you need a bit of weight around that belly of yours." Once again, a round of merriment seemed appropriate. Within a few minutes Ben arrived outside a tall imposing door. His pulse quickened as Hector knocked, the sound resonating like a drumbeat of fate.

"Enter," said a crisp and authoritative voice from inside, "state your business."

Hector opened the door with a practiced flourish and stepped inside, removing his hat. "It's midshipman Hector, captain," he responded, "I've got the young conscript, Ben for your appraisal, if you recall.

There was an uncomfortable silence for a few moments which gave Ben a little time to look around his surroundings.

It was a busy ship, it was also noisy, but seemed full of good cheer, nevertheless.

"Wel, bring him in Mr. Hector and let's look at him," The voice was smooth yet edged with steel. Hector grabbed Ben's hat off him and shoved it under his arm and pushed Ben into the cabin. Ben stumbled forward. In doing so he almost fell onto the captain's desk, but he couldn't help noticing the rugged splendour of the cabin. No gilded opulence here only the rugged beauty of fine craftsmanship. English oak panelling gleamed in the sunlight that streamed through a narrow porthole. Engravings of ships and battles adorned the walls in a magnificent beechwood, the craftsmanship was truly superb. It was here that he also noticed that strange perfume smell, it was the same enigmatic one that Hector also had about him. The quarters were also clean and tidy as you would expect. Ben was surprisingly impressed. The captain was not what Ben had expected, He was younger, perhaps in his early forties with sharp intelligent eyes that missed nothing. His uniform was immaculate.

The captain regarded Ben with an expression that was impossible to read, his gaze sweeping him from head to toe. "My name is Captain Lewis Percival," he said this in clear faultless English, "and I am honoured to serve in His Majesty's Royal Navy." The captain noticed that Ben's head was virtually touching the low ceiling of his cabin. "Now, what's your name? You have got a name I take it?"

"I have sir, it's Ben," he replied.

The captain leaned forward, his piercing gaze locking onto Ben's, "And your last name? What is that?"

Ben hesitated, the lie teetering on his tongue. "Well, I haven't really got one sir," Ben stuttered out the reply. "But most people call me Ben Jackson, I never knew my parents," he went on.

The silence that followed was heavy, but the captain merely nodded, his expression inscrutable. "Very well, Mr. Jackson, we shall see what you are made of. I see you've acquired a tricorn hat," his voice was steady and deliberate, "is that yours?"

"No sir, I found it in the holding locker and picked it up;" His words faltered, and he glanced nervously at Hector and Ivan. Once again, he blurted out a response. "They didn't say I couldn't have it."

The last remark caused a ripple of amusement to spread through the room. Even the captain's stern demeanour softened as he let out a low chuckle.

"You're quite a lad Ben and I like you already," said the captain leaning back in his chair. "From now on you will be called Ben Jackson Tricorn. And mark my words for it is on this ship the Unicorn that you will make your name."

It was then at this moment that Hector politely interrupted, "Begging your pardon sir, I wonder if you've had time to consider what position might suit young Master Ben," glancing over to his young charge, "Sorry Mr Tricorn."

Captain Lewis reply came without hesitation. "Indeed, I have." His voice carried an air of finality, as though the decision had already been set in stone. "Given his stature and potential, I believe he could make a fine midshipman someday. But first," he paused, his eyes sharp and narrowing, "we need to get to know him better. See what he is made of. For now, he'll serve as my personal cabin boy, if that's acceptable to you Mr. Tricorn?" He looked at Ben askance.

Ben's throat tightened, but he nodded resolutely. "Thank you, captain, it would be an honour to serve you and the Royal Navy."

From that moment, Ben Jackson's life began its transformation. Over the years to come, he would find himself embroiled in adventures that would test his courage, sharpen his wits, and forge his identity. Behind the boyish bravado of 'Ben Jackson' lay the hidden truth hiding his real identity. Circumstance meant that Ben could never contact Florrie or Fiona or indeed anyone left in the Northeast, although naturally there were moments when she really wanted to. Things weren't always enjoyable on the HMS Unicorn, Celia under her alias Ben Jackson was now approaching eighteen years old and beneath the boys clothing was the body of a woman. Nevertheless, she was now developing into a fine seaman, Ben's secret was still intact, and he was becoming something more – a capable seaman and a trusted protege of Captain Lewis himself.

The captain sensing an unusual spark in Ben, had personally taught him the skills of navigation, swordsmanship and tactics. The boy's natural aptitude was undeniable. So much so that even the Admiralty had been informed of Ben's expertise. It was incredible really, that a lad of his age would gain such notoriety in such a short space of time. In the process of many battles, he was accredited with lots of personal victories against his adversaries. Most of which perished at the end of his sword or pistols. Ben wasn't afraid of close quarter fighting either and had many duels. People said he would do anything to get the upper hand, including biting, kicking and even eye gauging when required, nothing seemed out of his remit. Survival demanded ruthlessness, and Ben delivered. After battles he would often reflect, to himself of course, of his early home life and upbringing in the confines of St. Hildas Church. Those memories were distant now, like a shoreline receding into the horizon, but they never truly left her.

It was during one of these reflective moments that Captain Lewis came to see Ben in his quarters, his expression unusually grave.

"At ease, Mr. Jackson," said the captain, his voice low but commanding. He stepped inside and closed the door behind him. "I have need of a serious conversation with you," he looked over to Ben and his gaze never flinched away from the Midshipman.

Ben stood silently; his eyes fixed on the captain. The weight in the room was palpable.

"As you're aware we are sailing into the Bay of Biscay soon, to rendezvous with the Admirals of the Royal Navy." He paused letting the gravity of the words settle. "But before that, we have another task. Intelligence suggests we may cross paths with a French fleet. Our mission is simple – capture one of their ships, take prisoners, and secure whatever information we can."

Ben's heartbeat quickened, he listened intently but made no reply or sound. The captain's tone sharpened. He paused for quite a while, allowing Ben to contemplate, no doubt as to what he had in mind for him. "You see, Ben," said the captain, "Apart from myself, you are the only one aboard who can speak French, which I still find amazing," he went on, "That alone makes you invaluable to this mission." He hesitated, his sharp gaze searching Ben's face.

Ben couldn't and didn't mention to the captain he could already speak French before he came on board.

"Right now," he said, "we have a daring plan, one that could succeed spectacularly, or end in disaster. You, Mr. Jackson, will play a central role."

The room seemed to shrink, the captain's words closing in around him. Ben said nothing, but his mind raced.

"We'll assemble a longboat," Lewis continued, his voice calm but edged with intensity, "and a small crew. Some shipmates, especially Ivan, will approach one of the French fleet's ships, we want you and others to sail over there under the guise of deserters and then, somehow, if God is willing, gain what information you can and if the fates are kind try to make it back safely.

The enormity of the plan struck Ben like a wave. The risks were staggering, but something inside him stirred. A restless hunger for action, he was more than happy to take up the challenge. Celia had always wanted this. She had dreamed of being part of something larger than herself, of living a life that mattered.

"I'm ready, sir "Ben said at last, his voice firm.

Captain Lewis nodded, a faint smile touching his lips. "I thought you might be. We leave nothing to chance. Over the next few days, we'll finalize the details. Trust will be your greatest weapon, and secrecy your greatest shield Ben stood there, the weight of the captain's words settling like a heavy mantle. This was it, the moment when action and identity collided, Celia was gone. Ben Jackson, a name now whispered with respect and fear, was all that remained.

One or two of the most trust crew members discussed all the details of the ambitious plan. There was no disguising the fact it was very dangerous and more than likely could end in failure and death for all those involved, but one Ben was more than happy to participate in.

Well, this is what Celia had always wanted, this is what she was made for, she wanted action and as Ben Jackson she was now assured to get it.

As the Unicorn sailed ever closer to its dangerous rendezvous, one thing was certain, Ben's story. Celia's story was only beginning.

CHAPTER 24

The wind howled against the rugged Tyneside coastline, rattling the windows of Florrie's cottage as she sat motionless in her chair, staring out toward the black expanse of the sea. It had been nearly four years since Celia vanished, and though the world had moved on, Florrie's heart remained anchored in the past. She refused to accept that her daughter was lost forever. In the dim glow of the fire, her gaze flickered to the cup she had placed beside the hearth – waiting, as she always had, for Celia's return.

Her eldest son, Amos, now nearing thirty, had sworn to put his criminal past behind him. But old habits, like the tides, were difficult to resist. The temptation of easy riches still surrounded him, his old alliances with smugglers like Jack the Blaster a constant reminder of the life he was trying to leave behind. And yet, despite his mother's quiet dismay, the shadows of his former world tugged at him, whispering promises of fortune and danger.

Erasmus, in stark contrast, had found solace within the confines of the sacred halls of the church, and with respect to him was progressing very well. Under its vaulted ceilings and solemn hymns, he had carved out a life of virtue, his dedication bringing his mother the only semblance of peace she knew. Where Amos wavered, Erasmus stood firm, a beacon of stability in a family adrift in uncertainty.

The flickering candlelight cast long shadows as Billy Burns, still a police Sergeant, knocked gently at the door. Florrie welcomed him with a weary smile, setting a cup of tea in front of him as they fell into their familiar ritual of reminiscence. Celia's name hung in the air like an unspoken prayer. It was impossible to forget her, impossible to let go of the mystery that still gnawed at them. The memory of the discovery alone, abandoned in a barrel in the caves near Trow Rocks, haunted Florrie, a riddle without an answer. Who could leave a beautiful child on her own like that.

It was on one of those many occasions, as the fire crackled and the storm raged beyond the walls, Florrie was discussing the circumstances with her lifelong friend Mary when the conversation meandered through time, dipping into moments of shared history.

"Remember the shipwreck Florrie, "Mary mused, her voice barely louder than the whispering flames. "That was some night, wasn't it?"

Florrie nodded, the weight of memory setting on her shoulders, "Aye," she murmured. "I won't forget that night in a hurry."

Mary chuckled softly, lost in thought. Her eyes glowed with reflection as they settled on the fire. "No, nor me either," chuckled Mary. "Remember that boy they took up to the Priory."

Florrie frowned, her mind sifting through the layers of the past. "Aye, I do," she replied, "what about him?"

"I just wondered what had happened to him, that's all."

Silence stretched between them, the firelight painting their faces with shifting hues of orange and gold. Florrie contemplated for a few seconds, "He's probably dead now like. He's been missing a long time. As far as I know nobody has seen or heard from him since."

Florrie's vacant expression appeared to conclude matters. They both sat back in their chairs and almost simultaneously, and in perfect unison, shook their heads, as if to cast away the ghosts of the past. Neither of the ladies knew or were even aware of what had happened to the cabin boy.

Beyond the fire's dying embers, beyond the walls of that tiny cottage, the truth still lingered, waiting, hidden in the depths of time, refusing to be forgotten.

The Northumberland air was thick with the scent of damp earth and burning wood as Peter Bartholomew moved through the narrow streets of Wylam. The townspeople greeted him with nods and smiles, he was well-liked, respected. A skilled wine merchant, his mead was considered among the finest in the region, though no-one knew exactly how he achieved such quality. He never spoke of his time in the monastery, nor of the secrets he had taken with him.

Interestingly though, wine making was not his only passion. Steam engines fascinated him, strange fire-breathing beasts that seemed to herald the future. Whenever he had a free moment, he could be found in the workshops, hands blackened with soot, eyes gleaming as he studied their mechanics.

Peter himself was now almost twenty-eight years old, a small slim gentleman of what appeared to be middle class origins. He was now married to a local girl, and they had two children together. It was a happy family and unlike most of the population of the time were not destitute and lived in a delightful little house right on the edge of the river itself.

To the villagers, Peter was a simple man, a husband, a father. A devoted member of the community. Yet, in the solitude of his riverside home, where he would sit watching any logs or debris the river might float on the water's surface, his mind was not in Wylam. It was in the past. In another life.

Pierre. The name haunted him like a ghost. He had shed it long ago, reborn under the guidance of Father Bartholomew at the priory. But the memories of the sea, the shipwreck, and the promise he had made to Captain John Marcel refused to fade, Auriel Celeste. The child he had hidden, the life he had sworn to protect. Was she still alive? Could he still find her? The years had slipped away like water through his fingers. Perhaps too many.

Pierre, named by Father Bartholomew to save his life, kept in contact but rarely. The priest was in poor health now but between the two of them they managed to keep their secret. In quiet times at the Priory in North Shields, the two often discussed the wild Scotsman, Archie Macpherson, but never in the same breath did they mention Archie and Peter in the same context.

At the priory Father Bartholemew, aged and weary, wrestled with his own secrets. For decades he had protected Peter's identity, shielding the truth from those who might seek it. But the weight of unspoken words had grown too heavy.

One evening, in the flickering glow of the priory's great hearth, the old monk sat across from Archie Macpherson, a man whose name carried whispers of wild deeds and untamed lands. He passed Archie a tankard of mead, his hands unsteady, spilling droplets onto the wooden table.

"Not as strong as I used to be," the priest chuckled, though there was a shadow in his eyes. He took a sip, exhaled, then spoke again, his voice quieter this time. "In fact, Archie, between you and me, I haven't got much time left on this earth."

Archie remained silent, his gaze flickering to the enormous wooden cross that loomed over them.

Bartholomew raised his eyebrow, Archie leaned forward. A log crackled in the fire, sending sparks into the air. "He knows when, Archie," grasping his glass strongly "but he won't tell just yet," he laughed, they both did, "but there is something I want to tell you before I go," he added quietly, "I should have told you before now so I hope it's not too late."

Archie was intrigued, but listened quietly and patiently, they paused for a few moments while a young priest put a few logs on the fire. "Go on father, you have my full attention. Say what you must," he added.

Father Bartholomew nodded and took another drink from his glass; he dabbed his mouth with a handkerchief before proceeding.

"You know, many, many years ago, when the young cabin boy that was rescued from the Montpelier and apparently disappeared into the night?"

"Yes, I remember, they said he vanished into the night, what about him?" asked Archie.

"Well. That's what they believed." Father Bartholomew exhaled slowly, "but he did not perish."

The silence stretched between them.

Archie just nodded, saying nothing. The priest paused which seemed like ages before continuing, "We took him in at the Priory and looked after him. We gave him a new life."

The fire crackled, casting flickering shadows across the stone walls. Father Bartholomew's voice was low, barely more than a whisper, yet his words carried the weight of decades.

There was a touch of sadness and melancholy in his voice, filled with guilt and remorse that he had not let Archie know the full circumstances.

A cold wave passed through Archie. He had spent years believing the boy from Montpelier was lost forever. Now, this? "Where is he now, Is he still here?" Archie asked, "I need to speak with him."

Father Bartholomew lowered his gaze. When he finally spoke, his voice was almost drowned by the crackling of the fire. He shook his head. "He's been gone from here these last ten years," looking up to the sky added, "and hopefully he's built a new life for himself."

"Do you know where he may have gone," Archie interrupted, "It's very important to me, he may have so much to tell. This is important. He may have answers, things I need to know."

The old monk nodded and sat back in his chair, at the same time poking at one of the embers which had fallen from the fire, lighting up both of their features. Archie noted, in the little light that was there, Father Bartholomew was growing weaker and weaker by the moment, a sign which wasn't lost on Archie. Time was winning its battle.

"We can leave this for now, Father, if you wish," he went on, "we can resume tomorrow."

This last remark made the wily old monk smile, "Tomorrow Archie?" looking directly into his eyes, "I don't think there will be a tomorrow, not for me anyhow." He took another couple of deep breaths before carrying on. "You see Archie, if I had let anyone know of his whereabouts at the time, he would most certainly have been killed. I couldn't let that happen, times have changed now though. Now the story can be told."

Archie acknowledged the statement, "So, he has a name now then. He has got one, doesn't he?"

"Yes, he has" replied the father, "Yes, he's now called Peter Bartholomew, his last name being called after mine." Archie, as only he can, was absorbing the revelation. He wanted to press for more, but he could see the monk's strength fading fast. He hesitated, then asked, "Am I to understand that this Peter Bartholomew was once Pierre? The cabin boy?"

The priest gave a solemn nod. "Yes, that's right," replied the monk, "I'm truly sorry I didn't inform you sooner."

Archie clenched his jaw, working through the implications. "Do you know where he might be now. Is he even still in the area?" asked Archie.

"I believe so." the monk replied weakly," He left here for Wylam and hopefully start up a wine business. We drifted apart after a few years and lost touch; I haven't heard from him for some time."

Archie leaned back, deep in thought, his mind covering all eventualities and possibilities. The pieces were shifting, forming a picture he wasn't sure he liked. His mind moved quickly, calculating, predicting. "As it happens," he said slowly, "I still visit Wylam from time to time. It's a place I will visit very soon."

Father Bartholomew gave him a knowing look but said nothing.

He turned his attention to the monk "Let's have drink now father and discuss this matter no more." Archie, as good as his word, stayed with the monk for a few days and offered his help and support in any way he could, but unfortunately and not unexpectantly the good father passed away peacefully in his sleep.

He had died with his conscience clear. Archie, however, had work to do.

By sunrise, he was on the road to Wylam.

CHAPTER 25

The flickering candle in the monastery's chamber danced violently, casting long, spectral shadows against the stone walls. As Father Bartholomew exhaled his last breath, a world away, a storm-laden sky loomed over the Bay of Biscay. Beneath its rolling waves, secrets stirred.

The HMS Unicorn – a sleek, formidable vessel of the Royal British Navy – cut through the blackened waters, its crew braced for what lay ahead. Their mission was perilous; to infiltrate Bordeaux and sabotage a segment of the French fleet concealed within its fortified port. The air crackled with tension. France and Britain, locked in an unrelenting dance of war, had long vied for dominance. And while Napolean ruled the land with an iron grip, the sea belonged to Britain. Or so they believed.

Recent whispers, however, suggested otherwise. A new weapon – something monstrous – was being developed by the French. A cannon, capable of delivering five times the lead shot of its predecessors. If true, this advancement could tilt the balance of power irreversibly.

In the dim glow of his cabin, Captain Lewis Percival studied the tattered map before him, his expression impassive. Across from him stood a young midshipman, Ben Jackson – sharpeyed, lean, and battle-worn beyond his years.

"You do know why I chose you, don't you Ben?" Captain Percival's voice was a low murmur, edged with something unreadable.

Ben met the captain's gaze and ever so slowly, stated "Because I speak French quite well Sir?" Ben replied, rather curiously.

A wry smile tugged at Percival's lips. "That is part of it. But the real reason? Because I trust you implicitly." His voice dropped lower. "And if there is any man who can uncover the truth, it is you and Midshipman Hector." He spoke his words with true sincerity.

A quiet understanding passed between them. There was no room for failure.

He nodded in the direction of able mariner Ivan, a rough, tough seaman, and suggested with him on board they could fight at least ten Frenchmen. It was a small relief in a tense situation.

So it was, at midnight, under the cover of darkness, six men set out. Their naval uniforms had been stripped of insignia, their mission etched into memory – no maps, no documents which could betray them if caught, only crude outline maps. The rowed in near silence, their oars mere whispers against the ink-black water. The French coastline loomed ahead, jagged and foreboding. No moonlight guided them, only the rhythmic surge of the tide.

An hour later, they found what they were looking for – a secluded cove, its entrance shrouded by olive trees and thick undulating masses of seaweed. Here, they concealed their boat, camouflaging it with whatever the shore provided. Without a word all six men disappeared into the dark night.

Dawn broke with an uneasy hush. After only a few hours rest, moving in pairs, they crept through the countryside, guided only by the faint etchings on their maps. Their hearts pounded with the knowledge that discovery meant death – or worse.

Ben and Hector took the rear, their eyes scanning the landscape. Every shadow could be a sentry. Every rustling leaf, a spy. The French were close – too close.

The closer they got, the more Ben became aware of one thing, they were walking straight into the lion's den.

Ben and Hector moved cautiously along the hedgerows. Their breaths shallow, their senses heightened. As they pressed forward, a sea of French soldiers emerged in the distance – at least fifty men, possibly more, all armed – gathering in a vast field. The area was encased by crude imitation walls, an unsettling replica of some battlefield.

When daylight eventually broke through it was indeed a beautiful day, the sun was shining brightly and even though it could not have been more than 6am it was quite warm and very pleasant. As they were lying among the bushes Ben began to look around him and watched a couple of French kingfishers, small birds, native to this part of France, frolicking abut and doing nothing, just being themselves, no sign of animosity there, he thought, if only life could be like that.

"This must be the testing site," Hector murmured, adjusting his telescope. Yet what truly intrigued them were the three figures in civilian clothing, moving with purpose among the uniformed men. Scientists? Observers? Whatever the case, it confirmed their worst suspicions. Something significant – something scientific – was unfolding.

It was midday now. The sun casting long shadows across the field. They opted to remain hidden, careful not to betray their presence. This was when Hector stiffened. Just beyond the soldiers, two figures ambled along a narrow path. Dressed as farm labourers, they seemed innocuous enough. But Hector recognised them immediately as they passed where three soldiers were testing their new equipment. Farm labourers they may be, he thought, but they looked very capable and different to what he imagined.

As they got closer into sight Hector very quietly spoke to Ben, "It's Ivan and Jack, for Christ's sake, what are they doing, so close," he went on, "they are going to be seen."

Ben, equally tense, kept his eyes fixed on the unfolding scene. "They have been seen," interrupted Ben, barely above a breath, "but nobody looks bothered, look they are just sitting down, they must think they are just farm labourers. "

Indeed, to everyone's surprise Ivan and Jack just sat down where they were their body language relaxed, exuding the casual indifference of simple onlookers The soldiers, dismissing them as mere peasants, continued their work. Two French soldiers approached Ivan and Jack. Ben and Hector held their breath. Minutes stretched into eternity as the confrontation unfolded. Then, to their astonishment, Ivan and Jack rose to their feet and just walked away, unhindered. Had they been lucky, or simply fearless? Whatever the reason, it was a masterful deception.

Suddenly, a shift in the atmosphere. The men in civilian clothes gestured towards the trees beyond the field. A moment later, gunfire erupted – sharp deafening cracks that shattered the uneasy stillness. Soldiers charged into the hedgerows, weapons raised, their faces drawn with urgency.

Hector gasped. "Look, there! Ivan and Jack again! The two men stood in the open, white flags raised in surrender. Ben clenched his fists. As the French soldiers closed in, Ivan and Jack raised their hands above their heads, motionless, awaiting their fate.

The accusation came swiftly; spies. Execution imminent,

Ben turned to Hector in sheer desperation, his eyes wild. "They say they want to kill them, what can we do to help?"

Hector, heart pounding, could only shake his head. He accepted there was nothing they could do this time. They both crouched down in the bushes and fell silent. As they watched further developments, they noted their other two shipmates, who till now had not be seen, were creeping toward the captured men being interrogated by the French.

"They are asking if there is anyone else involved," Ben muttered, "Hector, is there anything we can do to help? We must act."

Both men had now loaded their pistols and were ready for action, Hector shook his head in response. I don't think we can do anything now, he thought.

Without speaking he tugged on Ben's tunic to get his attention, "Look Ben," he breathed, "there's John and Wilson, they're walking straight toward them, what on earth are they doing?" The two men, defying all logic, were advancing on the remaining soldiers guarding the strange artillery.

Answers didn't take long to arrive. Chaos. Gunfire again erupted. Muzzle flashes split the air. Soldiers reeled, clutching at wounds, falling in confusion. The French turned their fire on John and Wilson, who had emerged in the crossfire. The soldiers fired indiscriminately and made their way to the centre field. While all this confusion was happening Ben and Hector remained hidden observers.

From what they could see John had been fatally wounded, his body crumbling into the dirt, leaving Wilson free to join his comrades under attack.

This crew of six men had been chosen well by Captain Percival for their individual skills and outright bravery, however unkempt they may have looked they were experts in survival and feared no-one. Able seaman Wilson for instance was a crack shot with the musket; it was said he could shoot a sparrow out of a tree from a hundred paces. This skill was about to become invaluable. Wilson managed to join his two companions Ivan and Jack, both were suffering minor injuries. They were now outnumbered by the French force but had managed to find a high spot further up the field, surrounded by huge rocks and various shrubbery, but however good their cover was they knew they couldn't hold out too long against such great numbers as the French artillery.

The battlefield was chaos – screams, gunfire, and the acrid stench of smoke filled the air. Amidst the carnage, two more figures moved like shadows. Ben and Hector, silent and precise, navigated toward their embattled comrades. Even Wilson's sharpshooting could not reduce the French soldiers' advantage, even his skill couldn't stem the tide of French soldiers bearing down on them. Their position was crumbling. To their credit, however, they were not about to give up their position any time soon.

Midshipman Hector scanned the scene and noted there were only about thirty soldiers left standing. Two civilians, possibly engineers most likely. And then, his eyes locked onto something else.

An experimental cannon.

While assessing the situation he nodded silently to Ben and made a sign; his hands flickered a rapid series of gestures. Ben understood instantly. The two French engineers stood perilously close to their prized weapon, oblivious of the danger creeping up behind them. A lone legionnaire stood between them. Eyes locked on the battle ahead. None of them saw their executioner's approach.

Hector moved first. A flicker of steel, a muffled gasp. The first engineer crumpled. At the same moment, Ben struck the soldier, but in the struggle, the Frenchman's bayonet slashed deep into his thigh. Pain lanced through him, but with a final, savage thrust, Ben silenced his opponent, severing his spinal cord.

Breathing heavily and trying to recollect his thoughts, he staggered back. He said to Hector in a matter-of-fact sort of way, almost an afterthought. "I think I have been cut."

Hector looked over to his companion, he was breathless himself, but he managed to say "Aye, you have lad, we'll see if we can bind it and make a good repair when we get back to the ship." He privately admitted to himself it was not looking good. The bleeding was bad, too bad.

Kneeling, Hector stripped a thin leather strap from the dead soldier. He needed this for Ben to stop the bleeding.

As he removed the strap he spoke to the dead soldier, "You won't be needing this anymore lad, we are going to put it to better use," he muttered, his voice flat. As he worked his eyes met the lifeless stare of the fallen legionnaire, he couldn't have been more than eighteen. His final expression was frozen between terror and acceptance as the remnants of his last tears glistened on his face. He noticed Ben was staring at the young guardsman, seemingly in a moment of sadness and despair, "That's war for you Ben" he said, "horrible I know, but it's nothing personal."

Hector's last remark seemed to jolt Ben out of his reverie and spur him into action once again. "Look at this canon, Hector," he said as he removed one of the engineer's arms from around the barrel, "five barrels 45-millimetre grapeshot and a crank handle which I assume you turn once each barrel has emptied. " He swallowed. "This thing could tear through entire regiments."

"Aye, you're right Ben," said Hector, "in any enemy hands, these could be lethal. They could kill hundreds of our soldiers against one of theirs." As though in unison they both simultaneously looked at each other with wry smiles. "Are you thinking what I'm thinking Hector?"

"I'm way ahead of you lad," Hector said. "Quickly let's load it up and see if it works."

They worked fast. Loading the weapon, adjusting the sights. Then they turned the cannon toward the battlefield.

Meanwhile, farther up the ridge Ivan and his two remaining companions were struggling badly and just about managing to hold off the superior numbers of the French force, they were fighting as hard as they could but truthfully were now in a crisis with only Ivan not injured.

Ivan spoke first, "if we survive this," he muttered through gritted teeth, "remind me to never volunteer for anything again."

A weak chuckle from his companions, then silence. Suddenly - A deafening roar split the battlefield.

The air vibrated with the relentless, mechanical thunder of the cannon. A storm of lead tore through the French ranks, bodies dropping in clusters. Thick smoke swallowed the field, white clouds rolling like mist over a battlefield turned slaughterhouse.

Ivan from his lofty position managed to drag himself round to obtain a better view. He shielded his eyes, his heart pounding. He turned toward the source of the devastation, toward the impossible sight of Hector and Ben, standing firm behind the cannon.

To his amazement and astonishment, the huge gun he had seen only hours earlier was fast becoming a circle of fire. The noise was truly devastating. The French forces were now dropping at an alarming rate, reduced now to a few survivors. Some dropped their muskets and fled into the distance. The firing ceased. The silence that followed was eerie.

The trio of British seamen just watched in amazement. Hector and Ben waved their companions down to their position. They were safe at last, out of the six volunteers only five remained but their mission was accomplished. Their work though was far from done. They had found the mysterious weapon which they were very impressed with and drew a couple of pictures of the great iron beast, as they called it.

They didn't have much time left, and they knew it, escape was of paramount importance. They gathered bits and pieces of the gun before setting off for the small boat.

"How's your leg now Ben," asked an overly concerned Ivan, "can you walk?" he added. He looked up as he said the words.

"Not really" answered Ben, "I feel very weak, but I will manage."

The last remaining members of the expeditionary force looked at each other but said nothing. They all knew the truth. It was touch and go for their young friend.

Ben was in a bad way, no doubt about that. They had to get him back to the ship almost immediately, otherwise Ben Jackson's days on this earth were numbered.

Time was running out and survival was still a gamble.

CHAPTER 26

"They are back, Captain, look on the starboard side," Perched high in the crow's nest, his fingers clenched the yardarm, his body pressed into the balustrade for stability the young lad was in a precarious position, the wind was threatening as his eyes, sharp and calculating, investigated the approaching craft but his exhilaration kept him firm.

"Hold your position there, lad," Captain Percival's voice sliced through the howling wind, "we can see them," he added, his expression frozen for a moment, "keep your wits about you! we don't need you falling from there, "he shouted again.

Upon hearing this last order, the young spotter released his hold on the rope, sat down, exhaled and smiled to himself. His pulse pounded in his ears as he caught sight of familiar figures among the crew returning in the small boat. Ben Jackson was safe. 'Thank God' he thought, 'they are all back safe and sound', especially Ben who had become his friend.

As the crew rushed over towards the railing, unease spread like a storm cloud. "Something's wrong," one sailor murmured.

"There are only five of them," another observed grimly.

While another shipmate yelled, "one's badly hurt," his eyes were scanning the approaching vessel. The small boat's movement didn't help matters and the heavy sea spray was causing difficulty. He could just about make out Hector and Ivan who were doing their best to row the small craft as well as they could, especially in the rough conditions.

Through the mist Able Seaman Wilson, his normally clean shaven face now rough with stubble, clutched a motionless figure.

"It's Ben Jackson and he's hurt," he shouted over the wind. "He's in a bad way sir," said one of the ship's crew.

Captain Percival didn't move, didn't speak. His gaze, cold and unreadable, remained fixed on the approaching boat. Only when it was mere yards from the ship did he turn on his heel.

His orders came out clipped, calculated.

"Take them to the sick bay." The disappointment in his voice was all too apparent.

He strode away without another word, but the tension in his shoulders betrayed him. A final command rang out.

"Midshipman Hector – report to my quarters immediately."

The men aboard the small craft scrambled onto the deck of HMS Unicorn, sea-worn and weary. They were welcomed with relieved pats and murmured praises, but all eyes remained on Ben, whose face was ashen, his breaths shallow.

"Welcome back lads, glad to have you back on board," said one of the worried crew members.

Ben, however, was being handled very, very cautiously as he looked in a bad way, gaunt and white as a sheet. "Easy," Ivan cautioned, "mind his leg, he's lost too much blood already, try not to put any undue weight on it, we can't have him losing any more," The crew didn't need the warning. Seasoned hands carefully lifted Ben and rushed him toward the sick bay, the doctor already waiting, his eyes sweeping over the wounded man with a practised intensity.

Doctor Winstanley barely acknowledged the others as he worked.

"He's lost significant blood," he muttered. "If it continues, we won't be able to save him." He glanced up, meeting the anxious gazes of the surrounding men. A deep breath. A decisive nod. "Strip him down, but don't touch the tourniquet."

The ship's cook, Harry, also the doctor's trusted assistant, grunted in response. "Aye, Doc. leave it to me."

Above deck, Captain Percival stood alone in his quarters, his fingers tightening around the edge of his desk. The weight of command was one he bore without hesitation, but tonight, it felt heavier.

A knock shattered his reverie.

"Midshipman Hector, sir. Permission to enter." The voice was steady, familiar, welcome. "Granted."

The door opened, and for a moment, there was no rank between them. Only two men who had faced death together.

The captain spoke first, his voice quieter than usual. "How is he?"

Hector held his gaze. "The doctor believes he can save him."

Captain Percival's shoulders eased, a rare smile ghosting his lips. "Good." A pause. "Very good."

The captain was obviously worried, his voice full of genuine concern, he went on "he's been like a son to me, you know," he added quietly.

"I know," replied Hector "and I fully understand your concern, but he is now in safe hands with Doctor Winstanley."

The words weren't lost on Captain Percival, "Excellent," he replied, "excellent" he repeated. He poured himself and Hector a small glass of rum and gestured for his young friend to have a drink before saying "Now, tell me about your excursion, how did it go?"

Hector raised the glass to his lips and finished the contents in one quick movement. He met the captain's gaze.

"Well, Captain," he said looking directly at him, "we found more than we could ever dream of," he paused for a couple of seconds, "much more, actually."

Before another word could escape his lips, a thunderous knock rattled the cabin door, the sound urgent, desperate even.

Captain Percival's eyes flicked toward the door, his patience thinning. "Enter, what's so urgent, damn you?"

The door creaked open revealing a pale, trembling able seaman. His hands clutched a bundle of cloth, its edges soaked in deep crimson. The fabric dripped, leaving uneven splatters on the wooden floor. his gaze darted between the captain and Hector, never settling, as though he were a rabbit caught in a hunter's sights.

"Spit it out, man!" Percival snapped," what's the matter with you, cat got your tongue? What's the news on Ben? Is he alright? For God's sake, is he alive?"

The intrepid messenger paused for what seemed an eternity. A bead of sweat rolled down his temple. He swallowed hard. The steely eyes of Hector and the captain seemed to stare right through him before the hapless messenger blurted out, "They've stopped the bleeding sir, and they've fixed the wound, or stitched it or something," he added. He was stumbling and slurring his words as he continued glancing between the two men.

"Well, that's good, isn't it?" retorted Hector, "At least he's going to be alright now," he nodded almost to himself.

The silence stretched unbearably. Then, the seaman took a low steady breath, squared his shoulders and delivered the words that would change everything.

"That's the trouble sirs," he answered almost reluctantly. It was ages before he could gather up the right words, "He," he said, meaning Ben, "is she. Midshipman Ben Jackson is a woman."

The cabin fell deathly silent.

Hector's brow furrowed. "That's absurd," he said, "Ben's as tough as iron, nothing like a." He stopped short, as if the words physically caught in his throat.

The captain, pale-faced, sank into his chair. His mind reeled, trying to piece together the impossible. "How," he breathed. "How did we not know?"

Minutes later, Dr. Winstanley entered, looking just as dumbfounded as the rest. He confirmed the unthinkable. Ben Jackson – the boy they had trained, fought besides, trusted – was, in fact, a young woman. The implications clawed at the captains' mind.

Another sharp rap at the door jolted them. A second messenger, breathless stepped into the room.

"Begging your pardon, sir. Ben Jackson, whoever he or she is has regained consciousness and wants to see the captain."

Captain Percival removed his hat, wiped his brow and nodded without speaking, his face, however, was a picture of bewilderment and disappointment if truth was known. "We best get down there then, we can't put it off any longer." He looked at his midshipman and Dr Winstanley directly, "Are you ready?"

The walk from the captain's cabin to the sick bay was brief, yet it stretched impossibly long. The weight of the revelation slowed every step. Ben, no, not Ben, was now sitting up in a makeshift bed, propped up by two very large pillows. He still looked pale but alert.

Captain Percival, after gathering his thoughts once again, quietly addressed his young midshipman, "How are you feeling now, lad," the words felt unnatural, forced.

Ben took a deep breath, considering his thoughts before answering, "Yes, thank you for asking sir, I am okay." With a half-smile he added, "it looks like I am going to live." With a tired expression his eyes wandered over to his friend, midshipman Hector, "Sorry sir," he said quietly, "I have, to my shame, deceived you all." Once again, he diverted his gaze to the captain. No one spoke immediately but Ben's sincerity was there for all to see. "I am not Ben Jackson," he said.

A pause. The air thickened.

"I am, in fact, Celia Trevelyan, the daughter of the vicar Tobias Trevelyan and his wife Fiona. We originate from the North of England near Newcastle." The name landed like a cannon shot. The room felt suddenly smaller; the air thinner. Ben stopped speaking at that moment and waited for his shipmate's response.

Ben or Celia as she was now, was in shock herself and there was no denying she was a female, a young girl. Captain Percival gathered up his immediate thoughts and decided all queries could not possibly be answered in such a short time, certainly not to everyone's satisfaction, that was for sure. It was agreed by everyone there present, including Celia, that all questions that may be asked were to be written down first and answered over a period of days. It was at this point; however, Celia thought it best if just for a fleeting moment her captain and her friend Hector would know just who she was.

Slowly and gently, she loosened her tunic revealing a young lady's bosom, therefore putting to rest all doubts that she was in fact a lady. There was, however, one question everyone wanted to know, why had she done it at all. Celia thought for a few seconds before answering, "I will, given time, answer everything," but paused once again, as though deep in thought, she closed her eyes and buttoned up her tunic.

For the first time a tear was noticed running down her cheeks, but she wiped it away quickly.

"I was abandoned as an infant, found in a wine barrel on a beach near Trow Rocks I never knew who my real parents were." A shadow passed over her face. "I ran away to sea, hoping to find them." She had been told of this event some years later by her half-brother. It was from then on that she desperately wanted answers. Those strong feelings never left her and caused many a sleepless night. She had asked all who knew her and all her circumstances what they knew, she then decided she had to find out for herself. Her plan was to run away to sea in any way she could in the hope that she may indeed find her parents and her true self.

"And did you?" Hector quietly asked, "find yourself?"

Her piercing eyes met Hectors." Regrettably not" she replied, "but I'll never give up."

It was at this point that Captain Percival postponed the meeting. He gently patted her on the shoulder and added with all sincerity, "We must, of course, inform your parents Celia, you do understand that?"

Celia thought for a while before replying, "Of course, you must," she said. "I still love them and all my family very much and I am looking forward to being reunited with them."

Exhaustion claimed her, and she drifted into sleep. But the storm of questions had only just begun.

CHAPTER 27

It was a beautiful day Mid-June 1815. The dawn sun, although a rare visitor to these parts, cast its golden fingers over the bay. The water shimmered, reflecting a sky bruised with the remnants of night. A lone Royal Mail boat sliced through the harbour's glassy surface, gliding forward with the incoming tide. The infamous Black Middens, jagged and merciless, loomed ahead.

Suddenly the captain yelled out to his helmsman, "Ten degrees port side, sir," his voice cracked through the crisp morning air," and then keep a straight tack afterwards."

"Aye, aye! message understood, holding steady" a rough voice replied.

With measured precision, the small ship threaded its way past the treacherous rocks and entered the River Tyne. As the small boat neared the numerous berths that were beside the river, the captain once again shouted out his orders.

"Portside berth, Mr Ablett," he said quietly, "and let the foy boatmen take over after that, if you will sir," he ordered.

The ship nestled securely between the middle and east docks close to the Trinity Church in the area known as South Shields. A modest crowd had begun to gather along the quay, drawn by the spectacle of the Royal Navy's colours snapping in the morning breeze. Ropes were thrown, bollards secured, and within moments, the deck erupted into disciplined chaos. Mail sacks were heaved onto the dock, letters bound for distant homes and foreign shores. Yet, among the cargo, one passenger was far more precious than any parcel.

Celia Trevelyan stood motionless; her heart was hammering against her ribs. For weeks the mail boat had been her home, but it was nothing compared to the towering HMS Unicorn, the ship that had been her world for three long years. Now, as she stepped into the full glare of daylight, an audible gasp rippled through the spectators.

Dressed in fine garments befitting her identity, Celia was unrecognizable to those who had once known her. The dishevelled, sunburnt boy she had pretended to be – Ben Jackson, midshipman of the Royal Navy – was gone. In his place stood a striking young woman, golden haired and graceful, stepping onto solid ground for the first time in what felt like an eternity.

The crew stood back in acknowledgement, giving her passage. A wooden plank had been laid out, a bridge between her past and present. She hesitated only a moment before stepping forward.

The captain appeared at her side before she finally left, his voice low. "Nervous?" Celia smiled, looking up at him, "A little," she replied, "but very happy all the same."

Although Celia's family had been informed of her survival a few weeks earlier they had been given no warning of her arrival. This homecoming would be on her terms. Yet the hushed murmurs of the crowd soon escalated into frantic whispers.

Then suddenly, cutting through the morning air like the sharp edge of a cutlass, a voice that could be heard as though no one was there at all.

The frantic voice wavered between disbelief and certainty.

"Celia," she said, "Celia Trevelyan is that really you? I knew you'd come back," she sobbed, "I just knew it." Her belongings tumbled from her hands as she fell to her knees, her weathered face streaked with tears.

Celia was beside her in an instant, collapsing into the woman's arms, their embrace silent but electric with emotion. Around them, the dock seemed to fade, swallowed by the gravity of the moment.

They were both kneeling on the rough cobbles, both oblivious to watching spectators, both women were crying and wailing out of pure joy and acceptance. They were only yards away from St Hilda's Church and the sound of the two women's crying finally caught the ears of Fiona, the vicar's wife and Celia's adoptive mother, she had been busy preparing the prayer books for the afternoon service. She was gently placing them on each wooden pew and, of course, in a precise orderly fashion. She froze. The book in her hands slipped through her fingers, hitting the wooden pew with a dull thud. Then another. And another until she had none left.

"Celia?"

She screamed, almost hysterically, she barely recognised her own voice as she shrieked the name, bolting through the church doors. She raced across the cemetery towards the jetty. She could now see Celia and Florrie who were still locked in an embrace that transcended time.

She lifted her heavy skirt and made her way over to the dockside skimming past the many gravestones.

"Celia, Celia," she shouted, she was running as fast as she could with her arms stretched out, jumping over anything in her way as she finally reached her destination. Stumbling onto the jetty before finally reaching them, pulling them into her own desperate embrace. Now there were three, clinging together, weeping, laughing, their bodies swaying in an unchoreographed dance of joy.

The crowds watched in stunned silence, and then, slowly, a ripple of applause. It was a moment no-one present, would ever forget, it was like something out of legend, a story unfolding before their eyes that would be told and retold for years to come.

And it was only the beginning.

Many days passed with Celia now reunited with her family and friends. The stories of Celia's life as Ben Jackson began to unfold and almost none of them could believe the outrageous adventures she had experienced. Her exploits were so interesting and unusual they even attracted the interest of the new newspapers that were beginning to circulate around England at that time. The tale of the girl who had vanished into the sea, disguised as a boy, only to return as a hero, captivated the people.

The newspapers, their influence stretching across England, caught wind of the astonishing truth.

A young woman thought weak and delicate, who had defied all the odds to become a midshipman, on the redoubtable HMS Unicorn, seemed incredible.

Celia Trevelyan sat across from the journalist, the candlelight flickering in the dimly lit tavern. The ink-stained fingers of the reporter tapped anxiously on his notebook; his eyes sharp with curiosity.

"So, Miss Trevelyan," he said, voice barely concealing his excitement, "you claim you were found in a barrel as an infant?" There was a look of disbelief in his eyes as he made his queries.

Cerlia nodded, "Yes. That's why I had to leave. I had to find out where I came from."

The journalist scribbled frantically, his mind already constructing the sensational headlines. The Girl in the Barrel. A mystery that had haunted Tyneside for years.

By the time the article hit the presses, the entire region was abuzz, everyone was discussing the story.

"Well, you're famous, now lassie," Florrie muttered over her cup of tea, eyeing Celia warily, "everyone knows who you are now." She paused before adding, "I hope this means you will stop all this nonsense about finding your birth parents."

Celia just smiled and sighed before answering, her determination unwavering. "Well, for the moment, Aunt Florrie, perhaps. Who knows," she admitted. She went on in a softer voice "It's something I must continue to do." Sadness crept over her beautiful young face. "But search I will continue to do for the rest of my life." She took hold of Florrie's hand and looked deeply into her eyes with a resolve as strong as ever. No further words were necessary.

Florrie sighed. She knew arguing was futile. Celia was a force of nature, unyielding, relentless. Nothing would stop her.

That evening Florrie had an unexpected visitor. The heavy oak door creaked open, and in stepped Archie McPherson. He was older now, his once athletic frame softened by time was more rotund, but his presence was as commanding as ever.

He had been visiting the priory in North Shields and thought he would pop over and see his old friends.

"Florrie," removing his bonnet he greeted her, a grin forming beneath his bushy moustache. "Heard ye had a bit of excitement round here."

"Archie McPherson," she cried out, chuckling and gesturing him in. "Aye, that we have. Celia's got the whole of England talking."

Archie was great company; he hadn't lost any of his charm or wit and he was really pleased to see the Guttenberg family once more. He settled into the worn chair by the fire, watching the flames dance. "I wanted to see the lass, but I hear she's away?"

Florrie nodded, "Aye, she is, off for a few days with her father, the reverend and his wife Fiona."

"Ach, that's a shame," Archie murmured, "but no doubt we will catch up soon. I am here for a couple of weeks, so I am, so I will come back to see her then." After all the last time he had seen her, she was an infant in a crib.

Archie went on to explain to Florrie that Father Bartholomew, the monk, had died and was the reason he was down here in the Northeast once more. To be honest Florrie didn't know him but out of respect she had some heartfelt sympathy for her friend.

"Aye, it comes to all of us eventually" said Florrie, wiping away a tear from her weather beaten, wrinkled cheek, simultaneously removing the cork from a bottle of rum with her teeth and then spitting it into the fire. "Not the night though eh, Archie. Not before we've finished this," lifting the bottle high.

Archie just laughed, his friend certainly had his kind of humour no doubt of that. After a night of laughing and joking and discussing all topics, some interesting, some not. Archie leaned forward, lowering his voice he casually mentioned the wreck of the Montpellier all those years ago, she didn't say anything, it meant nothing to her really, but she listened out of politeness.

"Aye, what about it?" she questioned," Have you found something interesting like?"

Archie leaned forward, lowering his voice. "Well, you know that cabin boy from the ship, the lad they dragged up to the priory?" Florrie nodded without saying anything. "And then he escaped and was presumed dead, so they said, eh?" Archie spoke carefully and in a measured sort of way. He paused for a moment. "Well, he didn't vanish Florrie," he said, "and he's not dead either.

Florrie's heart skipped a beat, she didn't know why. "What do you mean? How do you know this?"

Florrie was now more than interested but still said nothing for the time being. Archie went on, "Father Bartholomew from the monastery took him in. They called him Peter. The lad's still alive, living in Wylam, or so we think."

Florrie interrupted once again, "Well, why should I care? It's not my problem. It means nowt to me."

Archie set his glass down with a deliberate thud. "Because the Count of Artois himself tasked me with investigating that wreck. He wanted to know what happened to his son Jon and his wife – the ones lost that night."

Florrie sucked in a breath. "So, you think this Peter knows something that might be relevant?"

"I hope so," Archie admitted, rubbing his temples. "Theres no-one left to ask. He's my final hope."

For a moment, they sat in silence, the fire crackling between them. Then, absentmindedly, Archie reached for the newspaper lying on the hearth beside him.

His eyes skimmed the bold headline; The girl in the Barrel. His fingers tightened on the paper. "

Something wasn't right. His instinct twenty years ago made him uneasy with the circumstances and this didn't make him feel any better.

A slow creeping realization slithered into his mind. There was always more to this story, more than a coincidence, more than just fate.

"Can I keep hold of this, just for a few days Florrie?"

She waved a hand dismissively. "Aye, take it." she replied, "I was only going to use it for kindling to light the fire with tomorrow."

Archie being Archie had one more drink before leaving, he needed to find Pierre, the cabin boy, before returning to Edinburgh, in the hope that any meeting would cast light about the shipwreck all those years ago. He needed to know the truth.

CHAPTER 28

Archie McPherson rode into Wylam, Northumberland, just as the Sunday bells tolled across the quiet village, their solemn echoes rippling through the crisp morning air. He had spent the previous night in Newcastle, gathering strength for what he hoped would be a meaningful encounter. The village was unlike the bustling towns he had passed through – here, everything bore a pristine order, an untouched charm. There was no scattered refuse, no discarded crates from the day's markets, nothing of the unkempt disarray so common in South Shields or Tynemouth.

The townspeople, dressed in their finest, streamed toward the old stone church, its slightly crooked spire a testament to the centuries it had withstood. Though a few slates were missing from its roof, the building exuded an air of resilience, as if time itself had merely brushed against it but never truly worn it down.

Archie guided his horse through the neatly lined cottages, their thatched roofs bathed in the golden light of the morning sun.

He smiled and nodded pleasantly to anyone he met along the way. "Good morning, sir," he said to one person, "fine day for it," he added as he looked toward the church, it's heavy oak doors now open to welcome the faithful. The village vicar was stood at its entrance, his ornate robes flowing in the breeze. The man's kindly face was lined with years of devotion, his eyes twinkling with familiarity as he greeted each congregant. Archie stepped forward, removing his bonnet as a sign of respect, "Good morning, good sir. A fine crowd you've gathered this day."

The jovial vicar replied, "We have indeed, and there's room for one more, should the spirit move you."

Archie laughed, "Tempting. But first I must see to my horse," he answered.

Just beyond the church, a stable stood conveniently placed. As Archie secured his horse to the weathered wooden fence, a large man emerged from the forge, his broad shoulders casting shadows over the stable yard. He was sweltering from the heat of the furnace and used a vibrant neckerchief to mop his face. His eyes narrowed at the sight of the newcomer.

The man's voice was deep and unyielding, "Not from round here, are you? Just passing through? Or is there business to be had?" his eyes flickered toward Archie's attire, lingering on the ceremonial dirk positioned for quick access.

Archie met the man's scrutiny with calm assurance, recognizing the man's caution. "Actually, I'm looking for someone," he replied, "a young man by the name of Peter Bartholomew. I understand the gentleman moved here some years ago, from Tynemouth to be exact."

The blacksmith exhaled sharply, then extended a massive, calloused hand. His expression remained unreadable. "Would it be a friendship you're asking or legal matters?"

Archie smiled and appreciated the blacksmith's caution, "Ach away lad, it's nothing serious. It's, I suppose, good news, I have for him," pausing before he went on, "at least I hope it is, and unfortunately, some sad news as well. You see," he said, "his adopted father has died, and I think he should know about it.

"Of course, of course he should," replied the blacksmith, "I'm the blacksmith around here and I'm Joseph." He spoke the words simultaneously as he reached out his large muscular arm.

Archie noticed it was full of bruises and minor burns, "I guessed you might be the blacksmith," he said, "and Joseph, is that the name you go by around here?"

A deep chuckle rumbled from the blacksmith's chest. He paused before going on. "No, I am known as Big Joe, especially by my friends."

"And I am Archie McPherson." Both men clasped hands in an act of friendship. A silent understanding. "So, you do know Peter then, he does actually live here?"

"Aye, he does that," said Joe, "you'll see him soon enough, he comes here every Sunday with his family, well, to the church that is," he quickly added, "not the stables, if you see what I mean."

Both men laughed again, and Archie was offered a mug of warm beer poured into a wooden container. It was unusual to say the least and, to Archie's surprise, very tasty. This time he laughed to himself. 'I bet young Medhi Aziz would have liked this' he mused.

Big Joe noticed he was enjoying the ale before stating. "It was Peter who actually introduced the warm beer around here, no-one had heard of it before." Big Joe then took a sip himself. "Apparently back in Tynemouth that's the way they always drank it."

"Who? The locals?" Archie asked in surprise as it was not something he had noticed.

"No, the priory monks, where Peter learned his trade, they were the ones who drank it all the time" Joe went on.

Archie absorbed every bit of information like a sponge, his mind piecing every bit together about Peter. The more he learned the closer he felt to moving forward. He kicked and scuffed a bit of loose hay from the stable floor as he moved across it. "Does he have a business nearby? A workshop perhaps or a brewery even?"

Joe's response was unexpected. With a subtle nod toward a family approaching them he simply said, "Well, why don't you ask him yourself, here he is now,"

Archie turned. A man, his wife and his two children were walking toward them all dressed up ready for the occasion. The church bells in the distance sent waves of warmth through the air. The sight of the approaching family, framed against the sun, carried an undeniable sense of purpose.

Joe turned to Archie, "Watch the kids in moment," he said, "they love this part."

Without another word, by the time the kids got to the stable door he yanked an old canvas cover from a large rusty cage. The cage was almost as tall as himself and virtually covered his workshop door. Once the cover was removed it revealed a large beautiful green and yellow bird. "Hello Joe, hello Joe," screamed the bird followed loudly by shouting "Is breakfast ready," the kids burst out laughing as they always did, their delight infectious.

Archie took a step closer, his curiosity piqued. "What kind of bird is that?" He was totally amazed.

Joe chuckled, "It's a parrot, straight from the colonies"

As if on cue, the bird let out another piercing cry, "Eggs and bacon, eggs and bacon," he went on. Archie was amazed, he could scarcely believe it. He had heard tales and such about them talking but never in his wildest dreams did he ever think he would see one.

"What do you call him, has he got a name?" he asked still marvelling at the creature.

Before Joe could reply the younger of the two children interrupted. "He's called Napolean, sir. After the French general because he swears a lot."

The parrot squawked again, this time with perfect timing, "bugger me, bugger me, there's Wellington."

Laughter erupted once more, rolling through the stable like a tide.

But Archie's attention had shifted. As the introductions were made, he had noticed the missing clump of hair from Peter's forehead, consistent with the stories he had been told many, many years ago. He also had a dark, swarthy skin, suggesting a more Mediterranean background. His grip on the young man tightened. Nevertheless, his command of the English language was impeccable. Archie, however, was certain this young man was indeed Pierre, the cabin boy from the shipwrecked galleon Montpelier.

After exchanging pleasantries and introductions, Big Joe mentioned why Archie was keen to meet him and indeed to inform him of a death. It was agreed by everyone that Peter's family go on to church first and then afterwards they would discuss the relevant details. It was, perhaps, fortunate that Joe's premises included a huge garden and stable area, where it was suggested by him that a meeting could take place there. Like most stables around it was untidy and unkempt, nevertheless, it had a certain charm, there was a large rough timber table situated in the middle with empty barrels indiscriminately arranged around. It was warm and dry and was perfectly adequate for the purpose they had in hand. The church bells suddenly rang out again, signalling the service was over.

Peter's wife and their two children went off on their own, leaving Peter and Archie to carry out their conversation. Big Joe, ever the silent observer, once again brought over two tankards of warm beer to his guests, studying the unease behind Peter's eyes respectfully leaving them to their privacy. Both Peter and Archie sat on a barrel and made themselves as comfortable as they could under the circumstances. Both men faced each other across the old table. Curious, they were, but in a relaxed manner.

Peter was the first to speak. "Well, Archie, what news have you for me that is so important." In doing this he rubbed his chin and then drank from the tankard of ale. "I trust it's very important with you, a Scotsman coming all this way." He paused before going on, "From Edinburgh, isn't it?" He asked the question with an air of curiosity and wonder.

Archie didn't answer immediately. Instead, he mirrored Peter's gesture. The silence between them stretched like a drawn bowstring. He took a large drink from his cup and with measured words said, "Father Bartholomew is dead."

Archie then fell silent, to let Peter gather his thoughts and wait for his response. He noticed the genuine sadness in Peter's eyes but no real sense of emotion, which did surprise Archie, he seemed too composed for genuine grief.

Peter eventually gathered his thoughts, "Did he say anything?" Peter asked, "this monk, Father Bartholomew."

"Like what?" Archie asked, "Did you expect him to say anything?"

Peter, surprised at Archies quick response, gulped slightly. "No, not at all, I just wondered."

The silence returned, thick and pressing. Archie leaned forward studying Peter's every move. Then, in a voice as precise as a blade, he spoke.

Archie playing with his tankard turned it around playfully to face Peter almost spilling its contents, his huge hands grasping hold of his precious ale. He looked Peter straight in the eyes. "He did say one thing Peter which was very interesting." Peter's fingers twitched, betraying the anxiety behind his otherwise impassive demeanour.

Archie did not look away. "He did say, for instance, you were Pierre the cabin boy from the ship Montpelier. "Archie's voice was steady, deliberate. "You were not Peter as you now claim to be." He took his eyes from his ale for a moment. He slowly and deliberately looked into and almost through the eyes of Peter, such was the intensity of Archie's stare.

Peter exhaled sharply, as if some unseen weight had just landed on his chest. Slowly, he brought his hands to his face, rubbing his temples, before letting them drop to the table. "Yes." he whispered, his voice barely audible. "That's me right enough."

The confession hung in the air like a ghost.

After a moment, Peter looked up, his expression shifting from shock to something else – curiosity. "So," he asked cautiously, "what else do you want to know? And more importantly, who are you and what interest could a Scotsman have with the fate of a French cabin boy?"

Archie took his time before responding. He leaned back slightly, letting Peter stew in his own questions. Then, at last, he said, "My full name is Archie McPherson. I come from Edinburgh. And I serve Artois Marcel, Count of Montpellier."

Peter stiffened.

Archie pressed on. "Nearly twenty years ago, the Count tasked me with uncovering the truth about his family – his son Jon Marcel, his wife Eleonore, and the ill-fated ship Montpelier." He narrowed his eyes. "You see, Jon Marcel was heir to the Montpellier throne. As of today – I am still searching for answers.

Peter was shocked, remaining silent, his face pale. The storm had arrived and there was no escaping it.

"Ask of me what you will. It is a nightmare I have carried for twenty years, and I need to tell everyone the sadness and despondency I have endured."

Archie's stomach tightened. Something in Peter's tone sent a ripple of unease through their conversation. Archie nodded at first and took out some notes he had written down previously which needed clarification. In doing so he removed his copy of the Northern Press article and threw it on the rough-hewn table. It seemed innocuous at this moment in time, Peter, although looking fully compos mentis was literally miles away and staring into Archie's eyes with a glazed expression. Archie however, wasted no time, he wanted to know everything, no matter how unimportant, he wanted to know every little detail. He went on, "How do you know if Captain Jon Marcel and his wife died. Did you see them die?"

"Yes, I was with them both as they took their very last breaths," said Peter, distressed but very relieved. "I couldn't save them or help them though, "he went on.

Archie gently interrupted Peter. "So, let's get this straight. Out of all the crew and people on board you were the only survivor on the night of the shipwreck. No-one else, mind, just you." Peter took an unusually long breath before answering.

His voice just above a whisper, "No, there was another," he paused for a moment, "there was another survivor." Peter was undeniably upset and struggling to come to terms with his replies.

Nothing was now making sense. Even Archie, normally a calm, cool investigator was showing signs of inward panic he couldn't explain, "But how is that possible, Peter?" Archie asked, "everyone on board was accounted for, you agreed with that yourself." Peter was nodding the whole time. "The official report you and the authorities went over and over, you yourself agreed to it and signed it as God was your witness," he said.

Peter took another huge sigh and covered his eyes with his hands, only this time tears could be seen running through his fingers and down his face. Suddenly he blurted out. "There was a baby, a baby girl," Voices were now beginning to be raised.

"What do you mean a baby girl?" Archie shouted out, very loudly The extra volume in the discussions alerted Big Joe to come towards the table. "What the hell's happening? What's going on?"

Archie temporarily stood up and shook his head, he hadn't regained his own composure yet, his mind was reeling with thoughts and possibilities. He suddenly leaned over the table towards Peter and gently removed his fingers from his eyes and asked, "Who was this child and where is it now?"

Peter squeezed Archie's hands before responding, "The child was the daughter of the Captain, Jon and his wife Eleonore. She was only three weeks old and was actually born on board. I was there at the birth."

Archie interrupted him again, "and yet, nobody on board knew anything about her, is that what you are trying to tell me?" He was puzzled to say the least.

"No quite the opposite," Peter said, "the child was supposed to be a surprise once we reached Edinburgh. The Count and Countess were not to find out."

A cold dread coiled in Archie's stomach.

Archie exhaled in exasperation and turned to look at Joe who,was staring with wide uncomprehending eyes. He then turned to Peter, "Well, we all know now Peter but only you know what happened to her." His voice dropped to a whisper. "She can't be alive. Not after all this time." Peter hesitated. A war raged behind his eyes. "Probably not." he admitted, "but I don't know for sure, she was still alive when the ship sank."

There was a silence. Heavy suffocating silence, broken only by the rhythmic hissing of the bellows.

Big Joe shifted uneasily, then almost absent mindedly – reached for the newspaper Archie had tossed aside, his fingers tightened around its edges, knuckles whitening.

Archie wasn't done. He couldn't be done. "So?" he pressed. "Did the baby survive? What happened Peter? Did she drown? Was she lost to the sea? Did she have any food, clothes, identification?"

Peter wiped at his tear-streaked face. "We placed her in a wine barrel, she had food and clothes and a coin or medallion of sorts which would identify her, "he admitted "It was the only chance she had. We sent it out to sea, hoping – praying – that someone would find her." He looked up, eyes pleading for understanding. "I was only twelve, Archie. I didn't know what else to do."

Archie's grip on Peter's wrist tightened. "And the barrel? Did it sink?"

Peter shook his head. "No. It floated away, drifted more like into the unknown. I had promised him I would look out for her if I could."

A sharp intake of breath left Peter exhausted when Big Joe interrupted. "A bit like this girl?"

His voice cut through the room like a blade. Archie nodded sharply. "What?"

Joe held up the newspaper. His fingers ran over the bold black headline. "The girl," he said slowly, as if tasting the words. "The girl found in a barrel at Trow Rocks."

Archie snatched the paper from his hands, scanning the article with fevered eyes, his head banging like war drums."

Petere's breath hitched. "What, what story is that?"

Archie's voice was hoarse, barely above a whisper. "She was found 24 hours after the shipwreck." He met Peter's eyes, the weight of realization slamming into him like a freight train.

"But no-one made the connection." A pause, a shift in the air.

"Not until now that is."

Peter hands trembled as he snatched at the newspaper, his pulse hammering in his ears. Could it be, could it really be Auriel Celeste, the daughter of his captain and Lady Eleonore. If this was the infant, he was duty bound to find and return her to her rightful family, who could, in fact, be the legitimate heir to the throne of Montpellier. A wave of disbelief crashed over him. Could this really be the lost infant.

For a moment, Peter couldn't breathe. He just sat there in a world of his own.

And then – laughter. ~~~A raw, unfiltered burst of it, rising from somewhere deep inside him. He wanted to shout. To embrace someone –anyone. The tears came fast, hot and unchecked. His body moved before his mind could process, seizing the nearest person Big Joe. He danced and pranced around the stable yard, tripping over all manner of debris, horseshoes, discarded tools and broken iron scraps He didn't care. Nothing else mattered.

"She's alive. He shouted, "she's alive." He grabbed hold of Archie's collar and pulled him close, "The Count Archie, The Count he must know he has a granddaughter."

Archie's face remained steady, but his eyes darkened with thought. "And so, he shall," agreed Archie, "once we confirm the evidence."

Peter just nodded, his chest still heaving with exhilaration. "There was a note," he blurted," left with her. And a medal, that will prove who she is."

We must go and see her," Archie replied, "immediately."

At that moment, Peter's wife and children returned from church, blissfully unaware of the recent proceedings. "What's up Peter, have you had one of your nightmares again?"

Peter turned, grasping her shoulders gently, his voice steadier now, but still thick with emotion. "No, Patricia," Peter answered, "No, not this time, I've had all my dreams come true," A long silence ensued. He could see the questions in her eyes. But there was no time to explain, not yet.

"You are going to have to trust me," Peter said, "but all will be revealed, I promise, you'll understand everything."

He took a moment to thank Big Joe before turning to face Archie. His pulse quickened again, the weight of destiny pressing down on him. "Well big man, Mr. McPherson, are you ready? Shall we go and find this girl in the barrel, the Countess of Montpellier.

Archie lips curled into a slow, knowing grin. "Indeed, we shall Peter Bartholomew," he murmured. "Indeed, we shall."

CHAPTER 29

Montpellier simmered beneath a veil of tension. Within the cold stone walls of the Chateau D'Artois, Count Artois and his wife Celeste sat cloaked in silence, shadows dancing across their faces as the sun dipped behind the vineyards. Time was slipping through their fingers – days, maybe weeks, before the weight of the crown would pass to a man Artois barely trusted, and certainly didn't love: his cousin Francois. Known across the region by a name that sent chills through servants and noblemen alike, The Blackheart.

Artois stared out through the arched window, his voice barely louder than the wind brushing against the panes "We don't have long, Celeste." He paused, the words fighting their way out. "The abdication will be forced soon and with no heir – the law is clear." The law had decreed with the absence of any direct family the existing position of Count and Countess and their future destiny must be handed over to his cousin Francois. Artois went on, "We must discuss the future, like it or not."

Naturally everyone knew all that was happening but felt compelled to discuss every detail daily, however painful and distressing it was to do so. Artois's cousin Francois was now back in Montpellier in readiness for what he thought was his expected coronation. To help him achieve his aims he brought with him a substantial number of soldiers and personal guardsmen, a garrison all ready for action, if need be. Artois and Francois were still on speaking terms although neither agree with the other on anything, in fact, they had nothing in common other than the throne itself.

Celeste said nothing at first. The name of their long-lost son hung between them like a ghost. The silence ached. "It should have never come to this. It could have been so different, if only our son Jon had survived the terrible shipwreck," speaking through her tears she added, "but, alas, it was not to be." Her words trailed off, lost to grief.

Artois just nodded; no words were necessary as the same thoughts had passed through his mind a million times. Unfortunately, acceptance of their fate was all they had left.

Outside, the golden rows of vines shimmered in the fading light, beautiful and oblivious to the tragedy within. Inside the silence thickened, until it was broken by the trembling chink of porcelain on silver. A servant, young and visibly shaken, stepped into the chamber. His tray rattled in his hands, though he tried valiantly to steady it. "Begging your pardon, your Excellencies but this is my first day here and truthfully I am nervous." As he poured out the wine saying, "I do hope you will forgive me." The two just smiled as they understood why a young man would feel that way, in fairness it gave them time to observe the server.

Artois regarded him with curious detachment. The boy's accent betrayed his origin. "You aren't from Montpellier then?" he asked. "Nor even France I'd wager."

"No, your excellency," he said, "I originate from Tunisia, from the same town as Mr. Aziz as a matter of fact."

The name stirred something in Artois. Medhi Aziz – trusted steward, loyal to the family for years. "Good man," he murmured, "you'd do well to follow his example."

Even as he said it, Artois's gaze drifted. He was already somewhere else, mentally pacing a path of regrets and impossible alternatives.

Then it happened.

The young servant was preparing to leave the sophisticated ambience of the inner quarters of the Palace, when there was a burst of chaos outside the chamber doors and suddenly the air was charged. The doors flung open, the guards lunging forward, pikes crossing with lethal precision to bar the entrance.

And yet the man who'd forced his way inside did not flinch. Medhi Aziz.

Dishevelled, breathless, eyes wide with urgency. Clutched in his hand a scrap of parchment, tightly rolled, no more than two inches long. His presence was a violation of protocol, but the desperation on his face overrode every law of etiquette.

"Hold," Artois commanded, his voice slicing through the tension like a blade. "Let him through. I trust this man."

The two guards let go of Medhi's tunic and allowed him to proceed.

"What news could possibly warrant this intrusion?" the Count demanded, though weariness dulled his tone. "I warn you Medhi … I can bear no more."

Medhi didn't kneel. Didn't bow. He simply stepped forward and extended the parchment.

"It's a message, sir," Medhi blurted out, "a message from Archie McPherson." The name cracked through the chamber like thunder.

Celeste's hand shot to her mouth. Artois froze. Outside, the wind whipped against the old stone walls of the chateau as though the past itself was clawing to get in.

Archie McPherson had been presumed dead for years.

And if this message was real everything was about to change.

Artois answered, “From Archie McPherson, you say?” Artois’s voice cracked like a whip through the chamber. His brow furrowed, eyes darkening with urgency. “Well, what does it say man? Read it out.” said an extremely frustrated Artois.

Medhi froze.

His eyes flickered to the corners of the room, the two guards at attention, the young Tunisian waiter still stiff with nerves, his tray forgotten.

“I, I can’t, sir,” he said stumbling slightly as he shifted his weight. “Not with other people in the room.”

“Then hand the note to me and I’ll read it myself,” said an agitated Artois. Medhi didn’t move.

Medhi, once again looked around the room. “I can’t even do that,” he admitted, voice low but steady. “It’s in code, you see,” he went on. “It’s a cipher developed by Archie and me many, many years ago in case circumstances such as these ever arose.”

For a moment, the silence pulsed with suspicion. Then Artois gave a curt nod. “Everyone out.” He ordered sharply. “Leave us. All of you, except the countess.”

The room emptied like a tide retreating, the door shutting with a final, echoing thud behind the last guard. In the quiet that followed, the only sound was the ticking of the old brass clock and Celeste’s unsteady breathing.

“Right then,” he looked at Medhi, “what’s the message, can we now proceed please.”

The Count, although agitated, was strangely also excited although he admitted he didn’t know why he should be, an ember of hope perhaps fighting its way through years of disappointment.

Medhi explained. The message came from Archie's own pigeon," He went on to explain, he used it to send messages very quickly over huge stretches of land and sea.

"Yes, yes, yes," interrupted Artois, "I understand all that, but what does it say?" He was now becoming even more agitated.

Medhi moved to the marble table, unfurling the tiny note with careful precision. He gently pushed aside a half-finished glass of Bordeaux and flattened the parchment against the stone. He stared at it for a long moment before speaking. "Archie says," he paused for a moment, "Archie says," he emphasised once more he looked up from the note looking at Artois and his wife, "You and Celeste have, in fact, a granddaughter," before anyone could interrupt, he went on, "and she's alive and well and living in England."

Time stopped.

The words seemed to hang in the air like smoke. For several seconds, neither Artois nor Celeste moved. Their expressions were blank, shocked into stillness. Then slowly, Celeste began to shake her head, her lips moving in a silent prayer, her hands trembling over her mouth.

Medhi made use of the silence. "Apparently," he said, "she is the daughter of your son Captain Jon Marcel and his wife Eleanore. Your grandchild was only weeks old when the ship, the Montpelier sank." He paused once again and said quietly "That was twenty years ago." Medhi then ceased speaking to let his words sink in.

Artois took hold of his wife's hand, his void crumpled and cracked, "How does Archie know this? How can this possibly be true," he whispered, gripping Celeste's hand as though it were the only thing anchoring him to reality.

Medhi recomposed himself and slowly began to explain the situation." There was only one survivor that night aboard ship, or so we were told," he then went on, "the cabin boy. Of course we are not aware of the details yet"

"Yes, that's right," said Artois, gathering his thoughts, "Pierre I believe he was called; I met him once here in the palace before they set sail --- twenty years ago."

Medhi nodded in agreement. "Well. As it happens, your son's wife Eleonore gave birth to a daughter only weeks before the sinking of the Montpelier. The situation was desperate and to save the child's life they agreed with the help of Pierre to put the child in a wine barrel, sealed it, and cast it into the sea, hoping it might stay afloat long enough to reach safety. Pierre has now admitted this."

By this time, the Countess Celeste, although listening intently was covering her face with her hands and mumbling, "Please God, let it be true," repeatedly.

Medhi paused and began shaking his head in almost disbelief himself. "I've seen the child, Your Excellency. With my own eyes. She's still alive and thriving."

"No!" Artois barked, his voice cutting the room in half. "No, how can that possibly be true? Why didn't Archie tell me this in his reports? Why has Pierre not contacted me?"

"Because" answered Medhi, "at the time, no-one could associate the girl found in a barrel with the actual shipwreck --- not until now that is."

"Who else knows about this?" demanded Artois, "if this message is, indeed true, not only do we have a granddaughter," grasping his wife's hand as he said so, "we also have the legitimate heir to the Montpellier kingdom of France, an undisputed heir at that."

The air in the chamber had transformed.

Moments ago, it was heavy with the weight of mourning. Now it buzzed with something else, electric excitement. Joy. Disbelief. Hope.

Count Artois, Celeste, and Medhi embraced without hesitation, without concern for rank or decorum. For the first time in years they laughed, eyes bright with something long forgotten. But now a glimmer of hope shone.

Then without warning, The Count's expression changed. The smile vanished. His voice dropped low, measured, precise. "We must keep this to ourselves, for now."

Medhi blinked, the joy in his chest suddenly tempered.

Artois continued, eyes scanning the room as if shadows might be listening. "Francois cannot know, not a word. No announcements. No celebrations. Not yet."

He stepped forward, placing a firm hand on Medhi's shoulder. "I want you to send a message to Archie. Thank him, but more importantly, tell him to bring the girl. Bring her here. The abdication is scheduled for July 29th at noon. We have less than three weeks." He paused, his eyes narrowing. "We haven't a moment to lose."

The mood remained buoyant but now underpinned with urgency. It was joy laced with adrenaline.

Without a word, Medhi rushed to the massive oak doors and pushed them open. He was gone in seconds, his footsteps echoing through the marble halls as he sprinted towards the stables.

Outside, the sun had reached its peak, bathing the courtyard in golden light. Montpellier's warmth was unforgiving, and by the time Medhi reached the stables, sweat clung to every thread of his linen shirt.

He skidded to a halt before a narrow stone turret where the pigeon keeper lived.

"Louis!" he shouted, voice hoarse. "Louis, come down! I have urgent need of your services."

From the top window, a bald head appeared, half-shrouded in the white splattering's of his profession.

"Medhi?" he called down, blinking through the haze. "What in god's name are you after?"

"No time!" Medhi cut in. "Urgent dispatch. It must go now. The fastest bird you've got."

Together, they composed a message. A brief coded note. Just like the old days. Only Archie would understand it.

When the parchment was secured to the bird's leg Medhi locked eyes with the old man. "This must reach him, no delays, and no-one, not a soul, can know."

Louis gave a solemn nod. In his world secrets were sacred.

The pigeon burst into the sky seconds later, slicing through the bright air like a bullet. It was gone before Louis could speak again.

Medhi wasted no time. He turned on his heel and ran back towards the palace. Back to the storm that was building.

That evening the atmosphere was almost celebratory. Quiet toasts were raised, plans were drawn.

Medhi would leave by sunrise with twenty hand-picked guardsmen, loyal, discreet, battle tested. They would intercept Archie and escort the girl home. The rendezvous was set just outside Paris, in one week.

In their elation no-one noticed the quiet figure moving silently through the hallways. The young Tunisian servant.

His face was blank. His movements efficient. To the untrained eye, he was invisible. But he had heard everything.

That night, under cover of moonlight, he slipped out through the back gates of the palace, disappearing into the narrow alleys of Montpellier's old quarter towards the encampment of Francois.

By dawn the message had been delivered. The Tunisian servant of Count Artois was indeed a spy planted by Francois himself to gain information – any information.

Francois's reaction was immediate and terrifying. He read the report in silence, his every muscle in his face locked with tension. Then he stood, slammed a goblet of wine against the wall and turned to his captain, his ever-present companion.

"There's an heir." He growled. "A legitimate heir." His voice was venom. "She cannot be allowed to reach Montpellier." The room fell silent. Francois stepped closer to his captain, his voice dropping to a whisper. "Send twenty men, --- no send forty. Elite.

Silent. Lethal. I want them en-route before sunset." He turned to the window, his eyes narrowing on the horizon. "If she arrives," he said coldly, "we lose everything." Then, almost as an afterthought he added coldly, "Do whatever must be done. The girl does not return alive." He lifted his eyes once more and said, "You understand?"

And just like that, the race had begun. Two forces. Two destinies. One throne. And only one would reach Montpellier in time.

CHAPTER 30

Northumberland, England – 9.17 a.m.

The old stone cottage sat crouched on the edge of the beach, its walls whispering stories no one had heard in decades. Florrie stood at the threshold, fingers tightening on the rusted iron latch, her breath fogging in the cool morning air. She had made her decision.

She was moving back in.

It hadn't been part of the plan originally; the place was to be sold. But the house, hand built by her late husband Anders, had other intentions. Its walls held not just memories, but echoes. And today, it would host something far greater than nostalgia, the return of her granddaughter, Celia.

Celia the girl who had vanished into the folds of the Royal Navy two years ago, shrouded in secrets and silence, was finally coming home. And this homecoming, Florrie decided, would not go unnoticed.

She cast her eyes around the room. "The party has to be here." She said aloud, sweeping dust away from the mantle with the back of her hand. "No other place would do."

Mary, her lifelong friend, came over the stone step struggling to carry a barrel of ale, the weight of it etched across her face. "What do you think, Mary, is the cottage big enough, or should we try somewhere else?" she asked her friend in all honesty. She smiled faintly, but the edge of uncertainty still clung to her. The fire hadn't been lit in years. As she knelt to strike a match the flames sparked with more than just kindling, they awakened the room.

Mary was listening but passed off the remark as totally irrelevant, "Of course it's big enough, Florrie, you worry too much, you do," she replied, pointing her finger at her, "always have." Mary then smiled. She had known Florrie for most of her life and they were real friends, inseparable really. "Here Florrie," she ordered, "give me a hand with this, we've no men left in our lives now," she said breathlessly, and with this last remark, winked at her friend. There was an air of inevitability about it all. Florrie had begun washing down the hearth after she had just settled the fire. "Men," she gasped, "no use for them Mary, I'm afraid." They both laughed. "Except for my two sons of course," she said as she picked up the shiny black pebble sitting on the mantle, small, unassuming but smooth as glass, given to her by Amos some twenty years ago. A symbol of something unfinished. Something quietly powerful.

"Still got that thing," Mary muttered catching sight of it, "Should have thrown it out years ago."

They both grasped hold of the barrel and lifted it on to the table. Florrie was way out of breath; she lay forward onto the table slightly. "No, Mary," she answered rather seriously, "that pebble is a constant reminder of my life here. Anders, the kids and, of course, Celia. She arrived here on the very day I received this you know," she said to Mary glancing round to catch a glimpse of her friend.

Mary's expression shifted – nostalgic but guarded. "Aye, I forgot about that Florrie," she said, "precious memories they were, all right. She paused for a while. "For our Becky as well mind, --- she had a say in Celia's upbringing when you couldn't be there."

Silence fell between them. Outside, the wind moaned across the sea like a mourning bell.

"Eeh aye," Florrie said, remembering the occasion with fondness. "Is she coming this afternoon, Mary? I hope so." Her request was full of anticipation.

Mary was busy fastening her apron when she replied, her movements brisk but careful. "She'll be here, don't worry about that, with Charley and the bairn, of course."

Florrie nodded in excited appreciation, she liked Charley and Becky and besides all were welcome that day. A sense of momentum was building. As if this day, this gathering, might unlock something long dormant.

Mary, who had now sorted herself out, was just standing beside the large wooden table, stacked with pies and cakes – culinary offerings to a homecoming goddess. "So, who is coming exactly? We aren't feeding the entire village, I hope." She laughed more in anticipation and desperation than anything else.

"Why of course not," Florrie answered quickly, "it's just a small gathering of friends and family who want to see our Celia again. Even Billy Burns is coming."

Mary was shocked and interrupted. "He isn't on duty I hope." She paused, "not with your Amos being here as well."

Florrie laughed, the sound of her voice uncertain, like a match trying to strike in wind. She went on, "No, he's not on duty, anyway he's bringing his wife Dotty with him" She looked straight into Mary's eyes.

And just like that, the temperature in the room seemed to drop a few degrees.

" Dotty," muttered Mary, all warmth and smiles vanishing from her face, "stuck up cow, don't like her one bit, --- never have, miserable old git."

"Ah she's alright Mary, once you get to know her," said a slightly disappointed Florrie. "Besides, the day's about Celia coming home and nothing else, certainly not about Billy's wife Dotty."

Mary, looked at her friend, measuring her words. "That girl's been gone a long time, Florrie. People change. They come back – different."

Outside, a gull shrieked across the sky like an omen. Inside, the black stone gleamed in the firelight, quiet, cold. And waiting.

The two women spent the next couple of hours preparing for the impromptu get together. Around mid-afternoon, everything that needed sorted was done. The two women seemed pleased with their day's work.

The sky held, just barely.

"The weather's kept canny mind, certainly better than yesterday at least," said Florrie, her voice low but steady.

Mary didn't answer right away. Her eyes flicked to the horizon scanning the line where the sea met sky, it was fine she admitted to Florrie, but she'd lived on this coast too long not to notice the signs. Clouds were gathering, that was always a worry on the Northeast coast. "It's fine for now," she mumbled.

"Well, another good thing," added Florrie, "it's not windy, you know how much I hate the wind."

Mary understood that last remark as both ladies had spent most of their lives outside due to their occupation and because of this had almost become experts at weather forecasting. Wind was always the enemy, more than rain, more than cold. Wind could turn a good day to disaster in minutes.

"Come on then," Florrie said, brushing imaginary dust from her skirt. "Let's go back inside, Celia will be here very soon with Fiona and the Reverend, and you know those two. Never late."

However, they were not the first to arrive. This time, Amos and his slightly grimy and enigmatic friend Gunpowder Bob had the honour of that distinction.

"Hiya Ma," said Amos enthusiastically, flinging his arms around his mother as he greeted her, "We've got some Portuguese wine for you." Saying this, he looked very pleased with himself.

"It's not pinched, I hope." Florrie asked with a face covered in anxiety and worry.

"Of course it isn't," Amos pulled a mock-offended face as he looked to Bob to give him some sort of back-up, none was forthcoming, however.

"Not on a day like this, Ma," he blurted out. He paused for a moment before laying the wine on the table. "Where is she anyway? She hasn't done off again, has she?" He laughed.

Florrie and Mary both looked agitated. "Don't say that Amos, even in fun. We couldn't go through that again." Florrie appeared to be visibly shocked by Amos's remarks.

Amos though, had already moved on, his laughter rang out light and careless, it meant nothing to him and even less to his friend Bob, they were there to have a good time.

Just then there was another knock on the cottage door, this one more precise. The door opened. And the whole atmosphere of the room changed.

In walked Celia, and for a moment, it was as if the cottage itself paused to remember. Celia now radiated a quiet power. Fiona and the Reverend Tobias followed closely behind.

Amos stared. Florrie and Mary just … looked. As if taking in a vision they couldn't comprehend.

Gone were the boyish looks she had to have during her stay in the Navy, there were no dishevelled clothes, scruffy shoes or anything to suggest she had lived the last couple of years in a rough environment as a boy. Her hair, although still short was golden and seemed to radiate light, her skin, although on the dark side gave off a porcelain appearance, perfect in every way, seemingly sculpted. Amos couldn't take his eyes off her, she was so elegant and beautiful.

Florrie and Mary at first just stared at this beautiful young lady before them. Instinctively, they took hold of each other as though watching a parade and marvelled at Celia's presence. It was a few moments before anyone spoke which strangely in turn prompted Celia to give out a nervous laugh as she awaited someone speaking.

"Sorry, our Celia, sorry, you just look so wonderful, you really do and it's marvellous to have you back, bloody marvellous," she grinned. With that she rushed over to her granddaughter and almost crushed the life out of her, such was her joy at having her back. "Enough of all that. Now, let's start celebrating." Celia laughed, returning the embrace.

Over the next couple of hours everyone Florrie had invited had arrived, naturally of course, a few uninvited ones too, but they were also made welcome. The day was going along nicely with even Amos and PC Burns seeming to have reached a truce.

It was rather strange, throughout it all though, members of the family and guests and various friends would momentarily stop what they were doing for no reason and appeared to stare at Celia, such was her charisma and beauty, she was the axis, as if she drew the air toward her. It was strange, really, that every time someone stared at her it prompted Florrie, Becky and Mary to nudge each other. As far as they were concerned Celia was theirs and they were so proud of her. Time was getting on now and apart from the immediate family most of the guests had left. Billy Burns was still there although Dotty, his wife, had opted to leave a couple of hours earlier, which pleased Mary more than she was willing to admit.

The wind outside shifted. Subtle, but unmistakable. Florrie noticed it first. She went to the hearth, crouching low to poke at the fire. Her hands moved fast and practised, muttering old words to the flames.

Then – a knock. Quiet, deliberate.

"See who that is will you Mary," she asked, "there's always one who doesn't make it on time."

Mary stood. Her hand met the latch, her boot gave the door its usual nudge. It swung open.

It was Archie McPherson and a stranger. And the room held its breath.

CHAPTER 31

"Hello, Archie," Florrie's voice cracked through the warmth in the room like a whip. Her eyes flicked to the clock. "I didn't even think you were coming, you're a bit late I must say." She looked back into the cottage. "I don't think there's much beer left either, although there might be a pork pie." Her laughter was dry, amused only by her own sarcasm.

Archie grinned as he knew all about Florrie's wit and happy demeanour. He removed his bonnet with a casual ease. He stepped inside, motioning to the doorway behind him. "I've brought a young gentleman with me, from Wylam." His voice was quieter now, almost reverent, Archie said gently pushing forward his nervous friend. With his hand still on his shoulder he went on, "He has something to say to all of you, to all of us."

He gave the boy a firm but gentle nudge forward now.

Peter who was thin and pale was visibly trembling; he clung to the brim of his wellworn hat like it was a lifeline. Archie looked around the room, glancing from face to face. "Is the wee lassie Celia not here then?" asked a puzzled Archie. He paused for a few seconds, "It's her we came to see," adding quickly, "especially Peter. In saying so he gently put his arm around Peter's slim shoulder as he attempted to reassure him.

The room stiffened. "Oh? and what has our Celia got to do with him then?" Her tone carried suspicion, and she eyed Peter with the scrutiny of someone who'd buried more secrets than most had heard.

Peter attempted to speak but Florrie's hand was already in the air.

"Save it." She squinted at him, and something in his face softened her just slightly. "If you're with Archie. That counts for something."

She turned, her voice booming, "Celia!" she shouted through, "there's a handsome young gentleman here wanting to see you." She laughed and added, "He's no prince charming though," she added quietly.

Peter was now standing awkwardly alone on the threshold, the wind still pulling on his coat. He gripped his rather well-worn hat a little tighter and carried on speaking. "I think – I think I may have news for her," he spoke mostly to the floor. "At least Archie and I think I might have. We're not sure."

Archie nodded his head in agreement and said, "It's worth hearing."

Florrie sighed and shouted out. "Celia, can you come through please, and stop dawdling."

A rustle, then footsteps before Celia appeared from the back room, ducking slightly as she entered and Peter froze.

"I'm coming Grandma, keep your hair on."

Florrie looked at her granddaughter with a look of distain, "Never mind all that, get yourself in here."

As she entered, Peter just stood there, silent and unmoving, staring as though at something divine.

Florrie was watching these proceedings with interest. "What's wrong with him?" she asked Archie. "He looks like he's seen a ghost or struck dumb."

Archie said nothing at this time, he was just as silent as Peter and apparently answered Florrie with just a shake of his head, no words were forthcoming.

"What, then?" exclaimed a bemused Celia, lifting both her arms up in frustration. "Who are you, and what do you want?"

Peter, to his credit, managed to retain his composure, grabbing onto Archie for extra support. He finally stepped forward and then surprised everyone present, he dropped to one knee. Tears, real tears began rolling down his face, and with a strong voice she managed to say, "Your majesty, I have found you at long last." His voice sounded cracked like dry ice under pressure. "Can you find it in your heart to forgive me for the long delay?" He then bowed his head down even further, and for a moment there was silence.

Mary blinked. "Is he daft, like?" she hissed. "What's he going on about. Your majesty?" She looked firstly at Celia who was just standing there, her hands trembling. She stared down at the boy kneeling before her, unable to speak.

Archie broke the silence. "He's not daft. And God help us he might be right." "Actually Florrie, Mary, Fiona," he said, "your Celia may well be of royal blood." He quickly went on, "But there's a lot to discuss first."

Confused murmurs rippled through the room like a spreading flame.

This time P.C. Burns interrupted, "Well, that may be, "Bill said, "but who the hell is he?" He was referring to Peter, "and what has he got to do with Celia?"

Everybody still left at the party was now stuck in the small kitchen, all mumbling and buzzing with anticipation. Archie now answered Billy, "This young gentleman we call Peter used to be called Pierre."

"So what?" interrupted Fiona, Celia's adoptive mother.

Archie pulled Peter back to his feet and steadied his companion as best he could. "Pierre here, was the cabin boy of the Montpelier, some twenty years ago." Archie went on to explain. "You know, the shipwreck that happened on the Black Middens." He looked towards Florrie and Mary at this point. "You remember that ladies, don't you?" This time, they said nothing, just nodded in agreement. "Unfortunately, it's going to take some time to fully understand what happened that night, so, I would request your patience and understanding." He tried to take in everybody's eyes and pleaded with them for their support. Each question was answered with honesty and full clarity.

Mary's voice was barely above a whisper now. "You're saying he's that boy that they dragged up to the Priory from the beach?" she queried, "you must have only been about ten."

"I was eleven actually, "Peter answered, "but yes, that was me dragged out of the waves."

"But you supposedly escaped or died, and you certainly weren't seen anymore." She quickly reiterated, "how's that?" She ended her cross-examination abruptly, looking over towards Celia who now was beginning to shake uncontrollably with each question and answer. Florrie also noted Celia's predicament.

"Sit the lass down," Florrie said, "and give her a drink," she ordered anyone who would listen.

Mary then resumed, "If I remember rightly, I saw a half-naked boy getting dragged up the beach that day," she paused again, "that would be you if what you say is true."

Pierre nodded before answering, "Yes, once again, that was me. I escaped into a nearby monastery with the help of Father Bartholomew. My position kept secret for almost seven years."

Mary, at this time felt as though she was Archie McPherson, asking all the right questions, and would only move forward if the questions were answered correctly. "I'm sorry to ask this question," Mary said, "but it is relevant ... could you turn your head around so I could see the other side of your face." Mary was receiving strange looks by now from all present, but Peter turned around anyway and faced Mary. She, at once, immediately saw the patch of scalp where no hair grew, a brutal souvenir from a longforgotten tragedy. "In the name of Jesus," she said, "it really is you, the cabin boy."

There were gasps of amazement from all present in the room. Mary went on, "But even if that is true," she looked at her friend Florrie, "what has that got to do with our Celia here? And how could you possibly know her?"

Eyes turned to Celia, who now stood like glass under pressure, visibly shaking. Florrie took one look and barked, "Someone sit her down again, for God's sake. And pour her a bloody drink."

A ripple of confusion passed through the others.

Billy Burns then joined in the conversation, "That's what I would like to know. What connection could there be."

All eyes were now locked on the hapless Peter or Pierre as he was now known, a figure holding a truth too long buried.

Archie joined in the conversation, "You've got to tell them son," he said, "this is probably the only chance you will have."

Pierre nodded in silence, inhaled slowly, measured. His gaze swept around the room and all eyes were upon him. He paused at Celia, who had stopped shaking, her eyes fixed firmly onto Pierre's, searching.

And then, Pierre spoke.

He explained how the ship, the Montpelier had set sail from Southern France with its cargo of wine and luxury goods on its way to Edinburgh and how the captain Jon Marcel and his wife Eleonore were the rightful heirs to the throne of Montpellier. His voice grew distant, as though he were reliving it.

There were gasps and Florrie reached for Celia's hand.

Pierre explained why they had kept the secret of the child, hoping to protect her from political enemies. They had hopes of a triumphant return. They planned to return home and reclaim their legacy. However, the shipwreck on that fateful night scuppered all their hopes, dreams and plans, it destroyed everything.

The room held its breath as Pierre relived the storm, he explained how his captain Jon Marcel eventually realised all on board would not survive, including of course, the infant child. The captain and his wife made the decision to put their baby in the barrel, seal it, and set it adrift in a last desperate effort. They hoped that someone, anyone ... would find her.

His eyes lingered on Celia. "That child was you."

Whilst he was saying this, he glanced to Celia, Mary, Florrie and Fiona. They all had glazed, disbelieving looks. He went on to say that if the child could be saved and safely returned, the position of Countess of Montpellier would be kept in the original family, indeed the throne of Montpellier would still survive. He gave answers almost before the questions could be asked. There were many more explanations and details that needed clarifying which Pierre answered to everyone's satisfaction. However, there was one question more important than any other which needed answering with honesty and integrity that was from Celia herself.

"So! she said, with an intake of breath," are you actually saying Pierre, you knew my parents?" She looked over to Fiona, "Sorry, Mother, but I need to know." Fiona nodded silently, granting her permission.

"Did you Pierre, speak to them?

"Yes, I did," replied Peter, "and I promised that one day I would find you."

With tears in her eyes Celia responded, "And did they love me?" she asked, "and did they try to save me by putting me in that barrel? Did they care?"

Pierre answered immediately, leaving no room for doubt, "First of all they loved you very much, unreservedly, and Louis and myself, helped Jon and Eleonore to place you in the barrel. The last thing I saw your mother do before we pushed the barrel into the sea was to hug and kiss you and whisper a prayer. She was crying uncontrollably"

The whole room now had a sense of melancholy, sorrow, reverence and revelation all round.

Archie stepped forward. "The barrel washed up on Trow Rocks all those years ago and found by Amos was, we believe, the same barrel."

"Well," interrupted Becky, Mary's sister, "that child could have been anyone, doesn't have to say it had to be Celia."

Upon hearing this Celia jerked her head sideways sharply. "I know it was me," she retorted, "it couldn't have been anyone else, I know it."

Pierre's eyes softened. "If this helps, while I was the cabin boy on board the ship, your mother, the countess, made me feel like part of the family. I adored her, everyone did, she was so beautiful. She was radiant. I could hardly take my eyes off her." He looked at Celia for a few seconds, before going on. "And now, standing here, it's like I'm looking at her again, your mother."

Celia's breath caught. Pierre stepped forward. "The countess," he whispered. "She lives on in you." Now he was gripping both her elbows.

There were no mistaking Pierre's remarks, everyone present fell silent.

P.C. Burns spoke first, voice low and tight. "Well, I'm thinking, can we verify what Pierre's saying?" He sounded deep in thought.

"Aye, like a note maybe," came from a non-family member, who was nevertheless an independent observer, and his suggestion carried weight.

"There is a note, actually," Florrie said quickly, eyes darting to Fiona. "You remember, don't you Fiona, that note?"

Fiona fingers trembled as she took a final sip of wine, she put the glass down clumsily, almost spilling the contents. "Of course I remember," she said, "I carry that around with me, all over, no matter where I am. I never travel without it" Fiona paused before rifling through her bag, finally pulling out a piece of leather, with what looked like a brass button in the middle."

"What's this Fiona, where's the note then?" asked Mary.

"It's inside, concealed within the leather, it's to keep things safe, you know."

Mary harumphed and shook her head, "Aye, that'll be right," she mumbled, Miss Perfect.

Nevertheless, Fiona was very quiet and visibly affected. She turned her attention to Florrie. "Remember Florrie," she went on, "we couldn't quite understand it or read it properly," Florrie nodded her head in acceptance.

"No, we couldn't," she answered," we even tried rubbing it on the slate, didn't we?"

Suddenly, Pierre interrupted at this point and was very serious. "May I see it, Mrs Trevelyan, I know exactly what was written on that piece of paper."

Fiona hesitated only a moment before handing over the now faded piece of paper, it was of course, almost unreadable.

Pierre unfolded the worn scrap. What remained of the ink was almost invisible. His face paled. He looked shocked as he instantly recognised the small and insignificant but very important piece of paper. There were still some letters left on the note, and he began to read out what he could. He looked up briefly. "Well, it's definitely from my captain and his wife." He looked toward Celia. "I know you have taken this name, but your actual name is Auriel Celeste, which means the golden girl, after an ancient Greek goddess who was said to be invincible."

Gasps filled the room. Charley Wilson rose to his feet. "That's, it then! Between your word and that note, what more proof do we need?""

"Nothing, no proof actually," answered Pierre, "and the fact that her grandparents may see a family resemblance once they see her, perhaps. But without the medallion..."

This time Celia interrupted. "Grandparents," she said, "I have grandparents." She turned to face Fiona; she was beaming. "May I see them?" she turned to face Pierre, full of anticipation.

Archie, this time managed to place himself in the middle of the room. Well, it's a good story, right enough, and I personally believe it's true, all of it, but after twenty years there's not a lot to go on legally is there?"

"Perhaps not," said Pierre, "but alongside the note that had been put into the child's clothing there was a gold medallion placed around her neck, an official seal, the Montpellier seal. It is, in fact, the only medallion like it in the entire world, it is unique. It cannot be copied or duplicated in any way. One of a kind." His voice drained away to nothing.

Everyone in the room was now stunned into complete silence. None more so than Celia, but she did eventually speak. "Does it make any difference, "she asked, "if my grandparents believe your story and the note, I am indeed their granddaughter, there's nothing more needed."

"Yes, that's true," answered Pierre, "and I am sure they will be more than pleased with what we have discovered." Pierre went on and asked, "Whereabouts is the medallion now?"

No-one spoke; no-one knew. "Florrie" he queried, "do you know anything of the medallion?"

"Nothing," she answered disappointed, "nothing at all."

"Well, in that case," Celia said realising the inevitable, "I am no more than a possibility," she spoke very quietly, "a nearly person, in fact, not quite there."

Pierre bowed his head. "Without this medallion ... all of this, everything we've said is just a story. Nothing more."

The room fell still, shadows from the fire licking the stone walls, reflecting flickers of disappointment on every face.

"Well," said Mary finally, slapping her knees, "she stays with us then. We are more than happy for her to stay, aren't we Florrie? She's, our Celia."

Pierres tone was solemn. "Without that medallion, all of this ... everything we've said is just a story, conjecture. Nothing more. I'm so sorry. She cannot inherit anything.

Not as Countess of Montpellier."

Fiona gripped Celia's hand. "At least now we know who your parents were. That must be of some comfort, but we must move on."

For a long moment no one spoke.

Archie broke the silence. "Pierre and I regardless, think we should take her to France. She deserves to meet them, and I have given my word to do that."

"If only we had the medallion." Pierre murmured. "It would change everything."

There was an overriding feeling of despair in the room. The flickering flames of the fire, every so often capturing the disappointment in everyone's faces.

Then someone moved at the back of the room.

Amos, who had been sitting in the corner in relative darkness had said nothing previously, suddenly he stood up and walked purposely right into the centre. All eyes were upon him. "Actually Pierre, that may not be entirely true."

"What are you saying," asked Pierre, "what in God's name are you talking about?"

There was silence for a few bone chilling seconds ... the missing medallion." Amos replied.

Pierre tried to interrupt.

"Quiet Pierre, let him have his say." Archie ordered.

"Thank you, Archie "said Amos turning his attention once more to Pierre. "The coin or gold medal," he went on, "I have seen it."

"You've seen it. How have you seen it?" Florrie shouted over everyone.

He put up his hand flat to temporarily silence his mother. "It may not actually be lost or missing, for that matter." All eyes were watching Amos now, which prompted Florrie to intervene once again.

Hands on hips, with an incredulous expression she said, "What could you know, that we don't about the medal?" She adjusted some hair that had fallen around her eyes. "You were only a child when you and Erasmus found the barrel and we all opened it together, you, me, Erasmus and your father. You know that." She pointed at Erasmus. She was beginning to sound frantic. She glanced around the room, and she got the notion people were beginning to feel rather uneasy. Nevertheless, she went back, "There was nothing else in that barrel, just the bairn, the clothes she was wrapped up in and the old note." She turned round to Erasmus. "That's true, isn't it?" she asked.

"I think so, ma" he answered. He looked up to Amos, "but I wasn't the first to see the barrel, was I?" he went on. "Amos was alone with the barrel for a few minutes."

Amos said nothing. Gunpowder Bob, his mate, was just as surprised as everyone else and he knew more than most about Amos.

Without saying anything more Amos went over towards where his mother was sitting. He placed his hand on her shoulder which she instinctively grabbed and pressed hard down onto herself, she said nothing, but inwardly hoped for some miracle.

At this point Mary was lighting as many candles as she could in the room, they needed to see this, everybody did. Strangely then, Amos asked his mother if she would pass her lucky black pebble, her favourite ornament, once of her most treasured gifts.

Pierre, not familiar with the family or their ways demanded to know what was going on. Archie raised his hands slightly with his palm facing straight out to calm things down a little. "Let the lad get on with things, Pierre, I've told you once." he said before turning his attention to Amos. "Carry on son, do what you must. Amos turned again to look at his mother. He couldn't make out if she was in shock, disappointed or just curious, or was she hoping that an answer, at last, could be found. Either way, after twenty years he was about to reveal his secret.

Amos received the pebble from his mother and handled it reverently, before saying, "It's quite heavy, ma, you've polished it so well. It's beautiful."

He stepped forward, placed it on the slate floor. Arranged it just so. "Pass the axe will you Bob," he asked quietly, "the one by the fire." Bob hesitated but handed it over.

Amos looked up at his ma, "I'm so sorry," he said, and with one crushing blow he cracked open the highly polished stone.

Everyone jumped back in shock, gasps erupted. Shards scattered like glass, filling the air with a strange, briny scent – like the sea. And there, gleaming among the fragments, lay a gold coin, in fact, the medallion of the Montpellier dynasty.

Peter lunged forward, lifting it with both hands. Her stared at it as though holding the holy grail, then looked at Celia, who was being comforted by Fiona. "This is it," he said excitedly, "don't you understand, all of you, this is the crest of the Marcel family. The key to the door of the Montpellier dynasty. It's possibly the most important crest of all France;" Pierre was unbelievably excited. Whoever has been given this by the departing heirs automatically becomes the next legitimate ruler of the second greatest family in France.

He turned, his voice rising, trembling with awe. "This is it," he whispered. "The crest of the Marcel line. The seal of Montpellier. The key to it all. The riches, The power."

He turned, voice rising, trembling with awe. "Whoever carries this, becomes the rightful heir. This medallion makes Celia the Countess Celeste of Montpellier. One of the most powerful names in all of France."

Pierre personally and gently removed Fiona's hand from hers. Still on his knees now he said, "Your majesty, your excellency, I am your loyal servant."

Much to the amusement of Florrie and Mary it must be said. But after much nudging and giggling even they knew it was all true.

Celia Trevelyan, the girl in the barrel, the mystery of twenty years, was no more. She was now Auriel Celeste, the daughter of Jon and Eleonore Marcel, the future Countess of Montpellier.

For a moment, time itself seemed to stop.

CHAPTER 32

Archie wasted no time in informing the Count Artois of the most recent developments, and with the help of Pierre they began to prepare to return Celia to her rightful family in France. He was, of course, aware of the dangers they were likely to face along the way. The war between England and France was now over but Archie knew the truth, there were pockets of resistance all over Belgium, France and Spain, with indiscriminate battles breaking out, irrespective of any legitimate reasons. These scattered factions clinging to chaos. Their path would be anything but safe. It was obvious they would need further assistance. Archie wanted reinforcements, maybe from the Count's private guards, but time was slipping away, faster than they could organize.

There was no time to wait. They would have to rely on their own.

"We need volunteers," Archie declared. It was agreed by all in the room.

"There's enough of us here to arrange that," insisted Billy Burns looking around the room. "Who's going to volunteer?"

Every male hand went up. That was expected, but there was a gasp of surprise when they realised Becky Wilson had her hand up too.

A stunned silence fell over the room.

"You can't go, Becky," Billy said, his voice caught somewhere between admiration and disbelief. "It's not practical, even if it is a fine gesture."

"Why not? Becky's eyes locked on his. "I can fight, better than half the men here. Maybe more." There was silence for a few seconds.

Charley, her husband grinned. "She's right. And that's without a weapon." Even P.C. Burns looked rattled. "You're serious," he said, mostly to himself.

More hands followed, Amos, Gunpowder Bob, Erasmus. Both brothers looked at each in appreciation.

Archie counted the hands. "Close, we could do with two more." "You've got me," Charley said.

"And me," shouted Tom, Becky's son. That pleased Archie immensely, especially since Tom was by far the biggest and strongest although the youngest in the group.

Billy nodded, satisfied. "Then we're set."

But the room wasn't finished. "No, you're not," said a strong female voice, "you've forgotten about me, with this many men, and the dangers we're heading into … " her gaze flicked to Celia. "She'll need another woman beside her."

All eyes turned to Becky, she stood there with arms folded defiantly, waiting for a response.

Celia addressed the gathering, "She does have a point, she's right."

Archie didn't respond right away. Then softly, too softly he said, "Then prove it, show us what you can do."

A murmur rippled through the room. Archie reached down, pulled a ceremonial dagger from his boot. Cold steel caught the firelight.

It was said once the dagger was pulled, blood had to be spilled.

He threw it. The blade spun end over end across the slate floor. It skidded to a stop at Bob's feet. Small but deadly.

"Pick it up," Archie said.

Bob hesitated, looking toward his friend Amos. It looked as though Amos he guessed what Archie was up to and nodded his acceptance.

Becky stood calmly beside the hearth. She looked disinterested and detached. Then Bob lunged at her.

Within seconds Bob was at her throat. Easy to get at now she had opened her collar due to the heat in the room. A mad gleam was in Bob's eyes, the crowds froze, not sure if this was theatre or madness.

Virtually a second before he could strike, Becky calmly stood to one side, she put up her left arm as a means of deflection and at the same time crashed a massive, gleaming copper pan down onto Bob's head, knocking him out instantly. Blood sprayed across the slate floor.

There were gasps and screams, but she wasn't finished as she ranged blow after blow on him, kicking him and screaming with frenzied accuracy. Her boot slammed into Bob's ribs, her voice a storm of fury.

"Enough, enough," shouted Archie. "He's had enough.

She stood panting, cheeks flushed, fists clenched, the pan bent in her hand like a war trophy. Charley smiled and turned to Billy, "See what I mean, and she's not even angry yet." Nobody argued with that statement. Archie agreed she had done enough to prove herself. Everyone agreed and there was no option to do otherwise, she was, indeed, capable of looking after herself.

Gunpowder Bob, groaning and bloodied, would later call it the most humbling moment of his life. He too, gave his nod of approval.

Over the following days, they planned, routes, supplies, signals. Every move was accounted for and every risk mapped. What lay ahead would be perilous. Everything had to be agreed to exacting military precision.

But their minds were clear. This wasn't just a rescue. It was war.

To them, this was their Battle of Waterloo, and they would fight it together.

CHAPTER 33

No one doubted the storm was coming. They all felt buzzing beneath their skin like static before a lightning strike, something big was about to happen and they all had to be ready.

The volunteers assembled the next morning, faces drawn and eyes hard. There was no time for ceremony. A leader must be chosen, someone from within and to the acceptance of the majority. Voices clashed in spirited debate until almost unanimously Archie McPherson emerged as the man to guide them through, with Charley Wilson, stoic and sharp-eyed as second in command. It was pleasing to note there was no major discord after the conversations.

Charley spoke first, "I'm sure we all know, before we can proceed, we need money, fast. And where are we most likely to get the money from? "He looked toward Archie for inspiration.

There was an unusual silence for a moment before Archie gave out a gravel sound from his chest before his measured reply. "Whatever we manage to raise," he said, "and by whom," he added quickly. "It would essentially only be a loan." His eyebrows raised. Pausing and with great sincerity he said, "The Count Artios would make sure of that." He then paused once again and turned to face everyone. "You have my full guarantee on that."

There was a wave of appreciation and nods. That was enough.

Finally, after a certain amount of discussion, it was agreed that Celia and Becky were to be given the task of raising the funds. They had less than two days to do so. The room buzzed with restrained energy. There was no time for hesitation, only execution.

Amos and Gunpowder Bob were the obvious recipients to gather up the weapons due to their previous criminal activities. This finally left the tactics and plans down to Archie and Charley, with the welcome help of Charley's stepson Tom. The plan was born from military precision and with a certain amount of desperation. Both things would be needed, plus a slice of good fortune.

Tom leaned over the roughly drawn map, his voice calm but certain. "If we travel as French refugees who are escaping the war-torn areas of Belgium and France, we have a good chance of going unnoticed, we should look no more than common migrants," he added. It was agreed their survival depended on every detail and it had to be perfect.

Archie and Charley had decided between themselves that the task ahead of them would not be easy and the seriousness of the situation was now beginning to sink in. Everyone within the small group knew their place and how important each position was. There would be no room for complacency.

Later that evening, Becky and Celia returned, breathless but triumphant. The Reverend Trevelyan had agreed to lend them the funds, admittedly after some lengthy discussions, Celia reported. There were smiles and handshakes all around the room.

Pierre couldn't hide his happiness and pride at this latest development; it seemed to him that the local community were now fully behind them. At last, he was not alone in his quest or his promise to Captain Marcel. After further negotiations they managed to obtain a covered in cart. It was an ugly old thing and battered, but mechanically sound. At last things were moving along in the right direction.

Momentum within the group was now building. Bob and Amos returned later that evening under the cover of darkness with a crate of unusual weapons, all obtained through their underworld connections. There were two or three pistols, a blunderbuss and various swords and knives along with a long-barrelled musket. All came with the necessary ammunition and tools for the mission.

Celia and Becky took a moment to relax and were enjoying a well-deserved drink when it was suggested they had to make themselves look like a couple of French commoners, unkempt, scruffy and fleeing oppression. Celia enjoyed this task immensely. She blackened her teeth, and somehow made warts appear on her skin. Their beauty disappeared beneath the grime and rags. They virtually became refugees, unkempt, frightened and above all, forgettable.

Pierre had to laugh, "There's one thing certain," he said looking at Celia, "you don't look much like a princess now." His gaze wandering over her.

Celia, at first, just looked at Pierre and then without a moment's hesitation she suddenly gurgled out a substantial amount of mucus from the back of her throat and spat out a collection of green coloured slime in the direction of Pierre and Gunpowder Bob followed by a volley of brutal French curses that sent Bob into fits of laughter and Pierre into stunned silence. Apparently, it had been discussed by Archie and Charley, the last thing they wanted was two attractive ladies within their group as they travelled through France. Celia's actions in the last few moments seemed to convince everyone, this part, in fact, would not be a problem; they were warriors in disguise.

In the meantime two strong horses were also acquired from the nearby farm at Whitburn. While Amos, Florrie's eldest son, was given the task to obtain a boat for their passage across the Channel. He readily accepted and vanished into the night, full of youthful enthusiasm and expectation.

The countdown had begun. Everything depended on the next 48 hours.

A carrier pigeon arrived just before midnight. Its talons clutched a roll of parchment sealed in dark wax. Archie unfastened it with practiced fingers, his eyes scanning the words with growing urgency.

Count Artois had written again.

'*Medhi awaits at the southern perimeter of Paris.' The note said 'From there, he will guide you to Montpellier. Time is critical. Any delay risks everything.'* It was signed by Artois.

Archie passed the note to Charley, his jaw tightening. Things were now becoming critical, and time was of the essence.

"Ten to twelve days," Charley muttered, calculating. "Even if we plan every move with military precision, that's cutting it close," he ended, with a worrying expression.

"Actually … that may be cutting it too fine," said Pierre, "even if we were to move tonight, I'm not sure we could make it in that time." He glanced over to Archie, "and that's if everything goes to plan," he added. Archie, for once, said nothing other than taking on board his colleagues' comments.

Everyone present was aware that Celia had to be in the palace with the medallion no later than July 29th at twelve noon.

It was now 18th July, and it now became obvious to everyone there wasn't a moment to lose.

Meanwhile further up the coast, nearer Marsden, Amos was totally oblivious to the new conversations, he was inside Jack the Blaster's hollowed out cave. He laughed loudly, slamming his mug on the warped oak table planning for the hire of a boat with his old friend and accomplice Jack the Blaster. To be honest there was more drink flying around than any negotiations. Their talks had been going for about six hours with no real urgency, not from either man.

The door suddenly exploded open. Erasmus burst into the room and sweating profusely, having ran the length of the beach. He was completely out of breath. Patrons turned to stare but he had eyes only for Amos.

"Did you manage to get the boat," He asked with a certain amount of desperation. "We're talking about it," replied Amos blinking rapidly.

"Talking? We only have about ten or twelve days, at the most, to reach Montpellier or all is lost. If we fail, all is lost." His expression said it all.

In the meantime, Jack who was listening intently, handed Erasmus a tankard of ale, "Get this down you lad, "he said, "I trust it will make you feel better."

Jack didn't have many visitors, but he was a genial sort of character, around fifty years old, but you couldn't trust him entirely, money was king with Jack, it was said he would do anything for a chance to get some. He didn't have many boats at his disposal, especially at such short notice, but he did have one boat in mind.

Erasmus ignored the tankard of ale, brushing it aside. "What's the fastest vessel you have, capable of getting us to France?"

Jack hesitated for a moment. "There's one a fifty-foot schooner, previously used for the coastal trade and it's very fast." He added, "If I remember correctly, it broke a few records in its day."

Under the circumstances this seemed perfect for the task ahead. It still had all its sails and was still afloat and more to the point it was still available.

Excitedly, Erasmus interrupted, "We'll take it Jack. Give him the money Amos, "he added quickly, "and let's get on with it. When can she sail ...?"

There was silence for a few seconds, "the problem is not the boat Erasmus," Jack said with a sombre stare, "it's been retired over two years now, been in dry dock, so there are no crew available ... just old Seymour, the boat's owner and captain and as you might expect he's quite old now, and almost certainly drunk as we speak, I would wager."

Both brothers now sank down onto their chairs, blowing air out of their cheeks in disappointment.

Erasmus had his head in his hands as Amos now turned to Jack, "We could be the crew, Erasmus and me," said Amos, "and Pierre, he's got experience, we'll make it work."

He looked up at Jack, his eyes full of hope but with little expectation. "We could do it, couldn't we Erasmus?" He looked at his brother as Jack stood there shaking his head, it just seemed too tall an order.

Jack looked at both men before making a statement. "I never thought I was a fool," he said quietly, "but it looks like I am going to be. Meet me at the Shields jetty at eight o clock sharp tomorrow. Bring everything you need ready for departure. We sail with the first tide. I'll convince old Seymour and explain the situation. You may be surprised but he was great mariner." He paused for a few seconds. "Especially when he was sober."

He winked at Erasmus as he spoke, but his eyes betrayed the weight of what they were attempting.

The two brothers wasted no more time. Back at headquarters, amid scattered maps and half-drained bottles Archie and Charley dissected every route, risk and every hour that remained. P.C Burns also added his considerable experience.

The race had begun. The night was a frenzied activity, every detail checked and gone over, everything and everybody agreed they were now ready, and they all relaxed for a few precious moments.

"So, Amos, "Archie asked, "how do we recognise this wee boat of yours?" He lifted his eyebrows. "Has it got a name? "he queried with anticipation.

Amos smirked. "Aye, it's called the Invincible."

Archie stared at him and let out a breathless laugh. "Perfect," he said. "Let's hope the name holds true."

CHAPTER 34

It was 6.30 a.m. The morning light cast long shadows across the worn cobblestones of the Shields jetty. A cold wind whipped in from the North Sea, sharp and foreboding.

The self-formed group of volunteers gathered all the essential belongings for the trip ahead. Bags were slung. Equipment checked and there was tension in the air.

Florrie and Mary were there with them fussing about as usual, with more than a little apprehension.

Florrie's voice cut through the air, "Now make sure you have enough to eat now, our Celia," Florrie said, standing there with her arms folded, "and keep away from all that foreign muck!" she went on. Her friend Mary, silent but equally anxious gravely nodded in agreement.

Celia and Becky nodded and just laughed, as they both knew the other women were naturally worried and it was their way of coping and, of course, showing support.

Celia retorted, "We'll be fine."

But the truth was – no-one knew if they would be.

By 7.30 after some minor mishaps, they made it down to the dock, where they first got a glimpse of the boat they were due to sail on, the Invincible. It wasn't beautiful but it was intact.

Billy Burns, after seeing it for the first time, spoke first. "Got to say my first impression, it looks in good shape." He went on, "It's a lot better than I expected."

Behind him Amos gave a rare smile, for once P.C. Burns acknowledged something he had arranged and it felt good.

The next few hours were spent mechanically loading the equipment they had brought with them onto the boat, with only the cart proving a bit difficult and they solved this by removing the wheels temporarily. They managed to get everything sorted, each person essential, each minute vital, and in no time at all they were ready to set sail.

When the last rope was tied down, Jack the Blaster as he was known, a rough but jovial character, stepped forward to introduce Seymour the ship's owner and captain, he thought him the best damn sailor in the North Sea. He went on to explain why the now retired captain was so excited about this trip and very grateful for the opportunity.

Seymour, standing at the helm only a few feet away, was listening intently. He seemed pleased with Jack's portrayal of him, but Seymour was a fine seaman and captain, he was white-haired, and weather beaten with eyes that scanned the ship like it was an extension of his body. He was more than capable of performing his duties. He wasn't particularly tall, around five foot seven and slightly over-weight. Typical in fact, of a man of seventy years of age, hunched and unshaven. He may have been of a certain age, but his mind was as sharp as ever, he knew the same as everyone else, if he kept off the rum, he would be fine. His presence radiated authority and everyone believed he was born for this.

Later that hour, Seymour interviewed the volunteers for the various crew positions, which were assigned quickly. It was agreed by everyone that Billy Burns and Becky's son Tom would remain on board for the return journey, much to Tom's disappointment, it has to be said, but they both knew the reasons why and accepted the decision.

The tide now, was beginning to change and was on the way out towards the open sea. The lines were released and the foresails were now unfurled like wings and filling up with the following wind. The Invincible was now under way and swiftly heading out of the River Tyne.

Pierre stood alone on the port side. His gaze locking on the Priory at North Shields. He was standing alone and silent, he was in a sombre mood.

Archie, upon seeing this moved slowly toward him and put his hand on his shoulder, "Bringing back memories, eh laddie?" he said quietly.

Pierre paused and nodded.

The calm waters were gently pushing against the ship as she glided past the now submerged Black Middens, the rocks of destruction.

"A far cry from that night," whispered Archie, "but your still here lad to tell the tale, and you've still a lot more to do." He squeezed Pierre's shoulder tightly which prompted him to turn around and face Archie.

"We all have, Archie," he said with determination, "all of us." Again, there was no response, as the two men watched the Tyne disappear and soon the Invincible was making good progress and sailing past the infamous Trow Rocks, where, indeed, the barrel and Celia were found all those years ago. They were leaving the Tyne behind.

There was a good following wind, and Captain Seymour was taking full advantage of the conditions, below decks Charley Wilson and Archie were going over the maps and the time schedules spread on the table which were so important.

It was then they discovered, perhaps landing in Belgium was not their best course of action.

Charley, brow furrowed, went on "I think we should consider moving further South and straight on to France and spend less time on the land, because we risk exposure." He was expressing all his fears; he could visualise all kinds of problems they might encounter.

Archie's thoughts were in full agreement with his shipmate, but it also had to be considered landing in France directly would have problems of its own. Not only dangerous but difficult.

"The French won't take kindly to that Charley," Archie replied, "in fact, they would take great delight in stopping us."

Charley agreed but added "I think we must consider it Archie, or time itself might run out and we would have done all this for nothing."

Both men fell silent for a moment, with only the sound of the North Sea waters splashing against the bow of the ship.

Eventually Archie accepted Charley's proposal on condition that they discuss their thoughts with everyone on board, and in particular of course, the captain, who after all, was in the position of losing everything if things didn't go to plan. They agreed the decision would be the captain's and the captains alone.

Captain Seymour listened to everyone's opinions intently and appreciated, if they bypassed Belgium and went straight on to France the new course would take off a couple of days travel. This, naturally, would be very beneficial to the cause. "It'll cut two days, but we're running blind," he said quietly. He, or Jack the Blaster, knew nothing of the promise Pierre had made to Captain Marcel or indeed the urgency to arrive at their destination any earlier than need be. Pierre recognised this and decided to tell the men everything. Both the men listened intently and without interruption, all this time the ship was speeding along towards to English Channel, with the coast of Belgium in its sights.

Pierre explained everything, his promise to Captain Marcel, the urgency, the stakes.

Captain Seymour spoke first, turning toward his friend Jack, "Well, having listened to that story, I feel we have no option but to carry on to France. It was obvious he was affected and hoping for some support.

Jack didn't hesitate, "Let's do it," he said. He looked up toward the heavens and said, "and may God protect us." The last remark made everyone smile and collectively they agreed. Jack turned to Archie and whispered, "God's protection, perhaps there's hope for us all then, I've never asked for that before." Laughter followed, but it was nervous.

The rest of the day passed without incident. It was decided Le Havre would be the best place to land with its natural harbour and quiet location, less guarded.

The two ladies, Celia and Becky didn't say much at this stage, other than to agree the sooner they landed the better. Soon the Invincible would pass from the English Channel and into French waters. Toward the unknown.

The Invincible was a fine ship and it was gliding through and over the waves toward its destination, its sleek hull skimming the water with a precision that whispered of both elegance and menace. She was a vessel that lived up to her name. ironically the ships name's meaning was the same in both English and French, so it would not gain unnecessary attention.

In a world where identity was often a liability the Invincible was invisible in plain sight.

On the upper deck, Amos and Erasmus, Florrie's sons sat shoulder to shoulder and surprisingly getting on very well, something they hadn't done for a very long time.

Their laughter echoing across the salt-laced wind. It was a rare harmony, almost unnatural. They were, sitting and chatting about nothing, laughing and joking about almost everything, their demeanour hadn't gone unnoticed. A fragile peace, but peace, nonetheless.

"It's strange, isn't it?" said Celia, "just watching them get on like that?"

Becky at first just nodded, she was busy untangling a coil of old rope when she suddenly looked up, "Aye, Florrie would have liked to see this she'd be really proud and so would Anders," she ended, "let's hope they don't kill each other before we reach shore." She grinned, showing all her blackened teeth.

Celia smiled faintly but now turned her attention to Pierre, who up to this point had sat alone, beside a couple of discarded weathered oak casks that had once held wine. He was watching, waiting, thinking.

Celia made her way over to him. "Have you not had your fill of wine barrels, Pierre," she asked, and pausing for a moment went on, "I know I have," she joked. Pierre laughed at the significance of her remark.

Celia hesitated, "What was my father like, Pierre? was he tall, was he handsome and what was my mother like, do I look like her?" Before Pierre could give an answer, she went on, "You see, I know nothing of my family. Nothing." She paused for several seconds before going on, "Was my father a brave person, or just like any other man facing death?" She knew full well this last question would get an honest answer.

He responded immediately, his voice strangely deeper in tone and resolute. His jaw tensed. "He certainly was not a coward or weak, not by any measure," he pointed his finger at Celia and left it there. "Your father was the bravest man I ever knew," he answered with great conviction.

Each word struck like a hammer blow, deliberate and final. He was about to go on when Celia lifted her hand, causing Pierre to pause.

"I know Pierre, I'm only joking," she said, softer now. "I know just how brave he must have been, but truthfully," she was now speaking quietly, "I do need to know everything. I need to know as much of my family as possible and indeed, as much as you know." Pierre was, by now, only too happy to help her and for the next couple of hours Pierre explained to her everything he possibly could, the past, the betrayals, the blood, the names that had been lost and the ones that survived.

As the Invincible glided toward the French coast and Le Havre. Paris, with any luck would be only a day or so away.

Celia, after her conversations with Pierre, felt as though she knew her birth family and couldn't wait to be reunited with them. Pierre though, although pleased for Celia, was only too aware of the time scale In reality, there wouldn't be a minute to lose.

CHAPTER 35

The Invincible arrived at Le Havre slightly ahead of schedule thanks mainly to Captain Seymour's expert seamanship, according to Charley Wilson and Archie's plans they would need all the extra time they could find, wherever it may come from. It still seemed possible they would reach their destination in time, but only just, and that, of course, was providing nothing went wrong with virtually no stopping on the way.

There could be no delays, no mistakes.

Billy Burns stepped off the vessel first, boots crunching on wet stone. He inhaled deeply, savouring the air before the storm. Addressing his companions he called, "The best of luck, lads," he said, nodding in the direction of the journey south, "You're going to need it," he added with conviction, "at least the weathers with you. You couldn't guarantee that in England," he laughed.

Meanwhile the others were busy unloading countless crates of gear, along with the two horses and one cart, which as expected, was proving very difficult, especially the jittery horses, who sensed something in the air. Naturally they did not want to move at all and were very nervous. Eventually, Jack the Blaster had an idea to temporarily blindfold the animals which did in fact calm them down substantially, nevertheless the unwanted shenanigans cost the group the best part of an hour, which was too much time.

Charley pointed out, every minute counted, and every minute lost would have to be made up, if possible. "We'll have to claw it back," he muttered. "Every damn minute."

Finally, the last items were unloaded and accounted for, and the farewells began. Captain Seymour, Billy and Jack were to remain on board for the return journey, along with Tom, who at this moment was standing at the rail, feeling restless.

As they cast off Tom, who was not happy had other ideas as he felt The Invincible slowly moving away. He watched the beach and his heart was pounding. He turned around and looked at Captain Seymour. "Sorry Captain, I just can't do it. That's my mother out there on that beach and who knows what she may face. I can't let her face whatever's coming alone." Without any further discussion Tom dove into the sea and swam toward the shore.

Seymour, with his hands on his hips froze, he stood motionless, staring toward the shore. He shook his head from side to side, but words were unnecessary.

Billy's voice broke the tension. "Can the three of us sail the ship back to England?" he queried, "is it even possible?" His expression revealing his fears. After all Tom was a big strong lad and would be missed.

Seymour turned to face Billy, his answer slow but sure, "We'll manage, it won't be easy Billy, that's for sure, but I've been in bigger scrapes than this before, I have every faith in you," he paused for a few seconds, "and in The Invincible, as well of course." With these few words Seymour embraced his two crew members. "Let's do it lads, let's go home." No more words, just action.

By now Tom had reached the shore and his mother, Becky, was the first to react. "What have I told you about having a mind of your own?" she snapped, though her eyes shone with something else. Fear, pride and love. Her remark stunned Tom for a second.

"Well, I am twenty-two," he replied, "I thought I'd start sometime."

They both laughed, they had to, really. The team was now complete. Their mission had started. All the plans and times were checked and double checked. The cart had its wheels refitted and the horses were at the ready, and it was still morning. There was no sign of pursuit and the morning light shimmered off the cart's frame.

They were slightly ahead of time, so they were good to go. Archie seized upon this moment to send a final message to Count Artois by his trusted pigeon. He explained their position and gave an estimated time of arrival, which would be at a little village called La Cavalari, where they hoped to meet up with Medhi for the final few miles. He took great pride in watching his pigeon vanish into the sky.

For the first time things were progressing well with little or no problems to speak of, it was approaching mid-day, and the road baked under the punishing sun.

Archie decided to stop and have a few minutes break, as he scanned the horizon. "How's it going Charley?" he asked, "have we gained any time?" He was genuinely concerned even break times would have to be cut or even stopped if time was slipping away.

"We are doing okay," answered Charley. He paused for a minute, "to be honest, I think the next twenty-four hours are crucial."

Both men looked at each other, the silence between them was heavy. Not from fear, but from understanding. They exchanged a brief glance, neither speaking. Words were no longer useful. Hope was all they had left.

Pierre approached, balancing a jug of water and a bundle of dried fish in his arms. Primitive rations, but most welcome, nonetheless.

"How are the girls coping," queried Archie "they seem quiet," he remarked glancing to where they were sitting. His voice was low, wary.

"They're alright," replied Pierre, "just tired, I suppose, we all are." Pausing he added, "which isn't surprising considering the circumstances."

It was at this point Charley couldn't help noticing a lone figure in the distance. He didn't think too much of it as the rider was about half a mile away, but he called over to Bob and Amos. "Who do you think that might be, lads?" He nodded toward the horseman. "Do you think he's watching us?" he went on.

Amos answered without looking up. "Could be," he said, as he randomly poked the ground with an old stick he had found. "We'll see what he does when we move, but for the time being we'll ignore him and try not to look in his direction."

They finished their meal and were about to move on when Archie instructed Pierre to shout out loud in French for Celia to get a move on. Celia replied in perfect French.

He hoped this action would have the desired effect on the lone figure sitting motionless on his horse. Archie's eyes never left the rider. It had worked, the figure shifted and turned. He disappeared into the distance. Nevertheless, it was a clear warning that no chances could be taken, a warning no one could ignore.

By the time next morning they had covered quite a few miles without incident. No more riders, no more interruptions, just terrain – open and relentless. The ruined farmhouse appeared like a mirage. Crumbling walls, no doors, no windows but a mostly intact roof. Shelter, finally, especially for the horses. They took it.

Amos and his brother were still on edge and could not forget the lone rider of earlier, so they suggested they had a permanent lookout to be on the safe side. It was agreed Bob and Amos carry out this important duty. Archie agreed instantly.

As they settled down for the night, they lit a fire with any spare kindling laying around and enjoyed some refreshment, however, amidst the small break in their travels Bob nudged his friend and quietly said, "Look out of the window, there's that lone rider again, only not alone this time. There's another two. He paused for what seemed like ages, "They've both got guns on them, as well," he said.

Amos leaned forward, slow, calculated. He nodded and agreed it was best to tell Archie.

"Aye laddie, I've seen them," said Archie, "they've been following us for a while now but have kept their distance."

"Who are they?" asked Bob. "Are they soldiers, do you think? They don't look very friendly," he went on, and their clothes didn't match any official uniform. "I wouldn't trust anyone, especially under the circumstances." However, the three horsemen vanished again – swallowed by shadows, but they'd made their message clear. They were being watched, tracked, possibly hunted.

Inside the farmhouse everyone had been alerted to the potential danger and knew they would have to be extra diligent. Celia checked that the gold medallion was still safe and sewn up in her makeshift tunic. It was still safe.

As they all settled down for the night as best they could Archie whispered to Amos and Bob that they should sneak away under darkness and meet up with them about ten miles further ahead with the intention of warning the group of any further danger approaching. "I want to know if anyone's coming before they find us." They both agreed and disappeared into the night.

Meanwhile, back in Montpellier, The Count received the message from Archie's pigeon carrier. "Look," he shouted, "they are here in France, they are little more than twenty miles away. Quick, make sure Medhi is on his way to meet them," he blurted out. The Count's happiness was unmistakeable. He hugged his wife, Celeste the Countess, and they unashamedly danced around the room, emotion overwhelming them both, oblivious to anyone who may be watching. Joy, raw and unfiltered echoed through the halls.

But outside, the night was growing colder and the danger closer.

"Medhi's already gone, Your Excellency, as your specific orders," said his Chief of Staff.

"Has he indeed," laughed the Count, "yes, of course he has," he laughed again. He took hold of his wife with both hands and gazed into her eyes, quietly saying, "Our granddaughter, Celia, our granddaughter is safe and coming home."

At this precise moment our intrepid vigilante group, including of course, Celia, were rudely awakened by the rush of many feet into the small farmhouse, with the sound of steel scraped from sheaths and gunfire cracked. Shouts in French tore through the night. The men who had been following them, along with others, overpowered Archie and his entourage.

They had been betrayed, surrounded and outnumbered.

Before anyone could react, masked men poured into the barn, weapons drawn. The intruders weren't amateurs, they were trained, co-ordinated and cruel.

"Down! someone yelled. But it was too late.

Although most of the shots were fired in the air, one of the shots hit big Archie square in the chest. He fell back instantly and lay apparently dead on the straw covered floor. Everyone else was quickly tied up, kicked in the ribs. Screams erupted and blood spattered everywhere. They were unceremoniously dumped in the corner of the barn. There was chaos.

Becky, like the others, was eventually overcome by the vicious blows from her attackers, she was forced to kneel and await her fate, breathless, defeated and helpless.

Eventually the small group were all tied up and secured and were looking considerably the worse for wear.

Their captors moved quickly and efficiently. The leader, tall and lean with a predator's gait, stepped into the centre of the room. His long coat was caked with mud and blood. A jagged scar ran down the side of his jaw. His eyes were pitiless.

"Right," said the leader of the attackers. He leaned against the wall breathless but never taking his eyes off his captors. "Am I right in thinking you are from England ----and one of you," he said as he looked towards Celia and Becky, "could be the countess elect of Montpellier?" he queried.

He laughed loud and cruel as he said this. "You don't look like royalty," he went on, "not dressed like that." He stepped forward and yanked both women to their feet and ripped away their cloaks. Underneath was fine linen and quality stitching. "Hmm, could be true after all then. His Excellency, The

Blackheart will be delighted." He circled them slowly, prodding and probing and making judgements.

The two ladies were, of course, unable to object. He grabbed hold of Celia's hair from behind her neck and jerked back her head, which prompted her to utter a small cry of protest.

"I think you may well be the actual princess," He whispered in her ear, "not that it matters, of course," then, for everyone to hear, "my orders are, to kill you." He looked around the room and smiled. "All of you, in fact. That's what I must do." He paused for a moment. "And I'm going to enjoy doing it."

With this last remark he let out a raucous laugh, loud and chilling. This was indeed a cruel and vicious human being.

He instructed the rest of his men to return to Montpellier and let the Blackheart know their mission was accomplished and the princess would not be arriving at the palace tomorrow. He smiled once again, looking at his hapless prisoners. He asked for one other soldier to stay with him to help carry out his duties. He was beginning to love every minute. Most of the raiding party exited swiftly, spurred by fear and obedience. The one remaining soldier was clearly eager to participate in the carnage.

The leader knelt beside Tom and grabbed his long hair, pulling his head back sharply. Whilst doing so he rubbed his face across the rough stone walls, this action prompted Becky to shout out.

"Leave my son alone, or I will kill you," she screamed. Louis, the tormentor froze. Then turned slowly and smiled.

"Such spirit," he said mockingly. He hauled her upright. His left hand clamped her cheeks in a vice grip, distorting her face grotesquely.

Becky's husband Charley interrupted, "Leave it Becky, it will only make matters worse."This desperate plea from Charley prompted Louis to turn his attention, once again, to Becky.

"Oh, I mean to make it worse. You like to threaten men, madam?" He drew her very close to himself, his other hand wandering all over her exposed body. "Do you like this, Charley?" he asked, laughing, his voice venomous.

Suddenly, two other soldiers burst back into the barn. "Sir, we must go back now. We understand The Count has sent a contingent of soldiers to escort the princess to the palace, they could be here any minute." The look of anguish on the faces of the accompanying soldiers suggested they should waste no more time.

Louis turned sharply. His grin faltered. "The Count's escort?" Louis replied disappointedly, his acknowledgement accepted.

Louis's face twisted in frustration. Then resolve. "Message understood," he said coldly. But the prisoners die first. They'll arrive too late. I'll give them a barn of ashes."

He turned to face the group once more, "We will be with you in an hour or so." With that the rest of Francois' force left at pace, in the hope of finding Medhi and the Count's own soldiers.

Louis once more turned to face his prisoners, "Just for the sake of it and pure pleasure, and for my amusement, of course, I have decided to hang our two young ladies here in front of all you men, and when they in the throes of death I will shoot all of you and then set fire to the barn." Louis was laughing loudly; he was loving this.

Within a few minutes Louis and his men had made up a hanging step from broken planks and barrels, with two ropes tied around the beams of the ceiling. "That should do," he said thoughtfully. He then proceeded to pull the two women to the gallows and put the ropes around their necks, but this time Becky and Celia said nothing, accepting their fate. The ropes slipped over their necks. Neither woman screamed.

They stood tall. Eyes shining with quiet defiance, a few tears of love for those they were about to leave behind.

Louis then spoke, his two pistols loaded and ready for action. He glanced over to the men tied up on the floor who were still struggling to get free. "These will be your last moments on this earth gentlemen, and for you too, of course, ladies." He had no sooner uttered these words when a terrific explosion was heard outside the barn.

Sensing danger, Louis moved toward Celia and Becky.

CHAPTER 36

Louis, a loyal servant to Francois, signalled to his companion. A heavy boot clanged against the barrels stacked under Celia and Becky. They toppled over with a crash, rolling away across the barn floor, while the rest of the group were watching helplessly and struggling to get free, their eyes wide with terror.

"They can't die like this, surely," Pierre whispered, his voice hoarse with dread. "Not now."

Suddenly, a loud pistol shot rang out, amplified by the hollow acoustics of the barn. A well-aimed bullet zipped through the air, a perfect clean shot, slicing through the dust-thick air. It struck the neck of one of the hapless soldiers with surgical precision, killing him instantly.

For once Louis's composure cracked, he looked to be in a panic, but before he could get hold of one of his own pistols another shot rang out, this time from the small window. It stopped him in his tracks. The bullet passed through his shoulder and imbedded itself in the wall, with plaster fragments and blood spreading everywhere. The speed and the shock of this attack surprised everyone into silence. Silence fell, tense and total.

The gun smoke at last subsided and the figures of Amos and Bob emerged from the shadows.

"Just in time then, I'd say," muttered Amos, as he glanced round at his companions who were all tied up. "Are you all okay?" His eyes, however, never left Celia and Becky.

There was a collective nod, they were alive but shell-shocked. Amos moved quickly to Celia and Becky, cutting their bonds with practiced urgency. They collapsed into each other's arms onto the floor, trembling but safe.

As they began to untie the rest of the group, Amos noticed Archie slumped in the corner of the room. "What's wrong with Archie?" he asked, "he's not dead, is he?" He looked very concerned.

"I don't think so," answered Charley, "not yet anyway," he added quietly, "but he's close."

There was silence in the room at this point, as all their thoughts turned toward their friend Archie, who was not in a good way.

The mood shifted. A quiet dread settled over the group.

Suddenly, there was another almighty scream that filled the room, raw and primal, this was followed by a sickening thud of heavy metal cutting into flesh and bone, blow after blow was heard and then deafening silence. Everyone looked over to where Louis had been wounded. Becky was now standing astride him, holding a huge wood-cutters axe, which was now dripping in blood, mixed together with particles of bone and the soldiers' uniform. Her chest heaved with each breath as she turned to face her friends.

"Well," she said, still panting from her exertions. "that's one soldier who won't give us any more trouble."

For a moment no one moved or said anything.

Her husband Charley and their son Tom simply stared at her without saying a word, totally bemused but not surprised.

At this point she dropped her axe, letting it clatter to the stone floor, and gave both her son and husband a fierce, silent hug of relief.

Apart from Archie, who was still unconscious and deathly pale, no-one was seriously hurt. But as the sunlight filtered through the broken slates of the barn roof, reality hit them hard.

It was now the morning of 29th July, the day of the ceremonial handover. The weather was good. It wasn't raining and it was bright outside. They all knew they had to be inside the palace no later than 11.30 a.m. as the official handover and contractual agreements were to be handed over on the stroke of 12:00 noon. After that, no matter how legitimate, any claims would be null and void and not entertained. A fact, of course, not lost on Francois the Blackheart, who was already situated in the grand square only a few meters away from the ornate ceremonial chairs and the glinting solid gold mace.

Francois had taken note of the four entrances to the square and made certain his soldiers were in position to stop any last-minute surprises or unwanted guests.

Shoot on sight was the order. Francois feared only one thing now – the return of the legitimate heir. Such was his dread of not becoming a count at this late stage.

Count Artois and Countess Celeste had arrived early, they were relieved their granddaughter was now alive, and they were soon to be reunited with her, although they were still very worried that she may not arrive in time. They scanned the horizon but there was no sign of her.

Polite nods passed between themselves and Francois with barely concealed hostility masked by the ceremony's strict decorum. The two factions sat barely three metres apart, yet oceans of history and hatred separated them.

Artois leaned toward Celeste and whispered into his wife's ear, "There are only a few hours to go, and we have had no information yet. It's touch and go I'm afraid, things aren't looking good." An air of resignation hung around like a morning fog.

At that very moment, a sudden stir rippled through Francois's private tent. Messengers rushed in and out. The air vibrated with urgency. It appeared to all present he had received some news, and judging by their own reaction it seemed it wasn't very good for Artois or Celeste. There was no secrecy about these proceedings, in fact, just the opposite, everything had to be open and above board, nothing, absolutely nothing could be done in secret, which was, of course, why the ceremony had to be held in the public square adjoining the palace. The ceremonial square was large enough to hold at least twenty thousand guests and still leave substantial room for any official ceremonies.

Francois suddenly emerged from his tent the expression on his face had changed. He stood tall and elegant. His smile, though wide, did not reach his eyes. He looked over toward Artois and beamed impressively. He had obviously had some good news.

His attire was impeccable: jet-black military regalia tailored to perfection, adorned with gold embroidery and ornate epaulettes. Knee-high leather boots gleamed in the sun their buckles shining like small suns. He looked like a man who had already been crowned.

Artois glanced over toward him and almost with resignation gave him a nod of acceptance in what appeared to be the inevitability of the situation. He grasped Celeste's hand in a moment of despair and whispered "We need a miracle now, I'm afraid, Celeste. We need it fast," as he glanced at the magnificent clock tower. Time was slipping through their fingers.

Just as he said those very poignant words, there was a fanfare of trumpets. The Royal Delegation from Paris had arrived. Clad in their traditional scarlet and gold, they marched with mechanical precision. The central official placed the final part of the golden mace on the ceremonial plinth, it would be here the next legal person, he or she, would become the new Count or Countess of Montpellier. Artois, of course, according to the rules, could no longer rule and had to abdicate, but any living descendant could, if they appeared before the final stroke of twelve.

It was done; the mace was whole. Apart from the precise notch in which the medallion would fit.

Artois pleaded with the officials, to wait a while longer, as his granddaughter was on her way with the official seal. Regrettably no further time was granted, much to the satisfaction of Francois.

Above them the clock loomed. The time was set for 12 noon and at that precise moment proceedings would begin. The time was so important that it had to be the very last strike of 12 o'clock when the gold seal had to be pressed into place.

The clock tower was a sight to behold, it was situated right in the centre of the square next to the ceremonial mace, it was accepted by everyone to be a magnificent piece of architecture. At the base of the actual tower there were four mounted horsemen complete with full armour, shields and swords. They were all constructed in the most beautiful white marble. The centre column itself rose up between them, a shining pillar of pure black marble, strong and unshakable, as strong as the earth it-self, and standing right on top of this magnificent monument was the ornamental clock itself, beautifully constructed of heroes and warriors of days gone by. In turn they all appeared to be guarding the clock face which housed a huge bronze bell. It would be at this very spot in about three hours the clock would announce the beginning of the inauguration, and with-it history would be rewritten.

Meanwhile, back in the farmhouse Pierre and the princess elect, Celia, were taking stock of the situation. Although they were now only twenty miles away from the palace, time was draining away like blood from a wound.

Charley paced near the old stone wall of the farmhouse, his expression grim. "It doesn't look good, Pierre, "he said flatly shaking his head, "even with fresh horses and a clear run, we won't make it in time." He didn't sugarcoat it. His demeanour was pure dejection. He thought a minute longer and then went on. "In fact, to be honest, there's nothing we can do." As he said this he looked straight at Celia, his face was a picture of disappointment and dejection.

Before anyone could respond there was a faint groan from the corner of the room. Just then, Archie, the wounded soldier had now regained consciousness. Erasmus, his friend was the first to notice. He rushed to his side, "Archie!" he shouted, "you're awake, are you okay?" His voice was filled with concern.

Archie was still dazed and hurting. He managed to get a few words out. "I think so, laddie …not as good as I would like though," he smiled. His hand moved weakly to the wound in his chest; he could feel the hole where the bullet had passed clean through, miraculously missing his heart, but he was in no condition to travel, he knew that much.

Becky and Celia came over and checked his pulse, cradling g his head and brushing dust from his hair. After further examination it became clear he wouldn't make the journey. Not with them. He wasn't about to die, not yet anyway, and everybody agreed they would make sure he didn't. He wheezed a few deep breaths; his face lined with anguish.

Even in his pain Archie asked a few pertinent questions, it was then he instantly knew they would not make it to the palace in time, especially if he was to go with them. He was breathing quite heavily when he said, "Look, lads and lasses, you know its impossible, we won't make it, especially if I am to come along with you. "He went on a bit more "Just leave me here, I'll be okay. You go and do your best, that's all anyone can ask." He groaned uncharacteristically as he struggled with the words.

Charley glanced over to where Pierre was sitting, who simultaneously looked towards the two ladies, their expressions said it all.

Becky spoke, softly but with steel in her voice. "We are not going anywhere without you Archie McPherson. We made a promise, we came together, and we will stay together," she said strongly, "and if necessary, we will die together." She took time to look around the room. There wasn't one disagreeing voice in the group. By now the time was flying past. There was simply no chance. Archie gave a heavy sigh but agreed. It didn't seem like a time for optimism anymore, all was lost. The clock kept ticking.

"One thing, I can't understand though," he went on to say," why didn't Medhi turn up. Why didn't he meet us as planned … it isn't like him."

"Perhaps, he was ambushed or even killed," Amos said quietly. "Even if he was here, it would be too late. At that point he suddenly looked up at Celia. She looked every inch the princess now, tall, proud, beautiful and aristocratic. She nodded her acceptance of the situation and took hold of Becky. Further conversations didn't seem necessary. The group had left the farmhouse and were now sitting outside, enjoying the sunshine, reflecting on events, when Bob, who had been messing about trying to light a fire suddenly looked up into the sky and noticed something strange. Something he had never seen before in his entire life. "What on earth is that, is it real?" He went on, "Is it my imagination?"

Everyone looked up.

Something drifted against the pale blue of the morning sky. At first it was a shimmer. Then a shape. A strange silhouette against the sun. Pierre squinted. "It looks like one of those hot air balloons," he said very excitedly. "I've heard of them, but I've never seen one. I wasn't even sure they existed."

Nobody answered, it was as though they were transfixed.

As it approached even closer, they could see a couple of people on board. "Amazing … people flying," said Erasmus," I've never seen the like, it's really amazing."

By now the whole group were looking and waving as the strange craft grew ever closer. It was dropping in altitude all the time.

"What is it, Pierre," asked Archie, who was still lying down, "is it friend or foe, and who's on board?"

Pierre was more excited than most, considering that back in Tyneside his interest involved working with steam engines and anything mechanical. He couldn't take his eyes off the fast-approaching craft. "It looks like a lone French soldier, according to his uniform," he said, "and a dark-skinned, well-dressed chap. They seem friendly enough and they are waving a flag with the letter A in the middle of it. It's a kind of tartan, like you would wear."

Archie's eyes lit up. "That's my Medhi," he said, grinning through the pain. "I knew, he wouldn't let us down," this seemed to cheer up Archie immensely, with more than a little amount of expected pride.

The balloon groaned as it scraped across the uneven ground, bumping and skidding until it came to a stop – less than ten feet away from the farmhouse.

It was indeed Medhi who jumped from the craft and immediately ran toward his friend Archie, for the moment ignoring everyone else. "Are you okay Archie?" he asked.

Archie smiled and clasped his hand. "All the better for seeing you my friend, but I have to ask, what took you so long?"

Medhi burst out laughing. Archie, his great friend, hadn't lost any of his humour. "There's a story to tell, "Medhi went on, "but we don't have time just now. The palace awaits." he said raising his eyebrows, so we must leave soon."

But it's too late, surely isn't it," protested Pierre, "we will never get there in time, what with the terrain, the river, Francois's men, who will be in wait for us. The horses too, they need to rest."

Medhi raised his hand, listening patiently and eventually addressed the group. "Well, the truth is, my friends, I wasn't thinking of going that way. We are not going through the ground we are going over it. He looked up to the sky and nodded in the direction of Montpellier, and ended the conversation with a huge grin.

The group fell silent as his gaze swept over them. "I can't take you all, the balloon won't carry any more only Celia, Pierre and perhaps Becky. The rest of you will have to follow on, especially you Archie," he explained.

Medhi was quickly introduced to the rest of the group. He remembered some of them by name, but they had now grown up, especially Amos and Erasmus, but he recognised Charley who hadn't changed that much. He asked about Florrie and Mary but there was no time to lose now. The wind was light but blowing in the right direction, towards the east coast and the Mediterranean Sea. They hurriedly collected up some wool and dry straw and made up a fire like the one in the existing basket. They quickly lit the concoction of fuel and soon the balloon was filled with hot air and began to rise. According to Pierre they still had two hours to get to the palace. It was, in theory, still possible.

Celia stepped forward. Steady but pale. Becky took her hand. Pierre helped them into the basket. The flame roared, generating enough heat and the balloon trembled as hot air filled the canopy.

Archie winced and held his breath as he watched, then called up to Medhi. "You bring her home, you hear? Or I'll come and find you, dead or alive." Medhi saluted him with a grin, "Deal."

The balloon slowly lifted from the ground, Pierre glanced over to Celia, who at this time was clinging on to Becky, obviously fearful of the situation. Pierre's thoughts wandered back to that fateful night when the Montpelier sank. He remembered the promise he had made to his dying captain, Jon Marcel. It seemed, at last, for the first time in years, he was delivering Celia back to her true family.

CHAPTER 37

Within minutes of boarding the craft the vigilante group were soaring above the clouds – an unlikely alliance of rebels, nobles and secrets. At the helm stood Medhi, his hands expertly managing the ropes and flames that held their fate aloft.

He turned to the others with a grin, masking the pressure behind his eyes. He had assured them all would be well. Lightly he said, "Everything's under control." He laughed and joked insinuating there would be no problems whatsoever. He promised, providing the wind was favourable, they would arrive at the palace just in time.

Pierre squeezed Celia's hand. Her skin was ice cold. She was nervous, her eyes were locked on the horizon, they held a mixture of anticipation and dread. He could sense the anxiety coming from the princess. There was a certain amount of excitement, of course, as no one had come across travel like this before.

"Not be long now, Pierre whispered, although all on board could hear what he was saying. He went on regardless," after all these years you are finally going home," he smiled and squeezed her hand even harder. Pierre was as excited and proud as Celia was, in fact they all were.

Celia didn't answer, she couldn't, but her trembling fingers tightened around Pierre's grip.

The airship's ascent was swift, the burn of the flame giving the basket a surreal but welcome amount of warmth.

Suddenly, Medhi pointed through the drifting cloud cover." Montpellier, look," he said, urgency and excitement creeping into his tone. "That's Montpellier over there."

The medieval city loomed on the horizon, its spires, towers and terracotta rooftops rising like something out of a forgotten age.

Pierre, who had been hanging onto the ropes all this time, leaned backwards onto the basket, he had never felt less safe in his life. Yet his awe overrode his fear. he marvelled at this new technology, this was a marvel, a moment suspended in history. Medhi's companion who said very little winked in assurance.

Becky, however, wasn't so sure, it was only hours ago she was watching seagulls gliding past the old wooden jetty on the quiet banks of the River Tyne. There of course, she felt safe and totally comfortable with her surroundings and now she could hardly believe she was flying high above the ground, even higher than any gull. She was unable to take in this incredible situation. She felt as though she would be sick at any moment.

As they approached the outskirts of the city, which was situated just beyond the walls of Montpellier, they began to descend, mainly by adjusting the temperature from the fire. Slowly at first, controlled by precise adjustments to the flame.

The palace came into view and Medhi suggested they fly around the city walls at least once to access information for a safe landing.

There was lots of rope pulling and attempts to shift the weight of the basket to steer the craft. They were now only about one hundred feet from the ground. They found themselves flying at a steady pace. Not unlike the speed of a galloping horse Medhi remarked.

"There," shouted Medhi once again, his voice full of excitement and his finger pointing in the direction of the Count's official tent. "Look, there's your grandfather and grandmother, the count and countess." He sounded incredibly proud.

Below them two regal figures emerged from a white and gold tent near the palace steps. Pierre turned his head sharply towards Celia, as she stood there motionless like a beautiful statue, crafted from the finest marble, she looked magnificent and resolute, save for a few genuine tears of happiness rolling freely down her cheeks. It was, indeed, a sight to behold. Her expression was unreadable. She looked every bit the princess she was meant to be, serene, radiant, but fragile as glass itself. Feebly, she managed a meaningful wave which, surprisingly, was greeted with thunderous applause from the people of Montpellier who had realised that the princess elect was returning to them.

As quick as the cheering came from the massive crowd, however, shots were being fired from Francois's musketeers and they were flying all around the flimsy basket, which proved no protection from lead shot, holes were appearing everywhere, and they realised they would have to land soon. Time was now running out very quickly, they had less than an hour to land within the square and present themselves to the official who oversaw the golden mace. By now the ropes groaned and splinters from the basket flew while Becky and her companions made attempts to duck out of the way.

Medhi threw caution to the wind and took note of where Francois and his personal guards were. They had started making their way over to the count and countess in an orderly fashion. Circumstances were now proving to be very difficult and very desperate.

Medhi remembered there was an ideal landing spot just outside the courtyard, but he also realised if he chose to land there, they would not make it in time. Possibly minutes over, that's all, but it would still be too late.

"Too risky," he muttered to himself. "We have to land in the square; we have no choice."

The balloon, now full of bullet holes was beginning to lose height, a little too quickly, he thought, and there was only one course of action he could take. There was nothing they could throw overboard to make the craft lighter, so they decided to make an emergency landing on the ceremonial square itself. It was agreed by all; they would position the balloon as near to the clock monument as they could. It was hoped Celia and Pierre could jump out of the basket once it was close enough and reached ground level. This wasn't as easy as it sounded, bearing in mind the balloon would be travelling at some speed. There were lots of pulling ropes to and fro and shifting weights in the baskets in order to gain some kind of direction and the wind had to be facing the right way. All these shenanigans helped to slow it down considerably.

Even with all this going on the balloon was losing height quite considerably, a lot quicker than they hoped. It was touch and go.

The team worked in frantic silence, redistributing weight, adjusting the flame. The balloon responded sluggishly while the wind fought them at every turn.

Pierre popped his head over the basket. "They are still firing at us Medhi," he said, "quite a few shots have ripped through the balloon." He looked worried, he was naturally quite concerned about Celia, when Medhi made his decision.

"You've got the medallion, Celia," he said as he held her steady in place. She nodded. "Yes, I have," she replied.

He looked at her straight in the eyes as though he was about to shake her. "This is it then," he said, "Your Excellency, this is now your time." He glanced over to Pierre. "And you too, there are no second chances now."

Almost immediately the craft hit the ground momentarily, there were gasps of fear and shrieks from the expectant crowds. Suddenly it bounced up again to about thirty feet high, throwing the passengers in and around the small basket. There was no stability now and the occupants had no control. Once again, the basket bounced off the ground. It was now showing signs of considerable wear. There were gaping holes where the wickerwork had come adrift. Celia and Becky were now just holding on to one another with eyes closed, hoping for the best and awaiting more instructions from Mehdi.

"Ready," he shouted very loudly, "Now jump," at the same time giving them an extra shove from the basket. They were totally oblivious of where they were and where they might end up. All they remembered was hitting the ground hard, while their momentum carried them further along in the square. Then without warning they came to an undignified stop, battered and bruised.

They were back on land though, they knew that much but they weren't safe. They had landed somewhere halfway between Francois's camp and the golden mace. Pierre, who had also jumped from the basket came running towards them. He was limping badly as he collapsed near Celia and Becky wincing in pain, the balloon and Medhi now once more soared high into the sky over the palace walls and temporarily out of sight.

There were well over twenty thousand people in the square. They had come to see something spectacular, something they would never forget, but no-one had expected this.

Suddenly, Francois the Blackheart, dressed in regal black with gold trim, seized upon the opportunity and acted first. He was calm and resolute. He ordered his private guards to shoot Celia and her friends dead, and not to give them a chance. "Shoot them, shoot them all," he demanded. He was pointing directly at Celia especially. "The Golden Girl, shoot her first."

Pierre was now sitting on the ground; his leg was hurting badly but was being attended to by Becky. Celia stood up and made herself as tall as she could.

She turned and faced the firing line without flinching. Dozens of musketeers stepped forward, their weapons raised. She anticipated there must have been about forty of them, all in blue and yellow uniforms. All battle-hardened soldiers.

And then she moved. Within a matter of seconds Celia ripped open her tunic and pulled out the golden medallion. "The seal of the family," she shouted. She held it aloft for everyone to see and everyone became silent. "I am, "she said in perfect French, "Auriel Celeste, the daughter of Jon Marcel and the granddaughter of Count Artois. I am, people of Montpellier," she paused," the rightful, legal heir and bloodline to the regal throne of Montpellier." This time she paused for what seemed ages before going on to say, "I am your countess."

There was silence for a moment or two, broken only by the shrill voice of Francois. "Shoot her, you fools'. Shoot her."

But no one fired. None of the soldiers moved, they looked at each other with uncertain glances. Beads of sweat dripping from tense foreheads as they considered their next move. Their fingers tightened around their muskets pointed at Celia, but no one moved there were only murmurings.

Francois was furious, his face twisted with rage, as he pushed and shoved his men, who up until this moment had been fiercely loyal to him and would have done anything for him. Suddenly though, one by one the soldiers lowered their arms. Some took off their hats and began cheering. "Viva Celia," they shouted. Eventually this action was followed by them all, which enraged Francois. His evil looks returned with a vengeance.

"Traitors," he hissed, shoving his men aside. "Then I will kill you myself," he said as he snarled and spat out his defiance, grabbing a cutlass and edging toward the unarmed Celia.

Amazingly she didn't move. Instead she calmly handed the medallion over to her trusted friend Becky and smiled.

She took hold of her other hand and said very quietly, "Every beginning, however grand, must eventually end," she murmured, but winked at her friend and almost growled as she said with fierce determination, "but not this time."

Fate once again intervened as one of Francois's soldiers kicked over his cutlass towards Celia. "Let her die with some dignity," the man muttered, gaining approval from his companions.

Unfortunately, Francois was an expert swordsman, probably the best around, there was no doubt about that. He had killed many people during his lifetime, never mind this upstart of a young girl, he would not allow her to stand in his way.

He looked across the square to where the cutlass had landed. He nodded and with a twisted grin he said, "Good, a little sport to end this fiasco. Excellent."

He advanced, blade poised. Behind him Count Artois struggled against the guards, shouting his protests, but the crowds had engulfed him.

Celia picked up the cutlass with her right hand and held it high. This brought an immediate cheer from the eager crowd, there was no doubt whose side they were on. Francois took controlled steps toward his victim. He was now only feet away from Celia and he could see straight into her eyes, seemingly unafraid. He did think for once, 'what manner of girl could this be'.

Celia adopted the classic pose of a seasoned fencer, the right foot firmly behind the left and slightly off balance. Her left hand on her hip and her head just bent back.

This pose brought further cheers from the crowd; however, they were still impatient to see the outcome. Celia couldn't help, but look, at the palace clock it was 11.45 a.m. There was only 15 minutes to go. She, uncharacteristically, began to sweat. She then began to move sideways ever so slowly towards the clock tower to circle around Francois. However, without warning, like a bolt of lightning he struck first with a deft parry from his sword. Amazingly he caught Celia unaware and unbalanced. She stumbled slightly and allowed Francois to strike first blood.

He laughed cruelly as he shouted out, "The crimson nectar of a virgin princess. A princess who will never wear the crown. The colour suits you though." He gave another evil laugh.

He was enjoying this and while Celia was fighting back valiantly, she was, in all truthfulness, no match for Francois, no match at all and time was now slipping by with only about four minutes left on the clock. She was losing, and she knew it.

The scent of defeat hung thick in the air. She must do something she thought, and she had to do it now, although she didn't feel the blows so much, she was bleeding from several cuts and had administered none against Francois. Her tunic was now in threads, and she caught a glimpse of her grandfather slumped back into his chair, afraid to look.

Becky was still sitting on the ground with the injured Pierre and the crowd was quiet, all with the scent of defeat in their nostrils. She remembered back in time when Florrie and her adoptive mother Fiona used to argue, she remembered when her grandfather Anders used to give her courage when she needed it. She remembered every-one from her past who had loved her and believed in her and suddenly with a shrill and almost warlike scream she summoned up every ounce of her strength she possessed and charged directly at Francois irrespective of any danger.

She slammed full into his chest, temporarily knocking the wind from him, their arms entwined, and their cutlasses locked like the claws of a mythical beast. Their faces only millimetres away from each other. What could she do now, she asked herself in desperation. What would her captain from the navy on the Scorpion do now. He was a fine English soldier and her mentor. What would Becky, her friend, do under such immense pressure. She didn't need to think anymore she immediately bit hard into his ear, which made Francois scream out in pain and recoil back in shock.

Francois screamed. Blood spurting freely from his ear he lurched back. For once he dropped his guard and became human, vulnerable. Celia spat out part of his chewed ear and freed her cutlass from Francois's grip and plunged it as hard as she could straight up beneath his ribs and into his chest. The steel sank deep. His mouth opened but no words came, only a wheeze. His eyes rolled up and over, all blood shot and vacant. He had a look of complete disbelief before dropping down on one knee, dead, before falling to the ground.

Celia had no time to contemplate. The great ornamental clock had now started counting down to the hour of twelve. The ominous great brass bell, unmistakeable in its clarity and inevitability, there was no time to lose.

Celia discarded her shoes and started running towards the ceremonial mace. Becky saw this and threw the medallion toward her. She caught it in mid-air. Her stride never slowing.

She dropped to her knees at the ceremonial altar, bloodied and breathless as she raised the medallion, the official seal, high in the air.

She had now reached the mace, totally breathless but still managed to breath the words, "I, Auriel Celeste, daughter of Jon Marcel, do rightfully claim the position of Countess of Montpellier."

Whilst doing so, she simultaneously placed the medallion within the special place in the golden mace. There was only one second to go. Her hands slipped away with the last chime of the ceremonial clock reaching 12.00 noon. An almighty cheer went up from the crowd present, along with thunderous cheers from everyone present.

The blood had been spilled; the throne had been claimed.

The civic dignitaries were only pleased to accept her nomination and they granted there and then for all to see the new and official Countess of Montpellier, the Rt Honourable Auriel Celeste. History would never forget this moment,

CHAPTER 38

The days that followed flew by and were easily some of the happiest times any of the Marcel family had ever encountered. For the unlikely band of rescuers from Tyneside, Montpellier had become a sanctuary. But, even amidst the happiness, laughter and light, a shadow loomed; soon, they would have to leave for home. Return to the world they came from. And with that return, confront everything they had left behind.

In the meantime, there were lots of discussions as to how and when this would happen. Pierre had many meetings with Count Artois behind the closed doors of a weathered chateau. Their discussions, though laced with formalities, were fuelled by a sacred promise. His vow to Captain Jon Marcel about the rescue of his daughter. Captain Marcel had promised rewards beyond measure to the person or persons who were instrumental in the return of his precious infant daughter.

Artois hadn't needed much convincing. In fact, he needed none. From the moment he heard of the promise his heart filled with pride that, even in the hour of their death, his son's primary thought had been the safety of his daughter, the future Countess of Montpellier.

Artois decided the financial rewards would be massive. Even more so for Florrie, Mary and Becky. He would make sure they wouldn't have to work again. They had, quite literally saved a dynasty.

Arrangements were drawn as to how the beneficiaries would obtain their rewards. Set against all these discussions,

Archie had agreed to accept the invitation from his friend Medhi to stay and live in Montpellier, as did Amos and Gunpowder Bob. Both of whom, of course, were rewarded handsomely for their part. They promised to live a life free of crime and settle down. Charley Wilson and his wife Becky were only too pleased for them as over the last few weeks they had become firm friends. Erasmus and Tom could hardly believe it but were only too happy to give them the benefit of the doubt. Now, however, it was time to leave and return home.

A final sunrise painted the Montpellier skyline as preparations were made. Their departure from Montpellier was filled with genuine regret along with a sense of true happiness from all parties involved. Celia, the new Countess had promised she would never forget her adopted family and would visit England soon and as often as she could. She wished everyone a safe journey home. One of the finest schooners that Montpellier possessed had been gifted to the departing party a vessel worthy of nobility.

As the sails unfurled, Celia, now Countess of Montpellier, stood at the docks her eyes shining with promise.

The journey home was swift, the sea unusually calm. As if the ocean itself recognised the gravity of their return.

They docked at Tyneside in the late light of September 1815. The news spread fast, and just about everyone in the South Shields area was there to greet their arrival. It was a celebration.

Among the first was Florrie, her weathered face breaking into a thousand smiles, and Mary of course, arms outstretched. A grinning, happy, Billy Burns was like a man reborn. It's even said that the Rev Tobias Trevelyan cancelled the Sunday service in order that he and his wife Fiona were there to greet them. Such was the importance of the occasion.

For the moment genuine tears of joy and happiness mingled with a little sadness as it was revealed some of the crew would not be returning. Amos, Florrie's' elder son, had chosen a new life in Montpellier.

Pierre, who had made all this possible lingered a couple of days with his new friends before returning home to Wylam, offering no explanation why. Although he never revealed his adventures to his own family, something he never ever did, he poured his fortune into a mechanical engineering company, specializing in all types of steam engines and in particular aerodynamics, engineering marvels that would one day change history.

Erasmus, now back on English soil, found love and together they built a new church near St. Hilda's for the local community, a sanctuary for the community that had raised him. The fisher folk came in droves.

Billy Burns retired with immediate effect and built a wonderful, detached house in Westoe Village, though he remained close to Charley and Becky Wilson who became land owning farmers.

Florrie and Mary, rich beyond their dreams, decided, they would remain well within the town centre and never far away from their old stone-built cottages on the beach.

Many years passed, both on Tyneside and Montpellier. The Countess Celeste was proving to be a very popular and a successful monarch. Meanwhile, back in South Shields, the locals were becoming used to the many changes that were happening all over Great Britain, particularly to the industrial area in the North.

Florrie Guttenberg and her best friend Mary were now in their late 70s, although Florrie was not in the best of health, her once-strong frame bowed slightly by years and illness. They remained great friends. but circumstances meant they did not meet up as much as they would like. It was possibly, this in mind, that made Mary arrange a meeting for old times' sake.

Mary suggested the old fish quay at the Mill Dam would be perfect as it was a place they spent many years. The air smelled of salt and coal. Somewhere upriver a foghorn groaned like a wounded beast. Memories of gutting the fish, filling the old barrel for a few pence per day, drinking tankards of ale and having a good laugh. Now of course, due to Count Artois' generous donations they were well-off old ladies with no need to work at all. The two friends arrived at the quay about mid-afternoon. They initially just stood side by side looking across the river toward North Shields and overlooking the infamous Black Middens, treacherous and foreboding rocks, sticking through the river like razor sharp stone blades ready to rip through any ship unlucky enough to encounter them.

Mary was the first to speak on this occasion. "Aye," she said, "times gone by Florrie eh." She paused, "It makes you think though, doesn't it? This spot used to be everything." It wasn't really a question so Mary wasn't expecting a reply, she was just talking, rambling you could say.

Florrie answered anyway, "Aye it does, Mary. Mind you, it just seems like yesterday." She turned round just in time to see her friend take off her shoes. "What on earth are you doing?" she queried.

Mary with a mischievous glint that belied her age did something unexpected. She slipped off her shoes and let them drop to the stones with a thud.

"Not thinking of jumping in, are you?" This last remark made Mary laugh and giggle, a bit like old times.

"Relax, I'm not jumping in," she answered quickly, "but take yours off as well and get sat down here next to me. Come on pet, one more time"

Florrie hesitated, she was in two minds if her friend would suddenly jump in or not, but after a few moments it soon became apparent Mary just wanted to dangle her bare feet over the side and cool them off in the sea like they used to do all those years ago. Florrie shook her head but moved, slowly, deliberately just to keep her friend happy.

The sea was cold, biting even, but they didn't flinch. They had survived colder things.

As they sat there, they both realised there wasn't much left of the original jetty now but there was enough to sit on as they pushed each other, jokingly. Sailing ships were now being replaced by horrible steam powered iron monstrosities, in their minds. Noisy, smelly and ungainly, so much, they thought, had changed. Even the few people on the beach were picking up coal as against the fine collection of sea creatures they were used to. Their thoughts and their memories took them back to the day the French schooner, The Montpelier, sank with the loss of all hands.

"Eh remember that night, Florrie? We never guessed what secrets that held did we?"

"No, we didn't. but we know now." She smiled as she glanced towards her friend. The memories came flooding back as though it was yesterday. The tide was now beginning to come back in and was starting to cover the Black Middens. The sun was fading behind the smoke-stained rooftops of Wallsend and their mood was becoming more relaxed in such a way it prompted Mary to say to her friend. "But we are rich now Florrie aren't we, you and me." Mary virtually looked through Florrie's eyes almost into her soul and added again with sincerity and real meaning. "But there again, you always have been."

"Have been what?" answered Florrie, almost immediately. "Rich, I've never had any money … Until now, that is, and you know that more than anybody.

Mary once again left the view of the sunset and looked into her friend's eyes. She said quietly, "Sorry pet. I didn't mean actual cash," she went on, "in all my seventy odd years, good and bad, I've never met a family such as yours."

Florrie never answered, she just listened. Her gaze had shifted, inward now, to the memories.

Mary went on, about Anders, her mother and her fish ship, about Amos and Erasmus, everything really and about Celia and in it all the love they had for each other." she said. Florrie never said a word, no doubt going over her life past and present. "That's wealth, that's the kind of rich money can't buy.

The silence returned, heavier this time. Wind tugged at their sleeves. The tide crept up the stones.

All this time Florrie had been clasping something in her right hand, as though it was as important as life and death itself, "What's that your holding?" Mary asked out of curiosity.

Florrie opened her fingers, revealing a piece of black ebony quartz. That's all it was just a broken stone she explained,

"That's all I have left of the pebble Amos gave me all those years ago." She paused, "As long as I live, I will always cherish this, that's my riches."

Mary didn't speak, she couldn't. Her throat tightened.

Once again both ladies were silent. The world had changed. But some things remained unmoved by time.

Florrie took hold of her friend's hand squeezed it lightly, but ever so gently and almost in a whisper said. "Thank you."

About the author

George Crozier is a retired gas fitter living in South Shields close to the setting of this story. He is also an amateur artist. Always wanting to become an author, this opportunity only came about during the COVID epidemic when he had time on his hands and he could realise his dream.

Printed in Dunstable, United Kingdom

77473239R00231